RETURNING TO EDEN

RETURNING TO EDEN

ACTS OF VALOR, BOOK 1

REBECCA HARTT

Book and cover design by eBook Prep
www.ebookprep.com

January, 2020
ISBN: 978-1-947833-89-0

Rise UP Publications
644 Shrewsbury Commons Ave
Ste 249
Shrewsbury PA 17361
United States of America

www.riseUPpublications.com
Phone: 866-846-5123

For all the devoted readers who have followed me into this new genre, especially Penny and Deborah, and for all the new readers just discovering me—welcome! It is my sincerest wish that you will lose yourself in the pages that follow. I hope this series resonates with you as it does with me.

FOREWORD

Most authors can easily name their favorite stories. Over a decade ago, under a different name and in a different era of my life, I wrote several books that have continued to live in my imagination. Yet, those books left out an element I believe to be crucial to the reality of their characters. Navy SEALs face peril on a daily basis. With injury and death always threatening, it makes sense to me that special operators rely on a higher power to give them courage. They must have faith in God's protection—or, at the very least, the assurance of an afterlife. With this conclusion in mind, I have breathed life into the bones of my most heart-touching stories. I present to you the *Acts of Valor* series by Rebecca Hartt.

GLOSSARY OF MILITARY ACRONYMS

CO – Commanding Officer
XO – Executive Officer
OIC – Officer in Charge
NVG's – Night Vision Goggles
NCIS – Naval Criminal Investigative Service
BUDs – Basic Underwater and Demolition/SEAL Training
NWU – Navy Working Uniform
PTSD – Post-Traumatic Stress Disorder
REM – rapid-eye movement

PROLOGUE

*W*ithout warning, a bullet strafed the concrete floor of the warehouse not twenty feet in front of Jonah, shattering the quiet of the sleeping fishing village of Carenero, Venezuela.

His first instinct was to dive for cover behind the crate he'd just pried open. Picturing the dozens of rounds for AK 47s packed inside, hiding next to the crate wasn't the safest option. Then again, almost everything in this warehouse—guns, grenades, rocket launchers—was flammable.

Heart pounding, Jonah dropped to the cool floor and elbow-crawled toward one of the many steel pillars holding up the catwalks and the tin roof. Putting his back against it, he tabbed his mike before the officer in charge had a chance to and hissed, "Sit rep."

"Two shooters." Sniper Saul Wade's situational report was as nonchalant as if they were out quail hunting. "Up in the crosswalks, northeast wall."

Jonah located the wall in question and, sure enough, two tangos armed with assault rifles crouched up there taking pot shots at them. With surprise, he realized they must have been there all along. His SEAL squad had broken the lock on the door on that same side of the warehouse. They'd fanned out, moving around for the past thirty minutes trying to find the four boxes full of chemical weapons, which per their intelligence, ought to have been right next to the door they'd entered.

No one had come into the warehouse after them. Ergo, the shooters had arrived there first.

Rat, tat, tat, tat!

Another barrage of bullets verified Saul's report, echoing in the vast, metal warehouse. In his earpiece, Jonah overheard the OIC, Jimmy Lowery, utter an exclamation of dismay.

"We need to retreat." Lowery stated the obvious with a wobble in his voice.

Jonah cursed in silence. The op had gone from bad to worse. Lowery's nervousness betrayed his lengthy absence from the field. As executive officer of the entire squadron, he manned a desk more often than he took part in assaults.

"Reaper and Mr. T, break to the east exit," Lowery instructed Saul and Theo. "Jaguar and I will be right behind you," he added, referring to Jonah by his codename. "Meet you at the—"

White noise hissed suddenly in Jonah's earpiece. *What the...?*

Fiddling with the wire, he slid to a standing position, hugging the pillar to maintain his cover. His coms could not have given out at a worse time. Luckily, Lowery had managed to spit out most of the directions. They were to rendezvous at the rally point, which was a ditch located halfway between the warehouse and their insertion point on the shore.

"XO, can you hear me?" Jonah tested his mike as he listened to Saul throw up a wall of fire so Theo could sprint to the exit. The unmistakable *blam-blam-blam* of Theo's submachine gun signaled Saul's turn to move. Moonlight flooded the warehouse briefly as both men slipped out the exit on the east side together.

Figuring Lowery was talking to him and getting no reply, Jonah crept around the safe side of the pillar to look for him. The silhouette of a man swung suddenly around the pillar. Jonah reared back but the butt of the man's rifle still made stunning impact with his left cheek and sent his NVGs flying. Blood flooded into Jonah's mouth as he staggered backward, tripped over a dolly, and crashed onto his back, smacking his skull. Darkness ambushed him. He clung to consciousness, trying to digest what was happening.

A pair of rough hands seized him. Blood poured down his throat, choking him. Too concussed to fight back, Jonah submitted helplessly as his attacker flipped him over then grappled his arms behind his back, securing them with a nylon zip-tie that cinched his wrists together.

What's happened? Jonah's guttural protests sounded like they were coming from someone else. He tried to form words, but speaking was beyond his capabilities. *What's wrong with me?*

His attacker did the same thing to his ankles, immobilizing him. Finished, the man clambered off him and hurried away.

Jonah listened to his stealthy retreat. He lay with his face in a pool of blood —his own. Then, over the ringing in his ears, he heard strange men speaking in hushed voices. Speaking English.

Friendlies, he thought. They were speaking English. But then he heard a wicked chuckle. Someone said, "Let's blow this place."

The hairs on the nape of Jonah's neck prickled. Dear God, he was going die here if he didn't take action. *Move. Get out.*

He didn't even know where he was. *Why can't I remember?*

Contorting his spine, Jonah managed to grab, with oddly clumsy fingers, the Gerber blade concealed under his pant leg. With difficulty, he sliced through the zip-tie around his ankles, then angled the blade the other way and freed his wrists.

It took every ounce of concentration to come to his knees and put the blade away. He spat something out of his mouth—a tooth. Craning his aching head, he pondered where he might find an escape. Then he crawled, staying on hands and knees to keep out of sight while weaving like a rabid raccoon through a maze of stored goods. The sound of voices faded. At last, he came to a door. To his relief, it opened when he pushed it.

Help me get away, God.

It was possibly the first sincere prayer Jonah had uttered to his Maker. It wasn't that he didn't believe. He'd just relied on his own strength to always get through. God had better things to do than to help someone like him. *I want to live.*

As quietly as possible, he slipped outside, dragging himself on his elbows as far as his uncooperative muscles let him. Finally, the darkness tunneling his vision overtook him completely, and he collapsed onto the sandy soil.

CHAPTER 1

*E*den immersed herself in the bath so that only her eyes and nose cleared the layer of bubbles. Her aching muscles softened in the hot water. Relaxing, she let herself go limp. Through half-closed eyes, she stared past the frothy bubbles at the framed photo where it stood behind a line of dancing tea candles. Bittersweet emotion stormed her as she stared into her late husband's eyes.

Even from a distance of a few feet, Jonah's eyes mesmerized her, just as they had when the two of them first met. Most men with nutmeg-brown hair had hazel or brown eyes. Jonah's were light green with a gold starburst at the center. Both the color of his eyes and his ability to see in the dark had given him his codename, Jaguar, which also happened to be the make of the car he drove. His gaze was uncannily direct, making her squirm whenever he'd stared at her, which had been quite often in the beginning. However, by the time he'd disappeared, only two years into their marriage, he'd scarcely given her the time of day. He'd been too wrapped up in being a SEAL and saving the world.

Eden blew the encroaching suds away from her mouth, sending a bubble into the air. It drifted a moment and then disintegrated.

"Like my love for you," she murmured, addressing the man in the picture.

He'd disappeared a year and a month ago. The Navy wouldn't tell her where he'd been or the circumstances surrounding his disappearance. All they'd told her was there had been an accident—an explosion, and Jonah hadn't exited the building in time to escape it.

SEALs will never leave a man behind, so his teammates had gone back for him as soon as it was safe. The only remains they had found was a tooth, Jonah's upper left canine. The Navy had immediately declared him MIA, missing-in-action. They'd expressed the hope that he'd been captured, but Eden doubted that. SEALs were trained to avoid capture, and Jonah, provided he hadn't been injured, would have taken his life before he let the enemy take him.

As time went on with no ransom note, no video boasting the captivity of a US special operator, the Navy began to sing a different tune. Then last week, a young officer had appeared on Eden's doorstep, bearing an invitation to Jonah's memorial.

The Navy had finally declared her husband dead. She'd been issued a death certificate. She'd reached out to his life insurance providers. Yet, even with thirteen months in which to consider the likelihood that Jonah was gone, it had still come as a shock to be handed a tightly folded flag at his memorial.

Ironically, on the heels of Eden's shock had come relief. She would never have to walk on eggshells again, the way she did whenever Jonah was around. She wouldn't have to give up the job that gave her so much satisfaction because he'd refused to let her work. She would raise her fourteen-year-old alone, as she should have done in the first place. With Jonah's life insurance money in the bank, their financial situation could not have looked more secure.

For the first time in a long time, the future was hers to enjoy.

With the benefit of hindsight, she had admitted to Nina Aydin, her best friend, that marriage to Jonah had been a mistake. She'd thought she needed him to redeem herself in her parents' eyes. She'd wanted her daughter, Miriam, to have a father. And, yes, she'd been over-the-moon in love with him. She had thought having a handsome, capable warrior for a husband would fulfill her. In fact, marrying him had left her lonelier than ever. Jonah, with his drive to save the world, hadn't had time for a wife, let alone a step-daughter.

Less than a year into their marriage, the man who should have been her knight in shining armor had practically forgotten her. Two years in, he was dead.

Now, it was finally over.

Nina, who was divorced herself, had applauded Eden's self-actualization. They had both agreed it was time to put the past behind her and to stand on her own two feet. She hadn't needed Jonah Mills to make her whole. She'd done just fine this past year on her own. Better than fine. And yet...

Even with her ears underwater, Eden could hear the words of the Natalie Cole song coming from her cell phone on the sink. *"Unforgettable, that's what you are..."* A thread of longing stitched through her.

She still missed him from time to time. Closing her eyes, she remembered the feel of his hands on her, his lips. His touch, his kisses had never failed to sweep her off her feet. His quick wit had always made her laugh. His intelligence had roused her respect.

"Unforgettable, in every way..."

He would never again call her back to him as he did time and time again, after each mission or deployment—with the inviting quirk of his mouth or the flash of his catlike eyes. She was free to go, to live her own life.

Emptying her lungs in a long sigh, Eden released her lingering regret and sank completely underwater to wet her hair. Only when her lungs strained for air did she surface. Sitting up, she reached for the shampoo.

The landline phone rang in another part of the house, reminding her to cancel the service. Jonah had activated it for security purposes. Yet with every incoming call being from a telemarketer, what was the point in keeping it? The ringing stopped as Miriam answered, and Eden clicked her tongue in annoyance. Couldn't she let the machine pick up?

With arms that shook with fatigue, Eden lathered her hair. She'd taught two body sculpting classes and a high intensity cardio class that day. She would need to soak in this tub for half an hour if she wanted to lift her arms above her head tomorrow.

"Mom!" The bathroom door slammed open startling her as Miriam marched in unannounced. "It's for you," she said, holding out the landline phone.

In the light of the candles, her daughter's face looked waxen. Or maybe her complexion was all washed out from the dye job she'd just given herself.

Mauve? "Oh, Miriam, your hair!" Eden cried.

"It's urgent," her fourteen-year-old insisted.

The size of Miriam's brandy-colored eyes sent a shaft of concern through Eden. Taking the phone, she leaned out over the edge of the tub so as not to drop it in the water.

"This is Eden Mills."

"Mrs. Mills, this is Commander Schmidt over at Portsmouth Naval Medical Center," announced a man with a note of apology. "Traumatology," he added.

Eden lifted her gaze to her daughter's shocked face. This had to be about Miriam. She'd acted out again, had to be.

"Ma'am, I'm calling to let you know we've got your husband here. It's a remarkable story, actually. He was picked up in the Gulf by a fishing vessel and used their radio to hail the US Coast Guard. They collected him via helo and flew him to Portsmouth this morning..."

The commander kept talking, but Eden couldn't hear him over the ringing in her ears. She hadn't heard much, in fact, after the word *husband*.

"I'm sorry." She cut him off. "I think you've made a mistake. My husband's dead."

"He's not dead, ma'am. He's been positively IDed as Lieutenant Jonah Michael Mills. He says he was imprisoned in Venezuela, and he managed to escape last week."

It could not be Jonah. Eden's mind flashed to the flag she'd received at his memorial.

"How...how can you be sure?"

"I understand this is coming as a shock." The commander's voice softened. "But you can rest assured we IDed him thoroughly before making this call. His commander has already been in to see him. All that's left is for his family to do the same. He is alive, ma'am, and in pretty fair condition, considering what he's been through."

Eden swallowed convulsively. Her first impulse was to cling to the freedom she'd been relishing mere seconds earlier. Guilt immediately pricked her. If Jonah was alive, this was nothing short of a miracle!

"I'm sure you'll want to get down here right away," the commander prompted.

"Of course," she said, all thought of her overworked muscles fleeing her head.

"There's something you should know, ma'am, before you see him."

The commander's hesitancy made Eden's pulse skip. She braced herself for more shocking news—maybe Jonah had been disfigured.

"He's lost a few years of his memory, apparently."

What?

"He doesn't have any recollection of a family, I'm afraid. This kind of thing is normal, I want you to understand. It's an indication of post-traumatic stress, nothing that can't be dealt with, probably not permanent, though we'll know more once the results of his CT scan are in. Why don't you come down to the hospital tonight, and I'll go into more detail with you?"

Shocked into silence, Eden stared at her pale-faced daughter. Jonah didn't remember them.

"Ma'am?"

"Yes," she said automatically. "I'll be there in about an hour."

"Traumatology is on the third floor. Just ask for Commander Schmidt, and I'll escort you in to see your husband. Maybe someone should come with you?" he suggested.

"I'll bring my daughter."

The commander hesitated, no doubt picturing a small child. "I don't know if that's a—"

Eden hung up on him, too overwrought to explain. The phone slipped from her numb fingers, thudding to the bath mat. The flames of the candles danced in the corner of her eye. Maybe she'd drowned in the tub and was experiencing hallucinations.

"Mom!" It was Miriam, bending over her with silvery-purple hair instead of chestnut. "It's Dad, isn't it?" she demanded, searching Eden's expression. "He's back, isn't he?"

Eden couldn't tell if the edge to Miriam's voice was excitement or stress. Maybe she was worried about Jonah's reaction to her hair.

Poor Miriam. When Eden had married Jonah, her daughter had been euphoric at the thought of finally having a father. She'd insisted on calling him Dad right away, even when it was clear that unsettled Jonah. Her disillusionment upon realizing he had no time for an adolescent daughter had been hard to watch.

"He doesn't remember us." Eden heard herself relay what the doctor had told her. "He's suffering some kind of amnesia due to post-traumatic stress."

"He was probably tortured," Miriam stated.

Eden's stomach lurched at the bald statement. Her daughter could always be trusted to call a spade a spade.

"We need to get to the hospital." She started to rise out of the tub.

"Mom, you need to rinse your hair."

Oh, yes, her hair. Twisting the faucet, Eden stuck her head under a cold stream of water, hoping to shake off her shock.

With Miriam picking out her clothes, she dressed in record time, brushed the tangles out of her long hair, and jammed her feet into her tennis shoes.

"You want me to drive?" Miriam asked, looking suspiciously composed.

"Yeah, right." Eden forced a laugh. For someone who wasn't even related to Jonah, Miriam was a lot like him. She took blows without a blink, seemingly unfazed by the harsher aspects of life—until her stress manifested itself in some self-destructive behavior, which usually sent Eden scrambling for a counselor.

"It's not that hard to drive," Miriam insisted, following Eden down the hallway and out the front door.

Eden drove the silver Jaguar that had been Jonah's exclusive property. It was nearly nine o'clock on a gorgeous August evening. Leaving the coastal community in which they lived, they chased the sun that was sinking fast behind the pine trees. Eden took Route 264 at eighty miles an hour, fingers clamped so tightly on the steering wheel she had to pry them loose to turn up the radio.

I should be feeling grateful, she thought, realizing she wasn't. The dominant emotion residing in her chest at that moment was confusion. How could this be happening when she'd just acknowledged she was better off alone? What kind of selfish woman did that make her, accepting Jonah's death when he wasn't even dead? If he really was alive, then God had worked a miracle! She ought to be feeling grateful, not confused.

I'm just wary, she decided. She didn't know what to expect. After all, Jonah had been imprisoned for a year, by a country that was no friend of the United States. Under its current dictator, Venezuela had allied itself with Iran and North Korea. What if Jonah's captors had let those countries take a crack at interrogating him? If they'd known he was a Navy SEAL, they would have worked him over to the point of nearly killing him.

God help him. Help all of us, actually.

Glancing at Miriam, Eden wondered if her daughter felt as torn as she did. Miriam appeared utterly composed, staring out the window at the Norfolk and Portsmouth skylines.

"It's going to be all right, squirt," Eden said, if only to keep them on line and communicating. The counselors had all stressed the importance of communication.

Miriam didn't answer. Glancing down at her daughter's hands, Eden noticed that her fingers were crossed on both hands, as if for luck. What was she hoping for? That Jonah would remember them? That he would be okay?

It wouldn't be that easy, would it? Jonah was the toughest man Eden knew —even tougher than her father. He'd been hardened by his horrendous childhood to withstand hostility. For him to have repressed his memories, something truly awful must have been done to him.

The irony of having been reveling in her newfound freedom when the call came in did not escape her notice.

Of course, I'll be there for him, she assured herself. She'd been raised from childhood to consider marriage sacred. As Jonah's wife, she possessed certain obligations. She would welcome him home as warmly as any wife should. She would help him to regain his footing, do whatever was required of her. But after he'd healed mentally and emotionally, after he'd reestablished himself on the Teams, she might yet ask him for a separation. His supposed death had proven she was happier without him. Having tasted her freedom, she could never be content returning to the life she'd led before, and neither could Miriam.

With that decision made, the tension in her shoulders eased. For the time being, her move toward independence would have to wait. Blowing out a shaky breath, she accepted what had to be done. For now, Jonah needed her.

The knock at the door startled Jonah out of a drug-induced lethargy. He'd been staring at the blank TV screen envisioning a baseball game he remembered watching three years ago, wondering how he could remember that and not remember the two years that followed.

"Come in," he called, struggling to sit up straighter with an IV in his hand.

The knock had been charged with purpose. Jonah's pulse quickened to think this might just be his wife and kid—the ones he couldn't remember. Dr. Schmidt had warned him they were on their way.

A bouquet of flowers preceded his visitor through the door. Over a bright yellow spray of lilies, Jonah recognized the commander of Blue Squadron, Captain Daniel Dwyer, and he started clambering out of the bed to salute him, not sure he had the strength to do it.

"At ease, Lieutenant."

Dwyer's words had him sliding his legs back under the sheets—it was so cold in the room! Marching in, the CO deposited the vase of flowers on Jonah's bedside table.

"From the office," he explained, setting his cap beside the vase, then dusting a fallen petal off his dress whites. Dwyer appeared to be dressed for some important function.

"How's the patient today?" he asked, giving Jonah his full attention.

Jonah had always thought Dwyer resembled John Wayne, except with a head of salt-and pepper hair and a thick mustache, all black, which suggested he dyed it. He remembered his CO asking him that very question yesterday, only he had been too tranquilized to answer.

"Better, sir," he said. "I apologize for not responding yesterday."

Dwyer shrugged off the apology. "There's no need to explain, Lieutenant. You'll have bad days and good days. At least you remember me." His gray eyes narrowed, an implied question in his statement.

"Yes, sir, of course." Jonah sat a little taller, wishing he felt stronger. "I remember being stationed at Dam Neck with SEAL Team Six, working with Blue Squadron as a troop leader, but that was over two years ago."

Dwyer's long stare struck Jonah as grave. "Mind if I sit down?" he asked, heading for the recliner on the other side of Jonah's bed.

"Of course not, sir," Jonah murmured.

Watching the CO round the bed, his concern rose. What if Dwyer asked him the same questions that the NCIS Special Agent had asked him yesterday? What if Jonah lost his cool again and started stressing so badly he had to be shot up with another dose of lorazepam?

Dwyer hitched his perfectly creased trouser legs before sitting, military straight, on the edge of the recliner. "Tell me what you do remember."

Jonah swallowed hard. Dear God, how many times was he going to have to do this?

"Of the last mission, sir?"

"No, no," Dwyer corrected. "I mean everything. Start with the beginning. Where were you born?"

Oh, okay. Jonah's anxiety eased, though he knew this was only a reprieve. At least his childhood—as much as he'd like to forget it—was indelibly etched into his mind.

"I was born in Missouri, sir, my parents' only child. My mom ran a business out of the house. My father was a preacher."

Dwyer nodded approvingly. "Go on."

Jonah heaved an inward sigh. His life had gone steadily downhill after the age of five. "When I was five, my dad was killed in a car accident."

Dwyer's flexing eyebrows conveyed sympathy.

"My mom moved to Indiana and remarried when I was eight." Jonah opted to skip over the next decade—years of being bullied by his stepbrother, at least until he was big enough to fight back. His teen years were spent breaking into people's houses and stealing items he could pawn until Sergeant Reynolds of the Evansville Police Department intervened and essentially saved Jonah's life.

Captain Dwyer didn't need to hear how Reynolds had talked the judge into letting Jonah join the Navy in lieu of going to jail. He'd been given the chance to redeem his sorry life, and he had made the most of it.

"I enlisted when I was eighteen. They made me an intelligence specialist. I attended night school, got my B.S. and went to Officer Candidate School, then straight to BUDs after that."

Dwyer nodded approvingly. He'd clearly read up on Jonah's personnel file, which meant he knew all these facts for himself.

With a prick of impatience, Jonah summarized the rest of his history in a few clipped sentences.

"I graduated with Class 295 in 2012. I remember everything, all of my SEAL qualification training, every objective and every mission, right up to the jumping exercise in Oceana when Blake LeMere never opened his chute."

In fact, the memory of that training exercise traumatized Jonah like it had happened only yesterday. The vision of Blake plummeting past him as his own parachute billowed open filled him with horrified helplessness. He could do nothing but watch LeMere tumble toward the earth, eventually hitting the ground feet first. An investigation of the incident later revealed he hadn't opened his chute because he'd been unconscious. How and why LeMere had passed out shortly after leaping from the plane remained a mystery. That he had died unconscious, however, had been a small comfort.

Dwyer's eyes narrowed. "That's the last thing you remember? Blake LeMere's death?"

Jonah wracked his brain for a single memory that might have come after. A sharp pain, startling in its intensity, lanced the left side of his face, driving deep into his eye.

He clapped a hand over his eye and doubled over.

Dwyer jackknifed out of his chair to put a hand on his back.

"You okay, son? Should I call the nurse?"

"No, I'm fine," Jonah grated.

Forcing himself to sit up straight, he pulled his hand from his face and blinked Dwyer into focus.

"This happens sometimes," he added, deftly shrugging the CO's hand off his shoulder. "Apparently I took a blow to my left cheek."

Dwyer stepped back, crossed his arms, and frowned at him.

Jonah felt compelled to reassure him further. "The doctor says my memory loss is probably temporary. I'll get it back," he added, holding Dwyer's gaze with determination.

"What about your captivity? Do you remember that?"

And here it came, the questioning he'd dreaded.

"Not really. I remember waking up and realizing my cell door was open. No one was around, so I slipped away without anyone seeing me and ran straight toward the ocean. I stole a boat to get away, and I paddled for several days before a merchant vessel came across me."

He glanced surreptitiously at his blistered hands.

The CO drew a deep breath, the sound of which cinched Jonah's gut with worry.

"Look," Dwyer said, uncrossing his arms and letting them fall to his sides. "I'm not here to pressure you." His big hand rested on the railing between them. "You've been through enough already. I just want you to know I'm concerned about you."

"Yes, sir. Thank you, sir." Desiring with all his heart to return to the Teams, Jonah held his CO's gaze steadily.

Dwyer looked at his mouth. "That blow to your face," he said. "Dr. Schmidt thinks that's contributing to your amnesia."

That was news to Jonah. He'd been told his amnesia was due to post-traumatic stress. The doctor must have gotten the results of the CT scan.

"Really?" The news bolstered his confidence. SEALs weren't supposed to suffer long-term effects of post-traumatic stress. If it didn't go away on its own, it became a disorder—PTSD—and that would prevent him from returning to active duty. Losing his memory from a blow to his head looked better, didn't it?

"The scan shows damage to your frontal lobe," Dwyer continued gravely. "I'll let Schmidt explain the results in more detail. It's just—" his commander hesitated then shrugged, "he said there's a chance you may never get your memory back. The loss could be permanent."

Jonah swallowed his dismay. Dwyer had said the word *permanent* like it was the worst thing that could happen to a SEAL.

"I'm sorry, son," the CO added, confirming Jonah's perceptions.

"Sir, are you saying if I never get my memory back, I can't be on the Teams? Even if I remember all of my training?"

Searching Dwyer's inscrutable expression, Jonah tried to guess the answer before his leader said it.

"That's not strictly up to me. And there's still the matter of PTSD. If you're diagnosed with that, you can't be undertaking missions, obviously. If it's less pernicious than PTSD, then your doctors, Vice Admiral Holland, and I will all have to clear you before you can return to active duty."

Who? Jonah tried to hide his confusion.

"Oh, you wouldn't remember." Dwyer grimaced apologetically. "Holland replaced Vice Admiral Leland last year. He's the new base commander."

So much had changed! Jonah gripped the bed rail to ground himself.

"Son, I don't mean to pressure you," Dwyer added, his face the very picture of remorse, "but I need to know if you recall the night of your disappearance."

Jonah had figured the questioning wasn't over. Just like the NCIS investigator, Dwyer wanted to know what had happened to him in Venezuela. SEALs weren't supposed to fall into enemy hands—ever. They were trained to avoid capture at all costs, even take their own lives before letting the enemy lay hold of them. Yet, somehow, Jonah had been captured rather than perishing in the explosion which, according to Commander Schmidt, was believed to have caused his death.

"Do you remember anything?" Dwyer asked him. "Anything at all?"

In a desperate bid to restore his CO's faith in him, Jonah blew out a breath and focused inwardly. For the barest second, an image formed—light blazing in the darkness—but then it receded, lost in the gaping hole of the past two years. He winced as the pain behind his left eye threatened to return. Eyes closed, he shook his head, unable to admit to Dwyer's face that he could not.

His CO clapped a heavy hand on his shoulder again. "Relax, Lieutenant. There's nothing to be ashamed of. Obviously, we're delighted you're alive. It's a miracle you're here with us again," he insisted.

Maybe I'm just depressed, Jonah thought, but Dwyer didn't sound all that delighted.

"Concentrate on getting your strength back. Things will fall into place after that," the man assured him.

Too choked up to speak, Jonah kept his mouth shut.

"I hear they're releasing you tomorrow," Dwyer added, stepping back.

Jonah nodded. The reminder that he was going home to a family he couldn't remember stole his breath momentarily. The last home he recalled was an apartment on base for unmarried military personnel. His only family then had been his brothers in Alpha Troop.

"Are the guys around, sir?" He looked up at last. "Saul, Theo, Bambino and...and the new ensign, Lucas Strong?"

"Strong's a lieutenant junior grade now," Dwyer said with a wry smile. "He stepped into your shoes as troop leader."

"Oh." Jonah tempered his envy with the logic that someone had to lead the troop.

"The men are training off the coast right now," Dwyer said, rounding the foot of the bed. "I've radioed the news of your return, and Master Chief Rivera is flying back as we speak."

The news came as a relief. Master Chief was exactly the man to have around at a time like this. Unlike the CO, Alpha Troop's highest ranking enlisted officer wouldn't undermine Jonah's confidence. He'd bully Jonah into remembering and suggest he get his act together if he didn't want to disappoint his teammates. Jonah looked forward desperately to seeing him.

Dwyer retrieved his cap off the bedside table. "You can expect Rivera sometime tonight or tomorrow. He's going to help you with the paperwork and such."

Tucking his cap under his left arm, he held out a hand for Jonah to shake. "It's good to see you back, son."

"Thank you, sir." The CO's grip felt crushing.

"Your wife will take good care of you," Dwyer added, releasing him. "She must be out of her mind with joy to have you back."

Jonah couldn't comment. Not only could he not remember his wife, but he'd seen his body in the bathroom mirror. He couldn't imagine any woman wanting him, period.

"I'll be in touch." Swiveling on his polished shoes, Dwyer headed for the door.

"Good night, sir. Thank you for the flowers," Jonah called, though he couldn't bring himself to look at them. Weren't lilies more fitting for a funeral?

When the door closed quietly in the CO's wake, Jonah fell back against the pillows, emotionally drained. Doubts assailed him, putting a weight on his chest that made it hard to breathe. He counteracted the pressure with deep, tactical breaths and the reminder to trust in God.

I'm here, Father. And I think I'm going to need some help.

Over the faint pulse against his temples, he listened for the voice deep within. Strangely, he couldn't remember what that voice had ever said to him, but he knew the voice was there. More than that, he knew the source of the voice had gotten him through captivity. It had given him a second chance. Like Jonah from the Bible for whom he'd been named, God had saved him from the belly of the whale and put him back on land for a purpose.

How can I get my memories back? Without them, he'd never return to active duty—Jonah was sure of that.

Insidious fear spread through him as he considered what might happen to him. Being a SEAL had taught him self-respect, self-control. It had given him purpose and direction. It had given him a band of brothers. If he couldn't be a SEAL, what was his purpose in life? Being a husband? A father?

When and how had he let that happen? His father's death and the years of abuse at the hands of his stepbrother had convinced him never to wed. He'd known he would be a lousy husband, a terrible father. Tenderness? Compromise? Those were alien concepts to him. What had he been thinking to inflict himself on any woman?

"You idiot," he muttered, running a hand over his face.

And for him to have a kid already. How irresponsible could he be?

A light knock at the door brought his tortured thoughts up short. His heart began to pound.

Guess I'm about to find out, he thought, breaking into a sweat.

CHAPTER 2

"Come in," Jonah called, cursing the weakness that kept him from jumping out of bed.

The hospital door swung inward. Jonah recognized the khaki sleeve of Dr. Schmidt as he held the door for someone. Hospital noises rushed in—the ringing of a telephone, a voice on the intercom paging a doctor, elevator doors chiming as they reached his floor.

Then a woman stepped into the room. The emotion storming Jonah's arteries had him clutching the railing next to him to ground himself. He locked onto her like a homing missile, causing her approach to stall. She stared back at him, the very picture of astonishment.

A single thought entered Jonah's head. *Well, no wonder I'm married.*

Amber-colored eyes framed by dark lashes assessed him warily. Golden hair tumbled down her back as far as her waist. Her nose and lips were delicately drawn. Her chin sported a tiny cleft in the center. She wore a white T-shirt that, however loose, failed to hide her neat bosom and trim waist. Tan capris accentuated slim, fit thighs, and a pair of sandals showed off a recent pedicure and peach toenail polish. He could not stop staring at her.

"Jonah?" she whispered, as if she didn't recognize him either.

Maybe there'd been a mix up. Maybe she wasn't his wife but some other lucky guy's with the same name.

He nodded his head, about to say the name the doctor had given him when a second female edged into his line of sight. *Wait, maybe this is Eden.*

Except the second visitor with purple, shoulder-length hair was more a girl than a woman. Taller and stockier than the blonde, their similar eyes betrayed a mother-daughter relationship.

This couldn't be his kid. He'd forgotten two years, not more than a decade.

Confused beyond words, he looked back at Eden and, remarkably, his panic subsided. Beyond a doubt, she was the loveliest woman he had ever seen. His concern about being married eased. Why not? He loved a challenge. Maybe he was up to being a husband after all.

Eden fought the urge to turn tail and run, but Miriam, who had followed on her heels, blocked the only exit.

Jonah dominated the chamber. She ought to have expected that. Whenever he went away and came back, it took days to get used to having him around. His aura took up an inordinate amount of space, not that he was a giant at six feet, one inch. All the same, his bed looked like a baby carriage with him in it.

Because it was expected, she inched toward him, waiting for him to say something. His stunned expression was so open, so unguarded, she questioned whether she was really looking at Jonah or some kind of look-alike.

Venturing closer, she inspected him for clues. He looked different in a hospital gown, anyway, with an IV stuck into the back of his hand. He was thinner than she'd ever seen him, yet the breadth of his shoulders still strained the short sleeves of the gown. His sunburned arms, roped with lean muscle, looked familiar. His cheeks, more hollowed than ever, sharpened his straight nose and high cheekbones. Yet, aside from a new scar on his upper lip and some cuts and nicks, he looked too much like Jonah to be anyone else.

She checked his eyes and that cinched it. Light green with a gold starburst at the center, those eyes were singularly stunning. Glinting with the same intelligence and intensity that had drawn her to him over two years ago, she felt herself being drawn to him even still.

"Hey," she greeted him in a voice thin with uncertainty. "How are you?"

Her mundane question prompted such a familiar, crooked smile any remaining doubt evaporated. He was Jonah, all right, though now he was missing an eyetooth. Without it, his perfectly symmetrical face took on a roguish, piratical look, making him somehow more endearing.

"I've been told I should be dead, so guess I'm great."

Every cell of her body reacted to the familiar sound of his rough-edged baritone. Her heart raced and her blood heated. Her body *knew* him, especially when he looked at her with such blatant appreciation. That same look had drawn her to him in the first place.

"You really don't remember me, do you?" For some reason, it shocked her to the core, but clearly, the doctor hadn't been exaggerating.

Her question prompted Jonah to scrutinize her almost desperately. She clutched her purse closer, supremely self-conscious.

At last, he shook his head. "I don't know how I could forget, but I'm sorry. I don't."

An unexpected hurt pricked her. To conceal it, Eden reached for Miriam and tugged her closer.

"This is Miriam," she said, making introductions. "She's your stepdaughter."

Eden watched Jonah's confusion clear. To her surprise, he extended a hand to Miriam and with a welcoming smile said, "Hi, Miriam."

Stepping past Eden, Miriam ignored his hand, leaned over the bed, and hugged Jonah fiercely.

"Welcome home, Dad," she blurted in a choked voice.

Over Miriam's shoulder, Eden returned Jonah's startled reaction. Clearly, neither one of them had expected Miriam to hug him.

When all he said was a mumbled, "Thanks," Miriam pulled away, belatedly self-conscious, and Eden heaved an inward sigh. Jonah wasn't any more prepared to be a father than he'd been two years ago.

Uh oh. Interpreting his expectant look, she realized he was hoping she would hug him, too.

Oh, dear. Eden glanced at Dr. Schmidt, who watched their reunion through perceptive blue eyes. She supposed she had to do the expected.

Steeling herself against his appeal, she bent over the bed, offering him a perfunctory hug and using her purse as an excuse to use only one arm. But she could not immediately pull back. Jonah had hooked his free arm around her shoulders and was holding her captive.

Burying his nose into her damp hair, he breathed her scent as if she were a flower. Her body blazed with heat as it always had. The smell of soap, rubbing alcohol, and a scent that was uniquely his weakened her momentarily, before she found the strength to withdraw from his embrace.

"Welcome home," she murmured, utterly discomfited.

Jonah's eyes narrowed, making him look more like the old Jonah. He could tell she hadn't wanted the hug to continue.

"Yeah, well…" He ran a hand through his thick hair in an uncertain gesture she had never seen him make before. "I'm sorry. I wish I remembered you."

"That's okay." Feeling guilty, Eden turned to Dr. Schmidt, pulling him into the conversation in order to ease the sudden tension. "He'll remember eventually, though, right, Doctor?"

By way of reply Dr. Schmidt crossed to the laptop mounted on a rolling platform.

"That's certainly to be hoped," he prevaricated, rousing the computer and logging in. "Apart from the PTS any soldier sustains in captivity, the results of Lieutenant Mill's CT scan show some damage to the rostral area of his prefrontal cortex."

Eden glanced at Jonah, then back at the doctor. "I have no idea what that means," she said.

With quick strokes on the keyboard, Dr. Shafter brought up several images of a human brain. She assumed it was Jonah's.

"You can see the darker areas right here and here showing dead tissue. Damage to this region correlates with the scar on his lip and the fact that he's missing his upper eyetooth. He clearly suffered a blow to the left side of his face. Now, the prefrontal cortex is responsible for such things as memory, complex cognitive functioning, social behavior, even personality. Granted, the damage we see here isn't very extensive, but it is irreversible. If Jonah's memory loss isn't a side effect of post-traumatic stress, then it may be permanent."

The doctor dropped his hands and turned toward Jonah with a grimace of sympathy. "I wish I had better news."

Jonah said nothing. His expression had turned to stone, making him look like the Jonah Eden used to know.

The doctor slid his hands into his pockets. "Still, we can't rule out temporary amnesia, as it is a common side-effect of PTS," he continued, "so we'll start with that explanation first and see where it gets us. The sooner you return to a normal environment, Jonah, the sooner your healing can begin. We'd like to release him tomorrow," he added, looking at Eden.

"Tomorrow?" she repeated, feeling ill equipped to take on a soldier who suffered from post-traumatic stress, a husband who didn't remember her, a man who was virtually a stranger.

"I'm prescribing extensive therapy," Dr. Schmidt continued. "Dr. Branson is a renowned psychiatrist whose specialty is in cognitive behavioral therapy. He'll drop by tomorrow morning just to meet you, Jonah. His office is on Oceana Air Base, however, which I know to be closer to your home, so you can continue to see him there."

Eden had to widen her stance to counteract her sudden dizziness.

Miriam shifted closer.

"Jonah, your first follow-up with Dr. Branson is—" the doctor stole a peek at the tablet in his breast pocket "—the day after tomorrow, Wednesday, at fourteen hundred hours. He'll give you his business card with the address on it when he drops by in the morning."

Eden swung a look at Jonah, expecting him to protest the need for any therapy. Instead he just returned her gaze.

"Is that okay with you?" the doctor asked her.

"With me?"

"You'll have to drive Jonah to Oceana," Dr. Schmidt explained.

"Oh."

"In addition to PTS, he suffers from Chronic Fatigue Syndrome—a result of sleep deprivation. Plus, he really shouldn't drive while on the meds he's taking. His memories could return to him at any time. Some of them could be jarring—dangerous, should he be behind the wheel of a car."

"I see. Sure, no problem," she assured both men. In reality, she already had a work conflict.

Jonah spoke up suddenly. "What can I do to get my memories back faster?"

Eden's lips quirked at the typical-sounding question. Home for a day and he was already chafing to get back into the field.

Dr. Schmidt leveled an admonishing look at him.

"You can't treat this like a mission, Jonah. So much of it is out of your control. Putting you in a familiar environment is the first step. Surrounding yourself with familiar smells, sounds, or situations ought to trigger some memories. Others will return in the form of dreams, though you'll have significant trouble sleeping, I imagine. A prescription of Prazosin will counteract that."

Eden pictured Jonah prowling through the house at night and quailed.

"There's bound to be an adjustment period," Dr. Schmidt allowed, "but you can bring up any issues you're having when you meet with Dr. Branson Wednesday afternoon."

Eden's knees jittered. Everything was happening so quickly.

"I'm sorry. What time did you say the appointment is?" She pulled her cell phone from her pocket to add it to her calendar.

"Fourteen hundred hours on Wednesday."

She would have to get Karen to cover her CORE class.

"Okay," she said, adding Jonah's meeting with the therapist atop the class she was scheduled to teach.

Dr. Schmidt waited for her to finish before putting a hand out to her.

"Eden, Miriam, it was nice to meet both of you. I'll leave you three to visit, and I'll see you tomorrow when you come to pick up Jonah—say, oh-nine hundred? We'll need you to sign some papers."

"Okay," she said again, though it was anything but.

The door shut behind the doctor, and the three of them were left alone.

Jonah probed Eden's expression and said nothing. Avoiding his gaze, she looked around.

"Someone brought you flowers?" she asked, spying a vase full of lilies on the bedside table.

"Captain Dwyer," Jonah said, frowning in recollection. "He was just here to see me."

"Oh, good." It relieved her to hear she wasn't solely responsible for Jonah's welfare.

"Master Chief's flying in tonight. I should see him soon."

Even better, Eden thought. The more support from his team the less pressure on her.

"You're still on IV," she noted, glancing at the needle taped to the back of his hand.

"Yeah, I've been enjoying a diet of plasma and antibiotics all day. They let me have toast for dinner. It was great." He sent her his crooked smile, then glanced at his feet almost shyly.

It was like looking at a ghost. "I can't believe you're alive," she heard herself say.

He glanced back at her. Was that hope she saw, tempered with the same wariness she felt?

Miriam, who was looking back and forth between them, spoke up suddenly.

"I knew you weren't dead."

"We went to his memorial," Eden reminded her daughter.

"I know." Miriam shrugged. "But I knew he wasn't dead."

Baffled by Miriam's conviction, Eden quickly changed the subject.

"Dr. Schmidt said a fishing vessel picked you up on the ocean?"

"Yeah, I, uh...," Jonah broke eye contact as his thoughts turned inward. "I nabbed some poor fisherman's boat and pointed it straight north, hoping to run into Curaçao. I hope I didn't ruin the man's livelihood."

Eden blinked again. For Jonah to think of someone else's well-being—aside from a teammate's—was completely out of character.

"You were in Venezuela all this time?"

He flinched at the question, raised his free hand, and rubbed his left eye. "That's probably classified," he equivocated.

His remote tone conveyed an unwillingness to talk about it. Glimpsing stunted fingernails growing back on several fingers of the hand rubbing his eye startled her so badly, she turned and walked toward the adjoining bathroom. Miriam was right. He had been tortured.

"Do you have everything you need here?" she asked, hanging up a hand towel and putting the lid on the toothpaste. "Can I bring you anything?"

"I'm fine," he said. "I'm only here for one more night."

With her back still turned, Eden heard him ask Miriam, "What grade are you in?"

Eden stilled at the question.

"I'm a rising tenth grader." This was said in Miriam's most sophisticated voice.

"Wow, high school. That makes you, what, fifteen?"

"Almost. I have a late birthday, September 8th."

Eden turned around in time to see Jonah shift his weight onto an elbow so he and Miriam were facing each other.

"Mine's in July," he said. "I remember turning thirty-three, but now I'm thirty-five with no memory of any more birthdays. Weird, huh?"

What was happening? Eden had never heard Jonah converse casually with

Miriam. Children were meant to be seen and not heard, he used to say. He'd certainly never asked Miriam for her opinion.

"I remember your thirty-fourth birthday," Miriam volunteered. "We had a party on our deck."

"We did?" He searched her face with interest.

"Yep, Mom threw you a surprise party and invited all your friends."

"Mom, huh?" His catlike eyes swung toward Eden, who felt her face heat.

"I like your friend Saul best," Miriam added.

Picturing the rough-and-tumble SEAL with a gold hoop in one ear and frightening tattoos on his arms, Eden expected Jonah to disapprove. Instead he said, "I like him, too. He's a really good guy."

A moment later, stifling a groan, he sank back onto the bed as if suddenly weary.

Eden returned to his bedside. "We should probably go. You need your rest."

With his head against the pillow, Jonah struck her as curiously vulnerable. His hair, in bad need of a haircut, had fallen over one eye, giving him a boyish demeanor.

"You just got here," he protested, but he sounded suddenly exhausted.

"I know, but you've been through a lot, and you'll want to save some energy for tomorrow. Besides, I need to make some phone calls and free up my work schedule."

A hint of her overwrought state must have crept into her voice for Jonah immediately apologized. "I'm sorry. I'm probably an unexpected burden."

"Not at all," she assured him. "I'm happy to help. Are you kidding? This is amazing…to see you again and…" Not knowing what else to say that wouldn't mislead him into thinking everything was hunky dory, she let her voice trail off.

"I'll see you in the morning," she said instead. "What time are they releasing you again?"

"Oh-nine hundred," he replied, proving there was nothing wrong with his short-term memory.

"I'll see you then," she promised, hitching her purse strap higher. Now what? Should she embrace him, kiss his cheek, or simply walk out?

She opted for a quick smile and a wave. "Come on, squirt."

Spinning on her soles, she practically ran for the door.

Miriam followed at a more desultory pace.

"It'll be all right," Eden heard her daughter tell Jonah.

Would it, though? Things were steady, calm, and normal when Jonah was supposedly dead. Now that he was alive again, with no memory of their brief, disappointing marriage, everything seemed off-kilter, unnerving, and a little frightening, if she were honest. There were way too many variables in this crazy equation for things to be all right.

CHAPTER 3

*J*onah's eyes sprang open. Save for a soft line of light under the door, he lay in a room steeped in darkness. His sluggish mind informed him he was still in his squalid cell in Carenero, Venezuela, and danger was coming, as it always did in the darkest part of the night.

A faint creaking sound, like that of cane being flexed, reached his ears.

Please, God, not another caning. He lacked the energy to endure that particular torture, not to mention the hours following as he rode on waves of feverish agony.

Jonah felt for a weapon, anything he could use to fend off his captors, to dissuade them from taking him—at the very least to slow them down.

As the creaking came again from somewhere close, Jonah's fingers closed around the handle of an object, one that was full of liquid. A silhouette loomed over him, suddenly, and Jonah tossed the contents of the pitcher at it. With a startled exclamation, his attacker jumped back. Jonah hurled the pitcher for good measure and scrambled out of the contraption he was in, tearing off some kind of creature—a snake!—that bit into the back of his hand. In an instant, he was on his feet with the contraption between himself and his attacker.

Cursing in Spanish, the man snapped on the light and yelled at him.

"Jaguar, it's me!" He gestured to his sodden T-shirt. "What are you trying to do, drown me?"

At the sight of his master chief, Jonah sucked in a breath of disbelief. He groped for the bedside table for something solid to hold onto. A few darting glances corroborated where he was: not in some dark cell, but in the Portsmouth Naval Medical Center facing his beloved master chief, who'd apparently just risen from the leather recliner by Jonah's bed.

"Santiago," he whispered, struggling to clear his head.

Santiago Rivera looked exactly the same—lean and swarthy, with hair one shade darker than his espresso-colored eyes. Rivera's look of outrage shifted into one of concern as he beheld Jonah's transformation.

"You're okay," he said, in that soothing manner of his that calmed even the greenest Navy SEAL during harrowing missions.

Rounding the bed cautiously, he looked Jonah up and down, taking note of every new scar, every outward sign of abuse. Pausing about a foot away, he laid a tentative hand on Jonah's bony shoulder.

"I didn't mean to wake you. I was trying to get comfortable." Rivera gestured at the leather recliner on the other side of the bed.

Jonah couldn't help noticing the man's rough appearance. In complete contrast to Captain Dwyer, Rivera looked like he'd spent the last six weeks aboard a coastal patrol craft. His black hair was overly long and curly, his chin in need of a shave. He wore an odiferous naval warfare uniform, with the jacket cast aside. The white T-shirt, sodden from the water Jonah had just tossed at him, was stretched and stained with sweat.

Nothing in the world could have looked more dear to Jonah. He knew a startling urge to burst into tears and to hurl himself into Rivera's arms. At the same time, he wanted to die for having revealed the pitiful state of his over-wrought nervous system.

"You're groggy from medication," Rivera said, justifying Jonah's overreaction. "Go in the bathroom and splash water on your face."

As an officer, Jonah didn't have to take orders from his master chief, but he gratefully obeyed, seizing the chance to pull himself together.

He doused his whole head in cold water, hoping it would help him shake off the dulling effects of the tranquilizer he'd been given. Drying off his hair first, he then scrubbed his face. With his composure restored, he carried a dry towel out to his master chief. "Here."

Rivera dabbed the wet spot on his T-shirt. Draping the towel over his neck, he reached for Jonah, turning him toward the light to better see him. His expression of tenderness put a lump in Jonah's throat.

"Am I looking at a ghost?" Rivera asked him.

Jonah laughed. "Yeah, maybe. I feel like I've been resurrected."

To his secret relief, Rivera pulled him into a wet embrace. It felt so good to be held. In fact, he couldn't remember the last time he'd hugged someone, apart from his cute but strange stepdaughter and that half-hearted embrace from his wife. The urge to weep rose up in him again.

At last Rivera set him at arm's length. His dark eyes glittered with tears as he inspected him more closely.

"I thought I would never see your ugly face again." In his lilting cadence influenced by his Puerto Rican heritage, the insult sounded like an endearment. "How can you be alive?" he added. "The warehouse exploded with you in it."

Jonah tried desperately to remember then shook his head. "I don't know. I can't remember the mission at all."

"There were four of you—you, Theo, Saul, and Lowery."

Jonah frowned. "What was Lowery doing there? Isn't he too senior to go on ops?"

"Lowery took Taylor Rex's place. You remember Taylor. His foot got crushed when that roof in Chiapas caved in. He's off the Team now."

Jonah did not remember. He shook his head with a sense of shame. "There's a lot I can't remember right now."

"You will," Rivera assured him. "Just give it time."

"What happened to Taylor? What's he doing now?" Jonah couldn't help thinking he might be the next man cut from the Team.

"He got a prosthetic foot and a therapy dog. He serves on the police force in his home town. In fact, I hear he's getting married."

"It's good to hear there's life after the Teams," Jonah mused.

"You're not going to be med-dropped," Rivera said with certainty. "Your memories will return, and the PTS will fade," he added, proving he had discovered Jonah's diagnosis.

Jonah latched onto Master Chief's optimism. "I hope so. Unless it turns into PTSD. Plus, they say there's some damage to my brain behind my left eye. Apparently, I took a blow to the face."

Rivera cocked his head and considered him more closely. "Maybe that's how you got that scar on your lip."

Jonah grimaced and showed him his missing tooth.

"Oh," said Rivera, then chuckled.

"The doctor says the brain damage is permanent."

Rivera's smile disappeared.

"I might never get my memory back."

"Never?" One of Master Chief's dark eyebrows shot up. "I didn't think you knew that word, sir."

Jonah smiled at the gentle ribbing. Rivera was exactly the man he needed around him right now. "I've lost two years of memories, though," he pointed out. "Who forgets that much?"

Master Chief had no immediate answer.

"Dwyer came to see me," Jonah added. "I got the feeling he's cut me already."

"No." Rivera shook his head with vigor. "The CO's thrilled that you're alive. He's retiring soon, that's all, so he couldn't care less whether you get your memories back. By the time you return to active duty, there'll be a new CO."

"I have to be a SEAL, Santiago," Jonah grated. A sudden shiver wracked his body.

"You're cold," Rivera noted. "Get back into bed. I'll call a nurse to put your IV back in."

Chagrined by his weakened state, Jonah climbed into bed, pulling the blankets over him as Rivera wound up the IV tube.

"I'd rather have some real food," he groused.

"I'll see what I can do," Rivera promised.

The edge of Jonah's pillow was wet from the water he'd tossed. Exhaustion swamped him suddenly, keeping him from doing anything more than shifting his head to a dry spot while shuddering under the blanket. He'd never felt more helpless in his life.

Recovering his strength and two years of missing memories seemed an impossible feat from his present perspective. But he was a SEAL, and a SEAL never gave up.

Suspecting Jaguar had fallen asleep, Santiago hung up the IV tube and looked down at the lieutenant. The shock he'd masked earlier washed over him. The once supremely confident Jaguar looked like a scrawny teenager. With zero body fat on his large frame, no wonder he was cold.

Exhaustion purpled the sunken sockets of Jaguar's eyes. Dark eyelashes fanned his sharp cheekbones. The pale, thin scar that hadn't been on his lip before the mission-gone-wrong seemed to reflect the light shining from the bathroom.

A fatherly affection rose in Santiago, making him want to pull the blanket higher over the lieutenant's shoulder and tuck it under his feet. He satisfied himself with switching off the light. Jaguar's pride had taken enough of a blow for the evening.

Lowering himself back into the leather recliner, Santiago bent to lace his boots so he could fetch a nurse. As he did so, he recalled the last time he'd seen Juaguar alive. He'd been boarding a UH-60 Black Hawk on route to the carrier *USS Kearsage* in the Gulf.

As Jaguar had ducked into the helo, followed immediately by Lt. Lowery, a feeling akin to foreboding had seized Santiago. When word had come the next day that Lt. Mills had disappeared following an explosion, Santiago's premonition had seemed like a psychic revelation.

But Jaguar was alive. Never in his wildest imaginings had Santiago considered he might have escaped what the other men described as a massive, planned detonation. To see him, resurrected, defied comprehension. It made his heart swell with gratitude. At the same time, a certain disquiet kept Santiago from rejoicing.

The failed mission had given rise to an NCIS investigation, yet so many questions remained unanswered. The only SEAL who might answer them was Jaguar himself—if only his memories would come back to him.

Eden watched Jonah pause in the parking garage at the Portsmouth Naval Medical Center to admire his automobile. Dressed in the jeans and T-shirt she'd brought from what little clothing of his she'd yet to donate to the American Veterans, he looked less like a starved prisoner-of-war and more like himself. The familiar sight of the car he'd owned before their marriage obviously cheered him. She worried for a moment he would inspect it for recent scratches or even comment on the fact that Eden was supposed to be driving the Jeep. Of course, for the time being, he didn't remember that. Clearly, there were perks to his amnesia.

Slipping behind the wheel, she glanced at the car's digital clock—nearly noon. It had taken two hours for the psychiatrist, Bart Branson, and then Dr. Schmidt to clear Jonah for release. Filling his prescriptions and signing paperwork had taken yet another hour. If not for Master Chief Rivera's calming presence, Eden might have spent the entire morning on edge.

Jonah had displayed surprising patience. She supposed he was too tired, depressed, or medicated to grow agitated when the process dragged on for an eternity. Just once, when reviewing the paperwork that declared him disabled, possibly a victim of PTSD, had she seen him grow visibly upset.

Reading the paperwork herself, she saw it would take the recommendation of his psychiatrist, Dr. Schmidt, his commanding officer, and the base commander before Jonah could be cleared for active duty. What's more, he had to be cleared within a twelve-month period to be considered. And if he failed to meet the rigorous standards imposed by Naval Special Warfare, he'd be relegated to a disabled status permanently.

Eden had shaken her head at the cruel irony of Jonah's situation. He'd been missing for more than twelve months, and now he had just twelve months' time to get over what had happened to him.

By the time she'd signed her life away by agreeing to ferry Jonah to and from his counseling appointments, her goodwill had nearly run dry. They still had a half hour's drive to get home and little to talk about, given that Jonah didn't even know them. Miriam's chatter began to fill the quiet car as she said aloud whatever popped into her head.

Concerned that Jonah would lose his patience, as Eden accelerated onto the highway she suggested, "Honey, why don't you be quiet for a while and let Jonah relax."

He turned his head to look at her. "I like it when she talks."

The assertion stunned her. Eden was still pondering how different Jonah seemed from the uptight husband she'd known when they drove into Sandbridge, prompting Miriam to blurt, "Guess which house is ours."

Eden turned left onto Sandfiddler Drive, reducing Jonah's options. The Atlantic Ocean, denim-blue and covered in white-caps, lay just beyond the ocean-front homes to their right. Even on a Tuesday afternoon in August, the beach crawled with tourists who'd rented out the wooden castles at the edge of the sea for their summer vacation.

Their own home, occupied year-round, was in less peril of being swept away by hurricanes, positioned as it was a hundred yards from the back gate of Dam Neck Naval Base.

"This one?" Jonah asked, indulging Miriam's request. He pointed at a fairy-tale beach house, complete with turrets and towers.

Miriam laughed. "No, not that one."

Eden studied Jonah with interest. Was he playing this game with Miriam because he had nothing better to do? In the past, his job kept him constantly preoccupied. He'd scarcely acknowledged her daughter's presence, let alone indulged her in a whim.

"Oh, I know," he said, sounding confident this time. "It's coming up now, that one on the left." He pointed out a beach home resembling a museum of modern art with its streamlined architecture.

Miriam hooted, enjoying herself. "Not that one, either."

Eden used the rearview mirror to glance at her daughter's dancing eyes. Hadn't Miriam been happier, like she was, when Jonah was gone?

With too much to think about, Eden guided the Jaguar around the bend. Passing two more houses, she swung into their driveway, next to the Jeep that didn't run.

"Whose car is that?" Jonah asked.

"Mine. I need to replace the battery."

"I can help with that."

Okay. Jonah on disability was going to be a whole new experience. "Thanks."

He studied their home, in no apparent hurry to get out of the car. Trying to envision it from his eyes, Eden studied the modest wooden contemporary perched atop a dozen fat pilings and wondered if he might be disappointed. It was two stories high, with a laundry room, shower, and workshop on the ground level. Wooden steps zigzagged up to the front door where a balcony wrapped around the right side of the home, overlooking the front yard, their neighbor's house, and the Atlantic Ocean, only a short walk away.

In the front yard, she had planted wildflowers on little mounds of fertile soil: valerian, chicory, and black-eyed Susans. They splashed color onto the sandy yard, creating an effect like a Monet painting. She glanced at Jonah to gauge his response and found him looking baffled.

Miriam leaned over the seat and peered at his profile. "You don't remember," she guessed.

"No," he admitted, on a note of disappointment. "But I like it," he added. "Especially the flowers."

Eden exchanged a startled look with Miriam. The Jonah they had known never slowed down long enough to notice pretty things, like flowers. With an inward shrug, Eden pushed open her door and jumped out, hurrying to help Jonah from the car.

That morning she'd dressed in a denim skirt and a peach top. Warm sand crept into her sandals as she rounded the car to open Jonah's door. Miriam had beat her to it, so she paused at the trunk to fetch Jonah's meager possessions.

The hospital had sent him home with a box that held the vase of lilies, a baby cactus given to him by his psychiatrist, and a business card from an NCIS Special Agent Lloyd Elwood. She'd tossed his prescriptions into the box making it easy to carry everything at once.

Shutting the trunk, she stared for a moment at the vision of Miriam assisting Jonah from the car and toward the house. Apart from the hug Miriam had given Jonah yesterday, Eden had never seen them touch before. Yet, there they were, touching shoulder to thigh, with Jonah's arm around Miriam's neck, leaning on her. Chatting casually, her daughter started with him up the many stairs.

Dr. Schmidt's words the day before came back to her all at once. *The prefrontal cortex is responsible for things like memory, complex cognitive functioning, social behavior, even personality.*

Oh, wow, Eden thought. Was Jonah different because of the blow to his face?

The challenge before her seemed suddenly overwhelming. Not only was she having to take in a husband she'd already buried, at least in her heart and mind, but for the next twelve months—unless he got his memory back—she'd be living with a virtual stranger.

You're on this, right, God? You know I can't do this without help.

Jonah heard a dog barking frantically inside the home he could not remember. The sound was as welcoming as the flowers growing in lush islands throughout the yard. It gave him the energy to keep climbing.

"We have a dog?" he panted, grateful for Miriam's slow, steady pace.

She craned her neck to glance up at him. "Yeah, you gave us a puppy before you left. You were going to train her to behave, but you never had time, so she's still a little wild."

Two unrelated things entered Jonah's thoughts. The first was Miriam had a dusting of freckles across her nose that made her look like a pixie. The second was she sounded worried about the dog's behavior.

"I can train her now," he offered.

"Excuse me." Eden squeezed past them carrying a box. "Let me get the door."

Both women struck Jonah as anxious. Clearly, he'd been gone so long he seemed like a stranger to them.

As Eden released the lock and cracked the door open, a golden nose appeared.

"Sabrina, back," Eden ordered, edging her knee into the door to keep the dog from rushing out.

But Sabrina had other ideas. Jostling Eden aside, she burst out of the house and scrabbled down the stairs at a run, heading straight for Jonah. Miriam threw herself in front of him, and the dog crashed into them both. Jonah staggered several steps backward, and his wife let out a cry of alarm, before he managed to catch both him and Miriam from falling.

At least he wasn't totally useless. He could still take on an overgrown pup.

Miriam tackled the dog, pinning her on the steps with what looked like a death grip.

"Are you okay?" she cried.

He looked from her to Eden, who stared down from the top step with deep concern in her eyes.

Squirming in Miriam's arms, the dog gave a yelp and a happy bark.

"I'm fine," he assured them both. Then he reached out a hand to pet the rambunctious canine.

It was obvious the dog recognized him—weird, though, because he would have sworn he'd never met her before.

"She remembers you, Dad!" Miriam said, breaking into a bright smile.

"You can let her go," Jonah said, bracing himself against the railing so he wouldn't fall.

The word *Dad* reverberated in his head, shaking him and humbling him at the same time. *How am I a dad?*

With reluctance, Miriam released her death grip.

The dog sprang from her arms and, for a full minute, Jonah suffered a barrage of affectionate leaps, barks, and licks. The dog's giddiness filled him with unexpected contentment.

"Okay, okay." Scrubbing the dog's ruff, he laughed out loud at the small but reassuring indication he belonged here. The dog knew him. The dog obviously loved him. Everything was going to be okay.

Thank you, good Lord, he thought. But then he looked up at his family, and his optimism wavered. Both Miriam and Eden were staring at him with their mouths hanging open.

What? he wanted to ask, but there were so many things he didn't understand about their relationship he decided to wait and to watch.

To everything there is a season, and a time to every purpose under the heaven.

"Does she need a walk?" he said to Miriam.

It was Eden who answered, firmly. "Yes. I'll get the leash."

Darting into the house with everything still in her arms, she came out a second later, bearing the leash. "Miriam, why don't you walk Sabrina while I get Jonah settled."

"Fine," Miriam groused, then amended with a wary glance at Jonah, "Yes, ma'am."

Jonah helped her to clip the leash on the dog. She then dragged Sabrina down the steps for her walk. The dog clearly wanted him to come, too.

"I'll walk her with you soon," he offered.

Realizing Eden had to help him up the steps now, he looked up to see her approaching him warily. Every cell in his body perked up at the promise of her touch. She slid a tentative arm around his waist, put her shoulder into his arm pit. "Ready?"

"Yeah." Appalled by the weakness in his legs, he ordered himself to climb the last few steps to the open door. That same flowery scent that had stolen into his nostrils when she hugged him at the hospital filled his head, making him take great big breaths as he fought to place it. He recognized her scent; he knew he did!

"Wait." He paused before the door, trying to ground himself.

"You okay?"

Up close, her eyes were like amber pools, so clear you could see the pebbles at the bottom.

"I just...I remember your perfume," he admitted.

Her lovely eyes widened. "But I'm not wearing any. It must be my shampoo. I've used it forever."

He wanted to bury his nose in her hair to make certain, but since that seemed more intimate a gesture than their current relationship allowed, he refrained.

Urging him forward, she shepherded him into the cool, fragrant house and then released him to pick up the box she'd brought in, carrying it toward the kitchen.

Jonah glanced around, recognizing nothing. A high, slanted ceiling complete with skylights sheltered the open floorplan. A floral couch and matching armchair were positioned around a bright turquoise ceramic chimney. A glass-top table and six chairs and sideboard comprised the dining area. The kitchen boasted cream-colored cabinets, gray granite counters, and an island with turquoise stools. None of it rang a bell.

Eden was setting his box on the island, so he made his way closer and sat heavily on one stool, watching her unload it.

"Shall we put your lilies on the table?" she asked, glancing his way as she carried them there.

Frankly, Jonah didn't care where the lilies ended up. Sudden exhaustion kept him from commenting. Swaying on the stool, he struggled to remain sitting upright.

Eden returned to the box. "What about the baby cactus? Probably the kitchen window." She crossed to the sink where a bay window looked out onto the deck.

"From Dr. Branson," she noted, reading the sticker on the side of the plastic cup. "Did you like him?"

Jonah thought back to the plump psychiatrist who'd evaluated him that morning.

"I guess." He thought the man had seemed both intrigued and perplexed by Jonah's memory loss.

Eden studied him in silence for a moment, then glanced at her watch. "It's time for one of your pills." She lifted his bagged prescriptions out of the box.

Jonah watched her read the labels intently. Finally, she set down one pill bottle and opened the other, shaking a small white pill into her hand.

He'd been told by his psychiatrist that a strict regimen of Sertraline by day would help his anxiety, while Prazosin would help to curb his PTS-related nightmares. Jonah balked at the idea of taking either medication. Yet with

Eden holding out a Sertraline to him, and wanting desperately to get his memory back, he took it.

"How about some lemonade?" she offered, spinning toward the refrigerator. Seconds later, she placed a tall glass in front of him, before pouring a second glass for herself.

A thick silence filled the pleasant kitchen. Jonah tossed back his pill, drank most of the lemonade, and put the glass down heavily.

"This place is really nice," he said, wanting to smooth out the tension between them.

"Thanks." She sipped from her glass, avoiding eye contact.

Jonah studied her with perplexity. "Look," he said, marshaling the strength to get his thoughts across, "I know it's asking a lot of you to take me in."

"This is your home, too," she interrupted. But her spine remained stiff, and the look in her eyes wasn't as welcoming as he would have liked.

"But...?" He knew there was more she wanted to say.

Thoughts ebbed and flowed in her lovely eyes. "But nothing," she insisted.

He released a short weary sigh followed by a chuckle. "Funny, I don't remember you at all, but I know you're not telling me everything."

Looking her directly in her eyes, he waited. At the same time, his abs flexed in anticipation of taking a fist to the diaphragm. If she told him what was really on her mind, he was sure he wasn't going to like it.

Eden's heart thudded. Was this the time to be honest with Jonah? Her plan was to welcome him back into their lives, to do her duty by him, and eventually, after he got his memory back—or in twelve months, whichever came sooner—she would ask him for a separation.

He was giving her that look, though, that demanded honesty. And she was so overwrought by his return, it was tempting simply to tell him the truth now. Why suffer through the pretense of being happily married when she could explain right away why he wouldn't be sleeping in her bed? She wet her dry lips, uncertain how to answer.

"Jonah," she began in a tight voice, "you've been gone a long time—thirteen months." She paused for a quick breath. "We were told you were dead. I have a flag from your memorial," she added, reliving her shock when it was given to her.

Glancing at his expression, she sought a reaction from him, but he was suddenly as enigmatic as a rock, like the old Jonah.

Feeling her hand start to shake, she quickly put her glass down. "Don't think we're not grateful to have you back—we are. Truly. It's just...Miriam and I got used to being alone. I got a job teaching fitness classes at the base gym, and I really like it," she added, hearing the defensiveness in her own voice.

"That's great."

His response threw her completely off track. Eden stared. "But you told me not to work."

It was Jonah's turn to fall silent. A crease appeared between his eyebrows, betraying perplexity.

"If you're worried I'm going to interfere with your job, I can always get an Uber to my doctor appointments," he assured her. "I'm assuming Uber is still a thing?"

"Yes." She waved aside his offer. "No, driving you isn't a problem. I can work my schedule around your doctor appointments."

His green eyes narrowed. "So what else is going on?" he pressed.

He'd been so agreeable about her job she couldn't bring herself to tell him their marriage was essentially over. They could have that discussion at the right time, somewhere down the road. *One step at a time,* she thought, twisting her hands together.

"I hope you don't mind sleeping in the study," she said quickly.

His mouth quirked as if he found the statement humorous. His expression seemed to relax.

"I can sleep anywhere," he assured her.

"That's true," she agreed, with a chuckle of relief that they'd gotten that discussion out of the way. To give him credit, Jonah was behaving quite amenably. "You look tired," she added. "Do you want to see your room and maybe rest?"

She sneaked another peek at her watch and realized she needed to leave him soon to teach her CORE class.

"Yeah, sure."

Watching him straighten from the stool, he reminded her of an old man, the way he moved. With a pang of empathy, she picked up his pill bottles for him and led him toward the front bedrooms.

"Here's where you'll sleep," she said, entering the study and putting the pills beside the daybed they normally used for guests.

Jonah ran an interested gaze over the diplomas on the wall and the books in the bookshelf, then he looked at the desk. "Is that your laptop?"

"We share it," she assured him. "Here, I'll write down the password so you can get online and do whatever." Grabbing up a pen, she scribbled down the password she used to log on.

When she looked up, Jonah was sitting on the bed, rubbing the bedspread like it was made of velvet.

"You think you'll be okay here?"

He looked around and then up with a wry smile. "Beats the hell out of the cell I was in."

Hope blew through her. "Do you remember it?"

He shrugged and looked away. "Not really."

Disappointed, Eden moved to the door. "The bathroom's right across the hall. You'll have to share it with Miriam, I'm afraid. I've put your toiletries in there in your overnight kit—I think you'll recognize it. Can I get you anything else?"

She could hear Miriam making her way up the steps out front—back already from what was obviously too short of a walk.

"I'm fine," Jonah assured her.

She watched him fall over and stretch out on his back, stifling a groan.

"You must be getting hungry," she added. "I'll leave you some lunch in the refrigerator."

"Eden."

The sound of her name on his lips made her breath catch. "Yes?"

Their eyes met, and she gripped the doorknob as reality crashed over her —he was actually here, back from the dead!

"You don't have to wait on me. I can feed myself."

The statement confounded her. The old Jonah would have told her to make him a pastrami and Swiss sandwich with brown mustard and a pickle, and to do it precisely like he asked. But why give him any ideas?

Miriam and Sabrina crashed through the front door. "I'm going to tell her to keep it down so you can rest."

"She's fine," he mumbled, even as his eyes sank shut.

Eden closed the door behind her and stepped out into the hall.

Considering the circumstances, their first day together wasn't going so badly. Jonah was being remarkably cooperative and easy-going.

It's not going to last, she told herself, even as she caught the dog from barreling past her to scratch at the study door.

"Miriam, Jonah's going to rest, and I have to go to work soon. You might as well take Sabrina for a longer walk so she'll calm down."

Still hanging up the leash in the entryway, Miriam's face fell. "He's sleeping?"

"Of course. He's exhausted. I'll fix us some lunch, and then I have to head to work. Make sure he eats when he wakes up. The doctor wants him gaining two pounds a week."

"Ugh. Fine," Miriam retorted, plucking up the leash again with evident disappointment.

Eden watched her call the dog back. "Honey," she said, approaching her and lowering her voice so Jonah wouldn't overhear her. "I know you're excited to have Jonah home." Why exactly that was so was a mystery to her. "But you need to...temper your expectations."

She searched Miriam's piquant face for comprehension. "Do you know what I'm saying? He's not himself right now. When he gets his memory back, things will be like they were before, and they weren't great, if you recall."

Miriam had stilled as she listened. With a firming of her lips, she snapped the dog's leash onto her collar and, without responding to Eden's statement, led the dog back outside, shutting the door quietly behind her.

Eden drew a shaky breath and let it out again. Miriam's loyalty to Jonah puzzled her. It wasn't like they'd ever had a relationship resembling that of a father and a daughter. If Miriam invested herself emotionally in Jonah at this juncture, she was bound to be disappointed when he became himself again.

"Lord, help me," she whispered, turning toward her own bedroom at the back of the house to dress for her CORE class.

CHAPTER 4

*J*onah gave a helpless groan. It didn't matter that his body felt devoid of strength, his mind numb with exhaustion. He couldn't sleep—not in this strange place. Not with Miriam wandering around outside by herself.

I'm stateside, he reminded himself. This was a resort area, not some Third World country where thugs ruled the streets. Besides, Miriam had her dog to protect her. Picturing the boisterous puppy, he had to admit Sabrina wouldn't provide much of a deterrent to someone bent on harming her mistress.

When thirty minutes passed, according to the old-fashioned alarm clock by his bed, Jonah rolled over and dropped his feet to the floor. Miriam ought to be back by now.

Standing up slowly, he weaved a moment on his feet, then made his way out of the study and down the short hallway to the kitchen, refusing to use the walls for support.

As he wandered into the living room, he was struck by the silence. It wrapped around him giving him an eerie sense of déjà vu. His gaze rose to the rear window where a view of the sapphire ocean captured his attention and calmed his disorientation.

Nearing the window, he took in the view. Missile detection drones standing inside of Dam Neck Naval Base rose from the dunes. He realized he recognized them. In the distance, he could make out the tops of several

familiar buildings, including the Shifting Sands Club where the SEALs sometimes enjoyed happy hour. Beyond Dam Neck, the coastline curved east,
providing him with the familiar skyline of the city of Virginia Beach. He knew
this place. He *did* belong.

Providing he could lay hands on his ID, he could even get access to the
base and its amenities. But he couldn't step foot into Spec Ops Headquarters,
not until he was no longer classified as disabled. He would remain an
outsider, much the same way he was an outsider in his marriage.

Reminded of Eden's distant hospitality, he returned his attention to the
inside of his home. His gaze touched on the tasteful furniture and the built-in
bookshelves looking for proof that he had lived here. There were a few home
décor items and lots of framed pictures of Miriam, but no pictures of himself.

His gaze alighted on the partially-open door off the living room, one he
assumed led to the master bedroom. The opportunity to explore while both
Eden and Miriam were out had him walking toward it. Maybe if he found
evidence that this was his home, he could let his guard down, enough to get
some badly needed sleep.

Pushing the door farther ajar, he peered inside. Eden's flowery fragrance
floated out, startling him again with its familiarity. The room was practical,
which pleased him. A queen-sized bed dominated one wall. The quilt and
curtains were earth tones. The four walls had been painted a soothing shade
of beige. There were more books here—romance novels—stuffed into a
cherry wood bookcase, most of them old and worn and covered with a light
layer of dust.

He eyed the bed, his body responding as he pictured Eden sleeping there.
The cherry headboard matched the bureau and mirror. He realized his
dresser, which was now in the study and presumably held some of his clothing, completed the suite. An empty space against the wall told him where it
used to be.

Surely there were traces of him in this room. But as he scanned the bookshelves and surfaces, he realized, apart from a collection of Tom Clancy
novels, there was no evidence a man had ever lived here. He couldn't identify
a single object he recognized as his own.

He probed deeper, driven by some nameless desperation. Surely Eden
hadn't obliterated all of him after she'd thought him dead. If she had, that
didn't bode well for a future with her.

He entered the walk-in closet and noticed a pull-down ladder that presumably gave access to storage in the attic. On a rack below the pull-down ladder, he found some clothing—a couple of dress shirts and slacks painstakingly wrapped in plastic, with two pairs of oxfords lined up on the shelf below them.

Are these mine? The clothing struck him as vaguely familiar. Yes, now he remembered. He'd had himself fitted at a men's clothier in Coronado after graduating from BUDs. He'd liked dressing up in his off hours. It had made him feel important.

Jonah reached under the plastic and rubbed the sleeve of one of the shirts. The quality of the fabric failed to impress him.

He turned away, dismayed to find so little of himself. Where were all his uniforms—his service dress whites and blues, his dinner dress, his work dress, and his collection of jungle and desert-camouflaged NWUs? Had she given them to a teammate? Maybe he could get them back.

As he stepped from the closet, his gaze went through the open bathroom door to the jetted tub set under a clouded glass window. The size of the tub impressed him. What riveted his attention, however, was the framed photo propped at one end, surrounded by several glass tumblers.

That's me! He approached the tub and studied the set up. The tumblers were for candles, all of them melted to mere nubs. Had Eden erected an altar of some kind, here in the bathroom?

He picked up the picture. While obviously him, the man in the photo seemed like a stranger. Dressed in woodland patterned NWU's and hefting an MP 5 submachine gun, he emanated supreme self-confidence. Between the hard glint in his eyes and the smirk on his face, he looked like a man too revved up to slow down, too self-absorbed to be thinking of his family.

Jonah's gaze swung to the mirror. As thin as he was now, the resemblance was scant. Stepping closer, he contrasted the other differences.

There were new marks on his face: the scar on his mouth from getting his lip split open and another under his left eyebrow. He had dark circles under his eyes and his cheeks were gaunt. Imitating the smirk of the warrior in the photo, the gap in his teeth reminded him he'd endured something life-threatening and violent.

Only the eyes were the same.

Leaning toward to the mirror, he stared into the gold-green eyes with 10/20 vision that had given him his code name.

A voice sounded in his head—Eden's voice, he realized.

For someone with such good vision, why can't you see what's in front of you?

He straightened from the mirror with a gasp, his heart beating fast. That was a memory!

Dr. Schmidt had been right. Being in a familiar environment was bringing things back—first her scent, now this.

But the disillusionment in Eden's tone kept him from rejoicing. What *didn't I see?* What had she been talking about?

He dared to think back. Was it Miriam? His gut said, *yes.* They'd been discussion Miriam, who'd done something wrong, something for attention, maybe.

Thinking of Miriam reminded Jonah she was still outside alone. Pricked by guilt, he returned the photo to the exact spot where he'd found it and moved as quickly as he could out of Eden's bedroom toward the front door.

Finding it unlocked, a second wave of vulnerability washed over him. He stepped outside onto the deck and shut the door. A warm ocean breeze ruffled his hair. Sunlight bounced into his eyes as he rounded the deck slowly, raking the immediate area for signs of Miriam and the dog.

Feeling terribly exposed, he sought the source of his uneasiness, even as he craved the reassuring feel of a weapon in his hand. A car moved along the street below, passing without slowing. Not a single person showed himself within a hundred yards.

There's no threat, he assured himself.

Hunting for Miriam, Jonah continued around the deck until he could see past the house next to them all the way to the beach, about a football field away. A clearly delineated footpath followed the line of the chain-link fence that hemmed in Dam Neck Naval Base. On that footpath, he was relieved to see Miriam being pulled in his direction, sled-dog style, by her golden retriever.

The relief he felt sapped the remaining strength out of him, and he dropped onto one of the many colorful Adirondack chairs scattered about. With his back pressed to the yellow chair, he tried to remember his thirty-fourth birthday Miriam had told him about—the one Eden had thrown for him. He thought he could picture his teammates standing around the grill holding red plastic cups and laughing.

The vision reassured him. *I do belong here.* If only he got that feeling from his wife, who had nearly expunged him from her life.

What was I doing married, anyway? He shook his head in disbelief. He knew the kind of man he was; the kind of ruthless drive he had to excel. He even knew why he'd pushed himself the way he had—to make up for his misspent youth. Given his family history, his father's tragic death, the abuse at the hands of his stepbrother, Jonah had known he'd make a lousy husband and an even lousier father.

Then he'd met Eden, who was obviously too beautiful to let slip through his fingers. He really couldn't blame his younger self for compromising his oath to stay single. On the other hand, SEALs suffered a 90 percent divorce rate. Had he seriously thought he could hold onto her?

Yet their story wasn't over, was it? He could make amends for being absent this past year and for some other mistakes he'd made before that. He liked what they had here, a lovely home, a little family. He'd never thought himself worthy of either but now that he'd seen what he could have, he didn't want to give it up.

Hearing Miriam chase the dog around the front of the house, he tried to get out of the chair but found himself too weak to move. The two of them thundered up the stairs and descended on him. The dog all but jumped into his lap, licking effusively until Miriam tugged her off.

"You're supposed to be sleeping!" she scolded, bringing Sabrina under control.

"I tried," he said.

"I told Mom you wouldn't like that mattress," she commented. The wind pushed her dyed hair into her eyes. As she caught it back, Jonah noticed four holes punctured into the delicate shell of her ear, devoid of studs.

"The mattress is fine," he assured her. "Do you always walk the dog that long?"

Her eyebrows pulled together. "What do you mean?"

Jonah tried again. "I mean, that's a good walk and all, but is it safe out there?"

Her mauve colored head tipped to one side as she frowned down at him.

"Safe from what?" she asked carefully.

Jonah had a feeling he wasn't making sense. Exhaustion tugged at him.

"Never mind." He tried and failed to get out of the chair.

"Stay there," Miriam said. "Mom made us sandwiches. I'll bring one out to you."

In a flash she was gone, presumably to stow the dog in the house, then fetch him something to eat.

Jonah made himself more comfortable. Sitting out of sight of the street, he felt safer. The wind ruffling his hair and the ocean roaring in the distance combined to soothe his anxiety.

Minutes later, Miriam appeared bearing a tray with two full glasses and two sandwiches on paper plates. She set the tray down on a nearby table before handing a plate to Jonah, who only then realized he was hungry.

"Water or lemonade?" she asked, holding up the two glasses.

Thinking she likely wanted the lemonade for herself, he said, "Water."

With a quick grin of gratitude, she handed him the water and lowered herself into the chair next to him.

Jonah eyed the contents of his sandwich. "My favorite," he declared, noting the thin layers of deli-cut turkey and a slab of what looked like provolone.

"I thought pastrami was your favorite," Miriam retorted, taking a huge bite from her own.

Jonah shrugged. "All food is good." That morning at the hospital, he'd had oatmeal for the first time in he didn't know how long, and it had tasted like heaven.

They ate in companionable silence for a minute. Then Miriam asked on a breezy note, "So what did Mom say to you?"

"What do you mean?"

Miriam flicked him a glance but didn't elaborate. "You want some advice?" she asked instead.

The question caught Jonah off guard. Not only did Miriam strike him as a potential ally, but she also seemed to know what the issue was between him and Eden.

"Sure." He drew out the word, not knowing what he was going to hear.

"Well..." She licked a bit of mustard off her middle finger. "I would take things slow, if I were you. You've been through a lot—obviously," she added, slanting him a look brimming with teenage wisdom. "And so has mom. She just needs time."

Really? Recalling Eden's wary reception, he had reason to doubt their relationship would get on track that easily. Given various comments she and Miriam had made and glances they'd exchanged, he had reason to believe he'd been a lousy husband, probably a terrible stepfather. To think he'd actually forbidden Eden to work! Had he been that much of a control freak?

Yet if Miriam was willing to give Jonah a second chance, maybe Eden would, too.

"All right," he said, smothering a burp. The sandwich was more food than he'd eaten in days, probably even months. It filled his stomach and weighted his eyelids.

"I think I should try napping again." Pushing to the edge of his seat, he was determined to stand and not to wobble.

Miriam took the paper plate out of his hand. She watched but didn't help, which he greatly appreciated. If he couldn't even get off a deck chair, then what good was he?

Powered by determination and chagrin over needing a nap in the first place, Jonah managed to stand under his own steam.

"What are you going to do?" he asked as Miriam set his glass back on the tray.

Straightening with the tray, she made a face of disgust. "I have a book to read—summer reading for school."

Her answer perked his interest briefly, but speech was suddenly beyond him. Nodding his approval, he tottered toward the front door, so exhausted he wondered whether he would make it.

Miriam hurried past him and silently held it open.

"Thanks," he managed, moving down the hall back to the study.

Seconds later, he shut himself inside, kicked off his shoes, and fell face first across the narrow mattress, crashing into a deep sleep that kept him motionless for hours.

Eden awoke to the sound of her doorknob turning. Her pulse spiked. Her eyes flew open to a room that was stygian-black, and no wonder. It was 2:12 in the morning, according to the digital clock by her bed. Fear streaked to her extremities, bringing her wide awake—not that she'd been sleeping very deeply. How could she with Jonah in the house?

Intuition told her the intruder wasn't Miriam. Sure enough, a silhouette peered through her opening door. She knew by his height and the breadth of his shoulders it was Jonah.

An unexpected, visceral desire shot through her, and she immediately squelched it, demanding, "What do you want?"

He froze at her tone, which she recognized was about as welcoming as the thorns on the cactus she'd set on her kitchen window sill.

In the dark, she could make out his eyes reflecting the glow of her digital clock.

"When did you get home?" he asked, sounding hesitant, relieved.

She pushed herself into a sitting position. "What do you mean? I've been home since six o'clock."

"Six?" he repeated. She could hear dismay in his voice.

"You were sleeping so soundly I didn't wake you up for dinner. Are you hungry now?"

She snapped on the light to get a better look at him.

Jonah jerked, overreacting to the sudden brightness. Lowering the hand he'd brought up instinctively, he sent her a sheepish grimace, then blinked at her with interest.

Too late, Eden realized she was wearing a sleeveless cotton nightdress that left little to the imagination. She pulled the sheet up over her chest.

"Are you hungry?" she repeated.

Dragging his gaze to hers, he visibly swallowed and said, "I can find something to eat. I didn't mean to wake you up," he added, venturing in a little farther. "I just…I didn't hear you come in. I woke up and the house was so quiet." He peered around her bed. "Where's the dog? I don't see her."

"She sleeps in Miriam's room at night."

"Oh."

She realized as he quelled a shudder that he was shaken—like seriously spooked by something. He'd been diagnosed with post-traumatic stress, a condition that would go away in time. But if it didn't, his diagnosis could change to PTSD, a debilitating and long-lasting disorder that would likely prevent him from ever returning to the Teams. God forbid Jonah ended up with PTSD.

Determined to chase away his demons, Eden tossed back her sheets and jumped out of bed.

"I think I need a snack myself," she declared, scooping up the robe she'd dropped on the floor and slipping it on, all the while conscious of Jonah's stare.

He stepped back as she sailed past him, headed for the kitchen. With his slow, determined walk, he trailed behind.

"I grabbed some Chinese on the way home," she chatted as she opened the refrigerator. "I'm not sure if you remember, but I'm a lousy cook." She kept her tone conversational, hoping to calm his jitters and put him at ease.

Jonah stood by the breakfast bar, watching her every move through eyes that missed nothing. Even with the robe on, Eden felt distinctly underdressed. But then he'd always had that effect on her, his stare so appreciative that her skin prickled. She needed to ignore their chemistry. Giving into it would only confuse her more.

"Do you like Kung Pao chicken?" She knew for a fact he did.

"I like all food," he declared with conviction.

She shot him an encouraged look. "Good, because you'll have to eat a lot of it to gain back the weight you've lost."

Ladling the leftovers onto two plates, she warmed up the first one and poured Jonah a glass of milk.

"Eat," she invited placing his plate before him and turning away to heat up her own.

Even with her back turned to him, she could feel his gaze drifting over her robe-clad figure. She bit her lip against the desire that tugged at her.

"Tell me about your job," he requested as he forked up a bite.

She stiffened automatically. Was he going to tell her to quit? Regarding him over her shoulder, she gauged his reaction as she said, "I teach fitness classes at the base gym—cardio, CORE, yoga, and body sculpting."

His gaze betrayed interest and appreciation as it slid down and up her body. Her muscles clenched as if he'd touched her.

"Keeps you in great shape," he noted.

"And hungry," she commented, keeping their conversation light as she took her plate from the microwave.

Occupying the stool next to him, she joined him in eating. Neither one of them spoke. A strangely companionable silence filled the kitchen. Eden sensed Jonah was calmer now, less agitated. She thought about the fear that had to haunt him any time he closed his eyes. That he was finally affected by the violence he witnessed in his line of work made him seem more human, more worthy of compassion.

"You know," she heard herself say. His head turned and she could tell from her peripheral vision she had his full attention. "Sometimes, when I'm...when I can't sleep—" She didn't dare to imply that he was feeling fearful. "—I read the Psalms. You know, from the Bible," she added, looking over at him to gauge his response.

Jonah had professed to being a Christian when she'd married him, but as far as she could tell, he never talked to God. She paused, waiting to see if he welcomed her words or not.

He nodded, seeming to accept her suggestion. "Book of Psalms, yeah." His thoughts turned inward. Suddenly, he started to recite a psalm, one she recognized but couldn't identify by number.

"'God is our refuge and strength,'" he murmured, apparently by rote, "'a very present help in trouble. Therefore we will not fear, though the earth should change, though the mountains shake in the heart of the sea; though its waters roar and foam, though the mountains tremble with its tumult.'"

Eden knew there was more to come about nations in an uproar and the world melting, but only one verse popped into her, so she said it out loud. "'God will help when the morning dawns.'"

He looked at her, then, his eyes widening with delight. "Yes, that's part of it. You know that Psalm?"

"Do *I* know that Psalm?" She just looked at him. "How do *you* know that Psalm?"

His forehead furrowed as he tried to remember, but then he winced and shook his head.

"I don't know. It was just there."

Amazed, Eden came to an interesting conclusion. "You've been reading the Bible."

He searched her gaze with continued perplexity. "In captivity?"

She shrugged. "I guess. You never used to cite scripture." She got a sudden idea. "Wait here. I've got a Bible by my bed."

Hurrying to her room, she snatched it off the bedside table and brought it to him, all the while hoping her idea worked.

"I think you should read this whenever you...can't sleep," she finished, again avoiding the world "fear" as she placed it in his hands. He started flipping through it. "The book of Psalms is—"

"Right after Job," he finished, finding it.

Eden couldn't believe it. Without question, Jonah had spent considerable time this past year acquainting himself with the Word. Something cynical inside of her shifted.

He flipped through several pages until he found what he was looking for. "That was Psalm 49." He skimmed through it in silence, then added without looking at her, "Dr. Schmidt said I would have nightmares."

So she'd been right. "Is that what woke you up?"

"Yes. But I didn't dream about the past. I dreamed I woke up in this house, and it was empty. You were gone—you and Miriam, both. Even the dog. You'd all been...taken."

When he looked back at her, the glazed look she'd seen in his eyes earlier was back.

"Taken?" A droplet of fear trickled down her spine. "Who would take us, Jonah?" she asked, comforting both herself and him. "We're safe here. You're safe here."

He dropped his gaze, looking down at his lean fingers where they curved around the edges of her Bible. He gripped it like a drowning man would grip a raft.

"I hope so," he finally murmured.

Oh, dear. What if his PTS was actually PTSD? She had never envisioned her confident, indomitable husband looking so vulnerable.

Without thinking, she reached for him, combing his overlong hair from his eyes. He stilled, clearly registering her touch, then looked up at her slowly.

The impact of his gaze startled her. Snatching her hand back, she moved away from him to clear their plates, dropping them in the sink to clean in the morning. Then she flipped off the light switch, making her intentions clear.

"Better get back to bed," she said. "You have a busy day tomorrow."

The next day was his appointment with Dr. Branson at the Oceana clinic.

"Do you work tomorrow?" he asked her.

Was that resentment in his voice? Eden locked her knees. "I have to cover for the instructor who's taking my afternoon class. We switched places."

Jonah nodded, seemingly accepting.

"I'll keep an eye on Miriam," he offered.

"Thanks." She drew out the word, wondering if that was his way of suggesting she didn't spend enough time with her daughter.

"She's...," he hunted for the right word, "wise."

Eden blinked. "You think?"

"Yeah. She seems to know stuff. Not sure I can explain what I mean."

Eden hummed noncommittally, unwilling at that late hour to discuss her daughter's struggles.

"She's old enough to stay home alone, but I appreciate you keeping an eye on her."

"No problem," he said with utmost sincerity.

"Okay, then." Her gaze fell to the Bible. "You can keep that," she said, nodding at it. "I have another one."

"Thanks."

His sincerity disarmed her. She reminded herself he was only on his first night home. Sometimes strangers treated each other better than married couples did—sad but true. Once he settled in, got more comfortable, Jonah would morph into the same demanding, self-absorbed warrior he'd been before, a man she admired but found hard to love, and even harder to live with.

"Good night," she murmured, rounding the island to head for her room. "You going to be all right?"

He smiled his crooked smile. "Of course."

"Good." For a second, she wrestled with the urge to say, *Welcome home.* That was what a loving wife would say. Then again, a loving wife would hold him in her arms and cradle him in their shared bed. She had relegated him to the study to sleep alone, with his nightmares.

Guilt pinched the tops of her shoulders. Without another word, she spun away toward her bedroom, shutting and, as silently as possible, locking the door behind her.

Closing her eyes a moment, she pictured Jonah the way he'd looked sitting in the muted light of the stove's surface lamp clutching her Bible.

"Father, please comfort him," she whispered. "Comfort him because I can't. I really can't," she insisted, even as her heart seemed to fold over on itself. She had loved Jonah with every ounce of her being, and he'd betrayed that love by putting his job first, by ignoring his stepdaughter, remaining emotionally aloof. She couldn't put herself through that rejection again.

With a sharp sniff, she drove back the tears that threatened and crossed to the bathroom to brush her teeth. Like she'd told Jonah, tomorrow was going to be a busy day.

∾

Using the light coming from the stove, Jonah read Psalm 49 a third time in its entirety. Verse 9 leaped out at him, so he read that one aloud, pitching his voice low to keep from disturbing his family. "He makes wars cease to the end of the earth; he breaks the bow, and shatters the spear; he burns the shields with fire.'"

Weapons. There was something significant about weapons. Something he had to remember!

Startled, he looked up from the Bible and thought back.

Almost immediately, pain pierced his left eye, driving back any memories that might have surfaced.

Grimacing, Jonah thumped a fist on the countertop, then flinched at the noise he'd made. Miriam and Eden were sleeping. He, too, should sleep as it was his responsibility to keep an eye on Miriam tomorrow.

Taking the Bible with him, he returned to the study.

Surprisingly, his middle-of-the-night interlude with Eden had been a pleasant one. Not only was his stomach replete, but he'd found comfort in her company and solace in the Word. Touched that she would share her personal Bible with him, he hugged it briefly to his chest before placing it atop his dresser.

He decided he could sleep now, without the nightmare reoccurring. If not, he would reach for the Bible and find another passage to act as a balm for his troubled soul. He wouldn't trouble Eden again. For reasons that pained him to imagine, there were limits to how much she would comfort him.

CHAPTER 5

"*M*rs. Mills, would you care to join us for a bit?"

Eden looked up from the article she was reading about PTSD in the armed forces. Supposedly, special operators like Jonah were less susceptible to the disorder, thanks to the rigid selection process and prolonged exposure training. But acquiring the disorder was still a possibility depending on a number of factors, including the severity of the trauma experienced. A year of captivity and torture probably qualified as severe.

Caught off guard by Dr. Branson's invitation, Eden regarded him a moment before setting the magazine aside.

"Sure," she said, willing to do whatever it took to keep Jonah from being diagnosed with the disorder.

Entering the office, the first thing she noticed was Jonah's pained expression. He seemed embarrassed by her participation. He had chosen what looked like the least comfortable chair in the room and was sitting ramrod-straight in it with his arms crossed.

No wonder Dr. Branson had asked her to join them.

Jonah's discomfort prompted her to take the seat next to his. Sending him an encouraging smile, she put her purse in her lap and waited for the doctor to begin.

Dr. Branson dropped into the wingback chair opposite. Leaning back, he interlaced his fingers and divided a friendly gaze between them. A pudgy man with a head of gray hair, his eyes made Eden think of the ocean on overcast days.

"Mrs. Mills," he began, "Jonah was telling me the last thing he remembers, and his recollections apparently end soon after the death of a colleague of his. Did you know Blake LeMere?"

"No. He died before Jonah and I met."

Jonah spoke up in a flat voice. "Do you remember how he died?"

Eden thought back to what Jonah had told her. "He never deployed his parachute. The coroner said he was unconscious when he hit the ground."

"Doesn't make any sense," Jonah muttered, evidently fixated on the memory. "I was with him when he jumped. He was fine—cracking jokes and everything. I don't see how he could have lost consciousness."

The doctor hummed thoughtfully. "A tragedy to be sure," he said, "but let's talk about how you two met. Jonah doesn't remember the occasion. Perhaps your description of the event will jog his memories."

Jonah's sidelong glance conveyed chagrin.

Eden hesistated. Her courtship with Jonah had been an ecastatic experience. The disillusionment that came afterward wasn't something she wished to relive.

Dr. Branson must have sensed her reluctance because he added, "It would be helpful to Jonah to fill in the gaps. That way he has some continuity and a context for the memories that return to him."

Fine, she thought, resigning herself to getting it over with. "We met in Annapolis at my parents' house. My father was one of Jonah's instructors at the Naval Academy." She met Jonah's inquiring gaze. "You remember Captain Evans, don't you?"

His surprise was almost comical. "You're Captain Evans's daughter? He was my favorite instructor! He taught military strategy."

Jonah's unguarded delight was encouraging. She warmed to her tale. "You were his favorite midshipman," she continued, smoothing all judgment from her tone. Her father had loved Jonah's unwavering drive. "After graduating from SEAL training in Coronado, you came back to visit him. That's when we met. I was staying with my parents at the time." She'd been going back to school to earn the degree she'd failed to get the first go round.

Jonah's thoughts turned inward. She could see him trying desperately to recollect their initial encounter. Interestingly, he didn't wince as he did when he thought of his captivity.

Dr. Branson inserted a request. "What was your meeting like? Could you recreate the scene for Jonah?"

Eden described the foyer of her parents' elegant brick home located on the campus of the Naval Academy and who was there.

"Do you remember Jonah's first words to you?" the psychiatrist prompted.

She pretended to think about it when, in fact, she remembered every single second of the magical moment.

"He said the usual things. Nice to meet you. Stuff like that."

Jonah gave a quiet laugh.

"Do you remember something?" his doctor asked.

"No," he said. "I'm just picturing myself staring at her. I probably couldn't talk at all."

The flattering comment heated Eden's cheeks. "Hardly," she drawled, correcting his assumption.

Jonah and the doctor both looked at her for clarification.

"What I mean is...you were never at a loss for words. Confidence could have been your middle name. You asked my father right then if you could take me out to dinner. It didn't occur to you to ask me first."

Jonah frowned.

Dr. Branson sat forward, clearly intrigued by their exchange. "So you went on a date that evening. Where'd you go?"

"One of the nicer restaurants in Annapolis," Eden said, naming it. At the time, she had thought the evening to be the highlight of her life. The October weather couldn't have been more perfect. "We sat outside, shared a bottle of Chardonnay. You had rockfish and I had the scallops."

Jonah shifted in his seat, clearly uncomfortable with his inability to remember.

"What were you wearing, Eden?" the doctor asked her. "What color?"

Supremely self-conscious, she plucked at a loose thread on her sundress.

"I'm not sure," she heard herself say, even as she pictured the little black dress she'd worn for the occasion. "I don't remember."

"Hmm." Dr. Branson's bushy eyebrows quirked. "How was the conversation? Did you hit it off right away?"

It dawned on Eden their session was sounding more like marriage counseling than therapy for Jonah's memory loss. "Well, of course we hit it off," she said, masking her sudden impatience. "Jonah was everything a woman dreams of. Handsome and smart, and he knew a hundred ways to kill somebody. What woman wouldn't be drawn to him?"

Jonah and the doctors' mutual silence informed her she hadn't hidden her sarcasm well at all.

"I'm sorry. I just don't see the point in discussing our first date when Jonah's missing two years of his memory."

At her apology, Jonah looked away, staring at a spot over the doctor's shoulders.

Dr. Branson's eyes had narrowed. "That's exactly why I brought it up," he explained. "Every significant event that Jonah has forgotten should be detailed for him. Any one of them might trigger his memories."

Chastened, Eden swallowed her chagrin.

"Why don't you give us the highlights of the time you spent with Jonah, right up to his disappearance," the doctor insisted.

Eden nodded. "All right." She thought a moment. "We dated for just two months. You were about to deploy on a lengthy mission," she said, glancing at Jonah. "So you wanted to marry before you went. We bought the house in Sandbridge, moved in, and then you left."

When he'd come back from his seemingly interminable absence, Eden had been overjoyed that her knight in shining armor had finally returned. Everything was going to be perfect. He would assume his role as husband and father and they would live happily ever after.

Only it hadn't worked out that way.

"When you came back, you became troop leader for Blue Squadron, so you were really, really busy," she said, trying to mask the disillusionment that still hurt. "The next year flew by. You were home maybe six months out of twelve." She shrugged, hoping to imply their marriage had been so brief, so uneventful, it wasn't any wonder he'd forgotten.

Jonah just listened, his gaze boring a hole in the opposite wall.

Dr. Branson's thick eyebrows nearly touched as he regarded Eden.

"Did you know Jonah would be gone so much?" he asked. "His absences must have taken a toll on your young marriage."

No kidding. She sent him a dry look. "I think I knew what to expect. My father was a fleet officer when I was growing up. My mother taught us both how to be self-sufficient."

"Both?" he prompted.

"My older sister and me."

"I see. What about your daughter?" the psychiatrist asked. "Jonah says you have a daughter—Miriam?"

"Yes, Miriam's almost fifteen. What about her?" she asked, then realized that the question sounded rude.

The doctor cleared his throat. "How did she handle Jonah's absences?"

Eden flicked a glance at Jonah's stony profile. "No worse than she handled his being at home."

The doctor looked like he might ask her what she meant when Jonah abruptly stood up from his chair, halting their conversation.

"I think we've done enough for one day," he said in the tone he used to lead his troop—no one argued with it. "I've got a splitting headache," he added, closing his eyes briefly to convey his discomfort.

"Of course. You should have told me sooner." Dr. Branson's tone was apologetic, perhaps even relieved. No doubt he'd felt Eden's tension and didn't know what to make of it. "We'll continue this discussion at your next session. In the meantime, you both have a little homework assignment. Preferably tonight or as soon as possible, I'd like you to review some photos together in the hopes they'll awaken memories."

He pushed to his feet to consult his appointment book, and Eden followed suit.

"Jonah, I'll see you again on Friday, at the same time."

"Wait." Eden protested before she could stop herself. "Can we do a different time of day? Morning maybe? It's just that I usually teach a two o'clock class, and the woman I'm switching with might not be able to switch with me again."

"I can take an Uber," Jonah offered stonily.

"I'd prefer Eden attend sessions with you." Dr. Branson frowned at his calendar. "Let me see if any of my morning patients can switch to afternoons. I'll give you a call if that works out. How's that sound?" He looked to Eden for her corroboration.

"Thanks," she said. "You have my number?"

He glanced back down. "Ends in 4292?"

"Yes."

"Do I have a number for you yet, Jonah?" He looked inquiringly at Jonah, who in turn, looked at Eden.

She had dropped his phone from her plan several months ago. Why did that now seem like some terrible betrayal?

"You have a phone," she said, picturing the non-descript Android in her top drawer, "but I'll have to add it to our plan again."

Jonah shrugged as if to say it didn't matter to him.

"Okay. Well!" Dr. Branson smiled and gestured toward the door. "You two enjoy the rest of your day. Don't forget your homework assignment. Eden, I'll be in touch about Friday."

"Thank you," she murmured again.

"Jonah," the psychiatrist called as Jonah trailed Eden out the door, "be sure to take your prescriptions regularly, as prescribed. That'll help you sleep at night and not in the day."

"Yes, sir," Jonah muttered.

As she waited by the exit, Eden cast a regretful glance at the magazine she'd been reading. All that information on PTSD seemed far more helpful than the session they had just attended.

Jonah held open the door for her—a courtesy that had been ingrained in him from his time at the academy—and she stepped outside. Afternoon sunlight blinded her. Finding her sunglasses, Eden slipped them on, while Jonah squinted. She'd donated his sunglasses about two weeks ago to the base thrift shop, along with many of his uniforms. Guilt stitched through her at the reminder.

"Sure is hot," she commented, wondering if it was too late to get the items back.

Once inside the Jaguar, she cranked on the air conditioner and snapped on the radio, making conversation unnecessary as she drove them home. To distract herself from Jonah's brooding silence, she planned what she would make for dinner. She had some pork chops in the refrigerator. Applesauce? Check. Corn on the cobb? Yes. She added that to a salad of mixed greens. Dinner was complete.

They were approaching Sandbridge when Jonah shifted in his seat so he could stare at her without turning his head.

Eden's pulse accelerated. The directness of his gaze made her skin feel tight.

"Who was Miriam's father?" he asked.

Startled by the question, she glanced his way, reading concern and curiosity in his expression. Deciding his question was a fair one, she focused back on the road. At least he was interested.

"His name was Zach Palmer. I dated him in college."

"Why didn't you stay with him?"

She gave a bitter laugh. "He didn't stay with *me*," she corrected. "When he found out I was pregnant, he vanished. My parents were horrified," she added, recalling their reaction with mixed chagrin and hurt. "They hunted Zach down, thinking they would force him to marry me. By then, I'd turned my whole life around. I wasn't the same person, but Zach still was. When my parents realized it, they insisted he sign paperwork abdicating his rights as a father."

Jonah frowned. "Why would your parents do that? At the very least, Zach had financial obligations."

Eden snorted at the thought of Zach sending her money. "Zach couldn't be responsible for himself, let alone a kid. Don't get me wrong," she qualified. "He was brilliant and funny, but he dropped out of college because he found his professors ignorant. He couldn't hold a steady job because his managers didn't know anything. He was the dead last person my parents wanted in my life or in Miriam's."

"What about what *you* wanted?" Jonah asked.

The question startled a glance out of her. She tried imagining the old Jonah asking it, and she couldn't.

"I understood my parents' concern," she assured him. "I knew Zach couldn't handle having a baby, and I wanted Miriam to have a better father, even if that meant having only God for a father."

Jonah lapsed into thoughtful quiet. "Did you love him?" he finally asked.

Eden's heart skipped a beat. Compared to how she'd felt about Jonah, her feelings for Zach had been more like friendship. "I thought I did, but I was young. I didn't really know what love was."

"Do you now?" he asked.

She glanced at him sharply, then looked away, uncertain how to answer.

"Eden," he said, in the same reflective voice. "I want you to know whatever happens between us..."

She held her breath waiting for him to finish his statement.

"I'll take care of you and Miriam, financially and otherwise."

Relief and gratitude intermingled at the unexpected offer. Then the realist in her pointed out his comment probably wasn't purely altruistic. He was at an all-time low in his life, stripped of his memory, with no job to give him self-esteem. What if he was only being thoughtful because he was afraid of losing his family on top of everything else?

"Thanks," she said with less warmth than he doubtless hoped for. "That's... decent of you."

Jonah faced front again, then stared out of his window, lapsing again into brooding silence. When Eden rounded the car to help him to the front door, he avoided her, tackling the stairs on his own.

Feeling rebuffed, she watched him move painstakingly up the steps. Granted, he moved faster than he had the day before, but he was a long way from being considered fit.

Torn between pity and respect, she suspected he was finally getting the picture. All was not well on the home front. He'd seen to that long before leaving on the mission from which he hadn't returned.

Good, she told herself. *Now he knows where he stands and he won't have false expectations.* As she climbed the stairs behind him, she tried shaking off her guilt. It wasn't her fault Jonah had been so aloof after marrying her. She didn't owe him any more than the year she had promised to devote to his well-being. When that year was up, she would ask for her freedom without a twinge to her conscience—or so she hoped.

～

Eden had talked Miriam into looking at a photo album with him.

Jonah sat on the sofa in the living room, not only disappointed that he wouldn't be sitting next to his wife looking at photos on her camera, but flat-out depressed from two things that had happened earlier that day. The first was Dr. Branson had told him he might have PTSD—the full-blown disorder that some veterans grappled with for life. His second insight was that Eden wished she'd never married him.

"I'm pretty sure Dr. Branson wanted your mom to do this," he said, loud enough for Eden to overhear as Miriam pulled an album from one of the built-in bookcases.

Eden turned a deaf ear to him as she loaded the dishwasher. Like a dutiful wife, she'd made supper and chatted politely throughout the meal. Even so, her emotional distance confirmed what Jonah had realized. Not only did she wish she'd never married him, but she wasn't invested in their future any longer.

Sure, she had offered him a home and her full support toward his recovery, but in her heart, she had decided to move on. Whatever she'd been doing in the tub with his photo—it had probably been something like an exorcism, in which she'd cleansed herself of him.

Honestly, he couldn't say he blamed her. He could tell from the comments both she and Miriam had made the old Jonah hadn't been easy to live with. He'd been neglectful, self-absorbed, even border-line abusive—not surprising, given his horrendous childhood. That didn't excuse him from not trying, though.

Ironically, he was more than willing to try now—except *now* was clearly too late.

Miriam threw herself down on the couch next to him and dumped an album on his lap. "These are the only real photos we have."

The gold lettering on the white cover suggested he was looking at a wedding album. He groaned inwardly and rubbed his stinging eyes.

"You know, squirt," he said, calling her by the nickname he'd heard her mother use, "I don't think I'm up for this right now. I think I need to sleep."

"It's like 6 p.m.," Miriam protested.

"I know." Chagrin made his face hot. He'd never be a SEAL again if he couldn't get a handle on his chronic fatigue. The Sertraline he took in the morning kept him calm and alert until, without warning, it stopped. Then exhaustion flat-out ambushed him.

Miriam shot a look at her mother, who watched them from the corner of her eye as she scrubbed the kitchen sink. Turning her brandy-colored eyes on Jonah, the girl asked, "Just this one album?"

Miriam's puppy dog look was impossible to refuse. "Okay," he agreed.

"Great." With a grin, she lifted the cover, showing him the first page of pictures. "Here's Mom getting her hair done for your wedding."

Jonah lost himself in close-up shots of Eden's face. According to the date on the front, their wedding had taken place in June, just over two years ago. Eden looked a teensy bit younger, a little curvier than she did now. Her golden hair had been swept up into an elegant chignon and shot with baby's breath.

"Who took these pictures?" he wanted to know.

"Aunt Phoebe."

"Your mother's sister?"

"Yep." Miriam turned the page. "And here's Mom putting her dress on."

Jonah's breath caught at the vision of Eden in a lace corset complete with garters and white stockings, preparing to slip into the wedding dress hanging next to her. Jonah felt his jaw drop.

Miriam shot him a knowing smirk. "She's hot, huh?" The whispered words weren't meant for Eden's ears.

"Yeah," he agreed. He couldn't believe what a lucky man he'd been. How stupid he was for letting her down, as he clearly had.

Miriam turned the page. "And here you are at the church waiting for Mom to come in."

The pictures of himself were like the one in her bathroom, except he was wearing his dress whites and not toting a submachine gun. The expression on his face was the same—supremely confident. No last-minute sweats for this guy.

The living room walls seemed to shift closer. Jonah sat back, averting his gaze to halt the sudden anxiety that squeezed him. Perspiration breached the pores on his forehead and made his shirt stick to his back. Seeing what he used to look like made him think he'd never be an active-duty SEAL again. Without that confidence, he'd be a danger to himself and the others in his troop.

Miriam scooted closer. "You want to see what I looked like then?"

The kid was good. Jonah glanced at her piquant face then down at the photo she was pointing to. There was a younger Miriam dressed in a yellow gown with chestnut colored hair curling by her cheeks, her eyes sparkling with excitement.

"Aw. You were cute."

"Are you kidding? I was hideous at twelve." In spite of her scoffing, she flushed at his compliment.

He studied the picture. "I like your natural hair color," he said, though it was the look in her eyes that grabbed him. She'd looked so hopeful.

She lifted a hand to finger her hair, and he caught another glimpse of the holes in her ear. "Well, I'm thinking of dying it back."

"Up to you," he said, giving her room to make the right choice. "What's with the ear piercings?"

A wary expression crossed her face. Dropping her hand, she gave a quick shrug and didn't answer.

"Does Mom know you did that?" He gave himself a start by calling Eden Mom, but it had slipped out naturally.

"Of course." Miriam's tone turned sullen. "Why do you think the holes are empty?"

He glanced at Eden who was putting away pans. "She made you take the studs out?"

"Yes."

Good for you, Eden. "Well, you must have guessed she wouldn't like it." He let the implied question hang between them: *So, why'd you do it?*

Miriam's slight frown informed him she wasn't comfortable with their conversation. All at once, she thrust the album onto his lap and jumped to her feet.

"I have to read." With that muttered excuse, she fled the living room, disappearing down the hall to her bedroom.

Eden straightened from putting a pan on the bottom shelf of a cabinet. "Where's she going?" she called. "Miriam!"

"Let her go," Jonah advised.

From behind the breakfast bar, Eden eyed him with disappointment, then dismay, probably thinking it would fall to her to go through the remainder of the pictures—a trip down memory lane she clearly didn't want to take.

Jonah stood up. "I'm really bushed," he said, cradling the album. "I'll look at the rest of these before I fall asleep."

The relief on her face made him want to cry. Was she that reluctant to spend time alone with him? In that case, he was fighting a losing battle, one he didn't want to lose. He liked what he had here—a beautiful wife, a cute daughter. Would God really taunt him with this domestic picture and then deny him the opportunity to keep it?

"Don't forget your medication," she called as he headed in defeat toward the study.

Following a brief shower in which he nearly passed out from weariness, Jonah dressed in one of the few T-shirts and boxers in his dresser before crashing onto the daybed. Recalling his promise to look at more pictures before falling asleep, he cracked the album one more time, picking up where he left off.

The wedding ceremony was apparently over. Here were photos of him and Eden coming down the aisle together, hand in hand, husband and wife. The overjoyed look on Eden's face hit him like a bullet shot at close range.

Wait one blessed minute! She had obviously loved him. Just look at that smile! Yet, during therapy today, she implied that they'd rushed into marriage because he was about to go wheels up for the next six months. She hadn't said anything about loving him.

But she so obviously had. A thrill of excitement chased through him, and he perused the wedding reception pictures looking for more proof. As she'd danced in Jonah's embrace, as they'd cut the cake, the desire and admiration shining in her eyes was unmistakable. Not only had she loved him, she'd apparently thought the world of him!

Dear Lord. The realization he had evidently killed that emotion hit him like a fist to the diaphragm. He closed his eyes and absorbed the blow. Of course he'd killed it. He'd known when he'd married her he lacked a role model for how to treat a wife or daughter.

And yet it was perfectly clear to him now how he should have treated them both.

Had the blow to his brain changed him that much? Surely not.

Husbands love your wives. The passage from Ephesians leapt into his head, causing him to look at the Bible lying by his bed.

Regarding it, he thought of dozens more verses and lessons instructing his behavior. It occurred to him suddenly that he *did* have a role model for how to treat those close to him. He had a loving Father who had dwelled in the darkness with him, even helping him to escape, and who would even now give him the grace to win his wife and daughter back.

With equal parts gratitude and hope, Jonah clasped his hands together pressing them to his forehead. He couldn't remember praying like this in his captivity, but the familiarity of the action told him he had.

"Father, thank you for being with me," he whispered fervently. "Help me not to lose what I have here. I know—" He shook his head in remorse. "I know I wasn't good to Eden and Miriam. I know I don't deserve them. But I promise to do right by them this time. Give me the grace and the time to prove myself. Shine through me, Lord. Help me show them I'm not the man I used to be."

He was not surprised to feel tears leaking from the corners of his eyes. He'd pleaded with God like this countless times in the past year. He must have.

"Thank you for hearing me," he added. Clearly, God had heard—and answered—his cries before. "Amen."

Letting his arms fall to his sides, he went limp on the bed. His marriage to

Eden wasn't over yet. It wasn't too late to be everything Eden could dream of in a husband. To be the father Miriam clearly wanted and needed.

Momentary doubts sprang leaks in his newfound optimism. But what if his PTS turned out to be PTSD, making him such a wreck he never became an active duty SEAL again?

Peace, child.

The calm quiet words etched themselves on Jonah's heart, assuring him it would be okay. God would look after them one way or another. He'd gotten Jonah this far. He would not abandon him now.

With a profound sigh, Jonah cleared his mind for the time being and fell soundly asleep.

CHAPTER 6

*E*den emerged from her bedroom the next morning to find Jonah in the kitchen whisking batter in a bowl. Sabrina's tail, which was all that Eden could see of her from where she stood, beat out a rhythm on the linoleum floor. The sight of him cooking stopped her in her tracks. Jonah had often suggested Eden work to improve her culinary skills, but he had never himself stepped foot in the kitchen.

"What are you making?" she asked, resuming her approach.

He shot her a boyish grin. "Waffles!"

His enthusiasm paired with a waggle of his eyebrows made her laugh despite her misgivings. He'd clearly retained his ability to charm her.

"Is Miriam up yet?" She glanced toward the front hall.

"Not yet. Hey, do we have any vanilla extract?"

"Yes, we do." She crossed to the spice cabinet and found it for him.

"Thanks."

His cheerful attitude bemused her.

"You must have slept well," she observed.

He cocked his head as if considering her statement. "I did, actually."

"Good, then the medication works."

His noncommittal grunt implied neither agreement nor disagreement. His gaze had snagged on the outfit she was wearing, linen capris and a brightly printed blouse.

"You look nice. I don't have an appointment today, do I?"

"No, I'm going out shopping, but I did get a text from Dr. Branson saying he can fit us in tomorrow at 10 instead of 2. This is for you," she added, pulling his wallet out of her rear pocket and laying it on the counter. "It's yours. Master Chief returned it to me shortly after you…disappeared."

He put down the whisk to flip the wallet open.

"My ID," he said, looking startled. "And my driver's license."

"Don't get any ideas." She raised her eyebrows at him. Then she drew his cell phone from another pocket. "This is yours. I'm going to reactivate your account. Hopefully you can keep the same phone number."

He looked at the black Android she held out to him as if he'd never seen it before.

"Is that okay with you?" she asked.

"Yeah, sure." He looked back at the stove. "You're not in a hurry, though, are you? I thought we could have waffles together as soon as Miriam wakes up."

"Oh." A feeling of confinement squeezed her heart. "Actually, I'm meeting my friend Nina for coffee in like—" she glanced at the clock on the stove "—fifteen minutes, so I have to run."

His disappointment was so apparent she had to touch his arm. "But Miriam will love having waffles. Save me one, will you? I'll eat it when I get back."

"Okay."

She dropped her hand and went to collect her purse by the door. The dog followed her.

"Not now, Sabby. Jonah, could you ask Miriam to walk the dog, please?"

"I can walk her," Jonah offered.

Eden pictured Sabrina dragging him down the road. But telling Jonah he wasn't up to walking an eighty-pound retriever was tantamount to daring him to do it, so she just said, "Thanks."

"How long do you think you'll be gone?" he asked as she pulled the door open.

"Couple of hours maybe," she answered, deliberately vague.

Once out of the house, she descended the steps quickly, savoring the illusion of freedom. It was hers no longer—at least not until her twelve-month promise was over.

Twenty minutes later, she found herself explaining as much to an incredulous Nina as they sat by the window in a very crowded coffee shop, having miraculously snagged the last table for two.

"I can't believe it." The dark-haired dance instructor ran a hand through her mane of midnight hair. "You were free of him, and now he's back!"

"Nina," Eden scolded, "that's an awful thing to say." Regret pulled a whimper out of her. Too bad that was exactly how she felt.

Nina, who had heard first-hand accounts of Jonah's callous behavior before his disappearance, whispered through the steam rising from her coffee cup, "What about the money from his life insurance policy?" Her dark eyes roved Eden's face.

"I have to give it back," Eden realized with a start. In the recent upheaval, she had completely forgotten about the large sum of money from Jonah's supplemental insurance policy. USAA had transferred it to her savings account only last week.

"No!" With a miserable groan, Nina thumped her mug onto the tabletop and covered her face with her hands.

"I'm so sorry," Eden said, patting her friend's shoulder. "I know how much you wanted those treatments." She had promised her friend she could help pay for in-vitro fertilization. Nina, who'd been told years ago she was barren, now desperately wanted a baby. Her abusive husband had walked out, leaving her divorced and destitute. Yet, her dream of raising a child grew stronger with every passing month. She'd planned to proceed with IVF treatments and raise the baby on her own.

"I know every round is like eighteen thousand dollars," Eden added.

Nina's slender hands dropped to her lap. "It's fine," she said with resolution. "I've saved enough money for one treatment. Let's hope that's all I need."

"I'll pray for you," Eden offered.

"Thanks." Nina's tone, as usual, conveyed her belief that prayer was a waste of time.

A minute passed in which the two women sat in silence, watching people place their orders and doctor their drinks with cocoa, cream, and sugar.

"So there goes your nest egg," Nina said, bringing up the subject of money again.

Eden shrugged. "It's no big deal. I have a steady job," she reminded her friend. "I can make enough money to support myself. Besides, I'm not leaving him just yet. I've decided to give it twelve more months—"

"What? You were telling me last week how happy you are to be single."

"I was, but I can't just leave him," Eden insisted. "He's completely vulnerable right now. Wait till you see how thin he is. It'll take him months to get his health back. NSW is paying him disability for a year. After that, he'll either be a SEAL again or they'll med-drop him with disability pay."

"So, he's getting a paycheck, then," Nina said with relief.

"Yes. I don't know how much of his usual salary it'll be, but I'm sure it's enough for us to live on, and I can save up what I'm earning in the meantime."

"That's good," Nina answered. "But you can't teach fitness classes for the rest of your life. You're thirty-four now, and the body starts to break down after thirty-five. I'm already having trouble with my hips," she complained.

"You're only thirty-six," Eden retorted. "Stop acting like you're getting old."

"I'm just saying, when the time comes, you'll need to ask for alimony," her friend advised.

Eden understood Nina's obsession with money. Her own ex-husband had fled the country, returning to his native Turkey to avoid paying her anything.

"And maybe child-support." Nina gnawed on her lip.

Eden thought about what Jonah had said in the car just yesterday.

"You're not going to believe this, but Jonah already offered to take care of me and Miriam, no matter what happens between us."

Nina's eyes widened. "You've already had this conversation?"

"He brought it up. I think he can tell I'm not completely invested."

"Wow." Nina considered Eden in astonishment while sipping her coffee.

"He's so different now," Eden marveled. "He's sweet."

Nina snorted.

"Seriously. And he talks to Miriam like he enjoys her company. He's like a totally different person."

Nina lifted a skeptical eyebrow.

"Remember, I told you he was hit in the face and lost a tooth? Well, the part of the brain that's responsible for things like memory and personality sustained permanent damage. He may never get his memory back," she said, stating her worst fears. "He may never be the same man."

"Well that could be both bad and good," Nina pointed out.

Eden agreed to a point then shook her head. "No, he has to get his memory back. He'll never be a SEAL again without his memory, and that would crush him." She added with feeling, "Being a SEAL means everything to him."

Nina sighed. "Just promise me you won't put your life on hold forever."

"One year," Eden promised. "I'm going to return him to his former glory, and then my conscience won't bother me."

Nina sighed. "Good luck." Stretching out an arm, she patted Eden's hand. "I know it can't be easy having him underfoot all the time."

Eden pictured Jonah in the kitchen making waffles.

"Actually, it hasn't been that bad yet. Like I said, he's different."

"People don't change their stripes."

Poor Nina. Her ex-husband had certainly darkened her view of humanity, men especially. At one time, Eden might have agreed. Her husband, though, was certainly not like Nina's ex.

"I'm not so sure. I think a year-long captivity would change me, though not necessarily for the better. He was tortured."

Nina gasped. "How badly?"

"His fingernails are still growing back from where they ripped them out. And he's so skinny and weak he can barely walk a hundred feet without collapsing."

Nina shook her head. "I'm so sorry. I didn't even think about that." Her eyes reflected concern. "Are you sure you can handle this? Isn't there someone in his troop who can help him?"

"I hope so. Master Chief Rivera helped at the hospital. He told me to call him if I need anything."

Nina went perfectly still at the mention of Rivera's name.

Eden's intuition niggled. "You know Jonah's master chief," she guessed.

"No." Nina's denial was immediate and forced.

Eden took note of her friend's lie but didn't press the issue.

"The rest of his teammates should be back soon from coastal patrol. When they're home, I'll invite them over."

She pulled Jonah's old cell phone from her purse and showed it to Nina.

"This is his phone," she said. "I need to zip over to Sprint and see if I can activate his number again. Hopefully, they can download his contacts from the cloud."

"Hopefully," Nina repeated, but she seemed suddenly distracted.

"I'd better go," Eden said, taking a final sip of her coffee. "Thanks for meeting me."

"Any time," her friend replied. "Good luck." Catching Eden's hand, she squeezed it adding, "Be careful."

As Eden left the coffee shop and headed for the Sprint store three doors down, Nina's words echoed in her head, giving rise to a strange feeling of premonition.

Be careful. Actually, there was good reason in her present situation to be cautious. Jonah had been through so much. Was he honestly as balanced and introspective as he seemed? What if he were to suffer an episode of some kind? What if he went off the deep end? His training made him a lethal weapon. Was she safe with him? What about Miriam? Should Eden be leaving her alone with him for hours on end?

Hastening her step, she all but ran to the cell phone store, then chewed on the inside of her lip as she waited for the attendant to restore Jonah's phone, putting it back on their family plan.

As soon as Jonah got his contacts back, he could invite them to visit, which would take some of the heat off her.

Thinking of Miriam's safety again, she called her daughter's cell phone while she waited.

"Hi, Mom."

Miriam's cheery answer immediately dispelled Eden's fears. "Oh, good. You're up."

"Yep, Dad woke me up a while ago. He made waffles."

"I know. How'd they turn out?"

"Pretty good, but we need more maple syrup."

"What's he doing now?" Eden asked.

"Walking the dog."

Concern reared its grizzly head. "By himself?" Eden glanced at the attendant, willing him to hurry up.

"I tried to go with him, but he said he wanted to do it alone. I watched them all the way to the end of the street, but now I can't see them anymore."

"Was Sabrina pulling him really badly?"

"No, she's good with him."

"Well, that's a relief. Listen, I'll be there soon. Call me if Jonah isn't back in fifteen minutes."

"'Kay. Bye."

Hanging up, Eden was glad she'd called. It was reassuring to learn that Jonah was still treating Miriam well. Once again, he'd exceeded her expectations. That couldn't last forever, could it? Oh, Lord, what happened if he hurt himself while walking the dog?

One flaw common to all Navy SEALs was their tendency to bite off more than they could chew. She didn't want Jonah setting back his recovery by taking a fall.

~

The wind whipped Jonah's hair into his eyes. The sun, still rising toward its zenith, cast a warm glow on the left side of his face. Though he walked at a brisk pace set by the dog, he closed his eyes briefly, imagining the sun to be God's healing wand, undoing the damage he'd sustained to the front of his brain.

Stumbling into a pothole, Jonah snatched his eyes open, then chided himself for his foolishness. A voice in his head warned him against letting his guard down.

Pay attention!

Until that very second, he'd been enjoying his exertion, reveling in the obvious fact that he was getting stronger, breaking an actual sweat from exercise. Sabrina had taken him at least a mile from the house, all the way to the only hotel on the isthmus. There were people every hundred feet or so, either walking to the beach or leaving their ocean-front houses to head out somewhere. He hadn't felt alone or vulnerable until the voice in his head warned him of danger.

Realizing he had gone far enough, Jonah stopped in his tracks and urged the dog to turn around. "Let's go back."

Fortunately, the retriever didn't seem to care which way they were going, so long as they moved at a fast clip. That was fine by Jonah. Apart from the strain on his lungs and legs, he was happy to get exercise. But with the voice echoing, *Pay attention!* in his head, he spotted potential threats everywhere he looked.

That woman on the deck of her home. Why was she staring at him? What was in her hand? She had a clear shot at him if that was a gun.

"Hey!" Some teenager yelled out of his car. Jonah nearly jumped out of his skin, only to realize the kid was calling his friend over.

I'm freaking out over nothing, he assured himself. *Just because Dr. Branson said I might have PTSD, that doesn't mean I have it.*

Just then his attention was caught by a blue Ford Taurus, parked on the opposite side of the street, with the driver still at the wheel. He knew for a fact he had seen that same car, same driver, watching him from a different spot, shortly after he had left his house.

Check the plates. Thanks to his superlative vision, he could make them out before the car backed up and pulled a U-turn. XUV-6821. Yep, same car, same plates. Someone was watching him. Alarm swam up Jonah's bloodstream to his heart as the sedan sped away.

The driver had realized he'd been made. And now he was driving in the direction of Jonah's house, where Miriam was at home alone.

Miriam! Jonah broke into a jog, then lengthened his stride until he was running. The dog started to run, as well, jerking the leash right out of Jonah's hand.

"Sabrina!"

With a happy glance back, Sabrina kept running, fortunately in the direction of home. Moreover, she was bright enough to avoid running down the middle of the road. Jonah gave up chasing her but kept up his pace. *Run! Run straight to the house and protect Miriam from—*

"From what?" he ground out, even as he gasped for enough oxygen to feed his weak thighs. His calves protested with each step. But logic alone could not eradicate his fear.

There was a threat. He knew there was, and he wasn't imagining it, either. The feeling had been with him for some time. He remembered rowing the stolen fishing boat, thinking he had to get home to warn others. If he could only remember what the threat was!

Sabrina rounded the bend in the road and disappeared from view. By the time Jonah took the turn, the dog was gone. Lungs burning, a cramp building in his right calf, he pushed himself to get to the house to see if the dog had arrived safely.

As he approached the house, Eden dashed out of the driveway, sprinting in his direction. Relief and concern jostled for expression on her face. She streaked toward him with the effortlessness of an athlete, inspiring his envy. Her long hair swirled around her shoulders as she stopped abruptly in front of him, catching him by the arm.

"Stop! Why are you running?" she demanded.

"Sabrina," he gasped, dropping his hands to his knees to catch his breath.

"She's at home," Eden assured him. "We thought when she came back without you that something happened."

Jonah forced himself to straighten. Lacing his hands together at the back of his head, he kept filling his lungs. If he told Eden he had sensed a threat, she would think he was crazy. What if he was? Maybe the man in the car was simply some tourist who'd realized he'd forgotten something and had to go back for it. Dr. Branson's concerns about PTSD might be right on target.

"No." He managed to insert a few words between each breath. "She just… got away…I tried…to catch up."

"Are you insane?" Eden demanded. "Jonah, you could barely walk yesterday. You're going to kill yourself running like that."

He didn't try to defend himself. Not only was she probably right, but her scolding gave the illusion she actually cared about him. He nodded, acknowledging his foolishness.

"Even if the dog hadn't come home, you weren't going to catch her any sooner by running after her. Come on." She propped herself under his sweaty armpit and escorted him the rest of the way to the house. All the while, Jonah wished he weren't perspiring like a madman. He kept his mouth shut, so he didn't also sound like one.

Half an hour later, he ventured into the living area smelling like Miriam's berry bouquet body wash and dressed in fresh clothing. His exertion had sapped his remaining strength. Eden, who was standing at the stove, looked over at him. Miriam, seated on the couch and watching a game show, waved him over. Jonah crossed to the sofa and flopped down next to her. The show was educational, he realized. Teens from local high schools competed by answering trivia questions.

"Do you know these kids?" Jonah asked.

Miriam held a finger up as the host asked, "What is the name of the mythical bird that rises from its ashes to new life?"

"The Phoenix," Miriam answered as one of the students hit the buzzer.

Her answer, of course, turned out to be right. Jonah experienced a sense of pride.

"An illness which, in Latin, means 'inflammation of the lungs.'"

"Pneumonia," Miriam answered, but the youth who'd hit the buzzer got it wrong. "Oh, come on, David," she groused.

"So you know these kids."

"Yeah, sorry." She gave him her attention as the show went to commercials. "I don't technically know them because they're upper classmen and I'm only going into tenth grade. But they're from my school. I'm going to be on this show one day."

"You should be," Jonah agreed. "Has anybody ever told you you're smart?"

Her face flushed a pretty shade of pink. "Yeah." She laughed self-consciously. "But not you."

What did she mean, not him? *Oh, no.* Had the jerk he used to be implied she was stupid or something? Jonah frowned and sat up straighter. A glance at the kitchen showed Eden ladling what looked like mac and cheese into two bowls. She pretended not to be listening, but the watchful look she shot him indicated she most certainly was.

"Look," Jonah said to Miriam. He spoke quickly so as not to cut into the show when it came back on. "Whatever I might have said to you in the past—just forget it, okay? I must have had issues. I'm sorry."

Even with the television babbling, the silence seemed to ring through the house. Miriam and Eden both stared at him like he'd grown horns. Then, to his confusion, Eden thumped two bowls onto the counter, snatched up what looked like a cell phone, and brought it to him.

"I have to go to work," she announced. "There's lunch for the two of you." She gestured toward the breakfast bar. "Here you go," she added, putting his phone in his hand. "You're back on the plan."

Looking down at the all-black Android, Jonah was struck by the strange sense of foreboding he had felt when she'd showed it to him that morning. He didn't want to hold it.

"Luckily, your old number was still available, and all your contacts were in the cloud, so now they're back on the phone."

"Thanks," he said, acknowledging the trouble she'd gone to that morning.

"Don't you want to check it out?" Eden prompted, as he laid it on the arm of the couch.

Not really. He forced himself to pick it up again and rouse the phone, but he could not recall the passcode.

"You'll have to set that up again," Eden told him. "In the meantime, use 0719."

Recognizing the month and day of his birthday, he followed her directions and the home screen appeared.

"I think you should call your master chief and have him over," Eden continued. "Or maybe he could take you out somewhere. Ask him when your friends come back."

Jonah lifted a dry look at her. It couldn't be more obvious she was desperate to get him away from the house, out from under her feet. But then who would keep an eye on Miriam while she was working?

"Thanks," he said again. In reality, holding the phone made him feel like he was holding a grenade with the pin just pulled. He set it back down on the arm of the couch and licked the moisture from his upper lip.

Eden regarded him with gathering confusion. "Are you good?" she asked him.

He nodded and pointed to the television to convey that Miriam's show was more important than their conversation.

With a firming of her lips, Eden conveyed she *knew* there was something wrong. Something entirely in his head.

Dear God, please don't let me have PTSD.

Only one thing could be worse than that—an actual threat. But what could it be? And what would happen to him and to his family if he didn't remember?

CHAPTER 7

*D*riving onto the adjacent Navy base, Eden replayed the scene that had taken place between Miriam and Jonah. He had apologized for having *issues*.

Recalling his words, she clapped a hand to her head in disbelief. The old Jonah had never once apologized, as he was never in the wrong, at least not to his way of thinking. The new Jonah hadn't only complimented Miriam on her intelligence, he'd hit the nail on the head about his former self. The old Jonah *did* have issues, but he'd never once admitted it until now.

How could anyone have changed as much as he had? Surely a blow to the brain wouldn't change him for the better. Maybe it was his memory loss that made him seem so different? What if he became exactly like he used to be when his memory returned?

Eden parked in her usual spot in the shade. A glance at the clock told her she was five minutes earlier than usual. She should use that time planning new and interesting exercise routines. Instead, she let the engine idle to keep the air conditioning blowing cool air in her face and pondered her circumstances.

Was it fair to Jonah to keep her plans of leaving him to herself? She thought of how Jonah had made waffles for them that morning. Didn't he deserve to know where his marriage stood before he invested too much of himself? Already, he seemed to be forging a special bond with Miriam.

Perhaps she ought to come clean with him, let him know she intended to split once he was able to look after himself. Given his comment about taking care of them the other day, she doubted he'd be shocked to hear of her decision.

"What should I do, Lord?" she murmured, searching her heart and her conscience while listening for a quiet nudge. "Please show me what to do," she pleaded.

Silence was her only response. Cutting the engine, she took off her seatbelt and headed into the gym for work, wondering all the while what Jonah's psychiatrist would think of her planned desertion.

Two hours later, Eden pushed into the house still sweaty from her work out. She faltered at the sight of Jonah and Miriam sitting side by side on the sofa. Jonah sat with his head against the back of the sofa, his eyes half-closed. Miriam was reading out loud to him—her required summer reading, *To Kill a Mockingbird*. Eden had been trying all summer to get her to start it.

Gratitude toward Jonah vied with guilt. He was doing it again—investing himself in his stepdaughter. He sent Eden a sleepy smile when she met his gaze, but Miriam, who was too caught up in the story to acknowledge her mother, kept reading. Eden left her purse inside the door and went right back outside to tend to her wildflowers. If they didn't get regularly watered, they tended to wilt and die in the sandy environment.

As she weeded and watered, she asked herself the same question she had entertained earlier that afternoon. Should she tell Jonah they were headed toward separation or let him figure that out on his own as time went on? Which tactic was kinder?

God wasn't giving her any clear signs, not so far as she could tell. She wasn't any closer to making a decision when she went back inside, even hotter and sweatier than she'd been an hour earlier. Miriam was still reading. Jonah slit his eyes and closed them again. Feeling sorry for him, Eden crossed quickly toward her bedroom and briskly showered. She had yet to make a decision by the time she emerged from her room wearing a comfortable, cotton romper.

Miriam reached the end of a chapter as Eden sidled up to the couch.

"How's the story?" she asked, as Miriam set the book aside.

Jonah scrubbed a hand over his face, visibly trying to rouse himself. He lifted his nose in her direction and inhaled.

"You smell nice."

His comment caused Miriam to snicker.

Eden repressed the pleasure that spread through her at his compliment. "How's the book?" she repeated.

"It's pretty good." Miriam's tone betrayed surprise. "We're like halfway through already."

Eden dared to meet Jonah's eyes. "Thank you," she said simply.

The slow, sleepy smile he sent her made her stomach cartwheel. "It's time for Miriam to walk the dog," she said briskly.

Her daughter groaned.

"I'll do it," Jonah offered.

"No." Eden dreaded a repeat of what had happened that morning. "It's Miriam's job to walk the dog. That was the deal we struck when we got a puppy."

"Fine." With a long face, Miriam pushed herself off the couch.

"I'm going to order pizza for dinner," Eden added, knowing that would motivate her daughter. "When you come back from your walk, we'll decide what kind to order."

Miriam headed straight for Sabby's leash. "Cool," she said, then looked over her shoulder at Jonah. "You want to come with me?"

He blinked as if he couldn't quite bring her into focus.

"I think Jonah needs a nap," Eden commented. She had thought about having a talk with him while Miriam was gone, but it didn't seem fair to tell Jonah the truth about their marriage when he was struggling merely to keep awake.

He sent her a look that was partly gratitude, partly self-directed frustration. "Don't let me sleep for more than an hour," he requested, pushing to his feet.

"Use the alarm on your cell phone," Eden suggested. She had yet to see him use his Android.

Mumbling something to the affirmative, he headed blindly toward the study. Miriam, who was snapping the leash on the dog, watched him disappear then sent a worried look at her mother.

"He'll get better," she said, reading her daughter's thoughts. Neither one of them were used to Jonah being anything less than invincible.

Exactly one hour later, Jonah appeared fresh-faced and visibly rested. It wasn't clear to Eden if he'd used the alarm on his phone or if the dog barking at the pizza delivery man had wakened him.

"Let's eat in the dining room," Eden suggested, as she transferred pizza slices onto plates. "Veggie or meat-lovers?" she asked as he went to get glasses from the cupboard.

He hesitated, looking momentarily at a loss. "Which kind do I like best?" he asked her.

"Veggie," she said, testing him.

A dubious look crossed his face. "No, I don't."

She laughed despite herself. "You haven't changed that much," she said, even though that wasn't true. The old Jonah had always known exactly what he wanted and had no compunction about demanding it.

With their plates and drinks, they all took a seat at the table and dug into their pizzas.

"Have you called your master chief yet?" Eden prompted.

Jonah shook his head and looked away.

"You should ask him when the others get back. If you want, we can have another party on our deck," Eden offered. Anything to involve Jonah's teammates in Jonah's life.

"Yes, a party!" Miriam chimed in.

Jonah regarded the deck through the nearest window. "Okay," he said with rising enthusiasm. He clearly seemed to like the idea. "Thanks."

Thanks. The word seared Eden's conscience. He obviously thought she was being kind, offering to celebrate his return when, in actuality, she wanted him to rely on someone else besides her and Miriam for companionship. Letting him think that everything was hunky-dory wasn't ultimately fair to him.

Making up her mind to be honest with him, she saw that Miriam was nearly done eating her second slice. "Honey, when you're done with that, can you put your plate in the sink and give Jonah and me a minute alone?"

Miriam froze with a bite of pizza in her mouth. She pulled it slowly out and, meeting Jonah's quizzical look, laid the remainder on her plate and pushed her chair back.

"You can finish eating," Eden protested.

"I'm not the one who needs fattening up." Without a backward glance, Miriam marched to the kitchen, dumped her uneaten pizza in the trash, put her plate in the dishwasher, and disappeared toward her bedroom, calling the dog after her.

Jonah, clearly puzzled by Miriam's abrupt departure, wiped his hands on his napkin and, with a tense look on his face, waited for Eden to explain herself.

She drew a shaky breath and let it out again. "I haven't been completely honest with you," she began.

He just looked at her, waiting.

"Please don't think you've said or done anything to bring this on because you haven't. You've been great. I have no absolutely no complaints about the way you've behaved or how great you are with Miriam."

"What was I like with her before?"

The abrupt question forced her to put off what she had to tell him. "You never would have let her read out loud to you."

"Why not?" He sounded genuinely perplexed.

"You said, 'Children should be seen and not heard,'" she said quickly.

Jonah smiled faintly. "My stepfather used to say that." With a look of self-loathing, he shook his head. "I can't believe I repeated it."

In spite of his semi-apology, Eden pressed on. "Things weren't great between us, either. When you were home, we disagreed a lot."

Her confession got his full attention.

Finding her throat dry, Eden swallowed in order to push the words through it. "I realized, after the Navy declared you dead, I'd made a mistake marrying you as quickly as I had." Her voice wobbled. Was this really the right time to tell him? "I wanted you for stability."

The words were true, but that wasn't why she had married him. "And you wanted me for a trophy, I think."

Falling quiet, she waited for his response. His face remained a mask. Then he blinked, averted his face, and stared out the window at the ocean. She watched him draw a measured breath, heard him let it out again.

"I'm not asking for a separation. Not right now," she qualified.

He stared outside with eyes that had lost their luster. "Let me guess," he stated on a bitter note. "You'll give me twelve months."

Guilt stabbed her in the heart as he looked to her for corroboration.

"Unless you get your memory back sooner," she confessed.

His laugh of irony twisted the knife in deeper.

"I'm so sorry," she added. "I feel terrible. You don't deserve this."

Jonah looked down at his hands. For a long time, he said nothing. When he finally looked at her again, his expression betrayed neither rancor nor betrayal. Yet there was something in his eyes she couldn't read.

"It's okay," he murmured. "Now I know why you want my teammates back in my life."

"Right." She swallowed down her guilt. At least, he seemed to understand.

Pushing his chair back, Jonah left the table, taking his dishes with him. Like Miriam, he put them in the dishwasher then retreated to his room without a word.

Eden sat alone at the table, thinking. She had done it. She'd told Jonah their marriage had an end-date, and he'd accepted her ultimatum with seeming equanimity.

Nina would be so proud of her.

Why, then, wasn't her heart winging at the prospect of her freedom? Instead it ached. She knew a ridiculous urge to chase Jonah down the hallway and tell him she'd spoken in haste. After all, twelve months was a long time. Who knew what could happen?

Pressing a fist to her churning stomach, she whispered, "Forgive me." Only she couldn't have said whether the words were for Jonah or for God.

Jonah lay across the daybed in the study stripped of energy and motivation. The pizza on which he had gorged sat heavily in his stomach.

His wife wanted to divorce him.

Okay, that was probably an exaggeration. What she'd said was, when he got his memory back, they were going to separate. But, basically, they were headed for divorce.

Why should he care? Aside from her heavenly scent, he didn't even remember her. He didn't know when her birthday was, what her favorite food was, or whether she was ticklish. The only thing he knew for sure was that he wanted her to welcome him into her world, into her bed. And not because he thought of her as a trophy. Certainly, any man would be proud to show her off in public, but that wasn't the reason he'd married her. He had loved her, hadn't he?

Thinking back to his wedding photos, he searched for an indication he'd been smitten. He had to have been or he would never have abandoned his private oath never to marry.

The album was still under his bed. He rolled over, reached for it, and set it on the mattress next to him. Coming up on one elbow, he cracked the cover, this time to look at pictures of himself.

The confident, possibly even arrogant smile he'd worn in every image disturbed him. Thinking back on his life, was he really that sure of himself? How could he have been? Life had leveled him some staggering blows. What if that confidence had been pure façade? Come to think of it, his love for Eden might have secretly terrified him.

Now that made sense. Jonah plumbed each picture searching for evidence of his secret insecurity. If he thought of Eden while working, his concentration might have been compromised. He could have endangered his own men, put the whole troop at risk. Oh, yes, he'd had every reason to fear his love for her.

As for his attitude toward children, it wasn't that he'd considered them a nuisance. Rather, he hadn't known what to do with Miriam. He could barely remember his own gentle father. His stepfather had completely disregarded him. Jonah's parenting toolbox had been consequently empty.

Little wonder he had been such a lousy husband and father. Who could blame Eden for thinking she'd made a mistake, for wanting her freedom?

With a groan of defeat, Jonah slapped the album shut and shoved it back under his bed. Rolling over, he faced the wall and closed his eyes. A sense of déjà vu washed over him, telling him he had searched his heart during captivity and realized his shortcomings. Had he remembered Eden then or had he already lost his memory? Just when had his memories been stripped from him?

Either way, he knew he'd had plenty of time regretting the way he'd lived and vowing to become a better man. In that lowest of low places, he must have called on God for help. And God, in His mercy, had answered.

"'To give light to those who sit in darkness and in the shadow of death,'" he whispered. The words were from the Bible, he decided. But how did he know them?

A sudden urge to seek comfort from his master chief prompted Jonah to roll back over and look at the door. His phone was still in the living room. Summoning the strength to get up and fetch it, he overheard Eden call the dog and leave the house, taking her on a walk. The opportunity to get his phone without running into her propelled him to his feet.

He hurried to collect it, carried it quickly back to the study, and sat on his bed texting Rivera.

Master Chief, it's Jonah. When did you say the guys are getting back?

Rivera responded in less than five seconds. *Tomorrow around midnight. They can't wait to see you. How are you holding up?*

A sound that was half laugh and half sob escaped Jonah's throat. *No memories yet,* he answered.

Give it time, Rivera replied.

The pressure grew behind Jonah's eyes. He knew Rivera was a profoundly spiritual man. He knew he could count on him to be supportive.

I need you to pray for me, Santiago, he requested.

I am. I will. In a separate text, he added, *Would you like to talk?*

Jonah's eyes went to the window. It was still light outside, but the advent of twilight made him nervous. Remembering the car that might or might not have been following him earlier, he had no desire to exacerbate his nervousness by stepping outside with nightfall on the way. On the other hand, it would come as a relief to talk to someone about his precarious domestic situation.

Can you come over here? he asked.

Sure. When? Santiago asked.

Jonah opted to wait till Eden got back from her walk. Then he and Master Chief would sit out on the deck so as not to disturb anyone. *In forty-five minutes?*

See you then.

Thanks. Instead of putting his phone down, Jonah typed a group text to the men in his troop with whom he felt the closest bond: Saul, Theo, and the youngest SEAL in Alpha Troop if not the whole Team, nicknamed Bambino. He added Blake LeMere's name automatically before remembering with a pang that Blake was dead. How strange that his death was a full two years ago! To him, it seemed like yesterday.

Look forward to seeing you all when you get home.

There was no response, of course. The men would be busy training right up to their return.

Noises from the next room had him putting down his phone. He could hear Miriam climbing her bunkbed.

Having peeked into the room on a couple of occasions, he pictured it in his mind's eye: a sturdy white bunkbed drowning in stuffed animals, pink walls, white furniture. The innocent-little-girl setup was ruined by posters of pop stars, rap musicians, and bumper stickers with slogans like ALL STRESSED OUT AND NO ONE TO CHOKE plastered at intervals along the wall.

Concerned by Miriam's departure from the table earlier, Jonah got up and approached her closed door. He gave it a light knock.

"Come in."

He saw her tuck a magazine out of sight as he poked his head into the room. "That's not your book," he chided with a smile.

"I left it in the living room."

"Want me to get it for you?"

"Not really." Her tone let him know she was sulking.

"We'll read together tomorrow," he promised.

Her gaze seemed to harden as she looked down at him.

"Will you be here tomorrow?" she inquired quietly.

He hesitated at the strange question. "Except for my appointment," he replied.

"What about a week from now? Or a year?" she pressed.

The suspicion she'd overheard Eden's ultimatum turned him cold, then hot as self-consciousness flooded him.

Stepping into the room, he crossed to Miriam's bunkbed and put a hand on the upper rail.

"I don't plan on leaving." He'd made up his mind the night before that he was going to fight for his marriage, and he had no intention of changing it. "I struggled to get home to you guys," he added, recalling suddenly his terrible thirst, the blisters on his hands as he rowed through inky darkness and blazing sun. The burgeoning memories encouraged him.

"I don't want to be anywhere else." Saying the words out loud made them terribly apparent.

Miriam swallowed but didn't say anything.

He didn't realized he was gripping her bed so hard until his knuckles protested. He immediately let go.

"Look, your mother loved me when she married me, right?" His mind flashed to their wedding pictures.

Miriam nodded, her gaze softening.

"Well, squirt." Jonah had to clear his throat to get the words out. "Maybe she'll fall in love with me again. What do you think?"

He wanted desperately for Miriam to agree. The corners of her mouth twitched toward a smile.

"Wouldn't hurt to try," she said, finally.

They both stiffened at the sound of Eden running up the deck stairs with the dog.

With a belated sense of propriety, Jonah backed toward the door, but Eden spotted him leaving Miriam's room as she emerged from the foyer. Their gazes locked.

"Everything okay?" she called with a worried look.

"She wants her book," he said.

Eden glanced toward the couch. "I'll get it."

Trailing her into the living room, he added, "Master Chief's coming over. We'll hang out on the deck so we don't disturb you."

"Oh, good." Her relief couldn't have been more evident. Picking up Miriam's book, she looked like she might say something more about the subject of their separation. Then she handed him the book instead. "Can you take this to her?"

In other words, she trusted him to return to Miriam's bedroom.

"Sure."

"There's some juice and beer in the fridge. Make sure you offer Master Chief a drink when he gets here."

The implication she would keep her distance wasn't lost on him. "I will."

"But no beer for you since you're taking medication."

"Right." He decided she had to care about him a little bit to say that.

Turning back to him, Eden added with a sigh, "Jonah, I'm really sorry about my timing. I mean, you've only been home for three days, and you're trying to get your strength back. I just...I didn't want to mislead you."

Seeing her so genuinely upset with herself, eyes bright with pent-up tears, he saw his chance to convince her to keep an open mind.

"No worries," he said. Then, before she could guess his next move, he stepped closer and put his arms around her, pulling her stiff body against him. "It's going to be okay."

At first it was like hugging a pole, but when he smoothed his free hand up her spine, she seemed to relax slightly. Then, to his relief, she looped both arms around his neck and hugged him back, tentatively but genuinely.

A groan of satisfaction stuck in his throat at their full-body contact. Her soft curves molded themselves against him, fitting perfectly against his larger frame. Something powerful and possessive rose up in him, causing him to tighten his hold.

Eden immediately squirmed free. "Miriam's waiting for her book," she reminded him.

Avoiding eye contact, she spun away and headed for her bedroom, shutting her door firmly between them.

Was that a win or a loss? Jonah wondered. Surely a warm-blooded woman like Eden missed being held by her husband.

A terrible thought occurred to him. Had she possibly found someone else to hold her in his absence?

His gut wrenched at the thought. Could that be the reason she was anxious to wash her hands of him? Did she have someone waiting in the wings?

No, no, no. Life couldn't be that unkind, not when he'd survived captivity and made it all the way home again.

Surely Master Chief would have kept an eye on Eden, if only as a sentimental favor to Jonah, whom everyone believed was dead. If rumors existed of Eden being with someone else, Rivera would have heard them.

Recalling the book, still in his hand, Jonah plodded back to Miriam's room to give it to her.

~

Eden closed her bedroom door, then sank back against it, her knees too weak to hold her.

Jonah had obviously retained his ability to waken her yearnings with a simple hug. His heat, his muscles, his scent all combined to undermine her aloofness and awaken her desires. She had just told him not an hour earlier she wanted to separate! Yet, here she was trembling from head to toe in the wake of his embrace.

She had experienced this before. With every homecoming, he had wielded his special power and melted her hardened heart. His siren song had called her back to him, again and again. She could not afford to let it happen this time. Whatever else occurred, from that moment on, she couldn't let him put his arms around her.

She would not give up her hard-won self-sufficiency over a mere hug!

With an oath to stay as far away from Jonah as possible, Eden pushed off the door and went into her bathroom where she couldn't be overheard, to update her best friend.

"I did it," she said when Nina picked up. "I told him I want to separate when he's better."

Her friend's gasp of approval blended with the click of the door as Eden shut herself inside her bathroom.

"How'd you tell him?"

"After dinner, I just put it out there." Sitting on the edge of her Jacuzzi tub, Eden pressed a fist into her churning stomach.

"How did he react?"

Eden thought back. "He said he didn't blame me."

"Really?" Nina sounded incredulous.

"I told you, he's not at all like he used to be."

"Oh, please. He's been home for three days," Nina reminded her. "He hasn't had time to revert to his old habits."

Eden spared a thought to how Jonah used to behave. "He hugged me this evening," she admitted. "He still has that power over me."

"Ugh!" Eden pictured Nina rolling her eyes. "Don't let him touch you, then. You know what'll happen if you let him touch you. You'll be all confused, and you'll back away from your plan to separate. Next thing you know, you'll be miserably married again."

"I'm already confused," Eden admitted.

"How? You were happy when he was gone. How can you be questioning that now?"

Eden closed her eyes and drew a deep breath. "You're right. It's just because he's so different."

"He's not different," Nina insisted. "If anything, he's exploiting your weaknesses. He knows how to get to you—through your daughter and through your body. Doesn't that sound like something he'd do?"

Eden thought about it. The old Jonah did whatever it took to come out on top.

"Yes," she admitted.

"See. You can't trust he's changed, honey. He's behaving himself right now because you are virtually strangers, and strangers behave themselves. But deep down, he's being true to form. He doesn't want to lose you, Eden—who would?"

"Right." Nina's words made sense. Could Jonah be using Miriam to make a good impression with Eden? If so, it would break Miriam's heart when she found out she still meant nothing to him.

"Listen, I have to go. I promised Miriam I'd watch a movie with her this evening."

"No worries. You did the right thing, Eden. It's kinder to Jonah to make your expectations clear than to lead him on."

"Yeah," Eden agreed. "Thanks." Ending the call, she lifted her gaze to the mirror.

Regardless of her friend's assurance, the woman gazing back at her looked distinctly torn.

CHAPTER 8

"What's happening, Jonah?" Rivera asked.

Jonah sat beside his master chief in the Adirondack chairs that offered a view of Dam Neck's beach. The sun was setting out of sight behind the house, but it painted the sky with golden bands morphing into peach then darkening to violet where the sea met the sky. From the deck, perhaps thirty feet above sea level, Jonah figured the horizon he could see was over six miles distant.

He'd entertained himself with such mathematical calculations while bobbing out in the Gulf, awaiting either rescue or death.

At Rivera's question, Jonah scrubbed a hand over his face to wake himself up. The nap he'd taken earlier clearly hadn't been long enough.

"I don't even know where to start," he admitted on a weary note.

Rivera took a thoughtful drag on his bottle of papaya juice.

"You're seeing a doctor?" he inquired.

"Yep, a psych named Branson."

The master chief frowned. "I would have thought you'd see Dr. Alexander. He's supposed to be the best. But I'm sure Branson is good, or the CO wouldn't have okayed him."

Jonah grunted. "Dwyer doesn't care who I see. He's washed his hands of me."

"I told you this—he cares. He's just retiring soon." Rivera, who was naturally demonstrative, reached a hand across the space between them and squeezed Jonah's forearm.

Jonah sighed despondently. "Thing is, no one understands why I've forgotten two years of my life. Amnesia caused by trauma makes sense. I went through some stuff, and I can see not wanting to remember it, especially if I betrayed military secrets."

Rivera scoffed at the notion. "Not you," he said with gratifying certainty.

Jonah glanced at the stunted fingernails on his left hand. "Well, thanks for that."

He didn't think he had, either. Ripping out his fingernails would've only ticked him off. He considered the scars on his back from the lashings and the telltale signs of electric shock torture.

"You don't remember anything?"

"Not yet. I'm supposed to call a Special Agent Elwood when I do." Eden had stuck the man's business card on the refrigerator.

"Ah, Elwood," Rivera said, clearly recognizing the name.

Jonah looked at him askance.

"He's been investigating the op that resulted in your disappearance. Everyone on the squadron has been grilled by him," Rivera explained.

"Really? I wish I could remember what happened." Immediately the ache behind Jonah's left eye began to build. "This is going to sound crazy, but I feel like there's something I have to remember. Something about weapons."

Rivera paused in the act of taking another sip. "Weapons?" He set his bottle down.

"Yeah. Was the op an interdiction?"

Rivera's dark eyes swung toward the horizon. "Yes," he said slowly.

His reticence made Jonah stiffen. "I guess you're not allowed to discuss it with me," he realized.

Rivera whipped his head back around. "Of course I can discuss it with you. You were there."

Jonah's tension left him. "So, what was the objective?" He pitched his voice low in the unlikely event someone was standing under the deck listening.

Rivera answered quietly. "We got word of some dirty bombs being stockpiled in a warehouse in Carenero, Venezuela. Four of you went in to retrieve them."

"Me, Lowery, Theo, and Saul," Jonah said, recalling what Rivera had told him in the hospital.

"That's right. It was supposed to be a simple operation, in and out, except the bombs weren't by the northeast wall where they were supposed to be."

"Faulty intel?" Jonah asked.

"I don't think so."

Rivera's answer sharpened Jonah's dulled mind. "What do you mean?"

"This was not the first time we went to pick up weapons, only to find them gone. It's happened so often now we've named the thieves The Entity."

"What do they steal?"

"Mostly dirty bombs, chemical warfare agents, the kind of stuff our Third World enemies would like to get their hands on."

"How would The Entity have gotten the same intel we have?"

Rivera shrugged. "Possibly someone in DIA is selling information?"

Jonah grunted in disgust. "It wouldn't be the first time," he said, recollecting two prior instances of DIA agents betraying their country.

"If not the DIA, then the leak is on our end," Rivera said with reluctance.

The certainty he knew something niggled Jonah again. He redoubled his efforts to remember, only to suffer the same lancing pain behind his eye.

Rivera watched him rub the side of his face. "It hurts you to remember?"

"Yes," Jonah gritted. "Every time I think about the op I get this sharp pain behind my eye. It's so frustrating. I don't get it."

Sensing Rivera's commitment to listening, Jonah unburdened himself of his private fears.

"This is going to sound crazy," Jonah began, "but I also feel like someone's watching me."

Jonah pictured the navy-blue Taurus that pulled a U-turn before he could get close to it.

"I don't feel safe stepping out of the house without a weapon." He scanned the area, suddenly uncomfortable merely thinking about it. "My doctor thinks I might have PTSD, the kind that doesn't go away."

"What do you think?" Rivera countered, neither agreeing with the diagnosis nor scoffing at it.

Jonah sighed. "I don't think PTSD is the reason I've forgotten two years. If it was just my captivity that I couldn't remember, then maybe. I can't even remember my marriage," he lamented, craning his neck to peer into the window at Eden and Miriam, both on the sofa watching a movie.

Rivera mulled over the question for a minute. "What's the last thing you recall?"

A vision of Blake LeMere plummeting toward the earth made Jonah close his eyes.

"LeMere's death," he said, meeting Rivera's gaze again. "To me, it could've happened last week. I can't remember anything after being told it was an accident."

"The incident was traumatic," Rivera pointed out. "Maybe your amnesia *is* trauma-related."

"Remember the autopsy report?" Jonah asked. "The coroner said LeMere was unconscious before he hit the ground. I just don't get that. We jumped together. He was feeling fine in the lineup, cracking jokes and saying he'd beat us all to the ground."

Rivera shrugged. "A sudden change in altitude could have made him black out."

Jonah clicked his tongue. "Hardly. We were at four thousand feet. He'd done a dozen high-altitude jumps without any issues."

"I don't know." Rivera sighed. "It's just one of those things that will remain a mystery—at least until the next life."

The master chief's reference to heaven made Jonah think about his newfound faith.

"Here's some irony for you," he relayed. "For years you've talked to us about how important it is to talk to God and give Him control over our lives."

Rivera's gaze sharpened with interest.

"Well, I finally get that now. I can't remember when I started talking to Him, but I know God's the reason I survived captivity. I know it's because of Him I made it home."

Rivera's smile cut through the gloom. "I'm so happy to hear this," he said with feeling. "Everything will be better now, wait and see."

Jonah thought about his failing marriage. "Yeah, I'm not so sure about that." He had to look away as pessimistic thoughts reclaimed him. On the horizon, sea and sky merged into darkness.

"Eden says our marriage was a mistake," he continued, unburdening himself. "She says she wants to separate when I get my memory back—or in twelve months' time, whichever is sooner." He glanced at Rivera for his reaction.

The master chief's smile had disappeared. "I'm so sorry," he murmured. Studying Jonah sidelong, he added, "I can see that's not what you want."

"Hell, no," he said with heat. "She's all I've got right now—her and Miriam.

I really like that kid," he added, more to himself than to his friend. "I mean, I don't blame Eden for being unhappy. You knew me, Santiago." He looked at his master chief. "Was I really as much of a jackass as I think I was?"

Rivera looked at him for a long moment. "Not at work," he answered carefully. "Everyone in the squadron respects you. But, from what I saw, you could've given Eden more attention than you did."

Jonah cringed inwardly. "How did I treat Miriam?"

Rivera thought for a moment. "I'm not sure. I never saw you two together much."

"Right." With a groan that came from deep inside him, Jonah closed his eyes and rubbed his left temple where an ache tapped. Hearing Rivera corroborate what both Miriam and Eden had hinted at undermined his confidence completely. What if it was too late to win them back? What if some other man was in the picture? He looked back at his master chief.

"You would tell me if you'd heard about Eden dating someone else this past year, wouldn't you?"

Rivera blinked. "Is that what you think happened?"

The fact his master chief had answered a question with a question alerted Jonah.

"You know something," he guessed. "What do you know?"

"Nothing," Rivera soothed. "It's nothing, I promise."

Jonah wasn't sure he believed him, but he trusted Rivera's judgment. If the man wasn't concerned, he shouldn't concern himself either.

"*No te preocupes*. Don't despair, Jonah." Rivera sent him a smile of support and certainty. "You say God brought you through captivity and safely home again."

"Right."

"Then He's got you. He isn't going to let your marriage fall apart, not now."

The words touched a place deep in Jonah's heart, soothing him.

"God brought you home for a reason," Rivera added. "Put your trust in Him, and remember He works *all* things for the good of those who love him. *All* things, Jonah."

"Yeah." Jonah nodded in agreement. A calm wind blew through his spirit. "Thank you," he said, holding Rivera's gaze to convey his gratitude. "I really needed to hear that."

"Any time. I will pray for you, night and day."

"Thanks." The last ounce of energy seemed to leave Jonah's body all at once. Closing his eyes, he dropped his head against the back of the chair again.

"You look exhausted," Rivera said. "I think I should leave and let you rest."

Jonah pried his eyes open. "Sorry. This happens to me every afternoon and evening. My meds run out of steam."

"It's okay. You're recovering." Rivera touched the top of Jonah's head as he stood up. "Stay here."

Ignoring the words, Jonah struggled to his feet, determined to escort Rivera to the steps.

With a shake of his head, Rivera let Jonah follow him to the recycle bucket by the front door.

"You take care, my friend," he said, laying the glass bottle in the bucket, then straightening. "Call me any time. When you're ready, we'll train on the beach or something, yes?"

"Sounds good." Jonah's words slurred together, he was so tired.

"Good night." With a brief hug, Rivera took his leave, running lightly down the stairs and across the yard. Watching his shadow race toward the street, Jonah realized he intended to run all the way to his house, about a mile and a half away.

I used to be able to do that like it was nothing. In that moment, just entering the house to get to his bedroom felt like a monumental task. He headed, instead, for the closest thing he could collapse on—a lounge chair on the deck several feet away.

He would take a nap here so as not to disturb Miriam and Eden's movie. When he awoke again, refreshed, he'd go back inside and take his nighttime medication.

That was his last conscious thought as his muscles went limp atop the chair's wooden slats.

A sense of impending danger preceded the sound of voices. Barking at him, they descended without warning, seizing him with rough hands and dragging him off his ledge. Pushed down a dimly lit hallway, shoved through a door, Jonah was grappled into a reclining chair. Familiar straps closed around his wrists, ankles, and forehead. A man on either side of him cinched the straps tight, keeping him immobile. It was time for El Jefe to try to break him again.

Not the electricity, Jonah silently beseeched, as sweat poured off him.

The dreaded footsteps of his tormentor made Jonah's heart pound. Give me strength, Lord.

El Jefe dropped his carrying case on the table. He opened it—click, click—and lifted the lid. Silence ensued as he ran his fingers lovingly over his instruments of torture, searching for the one that would finally loosen Jonah's tongue.

Jonah knew the kinds of questions that were coming. He'd been trained to answer them with misinformation. But these were questions he didn't know how to answer because he couldn't remember. Through bits of conversation and by process of elimination, he had determined where he was. But he couldn't recall a single detail of the op that had evidently taken him to Venezuela.

He knew his tormentor would ask him, "Who destroyed my warehouse?"

Jonah didn't know the answer, but the question suggested he and his teammates had been interdicting weapons when—obviously—something unplanned had occurred. Jonah had evidently been captured—impossible if he'd been conscious. He must have blacked out. Where were his teammates? How could they have left him there alone?

Jonah's captors believed the Americans had blown up their warehouse. El Jefe queried him endlessly, unleashing every punishment at his disposal until he wearied at his lack of success and sent Jonah to his cell.

"Unbutton his shirt."

The command filled Jonah with dread. His body coiled like a spring as the commander's assistants laid his chest bare.

Relax, he ordered himself. It wouldn't do him any good to resist the wracking pain wrought by the electric nodes being attached to him. He drew a steadying breath, counting seconds as he inhaled and exhaled. A humming sound filled the chamber as El Jefe flipped the switch on his machine.

All at once, Jonah realized the strap around his left wrist was compromised. In his many struggles, he'd managed to tear the seams that bound the leather to the armrest.

A miracle!

Strategizing the best means of debilitating the guards who flanked him, he opted to seize the man on his left first, dragging him across his body to act as a human shield while he freed his right wrist.

Cool fingers touched his chest as one of the guards bent over him. Now! Jonah jerked his wrist free, seizing the man's windpipe. A curtailed shriek filled his ears. Hands flew to his shoulders. Sharp nails dug into his flesh. Hair fell across his face.

A familiar scent layered his dream, but it didn't belong there. Questioning reality, Jonah felt the slats of the chaise lounge beneath his shoulder bones. He forced his eyes open and realized he was lying on his deck at home, and the guard he was choking was his beautiful wife.

With a cry of denial, his hand sprang open. She collapsed atop him, sucking air into her lungs like someone trying to breathe through a straw.

Oh, God. Oh, dear God.

Galvanized by horror, he launched them both off the chair. On his feet, he half-dragged, half-carried Eden to the door. Shouldering it open, he hit the switches. Light flooded the entryway, illuminating her pale face and her wide-open mouth as she hung in his arms struggling to breathe.

Stricken by what he'd done, he sank to his knees in the foyer and brought her to the floor with him. In the back of the house, the dog barked.

"Eden. Jesus, what have I done?"

No answer. Her enormous eyes shone with panic as she managed to suck another breath through her crushed windpipe.

"Keep breathing! I'm going to call an ambulance," he said, preparing to release her.

She fisted his shirt and mouthed, "No."

"I have to. You can't even breathe."

"I can." The hoarse words were followed by another painful-sounding intake.

The scrabble of paws heralded Miriam's sudden presence as she and the dog emerged from her bedroom.

"What's wrong?" she cried.

Jonah wanted to die. "I hurt her by accident. I was dreaming. Help me get her to the couch."

Eden waved them off and clambered to her feet by herself. They each grabbed an arm and escorted her to the sofa, where she sat rocking herself gently and, with a look of painful concentration, continued to wheeze on every breath. Sabrina ran back and forth, excited by the late-night stirrings.

"I'm calling 911." Jonah headed for the home phone sitting on the end table.

Eden tried to shake her head and winced. "No!"

Her hoarse protest made him hesitate. He glanced at Miriam for her input. She sat beside her mother, smoothing a hand up and down her spine. She lifted accusing eyes at Jonah.

"Should I call them?" he found himself asking the fourteen-year-old.

"What do you think?" Her hard voice matched the look in her eyes. "You want them to cart you off to jail for domestic violence?"

The harsh words made him blanch.

"Miriam!" Eden scolded on a whisper.

Looking at his stricken wife, Jonah cast his own cares into the wind.

"I'll go to jail," he decided. "I don't care. She needs help."

He started for the phone again.

"No!" This time it was Miriam who protested.

Shoving fingers into his hair, Jonah prowled to the kitchen and back.

To Jonah's surprise, Eden stretched out a hand of reconciliation as he approached her again.

Desperate for forgiveness, Jonah clasped her hand in both of his, dropping to his knees by her feet. Immediately, the dog came over to lick him.

"I'm so sorry," he stated. His eyes stung with helpless tears as he released her and put an arm around the dog to subdue her. "I didn't know it was you, Eden. I thought it was…other people. And they were going to…work me over."

Eden and Miriam both stared at him in a way that was fast becoming the norm.

"Did you remember something?"

Eden's hoarse question nearly succeeded in redirecting his focus. *Yes, he had.*

"That doesn't matter right now. Are you getting enough air?" His gaze went to her red, swelling neck. He couldn't believe, looking at it, that he was responsible.

"I'm fine," Eden said.

Miriam touched her mother's neck lightly. "Can you swallow?" she asked. Her tone sounded slightly less accusatory.

Eden tried to swallow. With a grimace, she succeeded. "Yes. See, I'm fine. I was just a little shaken is all." Her amber gaze met Jonah's glistening one.

"It's my fault," she insisted, her voice still husky. "I should have said something to wake you up, not just touch you like that."

"It's not your fault!" Self-loathing drove him to his feet, making the dog start barking again. "It's mine. I shouldn't have fallen asleep without taking my meds first. The doctor said this would happen. Ice," he added, as his training kicked in belatedly.

"I'll get it." Miriam darted off the sofa, Sabrina on her heels.

Dividing his gaze between his stepdaughter and his wife, Jonah wondered if his latest faux pas would have a lasting, negative consequence.

"Jonah."

Eden wanted his attention. She patted the spot Miriam had vacated. He eased into it, eager to do anything in his power to lessen her discomfort.

"What can I do? Can I get you anything? Tylenol maybe?"

"In a minute."

Miriam returned from the freezer with a blue medical ice pack. "Hold this on your neck," she told her mother.

Eden took it, and for the next few seconds, they watched her close her eyes and draw several easy breaths.

"See, I'm fine," she said, opening her eyes to look at them both.

Jonah went to hug her. *Why shouldn't he?* At least she would know his remorse was bone-deep.

She put her hands on his chest, preventing him. "Did you remember something, Jonah?"

Her question demanded an answer. Glancing at Miriam's set face, he decided it wouldn't hurt to play on her sympathies in the hopes of gaining some forgiveness.

"I did, actually." To his gratification, the dream was still crisp within his mind, and his eye didn't hurt when he tried to remember. "I was being questioned about—" He cut himself off. "That part's not important."

"What *is* important?" Eden prompted.

"I knew what they were going to ask because they asked it every time they questioned me. Thing is, I also knew I couldn't remember. I had no idea what I was doing there, or how I even got there. I had no memory of the op at all, which means I must have lost my memory *before* my captivity."

"That's odd." Eden looked perplexed. "You were fine when you went wheels up."

Jonah paused to let vignettes of the recent past flicker through his mind like a slide show.

"Well, guess what?" he said with an unpleasant shiver. "I can remember some of my captivity now."

Visions came of a squalid cell, dirt floor and cinderblock walls, a slit for a window, too high to see out of. He almost wished the memories had stayed buried.

"This is huge," Eden insisted, her own trauma seemingly forgotten.

"Yes," Jonah agreed.

"The blow to your face!" Miriam spoke up on a note of excitement. "Maybe it happened before you were taken captive. Maybe you lost your memory then."

Eden's expression cleared. "That has to be it."

A memory nudged the outer wall of Jonah's consciousness. He fought desperately to pull it closer.

"Oh, my gosh, you'll have so much to tell Dr. Branson tomorrow."

Oh, him. Eden's comment caused the memory to slip away.

"Yeah," he said, puzzled by his reticence where the doctor was concerned. He focused his attention again on Eden's neck. "You're sure you're okay?" he asked her.

"I'm fine," she assured him, managing a wan smile.

He studied her a moment longer, then regarded Miriam.

"How about you?" he asked. "You okay?"

She petted the dog in silence for a minute, then looked up and, in a firm voice, said, "I just want to say that if something like this ever happens again, I'll call the police myself."

Her protective spirit pleased him immensely, making him want to grin with approval. Instead, he sought to look remorseful and said, "I get that. And you should."

Miriam shrugged. "All right. Well, if you people are done with all the drama, we're going back to bed. Come on Sabby." She caught the retriever's collar and led her away.

"What time is it?" Jonah's gaze went to the kitchen clock. "Wow, it's two in the morning."

Eden started to rise from the couch. He jumped up to help her.

"I'm good," she murmured, extracting her arm from his grasp. "When I woke up and found your door open and your light on, I thought you might still be outside, so I went looking for you."

He grimaced. "I was so tired I had to lie down outside."

They eyeballed each other for a moment, Eden still holding the ice pack to her neck.

It occurred to Jonah, even if they were happily married, it wouldn't be safe for him to sleep in her bed. Heaven knew what manner of violence he was capable of until he got his memory back.

"Good night, Eden. I'm sorry," he said again.

Her gaze softened as she considered him. "And I'm sorry you were tortured," she whispered.

Rolling up on her toes, she planted a quick kiss on his cheek and retreated.

Hah. If she had any idea the kinds of scars he was hiding under his shirt, she would probably freak.

Safeguarding the memory of her freely given kiss, he decided to savor it. More than likely, a kiss on the cheek was all he'd ever get from then on.

CHAPTER 9

"**M**rs. Mills, may I borrow you for a few minutes?"

Not again. Eden hid her frustration behind a smile and lifted an enquiring gaze to the doctor. She was making inroads into the fascinating article on PTSD. Seeing Jonah exit the doctor's office and drop into a seat in the waiting room, she realized she wouldn't be joining him but rather taking his place. *Oh, dear.* He must have told Dr. Branson about her ultimatum. *Wouldn't this be fun?*

Setting the magazine regretfully aside, Eden sent a searching look toward Jonah but couldn't tell what he was thinking. Dr. Branson closed the door behind her as she entered his office. Sitting across from her, his denim blue gaze went straight to the bruise on Eden's neck, and his expression reflected dismay as he beheld what Eden had tried, and failed, to cover with makeup.

"Jonah told me what happened last night—or rather, early this morning," he corrected himself. "How are you feeling?"

"Fine." Eden shrugged and touched her tender neck. "I bruise easily. It's no big deal."

"It's not?" The doctor searched her face. "He's very aware that he could have killed you."

"But he didn't," Eden pointed out.

"And why do you think that is? I mean, in his mind, you were the enemy and you were a threat to him. He is trained to protect himself."

Eden counted the beats of her heart. She wished the doctor would speak in sentences and not ask questions to which he already knew the answer. "I suppose," she answered, drawing out the words as if they had just occurred to her, "he must have recognized me."

The doctor nodded profoundly. "Exactly. And my guess is he recognized you by your scent. He has told me more than once that he knows it."

Eden countered his comment with a thoughtful *hmm.*

"Are you—" Dr. Branson seemed to search for the right words "—afraid to stay in the same house with your husband, Eden?"

She narrowed her eyes at him wondering where he was going with the question.

"No," she said truthfully.

"Are you afraid to spend time with him?" the doctor added, closing an invisible noose around her.

With a burst of impatience, she opted to bring the elephant out into the open.

"He must have told you what I said to him yesterday. About wanting a separation," she added when the doctor merely looked at her blankly.

Branson's bushy eyebrows pulled together. "Actually, no. This is the first I've heard of it. You asked him for a separation?"

Darn it! She'd opened that can of worms for no reason.

"No, of course not. I mean, not right away. I explained that...we had probably married for the wrong reasons, and I'd realized while he was gone we're better off apart."

The doctor appeared stunned. "I see," he said, absorbing her news with several slow blinks. "So that's why you've been avoiding him."

"I'm not avoiding him," she protested.

"He told me you asked your daughter to look at family photos with him."

Eden had nothing to say to that.

"Not that he minded," the doctor added. "He speaks very highly of Miriam."

Nina's words of warning returned to Eden, keeping her from saying anything.

The doctor looked at her funny. "Do you disagree?"

Eden looked down at her hands. In her head, she could hear Nina's words: *If anything, he's exploiting your weaknesses. He knows how to get to you—through your daughter and through your body.*

"Look," she said to the psychiatrist. "I'm not trying to avoid Jonah; I'm simply wary of being sucked back into a relationship that wasn't working."

Branson sat forward and asked, "How's it working now?"

It was Eden's turn to blink. "I think it's too soon to tell."

"My thoughts exactly. Right now, Jonah needs your full support. If anything, helping him get his memories back will free you faster. With his memories intact, he can find his own way forward."

Eden swallowed against a dry mouth. The doctor's logic made sense, but it didn't come without risk. The more time she spent with Jonah, the more influence he exerted over her heart and soul—not to mention he might take it upon himself to kiss her. If he succeeded, she would likely be a goner.

"You want me to spend more time with him," she restated.

"Yes. Take him places he's been before. Expose him to sounds and sights, and especially to smells that ought to be familiar."

"Okay," she agreed with a shrug. "Honestly, though, we didn't go to many places together. We were only married for a year."

"I remember. But I'm sure you can think of a few places you visited together. If necessary, you could return to Annapolis, to your parents' house, where you met."

Eden's thoughts flashed to the message on her cell phone from her irate father.

Eden! Vice Admiral Leland just told us the news. I can't believe you didn't tell us Jonah was alive. Holy cow! Call us the first chance you get. We want to hear every-thing, and we hope you'll both come see us soon."

Both, not all. Her father's omission of Miriam in the equation had kept her from calling him back. Her parents would deny it vehemently, but they'd always viewed Miriam as somewhat of a familial embarrassment, not quite a legitimate grandchild, which upset Eden to no end. It didn't matter that Miriam had been a wake-up call for Eden and the reason she'd given her life over to God's care and keeping. God had forgiven her youthful indiscretions, but her parents had not. Better for Miriam to grow up not knowing her grandparents well than to have her face rubbed in her illegitimacy every time she met them.

"Mrs. Mills?" Dr. Branson called her back from her wandering thoughts. "I think you're right that Jonah's not a threat to you—at least not physically," he added astutely. "If you can afford to spend more time helping him to rehabili-tate, I am confident he'll get his memories back sooner, rather than later."

"He told you what he remembered last night?"

"Yes, it's very interesting. If you'll call him back in, I'd like to talk to him some more. He needed a break to shake off the emotions associated with what he shared."

"Oh." Guilt pricked Eden as she realized Jonah's stony expression earlier was a mask. He hid his pain so well it was easy to forget what he'd been through. A wave of compassion propelled her to her feet.

"I'll go get him."

Stepping out of the office, she caught Jonah peering out the window, as if watching somebody suspicious.

"Everything okay?" she asked.

He jumped at the sound of her voice and whirled. "Yeah, sure. You're done already?"

"Yes." She indicated the office behind her. "Dr. Branson says he wants to talk to you some more."

"Oh." Jonah's shoulders visibly stiffened. "I don't think I'm up to that. Can you tell him I need to leave?"

Eden felt the doctor's presence as he stepped up behind her.

"I'm sorry to hear that. Are you sure you can't give me fifteen more minutes?"

Jonah put a hand to his head and rubbed it. "I don't think so. I don't feel so good."

Eden noticed he was rubbing his right temple, not the side usually bothering him.

The psychiatrist sighed. "I suppose we can pick up on Monday where we left off today."

"How about Tuesday?" Jonah suggested. "We should meet Tuesdays and Thursdays, not Mondays, Wednesdays, and Fridays. It's not fair to Eden to have to give up three mornings a week."

"I would really appreciate that," Eden agreed.

Dr. Branson looked back and forth between them, then consulted the appointment book on his reception desk. "I do have an hour available on Tuesdays and Thursdays, but only in the afternoon, at four."

Jonah looked at Eden.

"I can do that," she assured the both of them. She would have to hurry home after class and hold off on her shower until she got back from Jonah's appointment.

"Very well. I'll see you Tuesday at 4 p.m." Dr. Branson scribbled their names into his book. "You two enjoy your weekend. I hope you get the chance to do something special," he added significantly.

Eden forced a smile. "We'll try." She held the door for Jonah, who kept a hand clasped to his head as if it pained him even to walk.

"You can stop faking now," she drawled as they slipped into the hot Jaguar.

Jonah dropped his hand and swept the area with an anxious gaze.

As she backed out of their parking space, Eden asked him, "What are you looking for?"

He cut her a chagrined look. "There's a blue Taurus that's been hanging around our neighborhood. I thought I saw it drive by here earlier."

Starting forward, she drove them away from Branson's office. Considering the unlikelihood of Jonah's statement, she recalled what she'd read in the article on PTSD—how it often manifested in the form of paranoid thoughts.

Her heart sank. "I doubt it's the same car," she told him.

Jonah lapsed into guarded silence.

Desperation prompted her to ask him, "Why don't you want to spend more time with Dr. Branson? You've left early two times in a row now."

Jonah drew a breath and let it out. "I expected him to have more to say about what I remembered last night," he admitted on a note of disillusionment. "Instead, he was fixated on how I could move during REM sleep. That's apparently a disorder that makes me dangerous. He wants me to double my nighttime medication so I'm not a danger to you."

Eden frowned. "That's weird. He told me he was sure you wouldn't hurt me. Besides, doesn't that medication repress dreams?"

"Yes."

"But you remembered so much in your dream. Why would you want to repress them?"

"He's concerned about too much too soon. Traumatic dreams could aggravate my anxiety."

Ah, so that was what was happening. Jonah's dreams were awakening paranoid thoughts in him.

"Maybe you should listen to your doctor and take two pills then," she suggested.

"I'll think about it," he said, obviously just to placate her. "What did the doctor mean about doing something special?"

Realizing Jonah had deftly changed the subject, Eden grudgingly explained. "He wants us to visit places we've been before in the hopes they'll bring back memories."

"Like where?"

She searched for an appropriate place to take him. "We used to walk on the beach out at the Back Bay Wildlife Refuge. Miriam rides her bike out there all the time, hoping to see the wild horses."

"That sounds fun."

"There's also the Mexican restaurant we visited every Sunday after church."

"We went to church?"

Surprised by his enthusiastic tone, she shot him a glance.

"Miriam and I always do. You would come with us from time to time."

"Infrequently, you mean."

She shrugged in agreement.

"Let's go together, this Sunday," he proposed, "and then we'll go to lunch like we used to. When I get my strength back, we'll go to the Wildlife Refuge."

She thought about his recently manifested paranoia. "Are you sure you're ready to be out in public?"

"If my psychiatrist thinks I'm ready, then I should be ready," he reasoned.

"He also thinks you should double your meds at night. You should do that, too."

Jonah said nothing, which meant he certainly would not.

Eden pictured him beset by nightmares and swallowed nervously.

"But I think I'll flip the lock on my door so you can lock me in at night," he added.

"What?" The suggestion astonished her. "Jonah, that's ridiculous. We can lock our own doors and save you the trouble. You're not going to hurt me."

"What about Miriam? Are you sure you can trust me not to hurt her, either?"

The question undermined her confidence. If he was paying attention to Miriam only to get on Eden's good side, perhaps he didn't care enough about her daughter to recognize her in his sleep.

At her continued silence, Jonah added, "I'll reverse my door handle when we get home."

"What if you need to use the restroom at night?"

He chuckled. "I'll pee out the window."

"Not on my flowers you won't," she said, then laughed.

"Then I'll text you when I want you to let me out."

Eden rolled her eyes. Locking Jonah in the study at night seemed a bit extreme. But, then again, if he did suffer from a behavioral disorder allowing him to act out his dreams, maybe it was better to be safe than sorry.

"If that's what you want," she finally agreed.

His hand landed without warning on her thigh, causing her to jump as her taut nerves overreacted.

"Thanks for putting up with me," he said, his voice gruff. Giving her leg a squeeze, he drew his hand back.

Eden's heart continued to beat erratically. Her body wasn't going to relax, was it? Ever since he'd hugged her the other day, her nerves had remained on high alert, yearning for another embrace, perhaps a kiss, or several hundred. Keeping him at arm's length was going to come down to willpower.

"Do you teach this afternoon?" he asked.

"Yes. Is that okay with you?"

If he would just act jealous of the time she spent working, it would be so much easier to resist him.

He shrugged. "Of course."

His easy agreement made her wonder if he really was a changed man. For a brief second, she imagined what life could be like should he continue to behave as he did now—considerate of her work schedule, helpful around the house, good with Miriam. Then again, wishful romanticism had led her to marry in haste in the first place.

She couldn't let idealism blind her to reality.

The fact of the matter was Jonah had been difficult to live with. Paranoia and possible PTSD were only going to make him that much harder to deal with.

Just wait and see, warned the realist within her. *You'll be glad you kept him at arm's length.*

～

Jonah couldn't keep his eyes open a second longer. He gave up waiting for Miriam to come home from her friend's house and collapsed onto the sofa. Sabrina sidled up next to where he lay and dropped onto the rug. Stretching out a hand, Jonah petted her.

The retriever's fur was soft and soothing. Her presence made Jonah think about therapy dogs and how they soothed soldiers with PTSD—not that he had it, even though Dr. Branson was starting to think he did. All the same, it wouldn't hurt for him to try sleeping with the dog. He considered the width of the couch, adjusted a few pillows, then scooted over to make space.

"Sabrina, up."

She was beside him in a heartbeat. With a wiggle of her entire body and a happy sneeze, she went still next to him.

"If you don't tell, I won't tell," Jonah promised. Likely the fur on the couch would speak for itself, but he would gladly take a lint roller to it if it meant napping and not lurching awake in a cold sweat.

Soon, the dog's steady breathing lulled Jonah into relaxing. Exhaustion pulled him down into unconsciousness.

Sometime later, Sabrina lifted her head, startling Jonah from his slumber. He glanced at the watch he'd reclaimed from his dresser drawer and saw it was already four o'clock. Eden would be home within the hour, and Miriam ought to be home by now.

He called her name just in case she'd arrived while he was sleeping, but there was no response.

The dog leaped from the sofa, clearly eager for a walk. Jonah rose more slowly, discovering he had a crick in his neck from using the couch pillow. As he walked into the kitchen for a glass of water, a sense of isolation crept over him. He hadn't realized how much of a comfort it was to have his family around.

Guzzling his drink, he eyed the note Miriam had left on the kitchen counter that morning. *Gone to Ian's. Back this afternoon.* Her large, loopy hand-writing underscored how young she was, but then he remembered that most of her classmates were older than she was. That meant Ian was likely fifteen years old, and Miriam had been with him almost the entire day.

A desire to check with Eden prompted him to find his cell phone. Locating it in his room, he looked for his wife's number in his favorites list, noticing as he did that Miriam's number wasn't there. He dialed Eden.

"Jonah?" She answered after one ring, on a note of concern.

"Hi, I'm fine," he assured her. "I'm just calling about Miriam. Shouldn't she be home by now?"

A weighty pause followed his question. "Well, she should, but it takes twenty minutes to ride her bike from Ian's house. I'd give her another ten."

"Where are you? Are you on your way?"

"Um, I'm at the thrift store right now," she said, rousing his curiosity as to why. "But I'll be home soon."

"Can you call Miriam and see if she's all right? I don't seem to have her number."

"Oh, you wouldn't since she got her phone last Christmas. Here, I'll give you her number."

"I'd like that." Considering Miriam had given him a wide berth since he'd choked her mother, it was up to him to close the gap.

"If she doesn't answer it's because she's on her way."

Jonah added Miriam to his list of contacts, made her a favorite, then called her number.

Her phone rang six times then went to voicemail. Jonah hung up and sent her a text.

Hope you're already on your way. Sabrina is waiting for a walk.

His gaze traveled out the window. It was still light outside, and he was perfectly capable of walking the dog himself. Then he remembered the blue sedan, and the fear he was being watched swept through him.

I have to get past this. I do not have PTSD.

Pocketing his phone, he went back to the couch where he'd kicked off his shoes and put them on. Sabrina encouraged him with a wagging tail and a wide-open mouth that made her look like she was grinning.

"Okay, girl, but no running off on me this time."

Stepping out of the house, he realized he didn't even have a house key. That circumstance reminded him of Eden's decision to separate. Thrusting negative thoughts aside, he raked a cautious gaze up and down the street.

Thunderclouds piled one atop the other threatening an evening storm that would, hopefully, bring cooler air in from the ocean. There was no sign of the blue sedan. Descending the steps to the driveway, he started along an eerily deserted street. The rumble of thunder in the distance only added to his sense of impending trouble as Sabrina pulled him in the direction of the ocean.

They made their way along the same route they'd taken before. Was it only yesterday? It felt like a lifetime had passed since then. He thought again of Eden's ultimatum and how it had led him to call his master chief. Was Rivera right? Would God salvage his marriage, even when he'd nearly choked her to death?

Lost in thought, Jonah passed the oceanfront homes without paying much attention to them. In contrast to the day before, the beach appeared deserted.

Vacationers had retreated into their shelter in anticipation of bad weather. Only a few cars passed him.

Lightning sizzled out at sea. Jonah counted the seconds before he heard thunder. The storm was still several miles distant, he figured. He would go as far as he had gone the day before, perhaps a bit farther, then turn around.

An undercover police car drove past him. Not only did Jonah recognize it as such by the extra antenna and tinted rear window, but he could just make out the uniformed officer at the wheel—square jaw and sunglasses. As the car drove past, Jonah lifted a hand to acknowledge the man's vigilance and to convey his own gratitude.

An ominous rumble of thunder had him looking up. He realized he had better turn around if he didn't want to bring home a soaking wet dog.

"Come on, pup." Halting in his tracks, he urged the dog to turn and retrace their footsteps, walking quickly in the hopes of beating the storm.

The crunch of sand under his tennis shoes merged with the rumble of the storm and the rolling of the waves onto the nearby shore. Jonah had nearly reached the bend in the road that would take him toward his home when the sound of an approaching vehicle had him stepping off the pavement to let it pass.

He could hear the car closing in. The sudden revving of its engine had Jonah glancing back to gauge what was going on. The same undercover cop car that had passed him minutes earlier was apparently backtracking, but to Jonah's surprise, the officer didn't give him any leeway. Instead, he drove straight at Jonah who, thanks to his quick reactions, managed to leap off the road, jerking the dog out of harm's way just before they both got struck.

The Challenger's right tires dropped off the asphalt. The car fishtailed briefly before jiggling onto the asphalt again.

"Hey!" Jonah yelled in astonished outrage.

He expected the officer to stop the car, to get out and apologize for nearly running him over, but the Challenger kept right on going, without so much as a flare of brake lights.

"Did you not see me?" Jonah railed. In disbelief, he watched the car go to the end of his street where it turned left and disappeared behind the home across from his.

Adrenaline powered Jonah with the energy to get home as fast as he could.

Did that cop just tried to run me over? Perhaps he'd mistaken Jonah's friendly wave earlier for an insulting gesture, and he'd intended to teach Jonah a lesson. Even that seemed absurd. He could have been killed!

Shaken and bewildered, Jonah continued toward his home. He was climbing the stairs to the door when the Jaguar turned into the driveway and Eden jumped out. Pausing in his ascent, he watched her round the vehicle in the outfit she'd worn to work—colorful spandex capris, a matching pink jog bra, and a lightweight warm up jacket. She looked so fit and spunky with her hair in a ponytail that he let go of the leash and descended the steps to greet her.

"Hey, can you help me?" she asked, rounding the car to lift the lid of the trunk.

"Sure." Figuring she had groceries, he was surprised to see two huge leaf bags in the back. She hauled one out and dumped it into his arms.

"These are your uniforms," she said. "I got them back."

"From the thrift store," he realized as she hefted the larger one in her own arms and still managed to shut the trunk.

"Yeah." She looked like she might say more, then sent him a grimace and brushed past him to head to the steps. "Did you get through to Miriam?"

Jonah tore his gaze from Eden's toned backside. "Er, no. She didn't answer, so I sent a text. I don't think she's responded," he added, recalling he carried his phone in his pocket. "We should go get her."

"I'm sure she's on her way." Eden greeted the dog and pushed the unlocked door open. She carried her bag to the sofa, and Jonah did likewise, dropping his load next to hers.

He immediately broke into it, pulling out a Navy Working Uniform with multi-color digital print camouflage. He was pleased to recognize it, even though the patch bearing his name had been removed. He tried not to think about how she must have felt in the first place, donating her dead husband's uniforms.

"She's with a guy all day long and you're not worried?" he asked, holding the soft fabric to his nose and smelling a scent he associated with Spec Ops Headquarters.

"Ian is her best friend. He doesn't think of her that way."

Jonah lowered the jacket he was holding. "He's a fifteen-year-old guy. Trust me, he does think of her that way. Besides, she hasn't done any reading yet today."

"Well, that's true, and school starts in less than two weeks."

"Let's go pick her up," Jonah suggested. "She shouldn't be riding her bike in the storm."

Eden glanced out a window. "Okay," she agreed with a shrug. "But you know, she's still mad at you for what happened last night. Maybe I should retrieve her myself."

Jonah started for the door. "If she's still at Ian's, I want to meet him."

"Technically you've already met him," he overheard her murmur as she hooked her purse strap over her shoulder.

Jonah kept his mouth shut. As he stepped out of the house, a moist breeze buffeted him. The sky was going to open up at any minute.

"Can I get a key to this house?" he asked, as Eden locked up behind them.

She cast him a quick look. "Sure."

"And log-in information to our bank account. I assume we share an account?"

She hesitated a split second. "Yes," she said again, as they went down the steps together. "Of course. I'll give you that when we get home."

They jumped into the car just as the first fat raindrops pelted the earth. In silence, they drove with the windshield wipers beating frantically to counteract the deluge.

~

They drove clear to the other side of Sandbridge without coming across Miriam on her bike. At last, Eden turned into an empty driveway. Jonah eyed the brick rancher, noting the weeds that overran the garden and two shutters that were hanging askew.

"Who does he live with?" Jonah asked as Eden put the car into park.

"His mother. He has an older brother who just moved out."

"Looks like Mom's not home. I'll go get Miriam," Jonah volunteered, exiting the vehicle.

One glance at the doorbell informed him it wasn't working. Jonah rapped his knuckles on the door.

A long silence followed his knock. He glanced back at the car, sharing a look of concern with Eden through the rain-specked windshield.

At long last, a soft footfall heralded the approach of an occupant. The door swung open and there stood Miriam with the house plunged in darkness behind her, her eyes wide and full of trepidation.

"What's wrong?" she asked.

Jonah caught a whiff of cigarette smoke clinging to her clothing. He inhaled slowly through his nose, making certain it was coming off her before reacting.

"You should have been home a while ago," he explained, keeping his conclusions to himself.

Miriam brushed the hair out of her eyes. "I know, but then it started storming, and I didn't want to ride my bike in the rain." The expression on her face was decidedly wary.

"We'll take you home now," Jonah offered. "The bike can stay here."

She stared at him with a shuttered expression. "Okay. Let me go tell Ian I'm leaving."

"I'd like to meet him." He let the tone of his voice convey he would accept no alternative.

Her chin went up. "You've met him before," she insisted.

"So I've heard, but I don't remember," he said succinctly. Reaching into the strange house, Jonah flipped three light switches at once. The light on the stoop did not come on, but the light on the living room ceiling did, along with a lamp in the corner. Both of them lit up a room that was slovenly at best, with trash littering the coffee table and several pairs of boy's shoes lying about.

"Now you won't trip," he said, explaining his actions. The fact of the matter was he wanted to see where Miriam was spending her time.

Without a word, his stepdaughter disappeared down a hall that clearly led toward the bedrooms. Jonah looked back at Eden, lifting a finger to indicate that this would take a minute longer. He stepped into the tiny foyer, leaving the door open behind him. The smell of cigarettes was stronger inside the house, leaving little question as to who had been smoking.

A minute later, Miriam appeared again with a gangly redhead in tow. The boy was just starting to grow toward manhood, relieving Jonah's fears a tad bit. He approached Jonah with his hands shoved into his pockets and an inability to look Jonah in the eye.

"Hi, Mr. Mills," he mumbled.

One point for greeting him by name.

"Ian," Jonah countered, holding out a hand and forcing the teen to shake it. "I hear we've met before."

"Yes, sir."

Ian glanced to Miriam for help. She was edging toward the door, clearly eager to pull Jonah away.

"I noticed you two have been smoking. Just cigarettes, I hope."

Ian's mouth fell open.

Miriam stilled and angled her jaw at him. "You think I'd smoke weed?" Her tone sounded offended.

"Nope." Jonah shook his head definitively. "But then I wouldn't think you'd smoke cigarettes either."

"She didn't." Ian came to her defense. "That was me, I swear."

Jonah looked to Miriam for corroboration, but she merely pressed her lips together and glared at him. Considering the two teens together, Jonah sighed and crossed his arms.

"Tell you what," he said. "I'll bring myself to overlook your lack of judgment provided both of you work for me tomorrow. We're going to sand the deck, starting at o'nine hundred."

He looked Ian in the eye. "Can I count on you to show up, Ian, or do I need to have a talk with your mom?"

Ian visibly paled. He and Miriam shared a private look before he answered, "Sure, I can work."

"I'll even pay you," Jonah added, feeling generous. He would know after checking his online bank account how generous he could afford to be.

Ian looked back at Miriam and shrugged as if to say, *What choice do I have?*

"Great. We'll see you tomorrow," Jonah said. "Come on, Miriam. Your mom's waiting."

"Bye, Ian," Miriam muttered as she followed Jonah outside.

The rain had let up slightly, but they still had to splash through several puddles to get to the car. Miriam cast Jonah a searching look as he opened the rear door for her.

As they shut themselves in the car with her, Jonah expected Eden to smell the evidence on her daughter's person, in which case he would let Miriam defend herself. However, with the defroster blowing cool air from the front of the car to the back, Eden apparently didn't smell anything.

Instead, she chastised her daughter for her tardiness. "You should have come home hours ago."

"Sorry," Miriam murmured.

Jonah could tell by her quiet tension she was waiting for him to rat her out. He kept his mouth shut on the subject, just as he'd stayed mum about what had happened to him that afternoon. Eden had enough to worry about with an unwanted husband who had memory issues and, possibly, PTSD.

"What's for dinner?" Miriam asked.

Eden groaned. "Oh, shoot. We need to go by the store or order takeout."

Apprehension cinched Jonah's stomach. "Let's do takeout again." He had no desire to mingle with the public without a weapon. "How about Thai?" he asked.

Eden looked at him askance, as if sensing something odd about his suggestion.

"Awesome," Miriam exclaimed. "I want pork spring rolls and that coconut soup."

Detecting relief and goodwill in his stepdaughter's voice, Jonah determined he was well on his way to mending fences with her. He wished he could win back Eden's love so easily. Then again, if he'd developed a disorder, maybe it was better for her to remain emotionally unentangled.

Eden turned the lock on Jonah's door handle, per his request. He had disassembled the knob and its components and put it back on so that the lock now faced the hallway. Confining him to his room at night did not feel right.

"Okay, I'm sleeping with my ringer on," she called through the closed door, "so I'll hear you if you need me."

"I'll be good," he assured her. "No peeing out the window," he promised, drawing a small smile from her.

Conscious of Miriam making her way to the bathroom behind her, Eden added a parting phrase. "Sweet dreams, then."

"Night, Eden. Goodnight, Miriam," Jonah called, his hearing apparently excellent.

"Goodnight," they both chorused.

"This is so weird," Miriam stated as she headed for the bathroom.

"His choice," Eden pointed out. "Good night, squirt," she added, pausing to kiss her daughter's cheek. "He wants you to lock your door, too," she added under her breath. "And let me be the one to unlock his door in the morning. You don't need to do it."

"*So* weird," Miriam repeated, thrusting the dog into her bedroom.

"It's just a precaution," Eden assured her. "Go take your shower."

"That's what I'm doing," Miriam assured her.

Memories of their evening spent together filled Eden's thoughts as she made her way back to her own room, turning off lights as she went.

If Jonah was pretending to like Miriam only to gain Eden's goodwill, why would he have insisted on meeting Ian? He must have known doing so wouldn't make Miriam forgive him any sooner. Eden's daughter thought of herself as an adult, even though she wasn't. She wouldn't appreciate Jonah poking his nose into her business—or would she?

Honestly, sometimes Eden suspected she didn't know her daughter as well as she thought she did.

Per Jonah's wish, she shut and locked her door. Crossing to her window, Eden was glad to see the rain had finally stopped. She lowered the blinds and undressed, all the while replaying the evening they had spent together.

They'd opted to eat their Thai food at the empty restaurant, rather than bring it home. Once back at the house, Jonah had suggested a board game, and Eden had brought out a game called Catan for them to play at the dining room table. Fighting yawns, Jonah had nonetheless kept Miriam interested and engaged. She'd even laughed out loud a couple of times—a balm to Eden's ears. By outward appearances, last night's choking had been forgiven and forgotten.

Thinking back on her year of marriage, Eden couldn't help but compare the family dynamics she'd just experienced to what they used to be. *What had changed?*

The answer, of course, was Jonah, because he wasn't ignoring Miriam like he used to. Instead, he was acting like a parent, and not an overly authoritarian one either. Good thing because Miriam would balk at that. He showed concern and fairness and—most importantly—an interest in his stepdaughter, something he had never shown before.

With sudden misgivings, Eden sank onto her bed. What if Nina was wrong? What if Jonah wasn't trying to get to her through her daughter? What if his interest in Miriam was sincere?

Well, then, great, she told herself. Miriam had always wanted a father, whether she admitted that or not. Jonah himself had promised to be there for Miriam, regardless of what happened between the two of them as husband and wife. It was a win-win situation, wasn't it?

Not for Eden. The main issue she'd had with Jonah was his lack of familial involvement. If he was suddenly the husband and father she'd always wished he'd be, what further sin could she hold against him to justify her desire to leave him?

Did she truly want to separate when things were going as well as they were?

Clasping her hands together, she closed her eyes in prayer, and tried giving the decision up to God.

CHAPTER 10

*J*onah stared at the patterns of light dancing on his ceiling. The last time he'd glanced at the clock it was just past midnight. He'd told himself if he wasn't asleep by zero one hundred hours, he would text Eden to let him out of the room so he could take his nighttime medication.

He had skipped his regular dose in the hopes of inducing more dreams. Dr. Branson's fear that nightmares would exacerbate his anxiety didn't deter him. He had survived his captivity; he could cope with dreams of it, especially if they brought back snippets of his missing memories. Possibly even his reason for forgetting in the first place.

Closing his eyes, Jonah sent up a prayer for peace, then concentrated on sleeping. One would think, given his absolute physical exhaustion, he'd be out cold by now, but his churning thoughts kept that from happening.

He now regretted logging into his and Eden's online banking right before bedtime. While he'd been pleased to find their cash flow looked healthy, the numbers he'd seen going in and out of their savings account had driven home what he'd been through—a symbolic death.

One month ago to the date, his supplemental life insurance company, USAA, had placed a huge sum of money in the bank for his surviving family. Little question Jonah had paid exorbitant premiums for supplemental insurance, but Eden and Miriam's financial security made that sacrifice worthwhile. He was pleased to find out he'd looked out for them.

What threw Jonah for a loop was the fact that all the money—three hundred thousand dollars—had gone back out of their account yesterday. Someone, presumably Eden, had informed USAA that Jonah was alive. He couldn't imagine how bitter she must have felt, relinquishing the money because the husband she now believed she'd married in error was back from the dead.

Three hundred thousand dollars.

It was hard to believe he was worth so much. And that wasn't even counting the money she would have received from Service Life Group Insurance, his primary insurer through the military—notoriously slow to relinquish benefits. It was true that Naval Special Warfare had invested a pretty penny to turn him into a highly trained operative, but was he worth that much as a human being? Probably not.

"Lord, how do I increase my worth in Eden's eyes?" he asked.

He had to believe he'd made headway during their board game after dinner when he'd let Miriam get a leg up on him. Eden's knowing glances suggested she'd seen straight through him. But what did such small, insignificant actions accomplish in the large scheme of things? They couldn't make Eden love him if she didn't already.

"Ugh." With a groan of frustration, Jonah punched up his pillow. In the same instant, the creaking of a plank outside his window caught his notice. Straining his ears, he heard it again. A tread on the stairs leading up to the deck yielded under the weight of someone ascending.

His heart pumping faster, Jonah slipped out of bed and crossed to the window. Pressing close to the wall, he tabbed the vinyl blinds to peer outside. Four large silhouettes drifted up the stairs, headed for his front door.

It could just be his troop members, who were due home any day, but why would they be so stealthy? And why would they visit him this late? What if the threat Jonah had been sensing was manifesting into reality?

A cold sweat bathed his pores. He had secured the front door himself that night and locked the sliding glass door in the dining room as a natural precaution against intruders. But mere locks couldn't keep assassins out if they were hell bent on getting inside.

Is this it, Father? Are they coming for me?

Jonah cast an eye around the study in hopes of finding a weapon. Eden had informed him, when he'd asked the other day, that none of his private weapons still remained in the house. He must have left all of them in his locker at Spec Ops.

Eden! The realization his wife and stepdaughter might also be in danger sent him lunging for his cell phone. Even as he began fishing through his drawers for dark clothing, he placed a call to his wife. To his relief, she picked up right away.

"I knew you wouldn't last—"

"Listen." He cut her off. "Don't talk. There are men outside. I think they might try to break in. I want you to hide. There's a pull-down ladder to the attic in your closet, right? I want you to go up it and pull the hatch closed behind you."

"Jonah." Her tone was disbelieving. "Are you okay?"

He ground his molars together. "Just indulge me, okay? If I'm wrong, I'll call you back and tell you so."

"I'm supposed to hide without Miriam?"

Oh, shoot. He was definitely thinking too slowly. He couldn't leave his stepdaughter vulnerable.

"No, no. Go wake her up and take her into the attic with you."

Eden made a funny sound in her throat. "What about you? What are you doing?"

He shoved his head and arms through the holes of a black T-shirt before he answered.

"I'm going to stop them."

"Your door is locked," she reminded him.

"I'm going out the window."

"Oh, my gosh." She sounded frustrated this time. "Jonah, this is crazy. Are you sure there are people out there?"

In the same instant, the dog, who was in Miriam's room as usual, gave a bark.

"Yes," he said. "Sabby hears them, too. Please, don't waste any more time. Get Miriam and take her up into the attic with you."

"Fine." Eden's tone stated clearly, *You are out of your mind.* "I'm going to get her now."

"Hurry." Maybe he was crazy. Maybe he was imagining there were men coming after him, but even the dog seemed to sense a threat.

Ending the call without another word, Jonah slid his phone into the pocket of his black jeans and jammed his feet into his tennis shoes. Raising the blinds at his window, he flipped the locks and slid the window open, engendering the barest squeak.

The steps outside his window stood deserted. A balmy, briny breeze greeted him as he removed the screen and placed it at his feet to put back later.

Just then, snatches of a whispered conversation reached him, raising the hairs on the nape of his neck. The men he'd glimpsed earlier were now standing on his deck. Provided he'd seen all of them, the odds were four to one. No doubt they carried weapons, while he did not. Jonah would have to catch them by surprise, take down two at once, and seize their weapons to fend off the other two.

Or he could call 911 and pray the police arrived before the men broke in.

Recalling his brush with the police car earlier, he decided he wasn't yet willing to test his sanity. If he'd hallucinated that entire scene, how could he know whether or not he was imagining intruders? Better to find out for himself than to be humiliated by law enforcement.

Ducking through the window, Jonah put one foot on the stair railing. The wood was slicker than he would have liked. Carefully placing his other foot down, he sidestepped as nimbly as he was able up the railing's steep grade, holding onto the wall of the house to stay out of sight of anyone on the deck looking down.

As he neared the front door, he realized the interlopers had gone around the house toward the sliding door in the dining room because he couldn't see them. Occasional whispers assured Jonah he hadn't imagined them. His heartbeat doubled and a cold sweat formed a layer between his skin and his T-shirt.

The railing, he realized, gave him access to the roof. He could climb on top of his house and make his way to the other side without anyone seeing him. With a bird's eye view, he'd be able to assess what he was up against and catch the interlopers by surprise.

Fortunately, the pitch wasn't steep, but the asphalt tiles were wet and slick. As he neared the sliding glass door, the whispered voices grew more distinct. They were speaking in English, which took Jonah by surprise. A snippet of conversation reached his ears.

"The tape's not sticking."

"Try looping it over something."

Struck by something familiar in the speakers' voices, and unable to imagine what they could be talking about, Jonah peered over the edge of the roof to look down. His gaze alighted on the tallest man, whose head was so close, the man would spot him if he so much as looked up. The breadth of his shoulders and the cleanness of his profile jarred Jonah's memory—Lucas Strong, the newest officer who had taken Jonah's place as troop leader.

Jonah's incredulous gaze flicked to Saul, whose long hair made him easy to pick out, then to Theo, whose dark skin blended into the shadows, then to Bambino, identifiable by his hooked nose. These men were his teammates and they were sticking something to the side of his home, not trying to break in.

Rolling his eyes at his overactive imagination, Jonah backed away from the edge and reassessed his situation. He withdrew his phone and quickly dimmed the lighting before sending Eden a text.

It's just guys from my troop. He added a smiley face emoji before pushing his phone back into his pocket. The truth was, although relieved his imagination hadn't been playing tricks on him, he felt foolish for not immediately guessing who the intruders were. He'd known they were pulling into port that day.

In any case, the only way to shake off his chagrin was to play a practical joke on his brothers.

Returning to the edge of the roof in a low squat, Jonah waited for one of the men to walk directly under him before jumping on top of him.

"Agh!" Lucas yelped as Jonah jumped onto his back. The former football player thrashed to throw him off. With sheer tenacity, Jonah held on.

Within the house, the dog started barking in earnest.

"It's Jaguar!" Saul exclaimed as Lucas went to slam Jonah between himself and the side of the house.

Jonah slid off Lucas's back and grinned at them.

"Sir!" Lucas wheeled around to gape at him. "You scared the crap out of me."

With joyous exclamations, Saul, Theo, and Bambino all rushed at him. Saul hauled him into his arms and squeezed the air out of him.

"It's really you," he marveled, releasing Jonah so the others could welcome him. A light went on in the house, shining through the sliding glass door to illuminate all five of them as they hugged and thumped each other's backs.

"Look at you, sir," Lucas said, looking Jonah up and down. "You look good."

It was so obviously a lie. Meeting Saul's pitying gaze, Jonah felt his throat close up. His men were clearly appalled to see him looking so thin.

"Plus, you still got it in you," Bambino said, in his thick Philadelphia accent, "springing on Strong Man like some giant cat."

Jonah looked at the young Tony Danza look-alike. "What about you?" Jaguar asked him. "You old enough to drink yet?"

Bambino shook his head with mock dismay. "Not yet."

Jonah grinned and their gazes went straight to the gap in his teeth.

"Oh, wow," Theo breathed. "Your tooth."

"Yeah." Jonah closed his mouth self-consciously.

"I have it right here." Saul's assertion confused Jonah.

With curiosity, he watched Saul pull a sturdy silver chain from under the collar of his camouflage jacket. Hanging from the chain by a silver wire was a human tooth, worn the way Saul's grandfather, a Creek Indian, might have worn a claw.

"That's my tooth?" Jonah lifted it with his finger.

"Yeah. We went back for you twenty-four hours after the warehouse exploded," Saul explained. "This is all we found. The rest was just charred metal and ash."

"Who knocked it out of me?" Jonah wondered out loud.

"How'd you survive the explosion?" Theo demanded in his deep voice.

Jonah looked into their mystified faces and shrugged. "I don't know. I can't remember."

"Take it." Saul unlatched his chain and freed the pendant.

"Thanks." Cupping the silver-mounted eye tooth in his palm, Jonah wished he could shove it back into his gums and restore his memory.

The sound of the sliding glass door opening kept him from explaining further. Eden stood in a white satin bathrobe, her long hair in disarray, and an expression of wry humor on her face.

Struck by her loveliness, Jonah nearly threw himself between her and his men to keep them from enjoying the view. Luckily, Miriam, who came up behind Eden, released the hound she was holding, and Sabrina claimed everyone's attention as she barreled out of the house to offer them a frenetic greeting.

"Well, I'm glad it's just you all," Eden said from the doorway. "Why don't you come inside and catch up?"

"Oh, no, no." They all protested in unison as they bent to pet the dog and to avoid looking at her.

"We came straight off the boat," Lucas explained. "You don't want us stinking up your house."

"We got your text, sir," Saul added, rubbing Sabrina's side, which caused her to collapse onto her back for a belly rub. "We wanted you to know we were home and were thinking of you *before* we all crashed for like twenty-four hours."

Affection wrung Jonah's heart. "Thanks guys. I had fun ambushing you."

They all chuckled at his success.

"We'll catch up as soon as you're rested," Jonah promised. "Head on home now and sleep your hearts out."

"Hooyah, LT," Bambino said, looking up at Miriam, who shook her head at his tentative smile and walked away, no doubt heading back to bed.

"Good night, sir. Good night, ma'am." Lucas sent Jonah and Eden a respectful nod.

Saul straightened from rubbing the dog and punched Jonah playfully in the shoulder.

Theo grabbed up the box they'd brought with them and the four men took their leave. Jonah had to lunge for the dog who'd leaped up to go after them.

"See you soon," he called, trailing them a short way with a firm grip on Sabrina's collar.

Eden joined him on the deck, and they both looked up at the welcome-home sign fluttering in the breeze.

"Well, that was sweet of them," she commented.

Finding it difficult to look at her, Jonah ushered the dog back inside, held the door for Eden, then locked it behind them. He was glad to see Miriam had returned to her room.

"Sorry," he muttered, forcing himself to turn around and face his wife.

She was biting her lower lip, her gaze faintly pitying. "Jonah, who's going to break into this house when there are two cars parked out front?" she asked him.

The naiveté of her question made him blink. She had no idea what kinds of people he encountered in his line of work—people who wouldn't bat an eye at slaughtering his family while coming to kill him. Nor did he wish to explain his absolute certainty someone was coming for him, and it wouldn't take them long to find and execute him. He didn't want to tell her that because he wasn't quite positive the threat was real.

"It happens sometimes," he said, evenly, "and I'd like to know, if something bad went down, that you would trust me enough to follow my directions."

She pursed her lips while tightening the sash on her white robe. "Okay," she grudgingly agreed. "Next time, I'll follow your directions."

"Thank you," he said.

"Now, can I go back to bed? I'm working the aerobic marathon tomorrow," she reminded him.

She had explained at dinner how once a year the gym hosted an aerobic marathon, and she would have to work all morning.

"I remember," he said. "Sorry to interrupt your sleep."

"That's okay," she said, switching off the light. "I'm glad it was just your teammates."

"I need you to lock me in my room," he reminded her.

She didn't quite succeed in stifling a sigh of irritation.

As he lay in bed a few minutes later, Jonah reflected how he hadn't exactly proven himself as stable, husband-material that night, let alone a man worth three hundred thousand dollars.

"Help me out here, Lord," he murmured, on a note of desperation, "before I screw this up completely."

At 7:30 the next morning, Eden stood outside the study door listening for an indication Jonah was awake. It was hard to tell through a closed door, especially since Jonah rarely snored. Hearing nothing but silence, she quietly turned the lock on the knob, freeing him to leave when he awakened, and then went to the kitchen to fuel her body for the hours of aerobics to come.

Whisking a banana energy drink loaded with calories, Eden sat at the breakfast bar and forced herself to drink all of it. Her gaze wandered to the window where the clear sky promised a hot sun. Her wildflowers would flourish today from yesterday's rain, but the weeds would grow back, too.

The cactus on the windowsill caught her eye. Slipping off the stool, she approached it to admire how nice it looked, transplanted from the plastic cup into a small, brightly glazed pot Miriam had made in middle school. Jonah must have done that some time when Eden was at work. Sitting in sunlight, the little plant appeared to be thriving.

Regarding it over the brim of her glass, Eden finished the last of her shake.

Something about the happy cactus put a tender feeling in her stomach. Was it a sign, like the kind she'd prayed for?

"Ready for the marathon?"

The question, murmured practically in her ear, startled her so badly she let loose a startled squeal, whirled around, and nearly dropped the glass she was holding. Sputtering and coughing as her last sip went down the wrong pipe, she glowered at Jonah who stood inches away.

"Please don't sneak up on me like that!" she said when she could breathe again.

"Sorry." He looked especially contrite with a lock of hair falling in front of his heavy-lidded eyes. His warm gaze trekked from her jog bra to her bare midriff, causing Nina's warning to echo in Eden's head.

Wearing a rumpled T-shirt and a pair of boxers, Jonah looked so huggable she had to turn back to the sink and rinse her glass in order not to give in to the profound desire to snuggle against the wall of his warm chest.

"You look like you haven't slept at all," she commented as she put her glass inside the dishwasher.

"I did a little," he said.

"Why don't you go back to bed?" She dared to face him again.

"I have to get to work," he insisted.

"On what?"

"The deck. Ian and Miriam and I are going to start stripping it so we can have a party without our guests getting splinters."

"Thank you," she said, meaning it. "Just...don't overdo it, okay? You've only been home a few days."

His mouth quirked toward a smile. Her breath caught as he raised a hand unexpectedly and stroked the side of her face with his thumb. The simple caress made her stomach swivel and her heart beat faster.

"I'm not the one headed to a marathon," he reminded her.

Under the spell of his caress, she saw his kiss coming and panicked. Once he kissed her the way he used to, she would forfeit her resolve to leave him.

"I should go." Sliding along the counter, she escaped around him and headed straight for her bathroom to brush her teeth and comb her hair.

With her electric toothbrush humming, Eden dared to look at herself in the mirror.

The rosy color in her cheeks said everything. She still found her husband impossibly attractive. She craved his touch. But her heart rebelled at the thought of suffering his neglect again. Eventually, he would get his memories back. He would return to his job and promptly start ignoring her the way he had after they married.

Her thoughts flashed to the cactus in the pot with the lapis lazuli glaze.

Or was it possible that Jonah could keep their love alive this time?

∼

Hearing a car engine over the whine of his sander, Jonah looked down at the street from the deck he was sanding and snapped the sander off. Alarm shot through him as he recognized the navy-blue Taurus following him the other day. His mouth went dry as it turned into the driveway, parking in the spot Eden had vacated.

Jonah set the sander down. "Miriam?"

"Yeah?"

His stepdaughter and her friend were sanding the railing with sanding blocks. Both teens were covered in sawdust.

"Go inside and get something to drink."

She looked like she might argue with him, but the look on his face had her closing her mouth and gesturing for Ian to join her.

"Who is that?" she asked, spotting their visitor on her way to the door.

"I don't know," Jonah admitted. "But I want you to turn the lock. Call your mom if anything weird happens."

The look on her face reminded him of Eden's expression the night before. *Great, now Miriam thought him out of touch, too.*

Jonah listened for the deadbolt to turn before descending cautiously to the vehicle. Awareness of his vulnerability kept him in a cold sweat. The car engine died and the door swung open. Out stepped an overweight, middle-aged man Jonah recognized right away as the NCIS special agent who'd visited him in the hospital. He chastised himself for his ungrounded fears.

Jonah stopped by the front fender. "Special Agent Elwood."

"You remember me. Good." Elwood looked him over as he shut his car door and approached him. "You're looking better every day."

"You've been keeping an eye on me," Jonah accused.

The man seemed pleased by his observation. "I'm glad you noticed."

"Of course I noticed. How can I help you?" Jonah kept his tone neutral. He didn't bother extending a handshake. This wasn't a social call, and the last time they'd met Jonah had needed to be tranquilized.

Producing a handkerchief from his suit pocket, Elwood mopped his brow. "I'd like twenty minutes of your time. Can I come inside?"

The question put a cinching sensation in Jonah's stomach. But leaving the man standing in the August sun in his dark suit would be rude.

"Come on up." He led the way to his front door.

At Jonah's knock, Miriam turned the deadbolt. If Elwood thought it odd Jonah had locked himself out, he didn't show it.

"You two keep working on the railings," Jonah instructed his stepdaughter, "while this man and I talk."

Miriam gave Elwood a thorough once-over. "We'll be right outside."

Jonah sent her a wink, loving her protective nature.

With the teenagers back on the deck, Jonah poured the investigator what remained of the iced-tea.

"Have a seat," he said, indicating the dining room table since he was too filthy to sit on the sofa.

Elwood picked the chair at the end of the table, and Jonah sat catty-corner to him.

"I've come to see if you remember anything yet," the agent began.

Returning the man's watchful gaze, Jonah got the impression he was very serious about his work, to the point of neglecting his health. Belly fat hung over his belt to rest on his lap. Given his sallow complexion, he probably didn't get much sleep. Nor did he appear to have much of a social life—not even a wife, given the absence of a wedding ring.

Maybe I'll look like him one day.

Shaking off the depressing thought, Jonah confessed, "I have, actually. I remember some of my captivity now. It's coming back to me in bits and pieces." He repressed a shudder at the unpleasant visions sluicing through him.

"That's good," Elwood said, looking more hopeful. "What about the mission?" His pale blue eyes searched Jonah's face. "Do you remember that yet?"

"No. Sorry," Jonah added as the agent's shoulders slumped.

"Well, that's to be expected."

Elwood looked like he might get up and leave, so Jonah took advantage of his presence to question him. "Are you investigating what went wrong on my last op or what happened to the dirty bombs we were after?"

The agent reassessed him through narrowed eyes. "Both."

"I hear weapons are continuing to disappear," Jonah prompted. "Any idea who The Entity is that's taking them?"

"Do you?" Elwood countered, giving nothing away.

Jonah's heart began to pound inexplicably. "I don't know," he heard himself say. "Maybe."

Elwood perked up, his gaze sharpening. "Explain that," he demanded.

Jonah wet his lips while wondering whether Elwood, like everyone else around him, would consider him paranoid for saying what his subconscious prompted him to say.

"I *feel* like I know something about the weapons, only I can't remember." He waited for Elwood to mock him. Instead, the man regarded him with perfect seriousness.

"Do you think your disappearance was an accident, Lieutenant?"

The eerie question spiked Jonah's adrenaline. He tried to think back, only to suffer the usual debilitating pain that kept all memories at bay. Clapping a hand over his left eye, he returned Elwood's stare through his right one.

"What kind of question is that?"

Elwood simply looked at him.

"My men would never have left me behind," Jonah insisted, letting his hand drop.

"And yet, you were left there," Elwood pointed out gently.

Jonah puzzled over the circumstances, unable to explain them.

"Saul found my tooth," he recalled, pulling the pendant out of his back pocket. For some reason, he was now carrying it around, like it was some sort of talisman.

Showing it to Elwood, he added, "Someone knocked it out of me. That's why I can't remember. That's when my memory went bad."

Elwood seemed confused "I thought your memory loss was from PTSD."

Jonah frowned. "PTS," he corrected the man. "Who says I have PTSD?"

Again, Elwood just looked at him. "My mistake," he said on a strange note.

Jonah shook his head. "No, my amnesia is from brain damage. A CT scan showed dead tissue in the prefrontal cortex, right behind my left eye, which is right over my missing tooth. Plus, I remembered something the other night that confirms such a possibility." He briefly described what he had realized the night he choked Eden, finding it easier to tell to Elwood than his psychiatrist.

Elwood's horrified expression was tempered with compassion. Jonah found him liking the man more than he had at their previous meeting.

"Ever since that dream," he added, "I can remember some of my captivity, and the crazy part is I remember *not* remembering. I had no memory of the op at all. Therefore, I must have lost my memory when I was hit in the face."

"That must have been why the enemy managed to capture you," Elwood commented. "You were unconscious or concussed already. Nothing else makes sense."

Jonah blinked. "That's true. I hadn't thought of that. Who knocked me out, if it wasn't the enemy?"

Elwood's expression hardened. "You need to remember." His stern tone, like an order from a superior, had Jonah eyeing him more closely.

Without warning, the agent leaned closer, pitching his voice to barely above a whisper. "What I'm going to tell you needs to stay between the two of us."

Jonah watched a bead of sweat trek from Elwood's temple to his double chin. He glanced out the kitchen window to see the teens still hard at work.

"Go ahead."

"Three hours in advance of your insertion into Carenero, your strike force was still aboard the *USS Kearsarge*, just north of Curaçao. Someone in the strike force placed a call on the ship's sat phone. That call went to a cell phone with global positioning in Carenero, Venezuela."

It was Jonah's turn to stare. "How do you know that call was from someone in my troop? There's a huge crew on the *Kearsarge*."

"You had that area of the ship to yourselves," came the predictable answer.

Jonah considered everyone who might have been there, from the operations officer to the boat crew who'd transported the SEALs to their insertion point, to his squad members.

"You're suggesting a member of my force called ahead to warn the Venezuelans we were coming? That's absurd."

Elwood's jaw tightened, informing Jonah he had said all he was going to say.

"Talk to your teammates," the agent suggested. "Find out who might have made that call and why. But don't let on what you know."

Pushing his chair back, he signaled his intent to leave.

"Lieutenant, if you start to remember more, I want you to call me, first thing." He laid a business card on the table, even though Jonah still had the original. "Don't talk to anyone and don't trust anyone," Elwood warned, pointing a pudgy finger at him. "Not your wife, your psychiatrist, not even your commander. You call me first, understand?"

"Okay," Jonah said, deciding he would trust the NCIS agent over anyone else. Following Elwood's example, he rose to his feet and headed for the door.

A thousand questions vied for articulation, but the agent already seemed to regret telling him about the phone call.

As Jonah escorted him outside, the certainty that he knew *something* coalesced in him. What was it? Could he possibly know who had placed the call to Venezuela? Did he know who was leaking intel to The Entity, allowing them to steal weapons in advance of the SEALs?

From atop his deck, Jonah watched Special Agent Elwood squeeze into his car and shut himself inside. As the Taurus backed out of the driveway, Jonah could feel his own determination building.

Rather than having spooked him, the agent's visit filled him with a feeling of invincibility. In Elwood's opinion—likely an informed one—Jonah's disappearance wasn't an accident. Somebody had targeted him. He hadn't failed the mission after all.

If that was true, then he'd survived something few men could. Wouldn't it beat all if he could come back from the dead to finger the person responsible?

CHAPTER 11

*S*weating profusely in his T-shirt, Jonah bent double to push the sander over the worn planks. The teens, who'd worked diligently up to about an hour ago, lounged in the Adirondack chairs, chatting. Jonah let them be. The sun beat down on his back. A bead of sweat dripped off the end of his nose. He was dying to take his shirt off, but he didn't want to scare the kids.

Snapping off the sander, he decided he would jog down the steps and douse himself with the hose.

Miriam looked over at him. "Dad, can we go inside and make sandwiches? Ian's getting hungry."

He hadn't needed to hear anything beyond *Dad*, which she hadn't called him since he'd accidentally choked her mother. He would have agreed to practically anything at that moment.

"Yeah, sure, if you make me a sandwich, too."

"Obviously," she said, in a cheeky manner he'd probably once taken exception to. He realized her tone meant she was feeling comfortable with him.

"Thanks." He waited until the teens disappeared inside. Then, instead of dousing himself under the hose, he stripped off his T-shirt, thinking he could put it back on when he heard the teens come out again.

As the wind wicked away the sweat on his torso, Jonah closed his eyes, giving thanks for the gift of life he'd been given. Opening them again, he sought the ocean, a sapphire swath stretching as far as the eye could see. The sweetness of creation broke over him, reminding him that, in God, anything seemed possible.

Master Chief's words from their conversation returned to him: *God brought you home for a reason. Put your trust in Him, and remember He works all things for the good of those who love him. All things, Jonah.*

Had God spared him so he could expose the traitor who was selling intel to the enemy? It seemed so. More than anything, Jonah longed to flush him out—not only to avenge his year-long captivity, but to prevent more weapons from falling into the hands of ruthless despots bent on propagating terror.

It wasn't too late to make a difference. With that thought, Jonah flipped the sander back on and continued the grueling work of smoothing splinters and rough patches until the planks felt like silk beneath his touch.

"Dad!"

Miriam's shout made him realize she'd been calling him for some time. Shutting off the sander, he straightened painfully and craned his neck, recalling belatedly that his chest was bare.

Dismay turned to mortification when he realized the teens weren't the only ones looking at him. Eden stood on the top step, clutching her water bottle to her chest, her eyes wide with consternation. He hadn't heard her pull into the driveway.

Well, shoot, he thought, as all three of them stared at him like he was a mutant. Starting toward his T-shirt he'd slung over the railing, Miriam intercepted him, shoving a paper plate at him.

"Thanks," he said, taking it in one hand and groping for his T-shirt with the other.

Miriam's gaze skittered over his chest. "No problem," she muttered.

Unable to put his T-shirt on while holding the sandwich, Jonah dared to look at Eden for her reaction. Her silence spoke volumes. Now that she'd seen what his captives had done to him, would she ever want to touch him again?

∾

Say something, Eden ordered herself.

A vision of Jonah's back seared her eyeballs and put a chokehold on her vocal cords. She had already guessed he'd been tortured by his captors, but she could never have imagined any one person being the brunt of so much violence.

His torso, puckered with scars of various dimensions, was horrible to behold. They dotted his magnificent chest like a constellation of stars, some still purple and healing, others small and shiny. Her heart wrenched at the sight, unleashing the urge to protect him.

The fervent and unexpected desire to throw her arms around him kept her stock-still and speechless.

At her continued silence, Jonah put his plate down and started putting on his T-shirt.

"Don't," she managed.

He stilled and looked over at her.

"You're covered in sawdust," she explained. "You'll want to shower first."

Just act like everything's normal. She tore her gaze from him to inspect the deck.

"Wow! You've practically stripped this entire half. I'm so impressed."

His quizzical look told her she was doing the right thing. At least he didn't look self-conscious anymore.

"There's just one thing you forgot," she added, propping a hand on her hips and feigning disappointment.

"What?"

"Sunscreen." She gestured at Ian, whose neck and forearms were a vivid shade of pink. "Redheads require sunscreen at all times. You could use some yourself, Jonah. You haven't been in sun like this in months. Why don't you call it a day and come in and cool off while I run Ian home?"

"I rode my bike," Ian volunteered, starting toward the stairs.

"Hey." Jonah kept the boy from bolting. "You did good work today. I expect to see you bright and early Monday morning to finish the job. I'll pay you then."

Ian's look of dismay made Eden's lips twitch.

"You can use this electric sander," Jonah added, enticingly. "I'm going to rent a bigger one," he said to Eden.

"Okay." With a shrug that bordered on enthusiastic, Ian mumbled a quick goodbye to Miriam and loped down the stairs.

Jonah went to pick up the sander, and the pain that flashed across his face raised a red flag.

"You overdid it," Eden scolded him. Of course, he'd overdone it. That was Jonah's modus operandi. He *always* over achieved.

"Stop everything," she ordered. "I'll clean up out here. You go inside and take a shower. Actually—" she deliberated a split second before adding "—I want you to use my tub. You need to soak or you won't be able to move tonight."

"I'm fine," he protested.

She pointed a finger at him, something she wouldn't have dared do in the past. "Don't argue with me." She kept her tone light, but she wasn't going to let him refuse.

Miriam snickered, then piped up. "I'll clean up out here. I know where everything goes."

Eden shot her daughter an astonished look.

"Well, thank you. I will take you up on that." She crooked her finger at Jonah. "You follow me."

Marching him through the house, she dropped off her purse and her water bottle and led him to her bedroom. Jonah had kicked off his shoes. He was clutching his T-shirt to his naked chest and looking uncomfortable at the thought of getting anything dirty.

She led him into her bathroom and ran water into the Jacuzzi tub while Jonah stood at the door watching. Conscious of her own sweat soaked, workout attire, she pointed to the laundry hamper in the closet. "You can put your dirty clothes in there."

He tossed his shirt into the basket. "How was the marathon?"

She focused on his face to keep from gaping at his naked chest.

"Honestly, it wasn't bad. Keep in mind the patrons are all just weekend warriors. We took it slow from the start."

Reaching for the Epsom salts she stored under her sink, she grabbed the carton and opened it.

"I'm envious of the shape you're in," Jonah admitted as she sprinkled some into the tub.

She could feel his gaze sliding over her as she adjusted the temperature and turned on the jets. A low hum filled the room. The water started to foam.

The desire to do something more for Jonah than just draw his bath had her plucking lavender oil out of the basket on the tub's edge and adding it to the water. As its soothing fragrance filled the room, Jonah started shucking off his pants, hastening Eden's departure. Sure, there'd been a time when he'd undressed in front of her without a second thought, but they weren't back there yet.

Yet?

"Take your time in here." She headed swiftly for the door and tried to edge past him.

At the last instant, he shot an arm out, blocking her escape. They stood mere inches apart, so close she could smell his familiar scent layered with fresh lumber. One whiff made her head spin.

"I repel you, don't I?"

The gruff question caught her off guard. "What?"

"I know what I look like. I don't blame you for running off. It's hideous."

His conclusions so dumfounded her all she could do for a second was stare at him. Then, since there was nothing she could say to convince him how wrong he was, she rolled up on her tiptoes and pressed her lips to his.

His eyes flared, but then his surprise gave way to a focused intensity that brought her heels swiftly to the floor.

Flustered by her actions, Eden fled the bathroom before Jonah brought himself to kiss her back. If he did that, she knew she would be a goner. She would fall right into his arms and his bed, precisely as Nina had warned.

Stupid, stupid, stupid, she berated herself as she helped herself to Miriam's shower and washed the sweat of a four-hour workout from her body.

She should not have kissed Jonah. She'd meant to reassure him. Instead, she was afraid she'd revealed her attraction for him.

Once he realized she wanted him, he would corner her when she least expected it, pressing his advantage. And she would give in because, in all honesty, she craved the feel of his arms around her, his weight pressing her down into the bed. Making love had been the one thing in their marriage that had never lost its luster.

"Now you've done it," she muttered. It would be so unfair to Jonah to split with him if they became intimate again. She had to ensure it never happened.

⁓

Jonah submersed himself in the big Jacuzzi tub until only his mouth and nose stuck out of the water. With his eyes shut, he envisioned himself in his mother's womb, an innocent life-form. Pity for the fetus he'd once been rose up in him. The poor little thing had no idea of the hardships that awaited him.

It's not over yet, said a voice in Jonah's head.

He mulled it over, taking comfort from the suggestion that happiness and rest would be his one day.

Surely goodness and mercy will follow me all the days of my life.

The comforting verse returned to him.

But will my wife ever love me again? That was a question to which he did not receive an answer. If his body had truly repulsed her, how could she have kissed him the way she had, so sweetly, so reassuringly?

Replaying the memory of her kiss over and over in his mind, he clung to it like a prophecy.

Soften her heart toward me, Lord.

In the sacred silence of the womb-like tub, Jonah was certain God heard him.

"I kissed him," Eden confessed to her friend as she laid her purchase, a pair of leggings, on the counter at Nina's studio, *Inspired to Dance.*

It was five o'clock. Jonah had slept all afternoon, exhausted from his labors on the deck. The minute he'd awakened, Eden had seized the excuse to run out and pick up something for dinner. Staying alone in the house with him, even with Miriam around, made her feel like a cat on a hot tin roof.

"You didn't!" Her dark-haired friend eyed her with dismay.

"I did. And all I can think about is kissing him again."

"Ugh!" Nina rang up the leggings on her cash register, even as she shook her head in disapproval. "Why, why?" she demanded. "You know once you give yourself to him, you're going to want to recommit."

"I know, but you should have seen what I saw today."

"It's $24.50. What did you see?"

Eden swiped her card, completing the transaction.

"His chest and his back. Dear God, Nina. He was brutalized!" Tears surged to her eyes as she pictured what she'd seen. "I felt so bad for him."

Nina put a hand over her heart. She was still wearing one of the leotards she commonly wore while teaching her ballet classes. "It must have been awful to look at."

Eden shook her head. "Not really. I mean, yes, the scars are hideous, but they hardly detract from his overall attractiveness. It's not the scars that bother me. It's the idea that, while I was celebrating Jonah's absence, he was being hideously tortured. I feel so low, so selfish for ever being glad he was gone."

Nina shuddered. "That's why I could never marry a SEAL."

"And the strangest thing," Eden added, noting Nina's comment, "is all those scars make him even more noble somehow. It's like…he suffered all of that just so he could come home to me. I know it's ridiculous."

"It *is* ridiculous," Nina agreed. "He loved heading out on missions. He could hardly wait to get away, remember?"

"I remember. But he's not the same anymore."

Nina leveled an admonishing look at her. "Don't you realize when Jonah gets his memories back, he'll be all about his work again, and he'll forget you even exist?"

"Will he?" Eden wasn't so sure. "I don't know. I think his captivity has changed him—for the better."

"How can that be? Being brutalized doesn't make people better. It freaks them out."

Eden considered how Jonah had reacted when his buddies showed up at midnight.

"That's true in some ways," she admitted. "Last night, some guys from his troop showed up to paper our house, and Jonah thought they were terrorists or something. He told me to hide in the attic."

"Did you?"

"No." She huffed a little laugh. "Can you imagine if I had awakened Miriam and told her we needed to hide? She would think Jonah's crazy."

"Is he?"

The question gave Eden pause. She thought of the article on PTSD describing associations between traumatic experiences, paranoia, and hallucinations.

"Of course not," she muttered. "He's still getting over what happened to him. I mean, can you blame him?"

Nina blew out a breath. "Girl, I can't believe you're letting yourself fall in love with him again."

"I am not! Trust me, my eyes are wide open. It's just that—Ugh!" she released the moan of frustration she'd been holding in all night. "I want to be with him. I miss the way it feels to be held by him and kissed by him. Don't you ever just ache for that?"

Nina looked off to one side and didn't answer.

"Have you ever been with someone who made you feel like you have to be with them again or you're depriving yourself?"

"Almost," Nina said on a forlorn note.

"Who?" Eden immediately demanded. As far as she knew, Nina had only ever been with the husband who'd cheated on her and abandoned her. Had she indulged in a relationship Eden didn't know about?

Nina looked back at her. "I can't tell you. You know him."

"It's Master Chief Rivera," Eden guessed.

Nina gasped. "How do you know?"

"By the way you reacted the last time I mentioned his name. Oh, my gosh, what happened with you two? You're perfect for each other."

"Don't say that," Nina scolded as she moved from behind the counter to turn off the lights in her studio. "He's a SEAL. I could never be with a man who disappears at a moment's notice possibly never to return again."

Compassion blew through Eden as she recalled that was what Nina's ex-husband had done. "But Rivera is so handsome and sweet! Jonah says he's a wonderful man."

"And he can dance," Nina added, turning back to face her.

"You danced with him?"

"Salsa night at the brewery," Nina replied. "He asked me to marry him."

The words startled a shriek out of Eden. "Seriously, he asked you to marry him? Why have you never told me this?" She thumped an open hand on the countertop.

Nina rolled her eyes and went to collect her belongings from behind the counter. "Because I knew you're react like you are right now."

"I'm sorry! I'm calm. I'm calm," Eden assured her. "It's just that—Wow, Master Chief is the most eligible bachelor on the planet. Why wouldn't you at least date him and see how it goes?"

Nina hooked her purse strap on her shoulder. "I already told you. He's a SEAL."

"I know, but he's bound to retire sooner rather than later. He's got to be close to forty."

"Forty-two," Nina informed her.

"Then he's got over twenty years of service. He can retire and get married. Then you can have the baby you want."

Nina snorted. "You make it sound so easy. I'm barren, remember?"

"Maybe you are; maybe you're not. It could've been Mehmet who was sterile."

"He got tested. It's all me. Trust me, Santiago Rivera isn't going to want a barren wife."

Eden opened her mouth to argue with her friend.

"No more on the subject," Nina warned, holding up a scarlet-tipped finger. "If we talk about him too much, I'm going to get obsessed the way you are. Now run off and get dinner for your family. One of these days, I need to show you how to cook," she added, heading for the exit.

Eden grabbed her new purchase off the counter and followed her friend to the door.

"I do want to learn," she admitted, stepping out into the heat. The smell of gyros coming from the Greek restaurant next door caught her notice. "But not tonight. Tonight, I think I'll duck in here and get takeout."

Nina turned to her and offered her a hug. "Be strong," she ordered.

Eden nodded fatalistically. "Okay. But only if you give Master Chief another chance."

Nina visibly blushed beneath her olive complexion.

"I don't think so," she murmured, turning and heading toward her trusty Honda Civic.

Watching her friend duck into her car, Eden contemplated playing Cupid. If she couldn't have her own happily-ever-after, maybe at least her best friend could. Then Eden could live through Nina vicariously. But she would have to be sneaky about it or her friend would be furious with her.

What could it hurt? she thought with a tingle of excitement.

CHAPTER 12

*J*onah was pleased to recognize a number of people in the congregation of the big non-denominational church they attended the following morning.

"Master Chief's here," he whispered to Eden as they stood singing with the praise band.

"He is?" She went up on tiptoes, craning her neck to see over the people in front of them. "I need to talk to him after the service."

Jonah wondered what Eden had to say to Rivera, but it wasn't the time to ask. Fixing his gaze on the projector screen, he mouthed the lyrics while listening to Eden's tuneful alto and Miriam's warbling soprano. A rich baritone voice drew his gaze over his shoulder, and he was startled to recognize Lucas Strong as the source.

The lieutenant junior grade sat two rows behind them in the company of a dark-haired woman who made a point of catching Jonah's eye. He sent her a respectful nod, wondering why it was she looked familiar. By the time the congregation sat and the pastor mounted the stage, Jonah had yet to come up with an answer.

The verses read by Pastor Tom strummed a familiar cord. Jonah knew he'd read them, though he couldn't remember when.

"So, let's talk about where to find God and where God finds you." Pastor

Tom tucked the Bible under his arm and paced from one side of the raised platform to the other.

"A lot of people find God in church." He gestured to encompass the modern sanctuary with its wide stained-glass windows and white-washed walls. "This is a great place to let God into your heart, wouldn't you agree?"

The congregation murmured their assent.

"On the other hand," Pastor Tom continued, "I know plenty of people who say the God of Creation found them at their lowest point in life. Some of them were lying flat on their backs, still drunk from the liquor they'd promised never to touch again. I know someone who found God on a park bench where he'd been sitting for hours because his family had washed their hands of him and he had nowhere else to go."

Jonah's throat closed up at the sudden recollection of how God had found him in a dank, squalid cell in Carenero.

He'd awakened to a pounding headache, having no idea where he was.

Why am I here? How did I get here?

The answers had never come to him. He remembered being puzzled by the fact that he could recall his childhood, becoming a SEAL, losing a friend in the form of Blake LeMere. But he'd never figured out how he'd fallen into *El Jefe's* grasp in the first place.

Caught in a hellish existence, he had survived only because of his prolonged exposure-training. Still, he remembered wishing every time he opened his eyes that death would claim him until, one day, a stranger in uniform slid his daily meal beneath the bars and stood there watching him wolf it down.

"Are you hungry, señor?" the man had asked, his voice gently compassionate.

Jonah barely glanced at him, pretending not to understand.

"I wish I had more beans to give you. But food alone will not save you." The stranger had reached under his uniform and produced a book hidden at the small of his back. Sliding it through the bars, he'd urged Jonah to take it.

Jonah had regarded him with suspicion. Perhaps it was a trap, and he would be punished for stealing what wasn't his.

"Take it and read it. Don't let the others see. This book will save you."

Some force within him had compelled him to get up, shuffle forward, and take what he recognized as a Bible. "Gracias," he'd murmured.

"God is with you," the man said in Spanish, and then he'd disappeared, and Jonah had never seen him again.

Heart pounding, Jonah realized he could recall reading in spindles of sunlight shooting through cracks in the adobe. He had read the Bible from start to finish. The words within had fueled him as surely as manna had fed God's chosen people in the wilderness. One passage in particular had given him the strength to endure his captivity.

For I am convinced that neither death nor life, neither angels nor demons, neither the present nor the future, nor any powers, neither height nor depth, nor anything else in all creation, will be able to separate us from the love of God that is in Christ Jesus our LORD.

Dumbfounded by the memory, Jonah scarcely registered that the pastor was talking about him until Eden elbowed him.

"...someone in our congregation who deserves to be recognized. A month ago, we memorialized Jonah Mills and commended him to the Father. This morning he sits in our midst, very much alive."

A wave of love broke over Jonah as the congregation responded with audible amazement and then applause.

"I think you should stand up," Eden said, her eyes bright with tears.

Jonah was already coming to his feet. Nodding in acknowledgement, he marveled that all these people who were strangers to him seemed so happy about his return.

"We are looking at a miracle, ladies and gentlemen," said the pastor, who jumped off the podium to approach Jonah and shake his hand. "Jonah, we prayed every week for you." His handshake was firm and sincere. "You are living testimony to the power of prayer. Welcome home."

Despite the lump in his throat, Jonah was moved to say something. He held up a hand and the sanctuary fell silent.

"I just want to say thank you to all of you," he said, projecting so he could be heard. "I don't know most of you," he admitted, "but I hope that changes." He paused to clear his throat and started again. "I want you to know, if God could find me in captivity and turn my heart to Him—if He could rescue me and bring me safely home again—then He can find you, too, no matter where you are in life, no matter how dark a place you might be in."

He nodded his certainty. "Thanks again."

As he took his seat, the congregation showered him with more applause. To his deep satisfaction, Eden reached for his hand, interlacing her fingers through his, and gripping him hard. Miriam, he noticed, looked from their hands to their faces and smiled.

Jonah lapsed into a state of contentment. His surroundings turned into a blur as the universe encompassed only him, Eden, and Miriam, smiling her little smile.

He didn't know what Eden holding his hand meant exactly, but it felt good. Even if she only did it for the benefit of others, her gesture had made him a happy man.

Yet the service eventually ended, and Eden let go of him as they filed out of the sanctuary.

"I need to talk to your master chief," she said, leading him toward the reception hall.

Spying Rivera on the other side of the big room writing words on a dry-erase board, Jonah watched her make her way over to him.

"Hello, sir," came a voice at his side.

Turning, he greeted Lucas and the familiar-looking brunette with him.

"You remember Monica Trembley, don't you?" Lucas asked. "She's a secretary at Spec Ops Headquarters."

"I thought you looked familiar," Jonah said, shaking Monica's slim hand. He couldn't pull up a single coherent memory of her, however.

She flashed her dimples while regarding him quizzically.

"I'm also Lucas's fiancée," she added pointedly.

"Oh." Jonah looked back and forth between the pair, aware that Monica was watching his reaction. "Congratulations. When's the big day?"

"April 15th," she said, making a point of showing him her ring.

Jonah masked his astonishment at the size of the diamond solitaire.

"You've got a few more months left to plan then," he said, making small talk. Rumor had it Lucas Strong was loaded from having played professional football. Jonah had forgotten until he saw her ring how wealthy he was purported to be since the man never flaunted his money.

"Sir, the guys and I want to get together with you," Lucas said, reclaiming his attention. "Any chance you can come by my place this evening?" His gray eyes conveyed a desire to discuss the mission and what went wrong.

Jonah saw an opportunity to fulfill Special Agent Elwood's request that he feel out his teammates about who might have made a phone call to Carenero while still aboard the *Kearsarge*.

"Sure, what time?"

"Nineteen hundred hours."

"Can I bring anything?" Jonah asked.

"Just yourself. Theo, Saul, Master Chief, and I will be there. Bambino's taking night classes. Maybe you could get a ride with Master Chief since he lives out your way."

"I'll go ask him," Jonah suggested. Monica's scrutiny was making him uncomfortable. "See you soon," he said to Lucas, then nodded farewell to his fiancée.

Monica answered with a wave of her fingers, "Toodle-oo."

Jonah came upon Eden and Master Chief in earnest conversation.

"But she would," she was insisting, making Jonah wonder whom they were talking about. "You simply have to be persistent. And creative," she added. "She's understandably gun-shy."

Rivera tore his gaze off Eden's face to acknowledge Jonah's presence.

"Glad you could make it this morning," he said, clasping Jonah's proffered hand and adding, "Your words were very moving."

"Yes, they were," Eden agreed, smiling at Jonah.

His hopes ascended another notch. She was praising him in front of his master chief. This had to mean she was giving him another chance. Remembering his purpose, he looked back at Rivera.

"Lucas says some of us are getting together at his house tonight."

Rivera nodded. "Yes, I got the invitation."

"Can you give me a ride?" Jonah asked.

"Of course. I'll pick you up at quarter to seven. Are you all staying for Sunday school? I'm teaching today." He gestured to the white-erase board.

Eden looked at Jonah. "Actually, we're headed to lunch. Are you still up for that?"

Weariness hovered on the fringes of his consciousness, but Eden's seeming change of heart kept it at bay. Going out for lunch gave him the chance to charm her some more.

"Yes, I'm fine." He nodded at Miriam who was browsing the cookie selection. "We'd better go now, though, before she loses her appetite."

"Miriam!" Eden hurried off to stop Miriam from snacking.

Rivera waited until she was out of earshot. "I don't know, Jaguar. She doesn't strike me as a woman who wants to leave you." He sent Jonah a knowing look.

Jonah let his private hopes show. "You think?" The memory of Eden kissing him the previous day linked with the memory of her holding his hand.

"I think," Rivera affirmed, practically winking at him.

They both looked at Eden who was pulling Miriam away from the table. Jonah's heart swelled with love and desire for her.

Please God, let me keep them both, he prayed.

Watching Jonah head out to lunch with his family, Santiago knew a moment's envy. Having witnessed first-hand the number of divorces on the Teams, he had avoided romantic entanglements intentionally, though that hadn't been easy. In his mind, he was married to the Teams. His family were the men of Blue Squadron, most especially men in Alpha Troop with whom he felt the closest.

But increasingly, and with the advent of his retirement creeping up on him, he had begun to entertain the thought of finding someone to share his life. A few months ago, on salsa night at the micro-brewery just off base, he had run into the woman of his dreams. In fact, his first thought when laying eyes on the brunette at the table next to his was, *There she is. That's my future wife.*

Recalling how he had bungled his best chance to be with the perfect woman, Santiago felt his face heat. To think he had actually proposed to a near-perfect stranger!

It was so unlike him—and yet, he was Hispanic, after all, and most Hispanic men were incurable romantics.

His rash proposal had sent the lovely Nina running. Thanks to Eden, Santiago not only knew her last name now, but he knew where she worked.

In Eden's words, all Nina Aydin really needed was a persistent yet gentle suitor. Given the nature of his work, Santiago certainly qualified as persistent. The men he worked with might not say he was gentle, exactly, but they didn't always see his softer side.

Rubbing his hands in anticipation, Santiago sealed his intention to pursue the brunette ballerina who'd evaded him at their first encounter. God willing, she would one day be his wife.

Eden noticed Jonah's head bob as he studied the menu. *Oh, dear.* Was he seriously falling asleep?

"You okay? We can go home, if you want."

Her question brought both Jonah's and Miriam's eyes up from their menus. Jonah's usually sharp gaze struck Eden as unfocused.

"No, I'm fine," he insisted. "Hungry," he added.

His answer didn't convince her, but Miriam, who sat next to him, looked so dismayed at the prospect of leaving the Mexican restaurant they frequented, Eden thrust aside her private concerns and looked back at the menu. She found herself wanting to eat something she'd never tried before, something new to go with the new life she was experiencing.

Making her choice she looked back at Jonah. "What you said at church today about God turning your heart to him. That was beautiful."

He blinked at her, his gaze softening. "Thanks."

"I'd never heard you talk about God before today," she added.

Miriam looked over to gauge his reaction.

He grimaced rather sheepishly. "I always figured I could take care of myself. But I guess there comes a time when we all need help."

Picturing him praying in a cell on another continent tugged at her heartstrings.

"I'm very glad God found you when he did," she said sincerely.

His searching gaze told her he was reading every possible significance into her statement.

"I'm sorry about the money," he said, unexpectedly.

"Money?" What on earth? "Oh, the life insurance." She waved a negligent hand. "Please." She shook her head at him. "You can't put a price on a human life."

He smiled rather bitterly. "I hardly think I'm worth that much, but I would like to be. I can work on it," he added.

His answer both worried and encouraged her. With him investing so much of himself into their marriage, could she ever really bring herself to leave him? "Is that why you're sanding the deck?" She raised an eyebrow.

"No." He shook his head in an exaggerated manner, making her laugh. "I want to host a Labor Day party, remember."

"I remember," Miriam inserted.

The waiter appeared to take their orders. As he walked away, Miriam asked him, "Do you remember this place at all?"

Jonah looked around intently. "It looks like places I've been before."

As with many Mexican restaurants, the interior was dimly lit, with adobe walls and wooden booths tucked into private alcoves.

"We came here every Sunday whenever you were home."

Jonah's brow furrowed as he looked around again, clearly desperate to remember something about the place.

"What matters is the present," Eden assured the both of them. Hearing her own words, she realized it was time to give Jonah a chance. With God anchoring their marriage, they actually stood a chance, didn't they?

The look he gave her was both grateful and hopeful—and sleepy. He put a hand over his mouth and turned his head away to hide an enormous yawn. All at once, Eden saw him stiffen. His yawn disappeared and recognition hardened his features. Following his stare, Eden was dismayed to see Lieutenant Commander Jimmy Lowery sitting alone in a booth on the opposite side of the crowded restaurant.

Jonah looked back at her, but his recognition of Lowery unsettled her. For some reason, he didn't seem to like the man. A frown now rode his brow ridge. He unfolded his napkin and set it in his lap, but it was obvious he was thinking about Lowery and possibly some rumors that existed. Master Chief hadn't wasted any time telling him, apparently.

Eden dared to put her cards on the table. She had nothing to hide, so why not?

"I guess you've heard he used to call me," she said, watching Jonah's reaction closely.

His gaze came up. He glanced at Lowery then back at her.

"When?" he demanded.

Oh, dear, she'd done it again—blurting confessions that didn't need to be said. Master Chief hadn't said anything, apparently.

"After your disappearance," she said, glancing at Miriam and asking herself belatedly if the subject wasn't appropriate for her ears. "He called several times a week. Showed up a couple of times at the house. At first, I thought he was simply concerned, you being a teammate and all. He said he wanted to make sure we were okay," she added.

Jonah sat straighter in his chair. His shoulders went back. The muscles in his jaw flexed. A portion of Eden's newfound confidence retreated. Suddenly, Jonah looked so much like the husband she used to know, with his jaw clenched and his emotions concealed, she had to wonder if he'd changed after all. He'd never been possessive, but he was territorial. She wouldn't put it past him to slide silently out of the booth for a quiet word with Lowery. He wouldn't make a scene, of course, but he'd certainly get his point across.

"What'd you say to him?" Jonah's voice sounded exactly the way it used to when he was upset.

Eden looked away, regretting her impulsive tongue. She had hoped never to hear Jonah's voice go hard and cold that way again.

She looked back at him, her own words terse and brittle. "I told him he was wasting his time. I think he finally got the picture."

Jonah searched her gaze for several seconds while Miriam's gaze went back and forth between them, her look of contentment gone.

"Is he the reason you want us to separate?" he asked.

The hurtful words hit her like a slap to the face. *And he's back*, said a cynical voice in her head. "I'm going to go wash my hands," she said, refusing to answer him.

"Wait, I didn't mean that," Jonah muttered with contrition.

Ignoring him, Eden scooted out of the booth and fled to the ladies' room.

Relieved to be the only patron in the restroom, she leveled a stern look at herself in the mirror as she washed her hands.

What are you doing? she asked herself. *Either you stick to the plan and stop misleading Jonah into thinking you're going to stay with him, or you go all in and give him the chance he deserves.*

She bit her lower lip. But what if Jonah was like the shallow soil of the parables and the seeds of spirituality withered and died, turning him back into the man he was before? Giving him a chance meant risking her heart all over again. He had broken it once before, was she really going to leave herself vulnerable?

She searched her reflection for an answer.

"I don't know," the woman in the mirror said.

Looking down at the sink she sent up yet another prayer for clarity. "Show me a sign, Lord. I still need a sign."

With an indrawn breath, she dried her hands and left the restroom to return to her family.

As she made her way to their table, she saw Jimmy Lowery from the corner of her eye catch sight of her and do a double take. She could see him track her all the way back to her table where Eden was pleased to see Jonah chuckling at something Miriam had said. As she slid into the booth across from them, he stretched a hand across the table and regarded her apologetically.

"I'm sorry," he said with convincing feeling. "It's not you I don't trust. It's him." He darted a look in Lowery's direction.

Just then, the waitress appeared, carrying their plates of food and sparing Eden from having to say anything. The rest of the meal passed pleasantly enough with Jonah darting only a few spurious glances across the room.

Eden was polishing off her second shrimp taco when Jonah looked up and abruptly lowered his fork. A shadow fell over the table, and Eden turned her head to find Lowery standing next to her.

"Hey, all," he said, nodding at the women and holding a hand out for Jonah to shake. "Thought I'd come over and say hi. Welcome home, Jonah."

"Thanks, Jimmy."

As the two men shook hands, Eden watched Lowery take note of Jonah's deteriorated condition. "I'm so glad to see you again."

His assertion could certainly have sounded more sincere. She held her breath, awaiting Jonah's reaction.

"Are you?" he asked.

Lowery stiffened, folding his arms across his chest. "Of course. I, uh, I had a recent chat with Elwood, the NCIS investigator. He says you're starting to remember stuff about the mission?"

Was he asking if Jonah remembered what had happened?

"I remember some of my captivity," Jonah answered carefully.

"That's good," the XO said. "Can't exactly talk about it here, though," he added with an awkward laugh.

"Right," Jonah agreed. "Thank you for checking on my wife while I was dead. I'm alive now," he added with a hard smile.

Jimmy let loose a nervous laugh. "So you are. Well, I don't want to interrupt. Enjoy your afternoon."

His gaze met Eden's briefly as he turned and walked to the exit. She didn't know Jimmy Lowery well enough to say for certain, but he struck her as rattled. *By what?* Did he think Jonah might turn jealous and pounce on him when he least expected it?

For his part, Jonah stopped eating. His expression was unreadable, but Eden could feel the tension radiating from him. Miriam was eyeing them watchfully.

"He mentioned an investigator Elwood," Eden said, thinking if they talked it might ease the tension. "Is that the man who left you his business card?"

Jonah took a bite out of his tortilla so he couldn't answer.

Miriam did it for him. "It's probably the guy who came by yesterday when we were sanding the deck."

Jonah nodded and swallowed but said nothing.

"What did you two talk about?" Maybe speaking would ease some of the stress she felt roiling in him.

"Just trying to figure out what happened to me," he said with food in his mouth.

She would like to know that, too. Obviously, there was more to the story than she'd been told. Was he really a new man because he'd let God into his life? Or would she start seeing the old Jonah emerge more and more frequently, as he was doing now?

What if he hadn't changed enough?

Wouldn't she be the fool, losing her heart to him a second time.

Keeping his expression as neutral as possible, Jonah drew deep, steadying breaths and kept the conversation going until his adrenaline subsided.

Seeing Jimmy Lowery up close and personal hadn't jogged any memories, but it had left him with the absolute conviction, for whatever reason, that the man had betrayed him.

Lowery was the reason Jonah had suffered unspeakable horrors at the hands of his captors. Bitterness beyond words twisted through him, tying his full stomach into knots. He lowered his fork, wishing he hadn't taken that last bite.

Why? Why would one Team guy ever turn on another? Such behavior was unconscionable, unbelievable.

Maybe because it wasn't real. Maybe Jonah was making it all up. PTSD played serious mind games with its victims, didn't it? Maybe Branson was right, and he'd developed the disorder. With his brain chemistry out of whack, Eden's remarks about Jimmy calling on her while Jonah was away were affecting his brain like a toxin, causing him to invent carcinogenic thoughts. What if those thoughts had no basis in reality—like the cop car running him off the road the day before.

Stop.

The tense and uncertain look on Eden's face gave Jonah the wherewithal to haul on the reins of his pessimism. None of it mattered right now. What mattered more than anything was ensuring his relationship with his wife and stepdaughter stayed on an even keel so they would give him the chance to prove himself.

The last thing he wanted to do was ruin this outing by giving voice to his strange convictions. He would run them by his most trusted teammates first, measuring his sanity by their responses. If they agreed with him that Lowery's actions that night were suspicious, then—and only then—would Jonah share his angst with Eden.

Pinning a smile on his taut face, he forced himself to take one last bite out of his enchilada.

"This restaurant is great," he stated with forced enthusiasm. "No wonder we used to come here."

CHAPTER 13

*J*onah and his master chief were the last to arrive at Lucas Strong's condo.

As they followed Monica into the dining room, Jonah's gaze went straight to the former tight end, sitting at the head of the table with Theo and Saul on either side. Even seated, Lucas Strong loomed over the average-sized men. His home was nothing out of the ordinary, except it was filled with the kind of high-end furniture and décor found at Crate & Barrel stores. Either Lucas had an eye for interior decorating or Monica had contributed her talents. The yellow lilies overflowing the vase in the middle of the table made Jonah think of his commander.

"There you are." Catching sight of the latecomers, Lucas pushed to his feet, and the others did likewise—an unnecessary show of respect, but heartening all the same. SEALs overlooked rank in casual settings. This was clearly their way of building up Jonah's self-esteem.

Lucas pumped his hand, then turned to Master Chief and added, "Great class today. I never knew that about Jonah."

"What about me?" Jonah asked.

"Not you," Lucas corrected his assumption. "The Biblical Jonah. God wanted him to preach repentance in Ninevah. In modern-day terms that'd be like God asking one of us to preach morality in Las Vegas. I can see why Jonah tried to run."

Master Chief chuckled. "At some point he realized there's no running from God."

"When he became fish food," Saul drawled, proving he knew something about the Bible, though he professed to not believing.

Lucas nodded. "I've had a Jonah-moment myself once," he admitted.

Jonah wanted to hear what that was, but Lucas went straight to taking their drink orders. Master Chief asked for a diet Coke. Remembering his medication, Jonah did the same.

"Have a seat," Lucas offered as Monica hurried off to fetch their beverages.

"It's my fault we're late," Jonah said, pulling out a seat next to Saul. No sooner was he seated than Saul hooked him by the neck. Pulling him close, he scrubbed his knuckles on Jonah's scalp. So much for formality.

"Bet you were busy with your wife," he grated in Jonah's ear.

Jonah's face heated. He was glad when Saul let go of him.

"Are you blushing, sir?" Saul's devilish smile widened.

"I was sleeping," Jonah clarified. "Can't keep my eyes open in the afternoon," he added with a self-deprecating grimace.

"Nothing wrong with that." Theo's deep voice held soothing undertones.

All the men nodded their agreement, their gazes sympathetic.

Master Chief, who'd seated himself across from Jonah, said, "You've got about a year of lost sleep to catch up on, Jaguar. We lost a little sleep ourselves, while you were gone."

A reflective silence fell over the table.

"I want to know about the night I went missing," Jonah said quietly.

Just then Monica returned to the room bearing two cans of diet Coke and two glasses with ice.

"Here you go," she said, placing a drink in front of Master Chief, then Jonah.

Dark, fragrant hair slipped over Jonah's shoulder as she leaned over him.

"Can I get you anything else before I *disappear*?"

Her sarcasm on the last word let them know she considered her exclusion unfair. Jonah could see why she'd be put out, considering she worked in Spec Ops as a secretary. But their conversation didn't involve her, and she hadn't been part of the op.

Lucas answered, "I think we have everything we need, sweetheart. Thank you."

She made a point of crossing to his chair and dropping a kiss on his cheek.

"I'll be in the bedroom," she purred. On her way out of the room, she cast a backward glance over her shoulder, and her gaze landed squarely on Jonah.

What the heck? His instinct for trouble stirred. First the touch, then the look. Was she seriously coming onto him with her fiancé in the room? Fortunately, Lucas seemed oblivious.

"Do you two live together?" he asked when Monica was out of earshot. How well did Lucas even know the woman he intended to marry?

"Oh." Lucas blinked at him and frowned slightly. "No. I mean, she's here a lot, but she doesn't live here."

"I'm just asking," Jonah added on a light note. He glanced at Master Chief, who heeded his cue to get the discussion going.

"So let's talk about the op. Jonah doesn't remember any of it."

Saul groaned. "We've been through this at least a dozen times with what's-his-name, the NCIS agent."

"Elwood," Theo answered, nodding his agreement.

"I'm aware of that," Jonah said. "I spoke with him yesterday. Sorry to whip a dead horse, but I need to hear your version of the story."

Theo gestured for Saul to narrate.

"All right." Saul propped a muscular arm on the table then launched into his story in his distinct, Oklahoma drawl.

"At zero hundred hours on 26 July, the boat crew took us from the *USS Kearsarge* to an inlet just north of the warehouse in Carenero. The sky was overcast, the moon was waning. Two hours later, we cut the lock on one of the warehouse doors and went in. We'd been told there were four boxes packed full of dirty bombs located at the northeast corner of the warehouse. But the boxes weren't there."

Theo shook his head as if recalling their perplexity.

"We fanned out to look for them," Saul continued. "Out of nowhere, we started taking fire from two shooters who were hiding all along on the catwalks above us. Lowery ordered our retreat. Taking fire and all, we left kind of helter skelter. No one realized you were still in the building till you didn't show up at our rally point. We assumed you didn't hear Lowery's order 'cause your headset sounded like it was acting up."

Experiencing déjà vu, Jonah touched a hand to his ear.

"Once we saw the shooters leave, we started to go back for you when the whole f—" With a swift glance at Master Chief, Saul cleaned up his language. "The whole freaking warehouse exploded, heat and shrapnel everywhere. No thanks to the arsenal inside, explosions went on for hours. We wanted to wait it out, but the sun was coming up, and the boat crew was on their way to pick us up. The next night we went back to look for you, or what was left of you."

Given the look on Saul's face, the experience had been gut-wrenching.

Jonah put a hand on the sniper's broad shoulder. "I'm sorry."

"That's when I found your tooth," Saul added on a somber note.

Eyeing the long faces around the table, Jonah decided it was time to share his theory of what happened.

"My tooth got knocked out," Jonah said into the sudden quiet. "I don't remember it happening, but it explains the brain damage to the front part of my brain, and it explains why I can't remember."

"If you were knocked out, how'd you get out of the building?" Theo asked.

"No idea," Jonah said with a shrug. "Maybe someone dragged me out. Maybe I was just conscious enough to get out."

"Lucky the shooters didn't end you," Theo commented.

Jonah skimmed the faces around him. "You don't think the shooters were locals," he realized.

"Would the locals blow up their own warehouse?" Saul countered.

El Jefe's question echoed in Jonah's head. *Who blew up my warehouse?* "No, they wouldn't," Jonah realized. "I thought maybe it exploded because of the arsenal inside. Wasn't it packed full of weapons?"

Theo, who was their explosives expert, inclined his close-shaved head. "Yes, but I've never seen gun powder explode in a neat line like that, not even when bullets are stacked in rows. Only C-4 does that. You want my opinion, that explosion was rigged."

"Now it makes sense," Jonah muttered to himself.

"Master Chief has a theory," Theo said, recapturing Jonah's attention.

Jonah looked at Rivera, who took a sip of his diet Coke, then put his glass down lightly.

"My theory is we stumbled across The Entity that's been stealing weapons faster than we can get to them. They drove us out of the building because they were planning all along to blow it up."

"Why would they want to destroy it?" Lucas asked.

"To cover their tracks?" Rivera suggested. "Maybe to destroy the rest of the weapons."

Jonah cocked his head, considering. "Why not kill us instead of driving us out?"

Rivera traced a line through the condensation on his glass. "Perhaps they don't consider us the enemy," he replied obliquely.

Jonah stared at him, wondering who he imagined The Entity might be.

But Rivera didn't elaborate. "Explain about the dream," he prompted, looking back at Jonah.

Turning his attention to the others, Jonah relayed the memories of his captivity that had returned to him the other night.

"I couldn't remember why I was there, so I must have lost my memory right before I was captured. Also, I was asked over and over again who blew up the warehouse. The question made no sense at the time, but now it does. I think you're onto something with your theory, Master Chief."

"Tell them the last thing you remember," Rivera said.

Jonah braced himself for a prick of pain behind his left eye, but it never came.

"It was right around Blake LeMere's death which was, like, a year before the op to Carenero ever took place."

Three men regarded him with bemusement and pity.

"That long ago?" Theo asked.

"Yeah."

Lucas looked confused. "Wasn't Blake the guy I replaced?"

"Yes, and I remember being introduced to you," Jonah added, thinking back. "I showed you around Headquarters. I don't remember anything after that."

Saul, who had fallen silent, murmured, "Blake was my best friend. Nicest guy you'd ever want to know. Smart," he added.

The others concurred.

"What happened to him was weird, though," Theo reflected.

"Effed up," Saul agreed.

"I was with him when we jumped," Jonah reminded them. "First me, then him, then Lowery. Just the three of us. I don't see how Blake could've lost consciousness after jumping. He'd jumped dozens of times before without incident, and there was nothing different about him in the lineup."

Though they'd moved away from discussing the operation, the sudden urge to share his suspicions of Lowery overcame Jonah suddenly.

"I think Lowery turned on me in the warehouse, guys," he stated baldly. "I think he left me there for dead."

Deafening silence followed his assertion. The men gaped at him, clearly taken aback by the seemingly random accusation. Jonah couldn't blame them for their shock. Betrayal wasn't a word that even existed in a SEAL's vocabulary.

Finally, Rivera asked on an even note, "Why do you think it was Lowery, Jaguar? Why would he do such a thing?"

Doubt assailed Jonah. What evidence did he have for his suspicions? Pressured by the men's doubt, he focused on the vase of flowers, thinking.

"I don't have any proof," he admitted. "It's just a feeling. I get that same feeling when I remember Blake LeMere's death. It's like betrayal. I felt it overcome me when I ran into Lowery at a restaurant today. By the way, he seemed less than happy to see me."

Saul narrowed his hazel eyes at Jonah. "Are you sayin' Lowery had something to do with Blake's death, too?"

Jonah swept his gaze around the sea of hard stares. He hadn't been saying so at all, but he realized with a start that, yes, he suspected Lowery in that situation, too. After all, Lowery had been alone with Blake just prior to his jumping.

"I don't know." He qualified his accusation. "All I know is how I feel. Lowery was alone with Blake right after I jumped. He could have done something."

"Listen." Master Chief cut into the conversation on a soft-spoken note of authority. "Let's talk about what we know for sure versus what we're speculating. We *think* the warehouse was rigged to blow. If so, we can only guess what motivated The Entity to destroy it. We *think* someone knocked Jaguar in the face. Who that was, we have no idea. We *think* Jaguar got himself out of the warehouse, avoiding death when it exploded, but he ended up in the hands of the locals. Beyond that, all we have is speculation."

An ache started to build behind Jonah's left eye. Ignoring it, he apologized. "Look, I'm obviously out of line to suspect Lowery. I'm sorry. I just feel like I know something about him, and I have to warn people. But I can't remember why or what for."

Master Chief studied Jonah. "Maybe NCIS will have more luck than us at discerning the facts," he suggested.

Jonah recalled what Elwood had told him, along with his precaution not to reveal what he knew. "Yeah, actually, he told me something I don't think he's told any of you yet."

Four sets of gazes sharpened. Elwood had asked him to question his teammates without letting on as to why, but that was impossible. "I'm going to tell you something that doesn't go beyond this room." He was certain he could trust every man present to be utterly discreet. "Someone in the strike force placed a call on the sat phone in the area of the ship we occupied that night. Whoever it was called a cell phone in Carenero."

He looked at Theo and then Saul. "Was that either of you?"

Both men frowned and shook their heads.

"Could it have been *you?*" Master Chief gently suggested.

"Me?" Jonah blinked. "I don't know anyone in Venezuela," he said, though in all honesty he couldn't remember whether he did or didn't. "You guys know me," he reminded them. "Do you think I could be party to weapons smuggling?"

He was relieved when they all answered in the negative.

"Okay, then. So, if I didn't place the call, and neither of you did, that leaves the ops officer, one of the boat crew guys, or Lowery."

The men's skepticism seemed to waver. Leveraging his advantage, Jonah added, "Suppose Lowery had a reason for wanting me gone."

"Like what?" Saul prompted.

Jonah hesitated. "Eden said Lowery called her constantly after my disappearance. He even showed up at the house a couple of times."

The men looked startled to hear that—all except Master Chief.

"Maybe he wanted a chance with her," Jonah suggested. "If Lowery placed that phone call, he could have been warning the shooters we were on our way."

Master Chief's eyes narrowed. "You're saying Lowery wanted you out of the way badly enough to try and kill you? Just so he could have a shot with Eden?"

"No." Jonah gave one more thought to Elwood's precaution. "I'm saying Lowery might be leaking intel to The Entity." A chill of certainty raced over him as he awaited the men's reactions. "Maybe I was on to him. Maybe I confronted him, and he turned on me in order to keep me quiet. Now that I'm back, I'm a threat to him again."

Four sets of eyes regarded him with skepticism bordering on consideration. It was clear they wanted to believe him, only they couldn't overlook his disabled state.

Growing hot with frustration, Jonah sought to convey his certainty. "Look, since I've been back, I've sensed that I'm in danger. Elwood thinks so too, or he wouldn't be watching my house the way he's been doing." He caught himself from mentioning how a police car nearly ran him over, as that just sounded bizarre and completely unrelated. "If Lowery comes for me, I want to be ready. Anyone have a pistol they can loan me?" he finished on desperate note.

Saul put a hand on his arm. "I've got you covered, sir. I've got a spare Sig in my trunk."

"Thanks." Jonah pictured all the weapons he used to own. "Are my firearms still in my locker at Spec Ops?"

Everyone looked at Master Chief, who grimaced apologetically. "Your locker was emptied."

"On whose authority?" Jonah thought immediately of the CO.

"Dwyer," Master Chief confirmed.

Jonah gave a bitter grunt.

"Because he's retiring soon," Rivera added, quick to defend their leader. "He doesn't want to leave any loose ends for his replacement."

As conversation shifted to who might take their commander's place, Jonah fell into reflective silence. Master Chief's theory that they'd run into The Entity left Jonah wondering who they could be. Were they modern-day pirates selling their booty to the highest bidder? Whoever they were, they had a contact on the inside telling them where to find the goods.

It has to be Lowery, Jonah thought.

The more he thought of Lowery as the traitor, the more certain he became. As squad leader, Lowery had the authority to call for a retreat, getting the others out of the building which he would have known was about to be detonated. Once Saul and Theo weren't around to witness his attack, he had turned on Jonah—possibly just to keep him silent, possibly so he could have Eden to himself, enjoying Jonah's life insurance money to boot.

In other words—murder.

A humming filled Jonah's ears as his suspicions solidified. He glanced around the table, wondering if anyone could tell what he was thinking. Should he persist with his theory Lowery had tried to kill him, or had he said too much already?

Listening to his teammates' lighthearted banter, he decided he had said enough on the subject. Master Chief had made it clear the evidence was scanty.

Wiping perspiration from his brow, Jonah cursed the missing memories that made it impossible to connect the dots between LeMere's death and his own experience. Aware that his silence was likely being viewed as anti-social, he forced himself to rejoin the conversation regarding the Labor Day weekend, which was fast approaching.

"You're all invited to our place for an afternoon barbecue. I'll be done sanding and staining the deck by then."

The men accepted his offer with enthusiasm. Making plans to see each other then, they thanked Lucas for his hospitality and got up from the table. At the door, Lucas clasped Jonah's hand gently but firmly.

"We're keeping the oil lamps burning for you, sir." His gray eyes brimmed with compassion.

"Thank you," Jonah said, struck by the man's sincerity.

En route to their parked cars, Jonah glanced back at Lucas's modest townhome. A curtain twitching at a second-story window let him know Monica was watching their retreat, Jonah's in particular.

Saul led him over to the trunk of his midnight blue Camaro, where he displayed the arsenal he carried there, including his Weatherby hunting rifle and several pistols.

"You can have this one," he said, handing Jonah a Sig Sauer P226, neatly stored in a paddle holster. "She's about ten years old but as accurate as ever." Along with the pistol, Saul handed him extra ammo.

Dropping the ammo into his pocket, Jonah drew the pistol out of the holster and examined it.

"Nice," he said, feeling safer already.

"You need anything else, sir, just let me know." Saul's hazel eyes glinted in the darkness, reminding Jonah of all the nighttime ops they'd done together.

"Thanks, bro." Jonah clapped him on the back before heading toward Master Chief's antique Ford Falcon. The old clunker had been covered in primer for as long as Jonah could remember.

As they drove away, chasing Saul's taillights, Jonah ventured to ask, "Santiago, did you notice the way Monica behaved toward me?"

The whites of Rivera's eyes betrayed his sidelong glance. "I noticed," he said with a hint of disapproval.

Jonah wrestled with uncertainties regarding his own behavior. "You would tell me if I was ever...*friendly* with her, wouldn't you?" He was grateful to the darkness for hiding his furious blush.

Rivera chuckled. "Trust me, there's nothing to tell, Jaguar. Monica did her best to entice you, but she never succeeded."

Jonah didn't bother hiding his sigh of relief. "Thank God. I mean, I know I wasn't the best husband to Eden, but I'd have to have been out of my mind to cheat on her."

"You didn't cheat," Rivera assured him. "Monica doesn't know when to quit, that's all."

Jonah watched Saul's taillights disappear. "Doesn't Lucas mind that about her?"

"I don't think he's notices," Rivera replied with a shake of his head. "I've thought about pulling him aside, but it's not really my business whom he chooses to marry."

Jonah cut him a curious glance. "You didn't advise me not to marry Eden?"

"Why would I do that?" Rivera countered. "She's the best thing that could have happened to you."

"Yeah," Jonah agreed. Picturing her at their home, spending time with their daughter, his heart billowed like a sail filling with wind. Strange how he couldn't remember their first year together. At the same time, he was kind of glad he couldn't. He didn't want to think of himself ignoring Miriam or hurting Eden with his drive to be a SEAL first, a husband second.

"How are things between you two?" Rivera asked.

Jonah thought back to her kiss the other day, the way she'd held his hand at church. A hopeful smile tugged at his lips.

"Good, I think, though I screwed up this afternoon, acting jealous of Lowery. Eden didn't like that."

"You've no reason to be jealous of Lowery," Rivera assured him. "Eden's only got eyes for you."

"I hope you're right, Master Chief."

Rivera's smile reflected the light of his dashboard. "I told you, God's got your back, Jaguar. He's not going to let your marriage fall apart."

"When you stop to think about it, that's amazing," Jonah reflected.

In the past, he'd relied strictly on himself to make his future work out the way he wanted it to. And look how that had turned out. He'd alienated his wife and ignored his stepdaughter. Without God teaching him what a loving father looked like, he still wouldn't know how to treat either of them.

"It is amazing to be known and fully loved," Rivera agreed.

Jonah pictured everything working out. Then the cynic in him asked how that was going to happen. Eden had told him in no uncertain terms she was leaving in a year. A few gestures over a couple of days might mean nothing. Then, too, there was the question of whether Lowery was a traitor. How was Jonah supposed to prove the man had turned on him? Worse still, what if he went after him again?

"Do me a favor?" Jonah asked Rivera as they neared his home by the rear gate of the Navy base.

"Of course."

"Don't stop praying for me."

Rivera's curious look prompted him to add, "My psychologist thinks I have PTSD. So, either I do, or there's something evil coming for me."

The look of consternation he received only heightened Jonah's uneasiness.

"I won't stop," Rivera assured him. Turning into Jonah's driveway, he peered at the lights in the windows above him then over at Jonah. "We're all here to help," he added. "Don't think for one minute you're alone."

Jonah managed a wry smile for Santiago's diplomacy. The man had offered unqualified support without touching on the subject of Jonah's mental and emotional fragility.

"Thanks. And for the ride, too," he added, pushing out of the car.

The shrill ring of Bart Branson's cell phone startled the psychiatrist out of a deep sleep. He groped for the light switch as he came awake. Picking up his phone, he winced to see who was calling. Did Spitz ever sleep at normal hours? If the man hadn't given him a job, Bart would have let his call go to voice mail.

"Yes?"

"Barty." Spitz's voice was like the crack of a whip. "You were supposed to tell me when the patient's memories started to return."

Bart pictured the patient in question, the Navy SEAL who'd come to see him twice since his evaluation at the hospital. Poor Jonah Mills was looking a good deal better after a week back in the States. Being with his family again had done him a world of good, even if he couldn't remember his wife or daughter.

"They haven't yet," Barty defended himself. "I mean, he remembers fragments of his captivity, but nothing significant and nothing relevant to the mission. I thought that was all you cared about."

"He's remembering more than his captivity," Spitz insisted.

How do you know? Bart wanted to ask. "If that's true, I'm sure I'll hear about it. I'm due to meet with him Tuesday."

"Christ," the caller swore. "Not tomorrow? I thought you met three times a week."

"Twice a week works better for the wife. She has to drive him, you know, and she works."

"Fine. Find out on Tuesday exactly what he knows. Take notes, Barty. I want details."

"Of course." Bart would rather find out how Jonah was getting along with his wife, who'd told him they were going to separate. Family counseling was his passion, not trauma-related therapy. A recovering addict couldn't pick and choose the practice he wanted, however.

"I'll call you right after our consultation. That'll be about 5 o'clock," he promised.

"Don't call."

"Don't? But I thought you wanted to know—"

"I'm heading to Oceana for a meeting Tuesday afternoon. I'll swing by and pick up a copy of your notes then."

"Oh." It already rubbed Bart wrong to be sharing a patient's private information, but this was the military, where things worked differently than they did in the civilian sector. Apparently, a SEAL's chain of command had every right to pry into his medical records, especially if those same records dictated whether he was fit for active duty.

"Okay," Bart hesitantly agreed.

With a terse, "Don't disappoint me, Barty," Spitz hung up.

Thirty years had passed since they'd gone to school together. Spitz had gotten that nickname because he swam so fast, like the Olympic swimmer, Mark Spitz. Taller and better looking than Bart could ever hope to be, Spitz had been assertive and confident even in high school. All those years in the military—Special Forces, no less—had forged him into a man of steely determination, devoted to keeping the world safe. Above all else, he detested fanatics and terrorists.

Good thing, too, Bart thought. If Spitz weren't one of the good guys, he'd be a villain like no other.

Putting his phone down, Bart sank back against his pillows, thinking. If it were up to only him, Jonah Mill's therapy would involve every aspect of the patient's life, not merely his memories. His chain of command, however, seemed completely preoccupied with finding out what really happened the night he'd gone missing. Someone's head was going to roll when the truth came out and, apparently, that truth resided in Jonah Mills's brain, and it was Bart's unenviable job to pry it out of him.

Whether those memories were better off buried didn't seem to matter to Spitz. He was too busy holding back the tide of terrorism to concern himself with one man's well-being.

CHAPTER 14

*J*onah stood at the landing to his deck, admiring his and the kids' handiwork. Their objective for the day was accomplished, leaving him with an entire afternoon free. He vowed he wasn't going to sleep it away, either.

Renting an industrial sander had made short work of their project. In less than two hours, the entire deck had been stripped down to unfinished hardwood. Miriam and Ian had gone straight inside to enjoy their reprieve by playing video games. Jonah was at loose ends.

Glancing at the sky, he prayed the storm clouds hovering out over the ocean wouldn't dampen the pristine planks of the deck. He'd like to start staining it that very afternoon while Eden was at work.

The door opened, curtailing his inspection. Jonah's pretty wife stepped out of it wearing black workout capris, a pink tank top, and carrying her purse and water bottle. The realization she was headed out to teach dampened his spirits. He'd been hoping to spend a little time with her before she departed.

"You have to leave already?" he asked, checking his watch.

She crossed to where he stood and gestured at the sander standing at the base of the stairs. "I thought I could return it to the rental place before I go in."

"Not by yourself," he protested. "It weighs like eighty pounds."

She shrugged. "I'll get someone to help me."

He put a hand on his chest. "Hello, I'm right here."

"But the rental store is closer to the front gate, and I'd rather not drive all the way back home again. I'm sure there will be someone who can help me."

Jonah was sure of it, too. He had to laugh at his ridiculous jealousy.

"Just let me go with you," he pleaded. "I'll walk home from the base gym. That's not far at all."

All at once, he realized he would have to go without the pistol Saul had loaned him. Virginia was a right-to-carry state, but military bases were a different story.

I'll be okay, he assured himself. Lowery would be at work, and he'd keep a sharp eye out for any undercover cop cars trying to run him off the road—if that had even happened.

Swiping the hair out of her eyes, Eden considered him for a thoughtful moment.

"I guess the walk home would do you good," she relented.

He grinned at her. "That's your way of saying you'd love my company, right?"

Her lips wobbled toward a smile. "Go grab your wallet and your phone," she ordered in lieu of an answer. "You don't want to make me late."

"No, ma'am," he replied, hurrying inside to grab his things and to tell the teens he'd be back in an hour or so.

Delivering the rented sander back to the shop proved to be a satisfying, if not highly entertaining, outing.

"We should go on dates like this more often," Jonah teased after they'd dropped off the machine and were heading up General Booth Boulevard toward Dam Neck's front gate.

Eden shot him a distinctly torn look. "You're a lot more fun than you used to be," she surprised him by admitting.

He could only imagine. "I think I took life a little too seriously. Forgive me?" he asked. He'd kept his tone intentionally light but still held his breath as he waited for her answer.

She tore her gaze off the traffic to look at him. In her face, he read cautiousness but also a willingness to move forward. Her expression alone freed him to breathe.

"Sure," she said, keeping her reply to the bare minimum. Jonah slowly exhaled.

As they neared the gate, Eden asked Jonah if he knew where his troop members lived.

Jonah thought for a moment and realized he didn't remember. "I only know where Lucas lives," he admitted.

Eden nodded toward an elegant, gated community as they drove past the entryway. "Your CO lives in there," she said. "Saul lives close to Oceana in the cutest little bungalow from the 1930s. Theo and Bambino share a condo out on Chick's Beach."

"How do you know all this?" Jonah asked.

She cast him a wry smile. "They all had me over at one time or another the year you were gone."

"Even Commander Dwyer?"

"Well, yes, along with everyone else, for his Christmas party."

"Wow." Jonah made a mental note to thank everyone for looking after his wife. "I wish I could have been there."

Eden's grip on the steering wheel tightened. "Me, too," she said with surprising sincerity. "I hate the thought of you getting tortured, Jonah." Her voice turned gruff with emotion. "No one in the world should have to go through what you went through."

Seeing the tears well in her eyes, Jonah reached for her hand and squeezed it. The memory of her freely given kiss the day before emboldened him to lift her knuckles to his mouth and gently kiss them.

"I'm a survivor," he assured her.

He saw her visibly swallow and gently tug her hand back. Then again, maybe she needed it to turn the wheel as they came to the intersection bearing them toward Dam Neck.

By the time they approached the front gate, Eden had sent him two more surreptitious glances. *Was she reevaluating their relationship? Please, God.* In his mind, Jonah repeated the prayer he'd prayed the day before in her Jacuzzi tub.

He was pleased to see the base itself hadn't changed one iota from what he remembered.

"I'm a few minutes early," Eden remarked as they passed the mini shopping mall and turned into the parking lot at the base gym. "Would like a tour?" she offered. "We've added new equipment in the weight room since you were last here."

"Sure." Jonah's uneasiness returned as Eden parked and exited the vehicle. Sweeping a cautious look around them, Jonah followed her into the building.

She led him straight to the employee office where she dropped off her purse and introduced him to her colleague, Karen, who was on her way out.

Next, she showed Jonah the new gymnasium floor where he remembered shooting hoops with his teammates. A couple of men did a double take as they looked in his direction. One of them waved a hand in acknowledgment, and Jonah nodded in reply.

"Did I know that guy?" he asked Eden.

She glanced behind her on their way out. "Um, I'm not sure."

He trailed her to the weight room.

"Still smells the same," Jonah commented as they stepped through the door into the large, well-lit space.

"Check out the new...," Eden's voice abruptly faded.

Following her gaze, Jonah stiffened at the sight of James Lowery working on his triceps with the pulley machine.

At their entrance, Lowery looked over and froze. The muscles in Jonah's neck and shoulders clamped. As Lowery broke eye contact, Jonah backed out of the room, his heart thudding painfully fast.

"What's the matter?" Eden retreated with him.

"You'd better get ready for work," he said, unwilling to share his suspicions when she'd rejected them once already.

"But you haven't seen the updated locker room." She searched his face with concern.

"I need to head home." He said the first excuse that popped into his head. "Starting to get really tired."

Concern knitted her smooth forehead. "You sure you'll be okay? It's at least a mile to the back gate."

Self-disgust welled in him. "If I can't walk one stinking mile, then I'm no good to anyone," he growled.

The hurt that flashed across her face kept him from immediately turning his back on her. Instead, he dropped a quick kiss on her cheek.

"Thanks for the tour," he said, softening his tone, then he walked swiftly toward the exit.

Vulnerability ambushed him as soon as he stepped outside. *I have to get over this*, he thought, cutting across the baking hot parking lot in order to take the swiftest route home.

As he crossed the street then struck out across the field, he heard a car door shut behind him. A nondescript vehicle eased away from the gym, onto the street he was crossing.

It's not Lowery, Jonah thought. Nonetheless, he lengthened his stride, walking as fast as he could across the grassy expanse, at least two football fields in size. Out of the corner of his eye, he watched the car drive up the road away from him.

Shaking his head in disgust, Jonah looked the other way, in the direction of the ocean. The storm clouds were edging closer. He thought he detected a rumble in the distance, which meant his staining the deck would have to wait for another day.

Approaching Regulus Avenue, which would take him to his home by the back gate, he blinked as a clod of dirt flew up from the ground not a foot in front of him. Only for a split second did he freeze and question what he saw. In the next instant his training kicked in. *That's a bullet!* His brain screamed the warning, and Jonah broke for the nearest cover—the ditch that lay between him and the road.

Thoop. Thoop.

Two more bullets, fired from a suppressed rifle, drilled into the ground at his heels. He dove face-first into the damp ditch, his heart in his throat.

This can't be happening. It was broad daylight, for goodness sake!

Spitting dirt out of his mouth, Jonah peeked over the blades of grass on the rim of the ditch to locate his assailant. For an unnerving minute, he could see no one.

"Where are you?" Just imagining a shooter existed would have been a worse scenario than being shot at for real.

The glint of a watch gave the sniper away. *There you are.* A man who had to be Lowery hid behind the trunk of a loblolly pine, aiming a suppressed rifle at him. Jonah surmised he had driven around the far side of the field then pulled off into the picnic area there.

For the moment, the shooting had stopped. Lowery was waiting for Jonah to stand up again so he could nail him.

Helplessness steamrolled Jonah, making him crave the Sig Sauer he'd been forced to leave at home. Armed with a pistol, he could at least send Lowery running for cover. Then again, without a silencer like Lowery was toting, the military police would be on top of him in a heartbeat.

That's it—call the MPs!

Jonah was digging his cell phone out of his pocket when he changed his mind. The minute they pulled up, Lowery would withdraw. What Jonah would describe to the MPs would sound crazy. Of course, he could search the grass for the bullets to prove his story, but what if he didn't find them? Did he really want his CO hearing his allegations and concluding he did have PTSD, and it was out of control?

The sound of an approaching truck had Jonah craning his neck in the opposite direction. At the sight of a public works vehicle coming up Regulus, he squirmed out of his once-white T-shirt and waved it overhead like a soldier surrendering to the enemy.

Lowery wouldn't dare risk shooting someone other than Jonah, would he?

Praying that was the case, Jonah heard the truck decelerate. Brakes squealed as it came to a stop. The driver's door opened and footsteps preceded the shadow that fell over him.

Squinting up into the worried, weathered face of a public works employee, Jonah said simply, "Hey there."

"You all right?" The brawny man looked him over, clearly confounded. His gaze froze as it fell upon Jonah's scarred chest.

Jonah twisted his face into a pain-filled expression. "I think I twisted my ankle when I went to jump across the ditch."

"Well, darn." The stranger's eyes had filled with compassion. "I'll help you," he offered, leaping down into the ditch without a second's hesitation to lend a hand.

Praying Lowery was smart enough not to involve a stranger, Jonah talked the man into standing behind him as he helped him to his feet. It was all Jonah could do not to peer over his shoulder as the worker escorted him out of the ditch and up to the road.

"Can I take you somewhere?" the man asked.

"That'd be great." Jonah seized the opportunity for a ride while thanking God heartily for His well-timed intervention. "I live by the back gate."

"That's where I'm headed," the stranger insisted, escorting Jonah to the passenger door of his truck.

Once inside, Jonah ducked his head below the window while pretending to examine his ankle. Hope started to replace the dread coursing through his bloodstream.

"Think you broke it?" the driver asked, as he slipped behind the wheel and put the truck into drive.

"I don't think so." Jonah did not breathe easily until they'd cleared the gate and turned toward his house. By then, he'd put his filthy shirt back on.

"You need help with the stairs?" the man asked as he braked in Jonah's driveway.

"No, no. You've done enough," Jonah insisted. "Thank you so much." He pumped the stranger's hand profusely.

"Pleasure is mine," the good Samaritan replied. "Thank you for your service, sir," he added with a hint of moisture in his eyes. The scars on Jonah's chest had obviously affected him.

Jonah sent him a rueful smile. The man probably wouldn't feel so grateful should he discover he'd been used as a human shield.

Stepping carefully out of the truck, Jonah stood at the bottom of his steps and waited for the utility truck to disappear before dashing nimbly up the stairs, only to find the door locked. With a sigh and a nervous look around, he rang the doorbell and waited some more.

The day Eden gave him a key to the house he would finally be certain he was welcome here.

At last the door popped open.

"What happened to you?" Miriam gaped at his mud-and-grass stained shirt as he darted inside.

"You would never believe me," he muttered, heading straight to his study. There he shut the door behind him before retrieving the holster and pistol he'd been loath to leave behind.

His fingers trembled belatedly—not so much from shock as from rage.

Had Lowery seriously thought he could shoot Jonah in broad daylight and get away with it? Actually, with the streets so quiet and most Navy personnel at work, Jonah could have been struck by a bullet and lain in the grass for hours before anyone noticed him.

Outrage morphed into relief. *At least I know I'm not crazy,* Jonah thought. Almost immediately, he second-guessed himself. *Or am I?*

What if he'd made the whole thing up? Like his near-miss with the cop car, the scenario was possibly too outrageous to be true. Who would believe it if Jonah told them Lowery had fired three shots at him, right there on Regulus Avenue in the middle of a work week? No one.

With a whispered curse, Jonah crossed to the bathroom to shower. As he lathered the dirt off his body, he forced himself to recall the event, second by second, analyzing it for evidence it might have been a hallucination. Dr. Branson had let him know hallucinations were common with PTSD.

"No." Jonah shook his head. He could not have lost touch with reality to such a profound degree. He knew what had happened was real. Lowery had seen him leave the gym, and he'd seized the chance to finish what he'd left undone in Carenero.

Reassured by his conclusions, Jonah rinsed and turned off the water. He made up his mind right then not to share his story with another living soul—aside, perhaps, from Special Agent Elwood. That man might believe him. Naturally, Jonah's teammates would be skeptical. And Eden, who was only just starting to trust him, would have one less reason to give their marriage the chance it deserved.

Reaching for a towel, Jonah's gaze fell to the Sig sitting in its holster on the counter next to the sink. "Never leave home without it," he told himself sternly.

～

On her way to Miriam's bedroom the following afternoon, Eden passed the study and glimpsed Jonah sliding a pistol into a holster hanging from his belt. She jerked to a stop and stared at him in disbelief.

Catching sight of her, Jonah raised an eyebrow in slight defiance and cinched his belt one notch tighter. The jeans were fitting him better, but he still had some weight to gain.

"Where did you get that?" she demanded in a hushed but incredulous voice.

Tipping his head toward Miriam's bedroom, Jonah put a finger to his lips and gestured for them to talk elsewhere.

Eden huffed in exasperation and continued toward Miriam's closed door. Knocking as she entered, she found her daughter atop her bunkbed. Sabby, who lay at the foot of the ladder, sprang up at Eden's entrance.

"Honey, we're leaving now for Jonah's appointment. Are you finishing your reading?"

"Yes." Miriam peered down at her.

"Good girl." Eden stood on tiptoe for a kiss. "Please walk the dog as soon as you're done with your book. If Ian wants to come over here after that, that's okay, but no going to his house."

"Whatever."

Pursing her lips together, Eden decided Miriam's agreement, albeit grudging, was good enough. She left her daughter's room and found Jonah waiting in the foyer.

The sun he'd gotten while staining a portion of the deck that morning made him look especially vibrant and virile, causing Eden's pulse to quicken as she neared him. She told herself she was just nervous about the gun he was openly wearing.

"Ready?" she asked, letting him know with a look he had some explaining to do.

He opened the door for her, then stepped aside and watched her dig in her purse for the car keys.

"I don't suppose you've made a copy of the house key for me yet?" he prompted, reminding her of his request the other day.

"Not yet," she said tersely, then turned to descend the stairs.

"We could stop at a hardware store and make a copy."

"We could," she replied noncommittally as she slipped into the driver's seat of the Jaguar.

Ever since Sunday at the restaurant, she'd been waiting for God to give her a clear sign regarding the change in Jonah. On one hand, he was attentive, considerate, and helpful around the house. On the other, the more strength he gained, the more she could sense his energy building. A huge part of her feared it was only a matter of time before the man who'd come home from the hospital, all vulnerable and amenable, would disappear. He was already back to wearing a weapon.

"So, what's with the gun?" she demanded, the instant he shut his own door.

"It's Saul's." Jonah's voice held a soothing tenor to it. "He's letting me borrow it."

"Why?" Eden was aware her own voice, by contrast, sounded sharp. She sought to temper her agitation as she backed out of the driveway and pointed them in the direction of Oceana Naval Air Base. Jonah was hardly a novice where firearms were concerned. He was an expert, in fact, and his owning them never posed a problem for her in the past.

When he didn't immediately answer, Eden glanced over at him only to find him deep in thought.

"What?" she prompted, looking back at the narrow road.

"I have something to tell you."

His tone alone made her stomach tighten. "Go ahead." Deep ditches on either side kept her from looking at him again.

"The NCIS investigator, Elwood, thinks there's a traitor in Blue Squadron. Someone's been disclosing the whereabouts of certain weapons to a third party. Those same weapons have been disappearing in advance of our interdictions, taken by someone we've nicknamed The Entity."

Eden processed the information with gathering confusion.

"I think I might have known who the traitor is. I think I might have confronted him, and I think he might have tried to have me killed."

"What?" The bizarre assertions struck her as unbelievable. "When?"

"A year ago when the warehouse exploded and again yesterday."

"What?" She glanced at him incredulously. Was that why he'd locked himself in his study most of the evening, emerging only once to join them for supper? Eden had assumed he'd been sleeping. "What happened yesterday?"

Jonah hesitated. "You're not going to believe me," he said almost morosely.

Eden wrung the steering wheel and drew a deep breath. "Just tell me," she pleaded.

He drew in an audible breath. "Remember how we ran into Lowery at the gym?"

She pictured the tense moment when Jimmy caught sight of them.

"He's the traitor in the squadron. He hit me in the face with the butt of his rifle and left me to die, knowing The Entity was going to blow up the warehouse."

Stunned, Eden processed the information, acknowledging that some of it made sense.

"But if you can't even remember, how do you know it was him?"

"I know because he fired three shots at me yesterday while I was walking home," he grated almost reluctantly.

She laughed out loud at the unlikely scenario, glanced over at Jonah, and, seeing his taut expression, abruptly sobered.

"Sorry," she immediately apologized. He looked tense enough to pop a gasket.

"I told you that you wouldn't believe me," he stated.

She forced herself to contemplate his allegations more closely.

"Why am I just hearing about this now? If someone fired shots at you on base, wouldn't the MPs have gotten involved?"

"Lowery's rifle was suppressed. Nobody heard it being discharged. He would have hit me if I hadn't dived into a ditch. I hailed the first vehicle to come along and got a ride home."

Eden fought to conceal her skepticism as she pictured the unlikely scene Jonah had described.

"Why didn't anybody see him?" she inquired.

"You know that picnic area near the gym? He fired from there, behind the tree line."

"I see." She tried almost desperately to believe him, but the scenario was so far-fetched. "You're saying Jimmy is the traitor selling information to The Entity?"

"Yes." Jonah's tone became remote.

Eden envisioned Jimmy taking such risks and shook her head. "I just can't see that," she protested. "He doesn't have it in him to undermine the system. He's not an independent thinker. He does what he's told—even if a woman tells him to do it. He's a pushover."

Out of the corner of her eye, she realized she had Jonah's full attention.

"How do *you* know that?"

If he'd asked with accusation in his tone, she'd have slammed on the brakes and told him to walk the rest of the way, but he merely sounded curious.

"Because he backed off when I told him I wasn't interested. Someone gutsy enough to betray his own troop wouldn't take no for an answer."

Her words rendered Jonah mute.

When she glanced at him again, he was staring out the passenger window, his jaw muscles jumping.

"Do you see what I'm saying?" she asked, wishing he would talk.

He turned his head, caught her eye, then looked at the road ahead of them. It had widened to two lanes, with businesses on either side.

"Pull over a second," he requested. "This next parking lot," he said, pointing to the entrance they were nearing.

"Why?" she demanded, glancing at the clock. "We're already late."

"Just do it," he insisted.

To her amazement, he reached over and grabbed the steering wheel, as if to maneuver the car into the lot himself. Eden braked and grudgingly pulled off the road into the lot. Stopping under the shade of a tree, she threw the car into park.

"Are you crazy?" she demanded, whipping off her sunglasses to look at him.

He leaned abruptly toward her, pinning her with his gold-green gaze.

Warning sirens went off in Eden's head as he caught the side of her face with his lean fingers, forcing her to hold his gaze even though his touch was gentle.

"Please don't call me crazy," he said very seriously and with a hint of hurt. "I have been through a lot, but I am not crazy."

"I didn't mean *crazy* in that way," she amended breathlessly.

Jonah's face being so close to hers made her heart beat erratically. Her gaze darted toward his lips as the desire to be kissed competed with dread.

"It's okay," he said, surprising her with his acceptance. "It's also fine that you don't believe me about Lowery. I wouldn't believe it myself if I hadn't been there. I do, however, need you to believe in my instincts. They're telling me I'm in danger. Can you believe that much?"

Eden nodded automatically. His thumb, tracing the line of her jaw, distracted her. It slid to her chin and over the cleft there, reversing the breath in her windpipe as he applied pressure, forcing her lips to part. An awareness-filled tension enveloped them as his gaze locked on her mouth.

In Jonah's expanding pupils, Eden could see a twin-reflection of herself, all wide-eyed in expectation of his kiss.

In the next instant, he dipped his head and pressed his lips to hers, drawing a whimper out of her. It wasn't at all like the prim kiss she had offered him the other day. This was hot and intense and it made her toes curl.

Help me, she prayed, not sure what she was praying for. At the same time, her lips softened in welcome under his.

A sound between pleasure and pain grated in Jonah's throat as their kiss deepened and their tongues twined.

Eden's head spun. She found her fingers in his hair, keeping him from pulling back, urging him to continue his advance.

Heaven help her, no wonder she had married him before truly getting to know him. The way he made her feel—so beautiful, so connected—was exquisite, perfect. If he could only kiss her forever and stop talking of treason and conspiracies.

Arching unconsciously, she anticipated the heat of his hand as it traveled from her hip, to the indent of her waist, and higher.

Without warning, Jonah withdrew. Pressing himself back into the passenger seat, he drew deep, measured breaths while scanning the area around him with watchful eyes. Did he expect Lowery to spring out of hiding and attack them?

With heart-wrenching insight, Eden realized this must be PTSD manifesting itself. Dr. Branson had warned her Jonah's PTS might manifest itself as the full-blown disorder. Flustered and confused, pitying him and wishing he could forget his fears and kiss her again, she stifled a sound of lament with a hand to her mouth.

"Sorry," Jonah muttered, avoiding her stricken gaze.

Not as sorry as she was. The realization of how profoundly damaged he was had ripped the rug of hope right out from under her. She had started thinking their marriage stood a chance. How could it, though, with Jonah convinced Jimmy was out to kill him? He wore a loaded gun, for heaven's sake, and looked like he would use it if the wrong person happened to walk up to their car.

Without a word, Eden reached for the gear shift and put it into drive. Clutching the steering wheel as if it were a life preserver, she drove them out of the parking lot as fast as she could without drawing attention to themselves. She could not get to the psych clinic on Oceana fast enough.

At this juncture, Jonah's psychiatrist was probably the only person in the world who could help him regain his equilibrium.

~

"Have you remembered anything new, Jonah?"

Dr. Branson's point-blank question was meant to draw Jonah out of his shell. Remembering Special Agent Elwood's advice to not trust anyone, Jonah shared a couple of memories that had returned to him, both to do with his captivity, neither having to do with the mission.

As he spoke, his thoughts returned to the kiss he and Eden had shared. However blissful, the kiss could not obliterate the look of panic on Eden's lovely face after telling her his suspicions of Lowery. He'd wanted her to understand why he'd armed himself with a pistol. He'd wanted her to understand why he felt a constant and encroaching threat. Instead, she'd concluded he had made up the story about Lowery shooting at him, which meant she thought Jonah a paranoid mess.

Worse was the nagging doubt that he might have imagined the whole episode, along with his close brush with the undercover cop car.

"I'm not crazy am I, Doc?" Jonah glanced at the doctor's face in time to catch his startled reaction.

"Why would you ask that?"

"Just answer the question," Jonah exhorted. "You said you think I might have PTSD. Do you think I'm a danger to myself? To society?"

The psychiatrist's thick eyebrows pulled together in a confounded look Jonah was fast coming to recognize.

"That's not my impression, no," Dr. Branson said slowly. "But then I don't know you very well. You're not exactly forthcoming with me."

Jonah chuckled humorlessly at the irony of his situation.

"Sorry." He pitied the man for being stuck with him.

"What about the mission, Jonah, or the year prior to that? Have any of those memories resurfaced?"

Considering the doctor a moment, Jonah could tell the man was earnest in wanting to help him.

"What's it going to take for you to clear me for active duty, Doc?" he asked. "Do I have to get all my memories back, or can I be cleared based on other criteria?"

Dr. Branson appeared to be caught off guard by the question. "That's not strictly up to me, I don't think."

"I was told my doctors would advise my CO of my progress. What have you told him?" Jonah persisted.

His question prompted a deer-in-the-headlights stare. "Well, nothing yet. Your treatment has barely begun, Jonah."

At the depressing answer, Jonah jackknifed to his feet and crossed to the window to peer outside.

Given the angle of the doctor's office, he could just make out the back of the Jaguar. The faint spume of exhaust coming out of the tailpipe let him know Eden, who said she would come inside to wait, was still in the car with the air-conditioner running. He'd stowed the Sig under the passenger seat as they were entering the base. She wouldn't toss it into some dumpster while his back was turned, would she? He could tell she didn't like him having it.

"How are things going with your wife?"

Dr. Branson's sincere-sounding question brought Jonah's head around.

"She thinks I'm paranoid," he muttered. He immediately kicked himself for saying that much.

"Why would she think that?"

Jonah crossed his arms at the predictable question and dropped his chin, thinking. He couldn't afford to mention his suspicions of Lowery. Instead, he brought up the incident with the undercover cop car.

"You think he actually tried to run you over?" Branson appeared intrigued by the story.

"Sure looked that way to me," Jonah retorted.

The doctor nodded thoughtfully, prompting Jonah to add that he thought some foes intended to break into his house the other night, but it was only his teammates, stringing up a welcome home sign.

"Hmmm." The doctor grimaced and nodded. "Don't be too hard on yourself. After a year of captivity, you're conditioned to expect a threat. The imbalance between the neurotransmitters' serotonin and substance P continues to make you feel a threat is imminent. That's why your meds are so important. They'll help you to reestablish that delicate balance."

"Sertraline makes me fall asleep," Jonah pointed out. "I want to go off it."

Branson flinched. "Not a good idea. You need to be patient," he urged. "You've been taking your meds for less than two weeks. Finding the balance I mentioned takes time. Whatever you do, do not stop the Sertraline."

Better not admit to quitting the Prazosin, Jonah figured.

"Perhaps I should talk to Eden," Dr. Branson offered, "and explain what I'm telling you. That way she'll be more patient with your recovery."

Jonah glanced bleakly out the window. "I don't think she's in the mood for a visit today."

"Did you get to visit a place you'd been before?"

"Yes, we went to a restaurant we used to frequent after church."

"And?" Branson prompted.

Jonah couldn't discuss the experience without bringing up his suspicions of Lowery.

"It helped," he said shortly. "Look, I don't have anything new to add. Eden's upset with my paranoia. I need to spend time with her right now and make things right between us."

Smoothing a hand over his nearly empty notepad, Dr. Branson heaved a soundless sigh.

"Very well. If you want to mend fences with Eden, and you feel it's urgent, then go." He lifted appealing eyes at Jonah. "But if it *is* up to me to recommend your return to active duty, you'll have to work with me harder at some point."

Jonah faced the doctor with an incredulous look.

"Are you blackmailing me?" He laughed at the absurdity of his situation.

Dr. Branson visibly blanched. "Heavens, no. I just want you to recover," he insisted.

Jonah wanted to believe him. On one hand, the psychiatrist seemed to be a genuinely caring individual. On the other, Elwood had advised Jonah not to trust him. So, for now, Jonah had no choice but to remain aloof and hope Elwood knew what he was doing.

The only other possibility made Jonah rake his fingers through his hair. His suspicions of Lowery could be a figment of his imagination. If that were the case, Dr. Branson would never clear Jonah for active duty, and Eden would grow weary of his paranoia and eventually leave him, just as she'd originally intended.

∼

In the middle of her conversation with Nina, Eden's phone chimed, signaling an incoming call. She peeked at her screen to see who it was.

"Oh, gosh, my father's calling again. I can't keep ignoring him."

"Go ahead and chat with him," Nina urged. "I have a class coming in anyway. Just promise me you'll follow your head and not your heart."

"I'll try," Eden said, but her heart had started to settle on the idea of making her marriage good again. Not even Jonah's paranoid thoughts about Jimmy could eradicate the hope that had been building in her. "Talk to you later."

Ending her call with Nina, she answered the incoming one.

"Hi, Dad."

"Finally," he said by way of a greeting. "I've only called you three times."

"I know. I'm sorry. We've been really busy."

"I can imagine." Her father's tone turned forgiving. "How's Jonah doing? I still can't believe he's back from the dead."

"Me neither." Eden relived her amazement. "He's doing pretty well," she answered. "He gets stronger every day."

Closing her eyes, she wished her relationship with her father was such that she could express her concerns and receive comfort, in turn. But they hadn't talked like that since she'd found herself with child in college.

"I hear he's having memory problems."

She didn't bother to ask how her father knew that. Vice Admiral Leland, the former base commander, was a lifelong friend of his.

"He remembers his captivity, now," she said a tad defensively.

"Poor bastard," her father muttered with feeling. "Why don't you bring him up this way while he's got time on his hands? We would love to see him."

Eden rolled her eyes. Her father was fonder of Jonah than he was of his own flesh and blood.

"I don't know if that's a good idea." For one thing, her parents would stick her and Jonah in the same bedroom, and he might accidentally choke her again. Or make love to her.

She swallowed against a suddenly dry mouth.

"Why not?" Her father started to browbeat her. "It'd be good for him to see the Academy again. Might stir some memories, get him back on track."

She pictured the Jonah she'd married, right there in the Academy's stone chapel. God forbid a visit to his old stomping grounds turned him back into the man he'd been before. At least the old Jonah hadn't suffered paranoid delusions that someone wanted to kill him. Maybe getting away from this area was exactly what he needed. Because he remembered Annapolis, he would probably feel whole there—whole and safe. Maybe that was the first step in getting over what had happened to him.

"I'll talk to him about it," she promised. "Perhaps we can come this weekend."

"That would be terrific." Her father's tone made it sound like a done deal.

"I'm not promising anything," Eden cautioned. "Jonah might not feel up to a visit."

"He'll want to come, I'm sure of it. Get back to me as soon as you can."

"Okay, Dad." Seeing movement in her mirror, Eden realized Jonah was rounding the car. "I have to go now," she added, hanging up abruptly. The next instant, he dropped into the passenger seat and shut the door.

"That was fast," she said.

He regarded her inquiringly. "Who were you talking to?"

"My father. He wants us to visit Annapolis this coming weekend."

"Hmm." Jonah swung a thoughtful look out the window. "Any chance you can take off work tomorrow?"

"You mean go up to Annapolis during the week?"

"If you can get away," he said.

"But what about your appointment on Thursday with Dr. Branson?"

"I'll miss it."

Eden didn't like the thought of that. "Jonah, you need help," she said as gently as possible.

A bitter smile twisted Jonah's mouth. "I think we should leave town for a while," he countered. At the same time, he bent to check that the pistol he'd hidden under his seat was still there.

A feeling akin to panic spurred Eden's heartrate. The article she'd read on PTSD had described the effects snowballing, and Jonah seemed more paranoid by the moment.

All at once, she felt incapable of handling her situation alone. Her parents weren't exactly the best people to turn to for advice but, apart from Nina, who else could help her navigate these waters? For some reason, God wasn't answering her prayers. Or, if He was, He was answering them with silence.

"I think I can get time off," she stated, making up her mind. "One of my colleagues was just saying she needed to make more money to pay for her son's tuition. I'll ask if she can cover my Thursday class."

"Let's do it, then. We'll go tomorrow." He seemed ready to take off right then and there.

Suddenly, Eden's phone gave a ring, visibly startling them both.

Eden frowned at the unfamiliar number, then answered on speaker phone so Jonah could listen, "Yes, hello?"

"Mrs. Mills?"

"Yes?" The male voice on the other end was unknown to her. She glanced at Jonah to gauge whether he recognized it.

"This is Officer Hammond with the Virginia Beach Police Department. I have your daughter here at the Seaside Market."

Eden and Jonah's gazes locked in surprise.

"I happened to catch her trying to buy cigarettes. Of course, that's not legal under the age of eighteen. How old is your daughter?"

Disappointment hit Eden like a fist to the stomach. She'd really thought Miriam was done acting out. "She's almost fifteen."

"Well, I'll release her this one time with a warning. You'll want to keep closer tabs on her from now on."

"Of course. You're absolutely right. Thank you," she said, hanging up. With a whimper, she met Jonah's gaze again and braced herself for his reaction.

To her amazement, he smiled encouragingly and said, "It's not the end of the world."

Unanticipated tears rushed into Eden's eyes. She had not expected Jonah's consolation and support, especially when he was so vulnerable. And in the past, he would have reacted the way most men in the military reacted, with bluster and threats of dire punishment.

Seeing her tears, Jonah stopped her from reaching for the shifter. "Wait a sec. Don't drive just yet. Why do you think she's doing this?"

Eden let him keep hold of her hand. It came as such a relief to share Miriam's struggles with an interested party.

"I don't know. She's done this kind of thing all her life, from shoplifting to punching a boy at school. More recently she pierced one ear all the way up the back."

"I noticed."

"The day we came to the hospital to get you, she dyed her hair mauve. Now she's buying cigarettes."

"Sounds to me like she's looking for attention."

Eden sighed and nodded. "I know. I'm trying to spend more time with her."

"Not from you," Jonah corrected, stroking her knuckles with his thumb.

Eden's stomach cartwheeled at the caress.

"You're a good mother, Eden. Don't take this the wrong way, but I think she needs more. I think she needs a father, too."

Given Jonah's gentle tone and the connection they were sharing at the moment, it was impossible to take offense. But, at the same time, she added another variable to her equation of marital uncertainty—Miriam needed a father. If Jonah was out of touch with reality, could he really fulfill that need?

"I know," she admitted.

"Let's not punish her," Jonah suggested. "I'm sure being caught by a police officer will deter her from buying cigarettes again."

"Oh, she'll think she's being punished when we take her to see my folks," Eden countered.

Jonah cocked his head. "Why's that?"

"Because they're strict and old-fashioned and they don't exactly treat her with respect."

Jonah looked shocked. "Why not?"

Eden's throat constricted. "Because she's illegitimate." It surprised her to hear herself telling Jonah something so personal. Stricken with PTSD or otherwise, he was so easy to talk to these days.

"That's not fair." His green-gold eyes blazed with righteous anger.

Was he faking his affront, or did he really care so deeply about Miriam's feelings?

"It is what it is," she said, swallowing the lump in her throat.

"You want me to drive?" Jonah offered.

Taking in his crooked smile, Eden had to laugh. His reasonable reaction to Miriam's situation and his efforts to cheer her them both heartened her. Looking down at their hands, which were still joined, she marveled at how capable and manly his hand appeared, stunted fingernails, scars, and all.

"Thank you," she said, pulling her hand gently from his gasp and shifting into reverse. "I'm good now," she added, though she wasn't really.

Jonah's reappearance had flipped her life upside down and inside out. She'd gone from wanting a divorce to thinking maybe Jonah was a new man, born again in the Spirit. For the first time ever, she and Jonah were on the same team where Miriam was concerned.

Yet the hope their marriage might survive was such a fragile one, threatened by his memory issues and, most especially, by what looked like PTSD.

How could he believe Jimmy Lowery had tried to kill him twice now? She resisted the urge to shake her head.

Since God seemed to be keeping silent, maybe she could ask her father to assess Jonah's allegations and advise her as to the severity of her husband's delusions. One way or the other, she needed to know if she should recommit herself to Jonah, or if she should proceed with her plans to separate.

At the end of a long day's work, Nina locked the door of *Inspired to Dance*, securing it against break-ins. The strip mall in which her studio was located wasn't exactly the safest of locations, and there'd been robberies at some of the other businesses.

Her vehicle, a twenty-year-old Honda, was parked five steps from the door. She made her way to it, cutting a casual glance to the right and to the left.

At eight o'clock in the evening, the August sun had yet to set, lending her confidence. She liked the summer months for exactly that reason. But autumn was fast approaching, and soon she'd be running from her studio to her car, using the remote to open the driver door, so she could leap inside and lock it again.

Honestly, being single was scary at times. Having to work until evening most nights of the week, plus half a day on Saturday, took a toll on her physically and emotionally. On the other hand, she'd once been married to a husband who refused to let her work, who'd stripped her of her confidence. She far preferred being independent to wearing the chains of matrimony.

Sliding fluidly into her car, Nina shut herself into the stiflingly hot interior, slid her key into the ignition and turned it. Nothing happened.

She turned the key again—still nothing. Was the gear in park? Had she left the lights on and used up the battery? No and no. In all likelihood, the old Honda, with nearly two-hundred thousand miles on it, had simply died on her. The aging car had been a source of concern more than once. She'd known she needed to replace it with something more reliable. But did this really have to happen now? Here?

Sweating copiously in the sundress she wore over her leotard, she pushed out of her car to escape the sauna-like heat, leaving her purse on the passenger seat. Sweeping the area for shady characters—they tended to visit the liquor store two doors down from her studio—she popped the hood before shutting her door. What she hoped to discover by peering under it, she had no idea. She didn't know the least thing about automobile engines. She'd been too busy over the years running a business to learn anything else.

It took her almost a full minute to figure out how to prop her hood open. Praying no one was witnessing her incompetence, Nina glanced around again. This time, she caught sight of a man standing in the shadows just outside of the Greek fast food restaurant.

As she bent over the engine, eyeing the myriad of mechanisms, she watched the stranger from the corner of her eye leave his post and venture in her direction. Her heart started to thud and, having just identified the battery, which looked all right to her, she straightened to face the unknown entity. Would he help? Or were his intentions dishonorable?

A gasp of astonishment filled her lungs as she recognized the stranger as none other than the man who'd haunted her every waking thought from the moment she'd met him.

"Santiago." She greeted him with all the poise that she could muster, swiping the hair casually out of her eyes.

"Nina," he countered, mirroring her small, somewhat ironic smile. Having been watching her for a while, however, he had her at a distinct disadvantage. While she was still flustered, her heart beating erratically at his unexpected apparition, he was calm and collected.

His eyes, a deep chocolate brown and rimmed with thick lashes, drifted lingeringly over her before settling on the engine of her car. "Having car trouble?"

Just as she remembered, his intonation betrayed the barest suggestion of his Puerto Rican roots.

"It won't start," she admitted, drinking in his appearance.

He was still dressed in his work attire, a blue and gray patterned uniform with a matching woven belt and calf-high boots. The sleeves of his jacket had been rolled to his biceps, baring his lean muscles and weakening her knees.

The bag of takeout he carried in his left arm explained his reason for being there. Pure coincidence, right? He couldn't possibly know where she worked.

"Perhaps it's the alternator," he suggested. "Or the battery. May I look?" He gestured at her engine.

"Please." She stepped aside, giving him leave to peer under the hood.

With his free hand, he delicately touched one component and then another, inspecting each with a keen eye. Nina's gaze hung on his arresting profile. From his expressive eyebrows, to his aquiline nose, to his mobile lips, he utterly appealed to her.

"Ah," he said, breaking the silence fraught with awareness. "Here's your problem."

Finding the bag still in his left arm, he added, "Hold this for me?"

As their hands brushed in the trade-off, Nina could have sworn sparks ignited, fueling her pulse. He clearly felt it, too, his gaze jumping to hers before he turned his attention back to the engine. As he ducked under the hood, working a small component loose, her gaze trekked from his lean waist to his firmly planted feet. She had to remind herself to breathe.

He's just a man. An ordinary man with expectations you wanted nothing to do with, she reminded herself.

"Here's the culprit," he said, straightening with a small plug in his hand.

"What is it?" she asked, revealing her abysmal knowledge of cars.

"It's a spark plug with a faulty wire. This is a sub-standard part, bound to give out on you. Who works on your car?"

She thought back to the last time she'd had repair work done and named the garage.

He gave a skeptical hum. "I know an excellent mechanic, who drives his own tow truck. Why don't I call him for you and he'll pick up your car tonight? I imagine he can have all the spark plugs replaced by tomorrow."

Nina pictured the sum she'd been hording in her savings account dwindling. At this rate, she'd never have a baby.

"I guess I don't have much choice," she muttered.

Santiago's small smile was encouraging. "It'll be okay."

Pulling out his cell phone, he dialed his mechanic.

As she listened to him relay her need for a tow and a repair, she decided her situation could have been worse. Imagine if Santiago hadn't come along. She'd still be staring at her engine, paralyzed by uncertainty. She supposed there were occasional moments when it was good to have a man around.

"Thank you," she told him as he hung up. Handing his food back to him, she released him to continue on his way.

"My pleasure. John says he can be here within the hour. Just leave the key and your contact info under the driver's seat, and you can leave. I'll give you a lift home."

The unexpected offer unsettled her. "Oh, no thanks. I'll stay until he gets here," she decided. "And then I'll catch an Uber."

Santiago's pleasant smile wavered. Reconsidering the bag in his arm, he said, "Would you have dinner with me until then? I've got enough for an army here."

Having been subject to the aroma of savory beef coming out of the bag, her mouth watered at the invitation. She surprised herself by saying, "Okay, but will you promise not to mention marriage?"

He laughed self-consciously. "I'm very sorry for that. I don't often drink, and the beer must have gone straight to my head."

She propped her hands on her hips. "Oh, I see. So it had nothing to do with me." *Stop it! Stop flirting with him.*

He flirted right back. "Okay, I admit it wasn't the beer. Your grace and beauty led me to temporary insanity."

"As long as it doesn't happen again," she warned.

He just looked at her, making no such promise.

Nina eyed the bag of food. "Do you mind eating in my studio?" She gestured to the building.

His surprise appeared a bit overdone. "Oh, do you work here?"

He clearly knew the answer already. Only one person could have told him that—Eden!

Cautioning herself to be on her guard, Nina didn't bother with an answer.

She collected her purse and led the way inside, flipping on the lights and locking the door behind them.

"This is where the parents wait," she explained, pointing out the various spaces. "The dressing room and bathrooms are over there. Here, I sell dance paraphernalia. My office is where I do my accounting. And the studio is in the back." She pointed to a set of double doors.

"Do you own or rent?" Santiago asked with seeming interest.

"Own." She indicated the tiny bistro table by the windows. As he pulled wrapped gyros out of the bag, she dashed to her office for some paper plates.

"Now, we can be civilized," she said.

To her bemusement, he held her seat for her.

"Thank you," she mumbled as he pushed it in, then sat across from her.

"Do you teach any adult classes?" he inquired as he took his first bite.

"I have a few adults in my advanced ballet classes. Why, do you want to learn to dance?"

"I would love to learn ballroom dancing. Don't tell anyone I said that until I retire," he added lightly.

"You're an excellent dancer." She recalled how they'd stolen the show on salsa night at the brewery.

"I would love to dance with you again."

His impassioned statement shortened her breath. She forced herself to take a bite of the gyro he'd laid out for her, to chew, and to swallow it.

"I'm afraid that won't happen," she answered apologetically.

A taut silence fell between them until Santiago broke it.

"Not all men are like your ex-husband," he stated unexpectedly.

Nina's eyes flew wide. "I see Eden's been talking to you. How much did she tell you?"

"Very little," Santiago soothed. "Just that you'd been mistreated."

Her face flamed, making her grateful for her Mediterranean coloring.

"I don't need or want your pity," she informed him.

He smiled the tiniest of smiles. "Good. I'm not interested in pitying you. I simply want to get to know you better."

Suddenly less ravenous, Nina put her gyro down. She wished she hadn't taken him up on his offer to share his supper.

"There's really no point," she forced herself to say. "I really can't...give you what you're looking for." The words wanted to stick in her throat.

"You can't enjoy a picnic on the beach with me?"

She knew he wanted more than that, yet he sent her such an innocent, appealing look she had to laugh.

"You're a manipulative creature," she accused.

"Of course I am." He admitted the truth with a self-deprecatory nod. "Years of practice making men do what I want without browbeating them."

The reminder of what he did for a living sobered her. She wished he weren't so terribly appealing to her. His quick wit, his sense of humor, his humility and gentlemanly behavior all conspired to make her want to spend time with him. But what would that accomplish?

Eventually he would ask her to marry him—provided she didn't scare him away first. And Nina had zero desire to shackle herself to another husband.

Her ex had been a Turk from the old country, with values that relegated women to mere chattel. Santiago may seem kind and amenable now, but he, too, was from a male-centric culture. No doubt, once she knew him well enough, she would see his true stripes. Right now, all she saw was what he wanted her to see.

"I'm sorry." She stuck to her guns. "I'm not interested in a relationship."

His smile faded. The sparkle went out of his eyes. She felt like she'd reached out and pinched him.

"Please don't look at me that way," she said when he kept quiet.

He looked down at his half-finished food for a minute, then back up at her.

"Please reconsider," he requested. "I can move as slowly as it takes for you to learn to trust me. There is no other woman in the world I want to spend time with more than you. Please don't take hope from me."

His plea cracked the thick layer of ice around her heart.

"Come enjoy a picnic on the beach with me one evening," he added when she continued to look at him, weakening by the second. "What about tomorrow? I'll pick you up right here after work."

"I teach every evening until eight. That's too late for a picnic."

"Saturday afternoon, then."

Nina couldn't think of an excuse to avoid the invitation. Eden had texted her with a request to pet sit for the next few days, but the dog could certainly stay by itself for a few hours.

"Leave me your number," she decided without much grace. "I'll text you and let you know if I'm free."

His eyes softened, then crinkled at the corners in a private smile.

"Good enough." With impressive efficiency, he dug a pen and a notepad out of the breast pocket on his jacket.

"You won't regret saying yes," he promised, scribbling down his number.

She wasn't so sure of that. As she eyed the number on the slip of paper, it occurred to her that she was under siege. With a Navy SEAL scaling her walls, her safe existence was about to be tested.

CHAPTER 15

*S*etting the table in her parents' formal dining room, Eden paid scant attention to her mother's soliloquy. Fortunately, Elke Evans required a minimum of feedback to keep a conversation flowing, and Eden's lack of response had gone unnoticed.

"We heard from Phoebe yesterday," Elke continued from within the kitchen. Through the wide opening connecting the two rooms, Eden saw her stick her head into the oven to read the meat thermometer. "She and Rick are coming for Thanksgiving this year with the kids. I told her you and Jonah would be here, too."

Eden rolled her eyes. It hadn't even occurred to her mother to ask if they had other plans.

Nor did her mother mention Miriam.

"Another half an hour on this ham," Elke determined, closing the oven and straightening to her full height. Whether from the heat in the kitchen or the pure pleasure of seeing Jonah again, Elke glowed. Taller than both her daughters, the native German looked nowhere close to her sixty-three years. In celebration of Jonah's resurrection, she had thrown herself into preparing a veritable feast.

Eden hesitated over the silverware she was pulling from the buffet. What if she and Jonah weren't even together at Thanksgiving? If he reverted suddenly to the man he was before, or if his delusions proved too much for her to handle, it could mean an end to the fragile bond they'd created. Her parents would be crushed, of course.

She heaved a sigh. What else was new? The only time she'd ever met their expectations was when she'd married Jonah.

"What's Phoebe up to these days?" she asked. She hadn't spoken to her perfect, older sister in months. Phoebe, who had married a lawyer and begotten two handsome boys, reminded Eden of her shortcomings.

As her mother filled her in, Eden turned toward the cherry-wood dining table to lay sterling silver utensils on either side of the china plates. In the center of the table, a bouquet of roses basked in the light pouring through the paned window. The roses made Eden think of her wedding day two years earlier and the hopefulness that had been in her heart.

How strange to realize she felt that same way now!

If only Jonah wasn't suffering from what looked like PTSD.

Coming to the end of the table, Eden raised her eyes and caught Jonah's reflection in the mirror. He sat beyond the living room in the glassed-in sunroom at the back of the house. Through the large panes beyond him, the immaculate lawn of the Georgian home swept down to the Severn River.

From where he sat, she could see his expression as he followed her father's words. By now she had expected he would assume his military demeanor—a narrow-eyed, thin-lipped look her father never failed to inspire in him.

But Jonah wasn't wearing that expression just yet. He merely looked respectful and attentive. Her thoughts went back to their arrival and how strangely hurt she'd felt when he recognized her father immediately. Then again, her father had been Jonah's teacher many years before she'd been Jonah's wife.

She was about to turn away when she realized Jonah was glancing at Miriam, who was seated in the living room. Turning her head, Eden looked at her, too. As she'd predicted, Miriam perceived their visit to Annapolis as her punishment for trying to buy cigarettes. No assurances to the contrary could convince her otherwise, and, now, she was staring glumly at a television show with the volume barely audible.

Eden looked back at Jonah's reflection. Miriam's long face had given rise to a slight frown between his eyebrows. *He's worried about her,* Eden realized. Nor was his concern purely for Eden's benefit. He hadn't noticed Eden watching him. He honestly cared about her daughter. He really was a different man!

A wave of affection buoyed her heart. *If that's not a sign, I don't know what is,* she thought, sending up a prayer of thanks for a prayer answered.

Smiling inwardly, Eden turned back to her task, thinking how wonderful it would be if she and Jonah could start over again and get things right this time.

Almost at once, she remembered Jonah's diagnosis, and her confidence faltered. How would he ever get better if he refused to talk to his psychiatrist? The article on PTSD suggested the disorder only got worse if it was left untreated.

What was worse—a husband too wrapped up in his work to find time for family or a husband who suffered imaginary fears?

~

Jonah found Commander Evans thoroughly informed about what was happening on Dam Neck. Then again, he was friends with the previous base commander, Vice Admiral Leland, who must have told him about the weapons disappearing.

"It happened again, didn't it, the night you disappeared?" he asked Jonah.

"I'm sorry, sir. Even if I could remember, I'm not at liberty to talk about that night."

"Of course not." Evans shook his full head of silver hair. "I can't believe you're sitting in front of me, alive and basically in one piece." His pitying gaze went to the stunted nails on Jonah's left hand. "NCIS must be having a field day trying to make sense of it."

Jonah shifted in his seat, uncomfortable with his memory loss and fighting to keep his eyelids from drooping. In Commander Evans's eyes, he'd always been on the cutting edge, informed about world events, with an opinion on everything. What would Evans think if Jonah admitted his primary concern at the moment was keeping his marriage intact?

Evans propped his elbows on his knees, pitched his voice in a conspiratorial whisper, and added, "I've wondered if your disappearance wasn't related to the thefts."

The words affected Jonah's heart like a defibrillator, bringing him wide awake and raising his blood pressure. He had wondered that very thing himself, but hearing the commander say it made it seem suddenly likely.

"What makes you say that?"

The question seemed to baffle Evans, but then his expression cleared. "You don't remember, do you?"

Blood swished against Jonah's eardrums. "Remember what?"

Evans leaned in farther and said on a low note, "You phoned me several nights before the op. You said you'd found some evidence or something that explained where the intel leak might be."

Goosebumps scrabbled up Jonah's arms and tugged at his scalp.

"I found something? What did I find?"

"I'm not sure." The commander's blue eyes blazed with interest. "You didn't give me any specifics, only that you had suspicions and you were casting nets. I had to wonder, though, when you disappeared a few days later, if you hadn't confronted the wrong person."

Dear God. Jonah picked up the glass of water next to him and with a shaky hand gulped down half of it. He couldn't remember a word of what Evans was telling him, yet he knew it to be true. He *had* found evidence. What kind? Where? He had confronted the culprit—Lowery. It had to be Lowery. Why else would the man have tried killing him again?

Mixed emotions twisted through Jonah. On one hand, having his suspicions verified meant he wasn't paranoid. On the other, the feeling he was in imminent danger ambushed him anew. His gaze went straight out the glass windows to the large, lush yard.

Trees and bushes abounded, offering cover to a potential hitman. Could Lowery have followed them up here? What if he was out there hiding even then, just waiting for a perfect shot? Jonah put a wary hand on the pistol at his hip, taking comfort from its protection.

The Commander's sudden bark nearly startled him into drawing it.

"How many times have I told you that's not a toy?"

Jonah followed the Commander's glare in time to see Miriam snatch her hand back from the chess set siting on the coffee table.

As Eden stuck her head out of the dining room to assess the situation, Miriam paled and stiffened but did not talk back.

Jonah seized the opportunity to mend some broken fences. "Is the board just for show, sir?" he asked, maintaining his deference.

"Well, no. I use it all the time," Evans admitted.

"Maybe you'd like to challenge Miriam to a game," Jonah suggested. "You play chess, don't you, squirt?"

"I know how," she responded in a tone that conveyed she would rather eat dirt than challenge the man who'd just yelled at her.

"Go up against me first," Jonah suggested. "Then winner takes on Grandpa." He looked back at Evans to gauge his response.

"By all means." The CO waved him away.

Jonah jumped to his feet and headed for the chessboard, rubbing his hands in exaggerated anticipation. A game of chess would help take his mind off his fears.

Miriam's expression brightened as he took the seat across from her. Glancing back at Evans's glowering expression, he called out, "Care to watch, sir? This could get ugly. Miriam's already beaten me at Catan. She must have inherited her grandfather's gift for strategy."

To his satisfaction, the commander rolled to his feet and settled onto the sofa, next to his granddaughter.

Half an hour later, with Miriam's queen poised for a checkmate, Eden ventured into the living room to announce dinner was ready.

"Checkmate," Miriam said, raising a triumphant eyebrow at Jonah.

Evans roared in approval. "By God, I don't believe it!" His wife joined Eden to see what all the fuss was about. "Did you see that, Elke? Your granddaughter just bested Jonah at chess, and I'm next."

"That'll have to wait until after dinner," Eden's mother informed him. At the same time, she cut an approving look at Miriam. "Kindly wash up, everyone, and head to the table."

The commander muttered for Miriam's benefit, "Aye, aye, Captain."

She quirked a smile at him.

Meeting Eden's watchful gaze, Jonah trusted she'd noticed how he'd conquered the generation gap, at least for today. He sent her a private wink, causing her eyes to widen. He realized she was looking at him the way she had in their wedding photos.

Did that mean she was giving their marriage the chance it deserved?

If that was the case, Jonah couldn't let Lowery get the better of him. Whatever it took, he had to remember why Lowery had turned on him in the first place, and he had to do it before the man succeeded in killing him on his third try.

∿

Returning from her shower in the hallway bathroom, Eden slipped into her parents' guest bedroom and drew up short at the sight that greeted her.

Jonah had drawn the blinds and turned off all the lights, save the one by the double bed. Using a spare blanket he must have found in the cedar chest, he'd made a bed for himself on the floor and was lying on it. Draped in a sheet and with his head on a pillow, he watched her response to his actions.

"You know I can sleep anywhere," he said with a reassuring smile.

With her hand still on the doorknob, Eden surreptitiously turned the lock. Her pulse, which had been thrumming for hours at the thought of sharing a room with her husband, quickened. She hadn't had the heart nor the gumption to mention to her folks that she and Jonah kept separate rooms at home.

She was glad she hadn't. What he had done earlier in the day, standing up for Miriam, had made her realize she'd been withholding her support, whereas Jonah had been giving his all. In an instant, she'd made a decision.

Jonah deserved a second chance. She didn't have to believe his allegations about Jimmy, but she could at least stand beside him and encourage him in his therapy. She could stop talking or even thinking about separating and start fighting for their marriage.

If they got through Jonah's recovery together, she would know they could get through anything.

Conscious of his watchful gaze, she crossed toward the bed to pull the covers back, only to realize he'd done it for her, a sweet gesture that further encouraged her.

"What are you thinking?" he asked as she slipped beneath the sheets.

Twisting onto her side, she plumped up the pillow until she could look at him. His catlike eyes reflected the lamp shining between them.

"I'm still thinking about the movie," she said, guarding her decision a while longer.

They had watched a DVD of *Unbroken* after dinner, a drama released several years before about a WWII soldier who'd suffered captivity in a Japanese prison camp.

"I can't believe my parents made you watch that."

Jonah smiled ruefully. "It's okay. Your father is a history fanatic. I get that."

She searched his expression for his true feelings. "Still, it had to have struck a little close to home."

His smile faded. "Are you worried I'm going to have bad dreams?"

She kicked herself for misleading him into thinking that. "No, not at all—"

"I can slip downstairs after everyone's gone to bed," he offered, coming up on one elbow as if ready to leave right then. "I can sleep just fine on the couch," he added earnestly.

His selflessness made her want him even more. "I'm not scared to share a room with you, Jonah."

His chest rose and fell as he held her earnest gaze.

"You know my scent," she added on a softer, more intimate note that brought heat into his eyes. "You're not going to hurt me."

They regarded each other in silence for a long moment. The air seemed to thicken as they realized nothing stopped them from coming together as husband and wife. Eden queried her decision one last time.

"Jonah?"

"Yes."

"I think you should sleep up here, with me."

She saw his Adam's apple bob as he visibly swallowed. "You may not get much sleep if I'm up there with you," he warned, his tone gruff.

Her face heated, but she answered with a careless shrug, "Sleep is over-rated, don't you think?"

"Definitely," he said, but he stayed put.

As Eden waited, anticipation turned into self-doubt. Didn't he want to share a bed with her?

"You're so beautiful, Eden." His murmured words, so full of conviction, banished her worries. "I love simply looking at you, talking to you. I want us to get to know each other better."

Returning his intense regard, Eden marveled at how such a familiar face could look so different—and not only because of the scars he'd sustained, nor the missing tooth.

Over the lump growing in her throat, she admitted, "It's so strange to me that you don't remember me." She relived her hurt feelings of how he remembered her father, yet didn't remember her.

Jonah frowned. "But I do," he insisted, soothing her concerns. "I have no specific memories of us, that's true. But I know the way you move, and the way you tilt your head."

She realized she was tilting her head even then and promptly straightened it.

"I know when you're happy and when you're tense. And I know you want me to make love to you tonight." His smile widened to a cocky grin.

She gasped in protest. "Oh, you arrogant SEAL!" She snatched up the spare pillow and launched it at him.

He caught it easily and tossed it back to her. "See, I haven't changed that much."

His words sobered her, reminding her of her greatest fear—Jonah reverting to the man he was before and causing her and Miriam to relive their disillusionment.

"You've changed completely," she stated, causing his smile to disappear.

"I hope that's a good thing," he said very sincerely.

She nodded as a lump in her throat formed. "I've been afraid," she admitted on a whisper.

He regarded her intently. "Of me?"

She licked her lips, betraying her nervousness. "That things would go back to what they were like before."

He grimaced. "That's not going to happen. I'm not the same man."

"I know that now," she admitted. "I'm not afraid anymore." The old Jonah wouldn't have stayed on the floor after being invited to join her in bed. He'd have thought of himself first, not her, not their relationship.

"I can never be the same man," he continued. "How's the verse go?" His gaze rose to the ceiling as he searched his mind. "In Ephesians, I think, the Bible talks about putting off your old self, being renewed in the Spirit and putting on the new self, which is created after the likeness of God." He looked back at her and smiled. "Not that I'll be perfect. But I'll try."

"I believe you," she replied. The fact that he could quote scripture proved he was a new man. Now, all she had to worry about was his PTSD.

He smiled at her with so much warmth in his eyes, she marveled at his restraint in staying on the floor.

"Did you love me when you married me?" he asked, shortening her breath.

She wasn't going to lie to him. "Very much."

"I made you fall out of love with me, didn't I?"

The lump in her throat swelled, preventing her from answering. She confirmed his words by virtue of her silence.

He nodded and, with a bittersweet smile, traced the hem of the sheet covering him, then looked up again. "I think you could love me again."

The words were uttered with just enough hopefulness to keep them from sounding arrogant.

Tears pricked Eden's eyes unexpectedly. Her heart swelled with affection to the point of bursting.

"I think so, too," she whispered.

"Cool." They grinned at each other for what might have been a minute or five. Eden had lost all sense of time. Their talk hadn't exactly been the kind of intimacy she'd expected that night, but she wouldn't have exchanged it for anything.

"Guess we should get some sleep," Jonah suggested on a regretful note.

Watching him recline on his bedroll, Eden agreed. "We've got a full day ahead of us tomorrow."

Her father had insisted Jonah come to one of his lectures, then tour the Academy with him in the morning. Her mother was dying to take Eden and Miriam shopping.

Eden reached for the light by the bed and turned it off.

"'Night, Jonah," she said into the darkness.

"Goodnight, beautiful," he replied.

The endearment brought tears to her eyes. He had called her that before his disappearance, but only when they'd made love. Surely, he couldn't remember that. Yet the words assured her they would be husband and wife, in every sense of the word, soon enough. Jonah, she realized, was merely waiting for her to say she loved him still.

Do I? she queried her heart. If not for Jonah's diagnosis and the uncertainties it presented, she might have told him that very night she still loved him. After all, God seemed to be giving her the thumbs up regarding her commitment to her marriage. On the other hand, she wasn't as trusting as she'd been two years before. Jonah wouldn't intentionally hurt her anymore—she was certain. But the trauma he'd sustained at the hands of his captors, paired with his memory loss, might prove too challenging for their tentative bond to withstand.

Still, she fell asleep with optimism for the days—and years—to come.

~

Sleep eluded Jonah, what with Eden sleeping so tantalizingly near to him. Listening to her steady breathing filled him with a sense of reverence and joy.

He was plumbing the dark corners of his mind, trying to remember his short marriage, when he slipped seamlessly into unconsciousness, where he dreamed he was attending Blake LeMere's funeral with the rest of his troop. *I remember, now!* he thought, nearly waking up in his excitement. He forced himself to remain in the dream.

The Navy chaplin stood at the head of the casket, speaking words of comfort and eternity. Then it was time for Jonah and his fellow SEALs to approach LeMere's coffin. Each and every one of them pounded a personal trident pin atop the lustrous mahogany lid. With his palm, Jonah hammered his pin alongside the others.

Touching the coffin jolted Jonah into remembering his suspicions. The only way for LeMere to have been unconscious after leaving the plane was for Lowery to have done something to him. He raked the sea of faces around him for any sign of Lowery's lean frame. It seemed like every man in Blue Squadron was there. Lowery, however, was conspicuously absent.

Disappointed, Jonah got in line to offer LeMere's widow his condolences.

Rachel LeMere, a delicate-looking woman with gray-green eyes and sandy hair, looked lost, overwrought. Recognition flickered in her bloodshot eyes as she looked up at him.

"Jonah," she whispered.

"Rachel, I'm so sorry," he said, embracing her in lieu of a handshake. LeMere's eight-year-old son stood next to her. Jonah hugged him, too, even as he tried remembering the kid's name. *Crap, what was it?* LeMere used to talk about him all the time.

As dreams do, Jonah's jumped to a time several months later. He was married to Eden, sitting on one of the stools at the island in his kitchen, opening mail. He'd gotten a thick padded envelope from none other than Blake's widow, Rachel. It had been mailed nearly ten months after Blake's death. Inside was a composition notebook and a handwritten message in lovely cursive:

Jonah, I came across this journal of Blake's in one of his boxes and I read it. I'd always suspected Blake's death was not an accident. Now I am sure it wasn't. I thought about sending this to Blake's best friend, Saul, but you were his troop leader, and Blake spoke highly of you. Please read his last entry and tell me if you agree with me. —Sincerely, Rachel.

Jonah opened what was clearly his teammate's personal journal and, following Rachel's instructions, read the final entry.

About a week ago, Lowery sent out a group email to the squadron. I had a question I thought others might also be able to answer, so I hit Reply All. Our old version of

Outlook exposes blind copied recipients that way, so when a name popped up that I didn't recognize, I figured Lowery must have blind-copied that person in the original. The next day I asked Lowery, "Who's Eddie Holms?" "Who?" He looked at me all nervous-like. "Eddie Holms. You blind-copied him in a group email yesterday."

Lowery told me Holms was a new first class about to join Alpha Troop. I was curious, so I looked the guy up, and I came across his obituary. What the heck? The man had been dead for six months. So, I went back and looked at other emails Lowery had sent out. I hit Reply All on those, too, and—guess what? He'd blind-copied a bunch of other guys I never heard of. This past week, I looked up all seven of them, and they're all deceased SEALs. How weird is that? Tomorrow, I'm going straight to the CO to report Lowery. I have no idea why he'd be sending logistical information to SEALs who used to be in various squadrons but are dead now. Makes no sense, but then Lowery has always been a strange one.

Shock spurred Jonah's heartbeat. In his dream, he leapt to his feet, pacing the length of the living room and wondering what to do.

"I knew it!" He clutched the journal, imagining what had happened. Lowery, who'd lived in terror that LeMere would report him, had figured out a way to murder LeMere while making it look like an accident. Why Lowery had been sending emails to deceased SEALs in the first place made no sense. Their email accounts had to have been disabled, which meant no one would have received those emails—or had they? What if the accounts had remained active and someone outside of Spec Ops was receiving confidential information?

That had to be it. That was how Lowery was leaking information! Jonah pressed the journal to his pounding heart. My God! He'd found the traitor, and now he had proof!

"Jonah!"

Eden's voice seemed to come from a distance. "Wake up, honey, it's just a dream." A tentative hand jostled his shoulder.

The word *honey* brought Jonah abruptly back into the present, though the jarring time travel left him momentarily disoriented. Opening his eyes, he flinched at what seemed like a bright light but was only the single lamp by the guest bed in Eden's parents' house. Eden herself kneeled on the floor next to him, the very picture of concern. Her long, golden hair fell over her shoulder onto his chest.

"Are you okay?" Her amber gaze was shadowed with concern—and not a small amount of wariness.

"Yeah." He cleared his gravelly voice and tried again. "I'm fine. It's okay."

"Were you having a nightmare? You were breathing so hard."

"It wasn't a nightmare." His thoughts went back to the revelation in his dream. "It was a memory."

"Really?" Her enthusiasm was tempered with worry.

"First a memory of Blake LeMere's funeral. Then later after I was married to you."

Her eyes widened. "You remember our marriage?"

He had to disappoint her. "Well, just one day. It had to have been a couple months after the funeral. I got something important in the mail." He caught himself from spilling out the details. Eden didn't believe Jimmy Lowery had it in him to betray his fellow SEALs. Jonah wasn't going to try to convince her until he had the proof to back it up. "Something LeMere's widow sent me—a journal."

Excitement had Jonah sitting up. He reached for Eden's hands and found them cold, a little clammy. She'd clearly been afraid to waken him.

"This is important," he told her. "Please tell me that somewhere in the house there's a composition notebook with a marbled blue cover. It's only half-used." LeMere's death had kept him from filling out the rest. "Please tell me you didn't throw it away."

Eden's gaze darted toward their joined hands, making him realize he was gripping her too hard.

"I don't think I did," she answered with obvious uncertainty.

"It's okay," he reassured her—even though it wasn't. "It's okay if you threw it away. You couldn't have known."

"Have known what?" she asked.

He debated whether to tell her what he'd remembered, or whether he should keep it to himself. "There's proof in that notebook that Jimmy Lowery betrayed the squadron. He may have even killed Blake LeMere."

The angle of Eden's eyebrows betrayed her skepticism.

"Never mind," he added. "We need to go home as soon as the sun comes up. I need to find that notebook."

Her protest was immediate. "Jonah, we can't go home. My parents have big plans for us."

"Your dad will understand," he assured her. "He and I were talking about this very thing earlier today. That's got to be why I dreamed about it."

Eden kept quiet, her disappointment palpable.

"I'm sorry, beautiful. I really am. We'll come back soon. Thanksgiving is just a few months away. This is important, Eden. This journal explains what might have happened to me the night of the op. I have to get home to look for it."

A lengthy silence followed Jonah's declaration. Eden's expression was distinctly torn. Desperate to retain the affection she'd shown him earlier in the evening, Jonah pressed an impulsive kiss on her unsuspecting lips.

She blinked and gasped.

"Trust me, honey," he pleaded, using the same endearment she had used for him. "You have to trust me. I'm not suffering an episode. I'm not crazy. I don't have a screw loose. There's a reason why I went missing for a year, why the Navy thought me dead. And there's a reason God brought me home again. I have to make this right. But to do that, I need the notebook, and I need to get to it before someone else does."

He listened to her draw a shaky breath and let it out again. "Okay," she agreed with mediocre enthusiasm.

"Thank you." He went to kiss her again, but she averted her lips so his kiss landed on her cheek.

"Are you okay to sleep?" she asked, even as she withdrew and rose to her feet.

"I'm fine," he assured her.

She looked down at him with a doubtful expression. "I guess I'll use the bathroom while I'm up," she said, picking her way to the door.

Watching her slip from the room, Jonah suffered remorse for having to cut their visit short, for making Eden suspect his anxiety was out of control. But there was no way around it. Once he found the journal—*Please, Lord, don't let Eden have thrown it away*—he would prove to her his suspicions were founded. He would take the journal straight to Special Agent Elwood, who would know exactly what to do with it. Eventually, Lowery would be arrested and prosecuted, and Jonah would be utterly vindicated for his suspicions.

Then Eden would have no more reason to withhold her love from him. Then she and Jonah and Miriam would finally become the family God meant for them to be.

CHAPTER 16

*L*eaving Annapolis at ten thirty the following morning, they drove straight into a rainstorm. Eden gripped the steering wheel until her knuckles ached.

It felt wrong to depart her parents' place so abruptly, especially when they'd planned so many activities. At least Jonah had kept his word in offering up their apologies. She'd overheard him say to her father with convincing urgency, "I remembered something important last night, something along the lines of what we were discussing yesterday. It was written in a friend's journal. I need to go home today and look for it."

To Eden's surprise, her father had agreed with Jonah's need for haste and then convinced her mother they should leave right away. She, Jonah, and Miriam had piled into the car shortly after breakfast, and now they were moving with the thick traffic, passing Fredericksburg.

Jonah, who'd seemed alert when they got up, sat with his head lolling on the headrest, eyes half closed.

"Tired?" she asked when their eyes connected.

He drew a sharp breath and scrubbed a hand over his face.

"It's my medication." His speech was slightly slurred. "I hate the stuff."

"So stop taking it," Miriam piped up from the back seat, where she was finishing *To Kill a Mockingbird*.

"That's not the answer," Eden countered.

"I think I should stop," Jonah agreed with Miriam.

Pivoting in his seat, he sent her an approving look. "You're almost at the end."

"Yep." It was apparently too gripping for Miriam to say any more.

Glancing over at Jonah, Eden saw his gaze go out the back window and narrow. "How long has that Charger been following us?"

She cut her attention to the mirror, considering the black sedan behind them. "I don't know. Half an hour, maybe."

Looking much more awake, Jonah faced front again. Out of the corner of her eye, Eden watched him reach up under his T-shirt and pull out the pistol he'd started carrying with him. Her pulse doubled at the sight of it, and her grip on the steering wheel wobbled.

"Easy." Jonah's soothing voice encouraged her to relax. He checked the magazine and put the gun away.

Glancing into the mirror, Eden realized Miriam had stopped reading.

"What's happening?" she demanded from the back seat.

"Nothing," Eden told her. *Jonah's being paranoid,* she thought to herself. She cut him a pleading look. "Please don't take that out in the car."

Dividing his attention between the road ahead of them and the mirror on his side of the car, Jonah ignored her comment.

"There's a visitor's center coming up in two miles. I want you to pull off and see if the car follows us."

"Jonah, we are not being followed."

He stayed quiet so long she thought perhaps he hadn't heard her.

"You're probably right," he finally said. "But I also have to pee," he added, lightening the tension in the car.

"So do I," Miriam said from the back seat.

"Fine," Eden agreed. Considering Jonah's suspicions, she eyeballed the car behind them, trying to see inside, but the downpour kept the windshield blurry, which distorted her view of the driver. Time dragged as they traversed the two remaining miles to the rest area.

At last, Eden guided the car off the highway, dismayed to see the Charger exit behind them.

"He's following us," she reported. Her heart gave an erratic beat. *What if Jonah was right?*

"Pull up as close to the building as possible," he instructed. Eden could hear the gravity in his voice, which did little to reassure her.

She parked between a soft-top Jeep and a pick-up truck with a dog kennel in the bed. She, Miriam, and Jonah all kept quiet as they watched the Charger creep past them. The Jeep to their left backed out, giving them a clear view of the Charger parking in a handicapped spot.

"Stay here for now." With that brief warning, Jonah opened his door and shot out of the car. Eden watched him stride through the rain toward the rest area. Instead of going inside, however, he ducked into the sheltered portico and hid behind one of the brick pillars. To the casual eye, he'd simply disappeared.

Eden and Miriam both regarded the Charger. The driver's door opened. Eden held her breath as she waited to see if Jonah's fears were founded. An umbrella opened, and then a silver head appeared. The oldest man Eden had seen in a while closed his car door and shuffled through the rain toward the building. Eden blew out a long breath and mentally rolled her eyes.

Her poor husband had been deeply scarred by his experience in captivity. Last night, he'd insisted he wasn't crazy, wasn't suffering an episode, but the evidence to the contrary was too obvious to ignore. He'd thought that old man was out to kill him, the way he thought Jimmy Lowery was trying to do him in.

"Dad's freaking out for nothing," Miriam stated from the back seat.

"Yeah," Eden agreed.

They sat in the car a second longer digesting the uncomfortable implications.

"I'm going inside," Miriam declared. Scrambling out of the car, she slammed the door extra hard behind her.

Eden flinched. This was so not what either of them needed or wanted right now.

～

Watching the old man make his way up the walkway, eyes on the cement in front of him for fear of falling, Jonah reeled a moment in self-doubt as he relinquished his conclusion that the man was an assassin.

With the adrenaline in his bloodstream draining away, Jonah let his head fall against the brick pillar. He didn't even want to look at Eden for fear of seeing her reaction. Before the old man could catch up to him, Jonah swiveled and marched into the men's facility to relieve himself.

Dawdling over the sink a moment later, he glared at his reflection. *What if I am crazy?* The grave-eyed man in the mirror didn't look haunted or confused. He knew exactly what was going on, when he wasn't drowsy because of his medication.

Recalling Miriam's advice earlier, Jonah pulled his pill bottle out of his pocket. Eden had set it on the sink at her parents' house that morning so he wouldn't forget to take it. Unscrewing the top, he waited for the other man at the sink to turn toward the hand dryer before upending the contents of his bottle into the sink. Watching the remaining pills swill down the drain, he suffered a twinge of his conscience for polluting the environment. But deep down, he felt relieved, in control again.

No hitman was going to catch him off guard because he was half asleep.

Stuffing the empty bottle back into his pocket, he turned toward the door, holding it open for the old man, who was also leaving. Probably would have made the man's day to hear Jonah had thought him a gun for hire. With a wry smile, Jonah stepped outside.

Seeing the Jaguar empty, he waited out front for Eden and Miriam to join him. They emerged at the same time, both of them wearing taut expressions, their eyes full of pity.

Jonah heaved an inward sigh, determined to clear the air immediately.

"All right, so I overreacted." He threw an arm around both of them, giving them each a squeeze. "It's not the end of the world."

He was pleased to see Miriam's quick smile in response to his mollifying. Eden, on the other hand, remained somber. He wished he knew what to say to reassure her. But, honestly, things could get a great deal worse before they got better.

The truth was—and he still believed it—he could be targeted without warning and at any moment. His only hope was to find LeMere's journal and use it to finger Lowery before that man took action against him again.

～

Eden stood at the study door watching Jonah rifle through the bookcase in frantic search of the notebook allegedly implicating Dwyer's XO. Picturing lanky Jimmy Lowery's tensely held shoulders and eager expression, she couldn't imagine him doing anything to upset the status quo. Yet, her husband was clearly convinced he'd betrayed him to the point of plotting Jonah's death.

With a look of disappointment, Jonah, who'd arrived at the last book in the built-in shelving unit, turned to look at her. "Can I look in your room?"

She gave a quick shrug. "Sure."

"Thanks."

She followed him as he strode to their bedroom. Watching him work through her private collection of books, she emptied her suitcase of the clothes she had packed but didn't get the chance to wear. When he reached the bottom shelf, she could sense his agitation rising.

Straightening, he raked a hand through his hair and touched his gaze on every surface as if wondering where else he might have put the journal. Wandering over to the bed, he startled her by sitting on it like he was accustomed to being there. As she tossed her dirty clothes into her bin in her bathroom, she saw him stand up and lift the end of the mattress.

"Found it!"

Eden looked from the marbled composition notebook he was clutching in his hand to his triumphant expression. She approached him in disbelief. Surely, that notebook hadn't been there for over a year. She'd stripped and remade the bed dozens of times and never noticed it.

Without a word, she watched Jonah flip through the pages, scanning them rapidly. His intensity caused her to turn cold. What if there was something to Jonah's suspicions after all?

She stepped closer, wanting to see the journal for herself.

"Is it what you thought it was?"

Glued to the words written on a certain page, he didn't answer right away. When he looked at her, his green eyes blazed with urgency. "I need to make a phone call."

Excusing himself from her bedroom, he headed back to the study.

Eden trailed him. Obviously he considered his business private but, as far as she was concerned, she deserved to know what was going on. She heard the study door close as she approached the front hall. Miriam was out walking the dog, whom they'd just picked up from Nina's house. No one would be the wiser if she stood outside of Jonah's room and eavesdropped. She had to know right now if his suspicions were real or only imagined.

Which would be worse, she wondered, as she inclined her ear toward the closed door—finding out her husband had lost touch with reality or discovering Jimmy Lowery had, in fact, tried unsuccessfully to kill him?

~

Accessing his contact information for Lloyd Elwood, Jonah got nowhere trying to call the man's cell phone—not even his voicemail picked up. Looking back at Elwood's business card, Jonah dialed the second number, then listened over the thud of his own heartbeat to the man's phone ring and ring. He was formulating a message in his head when a woman answered, sounding out of breath.

"This is Charlotte Patterson."

Jonah frowned. "I'm sorry. I thought this was someone else's number."

"This is Lloyd Elwood's office number." The answer betrayed a level of suppressed emotion. "May I ask who's calling?"

Figuring he'd be put through to Elwood after he introduced himself, Jonah gave his name.

"Oh," she said, "I know who you are." There was no mistaking the strain in her voice this time. "You're the Navy SEAL."

"Yes," he said.

She heaved a shaky sigh. "I'm sorry to tell you this, Lt. Mills, but Lloyd's dead. He was killed by a car on his trip out of town." Her voice quavered. "It was a hit-and-run. No one's been charged yet."

Patterson's distress was the first thing that penetrated Jonah's consciousness. Then the actual finality of Elwood's life. Then the implications of a hit-and-run. He sucked in a breath. Was it possible Elwood's death—if it had been intentional—had anything to do with Jonah's own situation?

"I'm so sorry," he murmured. He could tell from the woman's voice she'd been close to the man. "Do you work with him—did you?" he corrected himself.

"Yes, I'm familiar with the investigation involving your disappearance."

How familiar? he wondered.

"He was hoping your memories would start to return," she added. "Have they?"

He didn't yet know if he could trust this woman or whether her involvement might put her at risk, considering what had happened to Elwood.

"Was the hit-and-run an accident?" he asked instead.

"Oh, I'm pretty sure it wasn't," she said in a tight voice. "Lloyd wasn't dead twelve hours before his desk was emptied and the hard drive removed from his computer."

"Who took it all?" Jonah asked, appalled that Elwood's hard work might simply disappear.

"Men in suits. No one would tell me who they were or why they were there."

"Can you ask your supervisor who's taking over for Elwood?"

"Lloyd Elwood *was* my supervisor. And, right now, I don't know if I trust anybody. No one's talking about what happened to Lloyd, and I've been told to take a vacation."

With rapidly rising concern, Jonah moved to the window to peer down at the quiet street. If Elwood had been targeted for investigating Jonah's disappearance, then Jonah was probably next. The fact his memories were returning didn't need to be broadcast.

"Listen, I think maybe you should let this go," he suggested. Patterson sounded like she was still in her twenties. God forbid something bad happened to her, too.

"Hell, no," she growled. "I am not letting Lloyd's hard work be brushed under the carpet like nothing happened."

Jonah had to admire her loyalty, but he needed someone with experience to help him.

"You said his hard drive was taken. How are you planning to proceed without it?"

"I think that question is best discussed face-to-face, along with the reason for your call. Where would you like to meet? Name any place, bring anyone you want with you, and I'll meet you there. The sooner the better," she added intently.

Jonah hesitated. How could an inexperienced special agent help him when the organization she worked for told her to take a vacation?

"I have a powerful contact in the Defense Intelligence Agency," she added as if reading his mind. "I can help you."

All at once her inexperience didn't seem to matter. Not only was she motivated to avenge her supervisor's death, but she knew someone who might actually wield sufficient power to make a difference.

"All right," Jonah said, deciding to trust her. Looking down at the notebook in his hands, thinking of Elwood's recent death, it hit him like a punch in the gut that he'd been in this position before and look what had happened. The fear that had been growing in him since his return mushroomed.

Where are you, Father? Do you know what's happening?

Reviewing all the information at his disposal, Jonah came to a sobering conclusion. Elwood's mysterious death and the fact that men in suits cleared out his office suggested intrigue that went beyond Lowery disseminating intel to unknown recipients. Even though Eden was standing by Jonah's side these days, Jonah couldn't stay with her, not without putting her and Miriam at risk. What's more, he needed protection only a teammate could offer. That meant he had to leave, taking the evidence he'd just found with him, and ask someone like Master Chief to take him in.

With a shudder of regret, Jonah glanced over at the duffle bag he'd brought in from the car. He wouldn't be unpacking it anytime soon.

"Give me your cell phone number," he requested of the fierce, young investigator. "I'll text you the time and the place. And then we can talk."

~

The door between them kept Eden from understanding every word, but Eden could tell that Jonah's call just ended. She backed quietly away from the door, lest it open suddenly. When it didn't, she approached it again to hear what Jonah might be doing. It sounded like he was opening his dresser drawers, probably unpacking his bag. She figured it was safe to knock.

Momentary silence was her only reply before Jonah said on a subdued note, "Come in, Eden."

She stepped into the room and faltered to a halt. Instead of unpacking his duffel bag, Jonah was filling it completely with pretty much every item of clothing he still owned, apart from the uniforms she'd recovered.

"What's going on?" she asked. It looked like he was planning to take off somewhere.

Jonah stuffed a fistful of socks inside the bag before turning to look at her. The pained expression on his face made her stomach cramp.

"We need to talk," he said, gesturing for her to sit in the chair at the desk.

Ignoring him, she locked her knees in expectation of bad news. Jonah was leaving. His really did have PTSD, and it was even more serious than she'd thought. *Help me, Lord.*

He heaved a sigh as if reading her thoughts. "Look, I know you don't believe me about Lowery. Maybe you think you know him better than I do."

She gasped. "What is that supposed to mean?"

"Nothing," he said on a weary note. "You have a point. Lowery comes across like a rule follower. It's hard to believe he'd betray the squadron in any way, shape, or form. But LeMere's journal details information that's hard to ignore. And now Elwood, the investigator looking into my disappearance, is dead."

"What?" She hadn't seen that coming.

"He died in a hit-and-run just the other day. I don't think it was an accident."

Her jaw became unhinged as she interpreted his meaning. "You actually think Jimmy killed him?" It was hard not to mock the outrageous notion.

Jonah's face turned to stone. He took a step toward her, causing her thighs to flex with the urge to back away.

"Listen." His tone was subdued but deadly serious. "My memory may be shot full of holes, but my intuition is as strong as ever. I have felt since I escaped from Carenero that my life is in danger. That means as long as I'm living in this house, you and Miriam are also in danger. Since nothing happened to you while I was gone, I'm taking myself back out of the equation. I'm going to live with Master Chief until Lowery is arrested and I feel safe again."

Devastated, Eden could only stare at Jonah. Why would God have given her a thumbs-up on their marriage if He'd known Jonah's fears were going to get the better of him?

She tried one last time to reason with him. "What if your diagnosis is causing you to invent this threat?" she suggested gently. "Dr. Branson says—"

"Dr. Branson is a civilian. He has no idea what's been going on, and I'm not about to tell him."

With those words, Jonah eviscerated Eden's only support system. That left her all alone with her husband's PTSD ruining their lives—unless God knew something she didn't know.

Seizing that flimsy hope, Eden stepped abruptly toward Jonah, threw her arms around him and hugged him hard.

"Please pray before you do this, Jonah," she pleaded. "We need you here to complete our family."

To her relief, he welcomed her embrace, wrapping his arms tightly around her and burying his nose in her hair.

"I don't want to do this," he grated in her ear. The emotion in his voice was wrenching.

"Then don't," she said as she listened to his thudding heart.

"I have to." Prying free of her embrace, he crossed to the window and bent the blind to look outside. "Where's Miriam?"

"Still walking the dog," she answered, while cringing at the thought of Miriam's reaction.

"I should go before she gets back." He turned and crossed to the bed, zipping shut his bag.

Eden shook her head. "You have an appointment with Dr. Branson on Tuesday," she reminded him. "How are you going to get there?"

"I'm not," he answered, slinging his bag over his left shoulder.

"You'll be reprimanded if you don't go." Worse than that, he would never get over his condition without help and never be released for active duty.

Jonah sent her a ghastly smile. "What can the CO do to me that hasn't already been done?" He strode past her toward the door, where he turned and paused. "I will be back when this is over. Don't give up on us, Eden."

Tears sprang to her eyes. She was too disheartened to answer.

Miriam dried Sabrina's paws with the towel hanging in the mudroom. Hearing the front door open and close, she rehung the towel and urged the dog outside, toward the steps to the front door.

Jonah, who was coming down, slowed his descent, then stopped on the landing where the stairs turned. Miriam's gaze went from his dismayed expression to the big Navy issue bag he was carrying. He clearly hadn't wanted to run into her.

"Where are you going?" she demanded, blocking his way.

He seemed to have trouble answering. "I have to go away for a bit." His voice was soft and gravelly.

"Why?" She wasn't going to let him off without an explanation.

"To keep you and your mom safe."

"Safe from who?" she scoffed. "An old man?"

His mouth firmed at her low blow. "From the person who tried to kill me a year ago," he clarified.

The extent of his paranoia widened her eyes and made her breath catch.

"I'm going to stay with my master chief," he added, hitching his bag and giving her time to digest his news. "I want you to be good for Mom. You know what I mean."

One low blow deserved another, she supposed, folding her arms across her chest.

"Can I call you?" she heard him ask.

The question put a lump in her throat. She hugged herself and feigned a careless shrug. "If you want."

"I want," he said. Descending another step, he bent to pet the dog's head, then hugged her stiff figure, kissing her on the forehead. "See you, squirt," he added, sliding past her.

He hadn't taken a step before Miriam whirled and threw her arms around him from behind, halting his progress.

Please don't go. The words got stuck in her throat.

He stilled, putting a hand over hers and squeezing it reassuringly.

"I'll be back," he promised on a gruff note. "Be good for your mom."

Pulling gently from her embrace, he stepped off the stairs and, without a backward glance, started for the street.

Miriam watched him walk away with long purposeful strides that made her eyes sting. He stepped into puddles as if he didn't see them. It started to drizzle, but he didn't seem to care. She watched him walk clear to the bend in the road where he disappeared, not once turning his head to look back.

Rivera looked up from LeMere's notebook with ill-concealed disgust.

"We have to tell the CO."

Jonah directed his gaze across Master Chief's living room and out the wall of windows where the slate-gray ocean tossed fitfully beneath leaden rainclouds.

"I know," he said, wondering at his reticence. "But Elwood told me not to trust anyone with my memories except him. I trust you, of course. And I'm sure he meant Lowery, but maybe he meant the CO, too."

"Dwyer has to be told," Rivera insisted. "I can't keep something this big from him."

"Let's just wait and see what Elwood's assistant suggests," Jonah said.

Getting up from the kitchen table, he stepped up to the window to look out the front of the house.

As if on cue, an emerald green Mustang turned into Master Chief's driveway, parking behind his antique Ford, which sat in the carport beneath them.

"Here she is now." Jonah had texted Patterson his location only thirty minutes earlier.

He caught a brief glimpse of short red hair as the woman dashed through the rain from her car up to Rivera's front door. Letting Master Chief open his own door, Jonah stood back, assessing the young investigator as she introduced herself to Rivera and received his handshake.

"Charlotte Patterson," she said, leaving out her title.

Jonah hadn't been mistaken about the investigator's youth. She was probably in her mid-twenties. Still, she carried herself with confidence. Standing about six feet tall in pumps and dressed in a handsome black pantsuit that accentuated her athletic frame, she struck him as eager and ambitious, two traits that endeared her to him.

Cherry-brown eyes, bloodshot from grief, assessed him as he stepped up to greet her.

"Lieutenant Mills," she said, gripping his proffered hand firmly. He watched her absorb the scars on his face. "Welcome home," she added, not with pity but with a glimmer of determination. "Let's catch the bastard who tried to get rid of you."

Jonah had to smile. "Thanks." Not only did she carry herself like a man, but she also talked like one. "I'm sorry about Lloyd," he added, using Elwood first name the way she did.

Her eyes immediately clouded. "Yeah." She drew a sharp breath. "He said you would reach out to him when your memories returned. Are they back?"

Jonah shrugged. "A few. I called because I found something." He gestured to the journal, still perched on the table behind him. "Something that implicates James Lowery of leaking information."

"Excellent." Her face lit up with interest. Sparing a brief glance around Rivera's charmingly constructed but poorly furnished A-frame, she followed Jonah past the clunky, mismatched furniture in the living room to the kitchen.

"Can I get you a drink?" Rivera asked, joining them.

"Bottled water?"

As the master chief fetched a bottle from his fridge, Jonah gestured for Patterson to seat herself in front of LeMere's journal. Taking the chair next to her, he explained who it had belonged to and how the man's widow had mailed it to him.

With a thoughtful look, Patterson cracked the cover and thumbed through several pages.

"So the guy who wrote this is dead, too," she commented, twisting the lid off her water bottle.

"Yes. And the last person to be with him before his death was Lowery."

She looked up at Jonah sharply. "How did he die?"

Jonah explained the odd circumstances surrounding Blake's accident. "Read this here." He pointed out LeMere's recounting of how Lowery had been blind-copying emails to dead SEALs.

Patterson's russet eyebrows pulled together as she read the entire entry to where it ended.

"There's no more?"

Jonah shook his head. "No. LeMere died two days later in an accident."

Running a long, freckled finger over the lines of the entry, the investigator reread it.

"He must not have had the chance to speak with your CO."

"Of course not," Jonah agreed, "or Lowery would have been arrested by now."

She raised her eyes to look at him. "Plus, your commander never mentioned any of this to Lloyd when he interviewed him." She took a swig of her water.

"Elwood interviewed the CO, too?"

"Of course. Everyone from the top brass down, including Vice Admirals Leland and Holland." She put the bottle back down. "If Dwyer knew about the leak, he would have turned in Lowery as a possible suspect. Instead, he was the one held accountable for your disappearance, since it happened under his command."

Jonah hadn't considered that. "Dwyer was reprimanded for my disappearance?"

Rivera, who stood nearby, interjected with an answer. "His retirement was postponed six months. He would have been a civilian by now if you hadn't gone missing."

"Huh."

"We need to show Dwyer the journal," Rivera reiterated.

Jonah looked to Charlotte Patterson for corroboration.

Instead of answering, she took another sip of her water.

"It's unethical to withhold the journal from him," Rivera insisted.

"Is there enough evidence here to have Lowery arrested?" Jonah asked her.

Patterson eyed the journal, then looked up at him. "If we found the emails in question and verified LeMere's findings, then, yes. A warrant could definitely be issued for Lowery's arrest, citing the dissemination of classified material. Whether he brought about LeMere's death is another matter altogether. That would take longer to prove."

Hope pulsed through Jonah's veins. Once Lowery was arrested, Jonah could cease to worry he'd be targeted without warning. He could return to his home and to the family he longed to be with.

"Then you'll take over Elwood's case?" he prompted eagerly.

Silence followed his request.

"I can't," she finally said, lifting her cherry-brown gaze to his.

"Why not?"

"Because I'm not a special agent yet. I'm an intern."

Her confession stripped him of his optimism. "I thought you were Lloyd's colleague. Why else would he tell you so much, especially if you don't have clearance?"

"I have clearance," she clarified. "I just haven't gone through the Criminal Investigators Training Program."

Jonah covered his eyes and rubbed them.

"NCIS isn't going to help you anyway," she insisted. "Someone way up the food chain has done his best to keep Lloyd's evidence from coming to light. What I'd like to know is why. Don't worry, though. Like I told you, I have a powerful contact in the DIA. I can take this information straight to him, and he'll respond, I promise you."

Opening his eyes, Jonah exchanged a disappointed look with Rivera.

"Wouldn't it be faster," Rivera suggested, "to show the evidence to Commander Dwyer? He'll have Lowery off the squadron and behind bars in no time."

Patterson narrowed brown eyes at him. "Do you really think Lowery works alone? He's the tip of the iceberg. The weak link in the chain."

"You're talking about The Entity," Jonah guessed. "What do you know about it?"

"Not much," Patterson admitted, "but Lloyd was working on a theory. The fact that someone went to the trouble of killing him makes me think his theory was right."

Jonah exchanged a look with Rivera. "What was his theory?" he pressed.

Patterson bit her lower lip. "It's pretty scandalous. I'm not sure you want to hear it."

Intrigued, Jonah bent closer to her. "Yeah, we do."

The intern divided a wary look between them. "You need to keep this to yourselves," she warned. "Lloyd believed The Entity is a group of vigilante warriors; former, maybe even active-duty servicemen who are taking the nation's security into their own hands."

Patterson's words rocked Jonah on his heels. He and Rivera shared a look of consternation. A sharp pain pierced Jonah's left eye.

"My God, that makes sense," he murmured, then reeled at the implications.

Patterson pulled her phone out. "Keep that to yourselves for now," she cautioned. "Mind if I take pictures of these entries to show my contact?"

Jonah waited for Rivera's nod. "Go ahead," he agreed.

"You can show these entries to your CO if you must," she added, standing up in order to snap clear shots of the pertinent pages. "But hold onto the original and give him copies. The original will carry more weight if this goes to trial."

Slipping her phone back into her jacket, she regarded both men with a grimace of apology. "Look, I'm sorry I'm not what you expected, and I can't wave a magic wand to get Lowery arrested. But I know someone who can and will. I just have to give him the evidence Lloyd was collecting."

"How are you going to do that with Elwood's hard drive taken?" Jonah asked. "You would have to reconstruct his investigation. That could take months."

Patterson's lips curled toward a smile. "Lloyd had an iPad," she divulged, pitching her voice lower. "It contains all the findings of his investigation. He told me he had almost cracked the case. If I can find the iPad, I'm positive the DIA will want to finish the work Lloyd started."

Jonah glanced at Master Chief, who raised a dark eyebrow. The woman might be just an intern, but she had guts and a plan. Patterson took one more sip of her water. "Thanks for the use of your house, Master Chief," she said, leaving her bottle on the table. "I'd better get going," she said to Jonah.

Escorting her to the door, he held it open as she stepped outside, unmindful of the rain dampening her short red hair. Turning on the landing, she extended her hand for a parting shake.

"I'll be in touch," she promised.

"Good luck finding the iPad," Jonah replied. Without it, he couldn't see how justice would ever be served, at least not in this lifetime.

"Thanks." With a nod, Patterson turned and moved smartly down the stairs.

As she disappeared from sight, Jonah shut and locked the door. He and Master Chief stood a moment looking at each other in bemusement.

"So much for Lowery going to jail," Jonah muttered, shoving his hands into his rear pockets.

"Don't be so sure," Rivera comforted. "Anyone as determined as Patterson will get results eventually."

Jonah nodded in agreement, but he couldn't see how a mere intern was going to bring about justice, no matter who her contacts were. "Considering what happened to Elwood, I think we should say a prayer for her," he stated.

"I agree," Rivera said.

CHAPTER 17

*W*alking the dog on the beach, Eden looked up to realize she had plodded nearly to the other end of Sandbridge, where Master Chief Rivera's cottage sat between two enormous ocean-front houses.

She stopped abruptly, ignoring Sabrina's tug on the leash. The dog whined, wanting to join a family playing Frisbee nearby. The sun had fallen beyond the horizon, turning the sky behind the houses oyster-pink. Water swirled about Eden's ankles, shifting the sand beneath her feet until she sank into it. This was as far as she would go. A hot summer breeze lifted her hair and plastered her capris and T-shirt to her body.

Searching the lit windows of the master chief's little A-frame, Eden wondered if Jonah could see her, and whether he might run out to talk to her if he did. A wave of loneliness rolled through her. Two days had never seemed so endless.

Who could have guessed she'd have gotten so accustomed to his presence in so little time? Every moment spent with him had felt like an awakening. She had rediscovered him, falling in love with the man that he'd become. Yet, just when she'd realized she wanted her marriage to work, Jonah's PTSD had taken him away from her.

Even that would be acceptable if Jonah recognized he needed help. Instead, he'd turned his back on counseling and refused to accept that his suspicions were a product of the trauma he'd sustained.

Dr. Branson, whom Eden had called for advice, was surprisingly understanding.

He lived with more horror than you or I can imagine, Eden. His mind is accustomed to a constant threat. Just give him time.

Time was what she wanted to give—the rest of her life, as a matter of fact, but only if they were together. She had pledged herself to standing by Jonah through his recuperation, but the fact that he'd pulled away for reasons that were only in his head was too painful to tolerate.

The fear that nothing would ever be normal between them had usurped her faith that God would find a way. Although she'd received a clear sign from Him that Jonah was a changed man, Jonah himself refused to acknowledge there was anything wrong with him. If he didn't love Eden enough to attend his counseling sessions, what hope was there for their marriage?

In her heartbreak, she had stopped taking Jonah's phone calls—not because she didn't want to talk to him but because she could think of nothing else than the issue that was keeping them apart, and Jonah refused to budge from his decision.

Pulling her feet from the sand, Eden was startled to find the sun had dropped behind the rooftops, casting irregular shadows on the shore.

"Let's go back, Sabby," she said, urging the dog to turn toward home.

It wasn't much of a home now with Jonah gone. Miriam was there, of course, as sullen and morose as she'd been before Jonah's reappearance. Eden cringed to think what her daughter might do next in response to his recent desertion.

Poor girl. All she'd ever wanted was a father who loved her. Try as Eden might, there was nothing she could do to fulfill that basic need.

Don't desert us, God, she prayed as she trudged across the damp sand. The wind whipped her hair into her eyes. As she raised a hand to pull it back, the cell phone in her pocket rang. Daring to sneak a peek at it, she felt her heart squeeze when reading the caller's name.

As much as she longed to talk to Jonah, she couldn't bring herself to listen to his reasons for keeping his distance. His conspiracies about Jimmy Lowery were simply too far-fetched.

Declining his call with a push of her thumb, Eden accessed her favorites and placed a call of her own. If not for Nina's support and encouragement, she'd have fallen to pieces already.

Bracing herself for an encounter with Santiago Rivera, Nina Aydin drew a deep breath as she rapped on the door of his home.

Morning air, redolent with the scent of sand and sea, filled her nostrils. Waiting for him to answer, Nina turned her head to admire the sunrise. Santiago's home might be tiny, but the waterfront property had to be worth a pretty penny with such a view. Squinting at the golden sunrise, she listened for the sound of approaching footsteps.

To her relief, the door opened and there stood the man she'd come to see: Jonah Mills—not Santiago. His hair was still rumpled from sleep, and the jeans he'd obviously just tugged on were only halfway zipped.

"I'm sorry," she said, realizing she'd awakened him. "I thought you'd be up by now."

He blinked at her with evident confusion and not the slightest sign of recognition, causing Nina's eyebrows to shoot up.

"Oh, you don't remember me." It hadn't even occurred to her that might be the case.

"No, I'm sorry."

She'd never liked Jonah Mills, but his earnest apology roused her immediate sympathies, especially considering his amnesia wasn't his fault.

"I'm Nina Aydin," she said. "Eden's friend."

His confusion cleared in an instant. "Oh, of course. How is she?" he immediately asked. "She's not—" He faltered before admitting with chagrin, "She's not answering my calls right now."

Nina grimaced. "I know. That's why I'm here. I wanted to see you for myself."

Jonah's expression turned quizzical. He stepped back and opened the door wider. "You want to come in?"

"Oh." She plumbed the sunlit interior for signs of Santiago. "Are you alone?"

Jonah's eyebrows flexed at her hesitation. "My master chief's taking a swim, but he should be back soon."

Realizing she was dying to see the inside of Santiago's house, she said, "Sure, I'll come in," and brushed past Jonah into the open-concept living room. Her eyes rounded at the mismatched furniture, then darted toward the outdated kitchen. If not for the heart-of-pine floors, the soaring cedar ceiling, and the spiral staircase leading to more rooms upstairs, the place might resemble a bachelor pad.

Jonah wandered past her into the kitchen.

"Coffee?" he asked, making a beeline for the coffee pot.

"No, thank you."

With his back to her, Jonah poured himself a mug of fresh coffee then turned and eyed her through the steam.

"Why, exactly, did you want to see me?" he prompted lightly.

Already, in merely the few minutes they'd been face to face, Nina's question had been answered.

"I wanted to know if you were really as different as Eden said you were."

At the point of sipping his coffee, Jonah lowered his mug, not with surprise but with something akin to chagrin.

"I sure hope I'm different," he said fervently.

An incredulous laugh escaped her. "You really are," she marveled.

Gone was the overly confident, highly judgmental man she'd met on numerous occasions. This Jonah seemed completely human and humble.

"That's a good thing, right?" he asked, taking his first sip.

"A very good thing." She turned serious, recalling the true purpose of her visit. "Eden really loves you."

Her words had him staring into his coffee, hiding how strongly they affected him.

"I wish she would answer my phone calls," he finally said, lifting his eyes.

Nina pitied him. "That's between you two. All I know is she's afraid of being hurt again."

"Again?" he asked, making her regret letting the word slip out.

Ignoring the question, she countered, "She's hoping you'll keep your appointment with your psychiatrist. She wants you to be well."

A bitter smile twisted Jonah's mouth. He shook his head and thought for a moment. Nina could feel the powerful emotions rolling off him, though he held them firmly in check.

"I am well," he finally told her, in a voice so filled with determination and certainty she wondered for a moment if Jonah's paranoid beliefs might possibly be true. His smile turned grim.

"Since Eden won't take my calls, would you convey this message for me?"

"Yes." Guilt for undermining his and Eden's reunion these past two weeks pricked her conscience. The least she could do was be a go-between.

He started to talk, only to pause and clear his throat before trying again. "Tell her everything is going to be okay." His voice roughened. "I told her I'd be back, and I meant it."

Nina nodded. His determination roused her respect. "I will," she promised.

All at once the sliding glass door between the living room and balcony slid open. Santiago Rivera, wearing nothing but skin-tight swim-trunks and a towel slung around his neck, stepped inside.

Catching sight of Nina, he froze in astonished delight. "Hello."

"Hi." Giddiness spread through her, threatening her poise. She caught herself wanting to grin at him. Seeing him in the flesh, so virile and vigorous, she realized the real reason she'd come over hadn't solely been about Jonah. She'd wanted to see Santiago again. The idea of going on a date with him had morphed into a powerful desire to have his baby. The vision was so persistent she'd been driven to act on it, albeit subconsciously.

Moving past Jonah, she approached Santiago, fighting all the while to keep her eyes on his face and not let them drift toward his splendid chest and the six-pack abs he sported.

"Turns out I'm free this evening, after all, if you'd still like to go on that picnic." She was proud of how nonchalant she sounded when, in fact, her heart was trotting.

His eyes blazed with triumph. "Excellent. I'll pick you up at six if you'll tell me where you live."

She hesitated. "Pick me up at my studio," she suggested.

"As you wish." His smile of anticipation carved dimples into his lean cheeks.

All I want is a baby, she reminded herself. *A baby with dimples just like his.*

"I'll see you tonight then," she said. Tossing her long black hair over her shoulders, she looked back at Jonah. "Good to see you again," she said, surprised she actually meant it. Jonah wasn't at all the man he used to be. On her way to work, she would call Eden and apologize for not believing her on that score.

As she started for the door, Santiago rushed past her to draw it open. Military courtesy, Nina reminded herself. It didn't mean he would always be chivalrous.

"Until tonight," he said, his dark eyes warm with passion.

Not trusting her voice, Nina sent him a prim smile and stepped outside.

The sun painted a spectacular strip of gold across the sea. A flock of pelicans flew parallel to the shore, completing the idyllic scene.

Don't be a romantic imbecile, she warned herself and headed for her car. With four new and surprisingly affordable sparkplugs powering her engine, she drove away, determined to keep her attraction from clouding her judgment.

She wanted Santiago Rivera for one reason only. Convincing him to give her a baby without any strings attached was her objective. Falling in love with him was not.

Miriam regarded her reflection in the bathroom mirror through critical eyes. The dye was coming out of her hair turning it silver instead of purple. Her nose was too big for her face and dusted with freckles. Her mouth was too wide. She stuck her tongue out at her reflection.

Maybe she should dye her hair a different color or force studs through the closed holes in her ear. Her mother would have a cow if she did that. She'd be so upset she'd probably even call Jonah, with whom she'd refused to communicate, even though he called her all the time.

Miriam had watched with plummeting optimism as her mother ignored call after call from him. He'd called Miriam, too, but only once because she'd gotten emotional and asked him when he was coming back.

I shouldn't have done that.

Reaching for the jewelry box on the counter, she fished out the four sterling studs her mother had made her remove from her right ear. Were the holes completely closed up or was there hope of getting them back in there?

She tried pushing a stud into the first hole.

"Ow, ow, ow." The pain took her mind off Jonah's absence.

Silence seemed to echo in the rest of the house. Miriam felt most alone during the long hours her mother was away for work. Yesterday, she had sought refuge in the outdoors, hoping to distract herself. Unfortunately, every father in America was spending the last week of summer with his kids. All throughout Sandbridge, families frolicked in the sand and surf and shopped for souvenirs. Looking at them hurt.

I will never have a normal family. The thought ripped through her heart in the same instant the stud impaled the tender cartilage. The pain felt oddly satisfying. Ignoring the little rivulet of blood sliding toward her earlobe, Miriam picked up the second stud and moved to the next hole.

She had been so sure everything would work out with Jonah coming back into their lives. The fact he'd been alive when everyone thought him dead proved his marriage to her mother was meant to be. His being interested in Miriam and nice to her was an unexpected bonus. Truth be told, though, she'd have taken him back exactly the way he was. A distant dad was better than no dad.

The best thing of all was Mom had started liking him, too.

During their visit to Annapolis, Miriam had seen them look at each other with love in their eyes. Her hopes had soared. She'd been so certain her mother would forget her plan to separate from Jonah once he got his memory back. Having fallen in love with him, she would never leave him. Then Miriam would be just like the happy kids at school who had two parents.

That pipe dream had lasted right up to when Jonah thought some old man was following them back home.

The look on her mother's face lately said it all. Something wasn't right with Jonah. His year of captivity had left him thinking someone wanted him dead, the same person who'd tried to kill him a year ago. That story made no sense. He'd gone missing due to an accident. The enemy lived in a whole different country, which meant Jonah's fears were all in his head.

Anyway, that was what his psychiatrist believed, according to her mother.

Holding her ear still, Miriam gritted her molars to counteract the pain as she jammed the second stud through the resisting hole. It yielded with a stabbing pain, making tears spring to her eyes. She didn't have the guts to try the next two studs. Putting them back in the jewelry box, she raised a defiant gaze to the mirror and regarded her handiwork.

Two extra studs in her right ear didn't make her any prettier, she decided with a grimace.

The doorbell rang, startling her from her bleak thoughts. Who could that be? Ian wasn't allowed to come over while her Mom was out, and Eden wasn't due back from her Saturday afternoon grocery shopping for at least another hour.

With Sabrina emitting evenly spaced barks, Miriam wiped the blood off her earlobe with a tissue and left the bathroom to investigate.

Peeking through the narrow window by the door, her stomach lurched to see the same uniformed policeman who'd nearly arrested her earlier that week. Panic doubled the beat of her heart. The rule was never to answer the door while you're home alone, but this was a policeman, not a stranger. What's more, he'd seen her peeking out at him.

Assuring herself she'd done nothing wrong lately, other than re-pierce her own ears without permission, she turned the deadbolt, grabbed the dog's collar, and pulled the door open.

"Hello, again," said the officer whose square face she'd wished never to see again.

"Hi."

Glancing at the dog and dismissing her as a potential threat, Officer Hammond lifted his sunglasses from his pale eyes and peered over her shoulder into the house.

"Is your father here?"

Miriam's heart wrenched at the word *father*. "Not at the moment."

Lowering his sunglasses onto his nose he looked back at her.

"I'm sorry to be the one to tell you this," he said in a low voice, "and I don't want you to be alarmed, but your mother was in a car accident."

The blood drained so abruptly from Miriam's head her cheeks went cold and spots burst before her eyes. She clutched the doorknob for support.

"She's been taken to Sentara Hospital, and she's asking for you. Would you like a ride?" he asked, watching her carefully.

Miriam locked her knees to keep them from folding. "Yes." She looked down at the dog, whom she had yet to walk. "I'll walk you when I get back," she promised, patting Sabrina on the head.

"Better lock the handle behind you," the officer suggested as she slipped outside.

"I should get my cell phone," she said, hesitating. She'd left it on the bathroom sink.

"There's no time," said the officer.

The words turned her blood to ice water. "H-how hurt is she?" she stammered, chasing him down the steps to the undercover cop car he apparently drove.

Officer Hammond didn't answer. Instead, he opened the rear door for her.

"Hop in."

She didn't give a second thought to slipping into the back until she realized it was used for transporting criminals. Bullet-proof glass separated her from the front seats. Finding a seatbelt, she buckled herself in automatically. Shock slipped over her, numbing her thoughts and her emotions.

A single, horrifying prospect lodged itself in her mind. Not only did she not have a father but, if her mother didn't survive the accident, she wouldn't have a mother, either.

~

Santiago abhorred the dress Nina Aydin was wearing. Unrelentingly black, it hung from her shoulders all the way to her ankles. Sitting in the passenger seat of his Ford Falcon, she resembled a nun cloistered in a habit, except that her slim, strong arms were bare. He supposed he ought to be grateful for that small consolation.

At the moment, however, those lovely arms were folded across her torso like a shield, which he did not take to be a good sign.

She wore her long hair in a ponytail. Silver earrings shimmered on her earlobes and five assorted silver bracelets jangled on her left wrist. Slim black sandals failed to disguise the scarlet toenail polish on her elegant little toes. Over all, she looked more ready to attend a formal cocktail party than to sit on the sand enjoying a picnic.

His blue Bermuda shirt and cream-colored shorts were far more fitting for the occasion. Fortunately for them, it was a gorgeous evening, just cool enough to hint of the fall weather to come but warm enough to sit on the beach while the sun set behind them.

When he pulled into Back Bay Wildlife Refuge, Nina cut him a curious glance but said nothing.

He had chosen their destination for a reason. The refuge was unknown to most tourists. Its goal was to offer a sanctuary to sea grasses, wild ponies, and rare birds, not to take in revenue from visitors. In fact, the only other car in the parking lot was a Park Services Range Rover.

He pulled into the parking space closest to the beach path, cut the engine, and hopped out of the car to perform his gentlemanly duties, but Nina had already opened her door and was stepping out.

Accessing the trunk, he retrieved their picnic paraphernalia. While packing it, he'd anticipated the favorable result of their time spent together. She would realize they were destined to be a couple. They would marry and have two children within the next five years. Considering how resistant she was to a single date, he knew convincing her to share the visions in his head would be challenging—but then any good thing usually was.

She took the blanket out of his arms without being asked.

"I can carry it," he protested, hefting only the basket.

"Don't be a chauvinist." She angled her chin at him.

Strike one, Santiago thought, closing the trunk gently. Eden had warned him about Nina's mistrust. He would need to tread carefully if he didn't want to lose her before he even got off the ground.

"This way." Indicating with a smile the direction they should take, he escorted her down a sandy path toward the beach. The wind molded Nina's ridiculous dress to her body making it less of a sackcloth than it had first seemed.

He forced himself to avert his gaze. Seducing her wasn't his intention. He'd brought her here for one reason only—so she could get to know him better. Surely, once she realized he was nothing like her abusive ex-husband, she would give him a chance.

They came upon the ocean suddenly. The expansive view was everything Santiago wanted it to be, though he wished the waves weren't pummeling the shore with quite so much vigor.

"Let's try up here," he suggested, indicating a spot sheltered by the dunes. Putting down the basket, he took the blanket from Nina's hands and shook it out over the bowl of pristine sand, creating a surface as soft as a bed when he kneeled on it.

Kicking off his shoes, he watched Nina settle herself primly on their quilted nest. He was pleased to see she looked rather intrigued when he placed the basket between them and lifted the lid.

Drawing out the bottle of wine first, still gratifyingly chilled, he then reached for the corkscrew and glasses—not plastic cups, mind, but crystal goblets inherited from his grandmother, both carefully wrapped in a towel.

He unwrapped them and handed one to Nina. Her interested look was more bemused now, and touched with suspicion.

"Russian River Valley Chardonnay," he informed her as he popped the cork from the bottle then filled their glasses to the rim. "Have you ever tried it?"

"I don't think so. Do you drink often?"

The pointed question surprised him. "Only on weekends." Was she testing him?

Fortunately, his answer seemed to relieve her. He could only assume her ex had been a drinker.

Balancing his goblet on the sand, he pulled two containers from the basket and laid them out—cut veggies and dip in one; cheese and crackers in the other.

"Help yourself," he invited, waiting for her as she took a stick of celery before he selected a wedge of gouda and a cracker.

Crunch. Biting into the celery with her small white teeth, Nina chewed and crunched again, saying nothing.

Santiago cast about for something to talk about. The night they'd danced together at the brewery, there'd been no shortage of conversation. She seemed far more reserved tonight.

"Are you shy?" he asked as she reached next for a carrot.

She looked him in the eye then glanced away.

"No," she said self-consciously. "Not usually."

He sent her a crooked smile. "You don't have to be shy with me. Ask me anything. I'm an open book."

She swirled the carrot in the dip. "Have you ever been married?"

Satisfaction curled through him. She wasn't wasting his time with superficial questions.

"No. I didn't think it would be fair to have a wife and then leave her all the time. My job has kept me overseas much of my life. But since I'm planning to retire soon, that's no longer an issue."

Her wide-eyed stare assured him she was listening to every word he said.

"Then you plan to get married one day," she interpreted.

"If God wills it," he answered with a shrug.

One dark, elegant eyebrow edged above the other. "God's in charge of your social life?"

Her ironic tone dismayed him. So, she wasn't a believer. That might present a problem.

"Of course. He oversees every aspect of my life."

The statement seemed to puzzle her. "I've never understood that. You don't want to control your own destiny?" *Crunch.* She bit the carrot and chewed it as she waited for his answer.

He smiled ruefully. "My life would be a disaster if I tried to control it all by myself. That's way too much work. God does a far better job than I ever could."

He could tell by her mystified expression she had no source of strength to fall back on. His plan to marry her one day wavered. How would that work out to be with someone who couldn't understand the way faith worked?

"Eden says the same thing," Nina commented. "I wasn't raised to believe in anything." Lifting her gaze to the lavender sky, she added, "But I do."

Her confession relieved and encouraged him. "Then you believe in a Creator?"

"Oh, yes," she nodded. "I just don't talk to Him."

"You could try it," he suggested.

She laughed at the thought. "I'm afraid I would just end up yelling at Him."

He blinked at the unexpected confession. "Are you mad at God?"

Her focus turned inward. "I suppose I am."

"Tell me," he encouraged.

Her face hardened, and she turned her head to regard him. "Look, I'm not here to tell you all about my past. I'm not even here to get to know you better."

Her apologetic grimace took the edge off her words.

"Why are you here then?" He sensed a deep vulnerability in her, one she hid behind her thorns.

She looked down at the cheese plate and reached for a cheddar cube.

"I can't believe I'm going to say this," she muttered to herself.

"Say it," he encouraged. "There's nothing you could say that would upset me."

Hope vied with disillusionment in the big brown eyes she raised to him.

"One of the reasons I'm mad at God," she said, hearkening back to their conversation, "is because I can't have a baby. I've always wanted children, but I'm barren."

While her words disappointed him, the pain in her voice melted him. Scooting closer, he reached for her hand and squeezed it.

"I'm sorry." Keeping her hand in his, he waited for her to continue.

"However," she continued, her voice growing strained, "there's a possibility I could have a baby through in-vitro fertilization. I just need a sperm donor."

He stilled, suddenly aware of where their conversation was going.

"You want me to be the sperm donor?"

Searching his incredulous gaze, she licked her lips in a nervous gesture.

"Are you angry with me?"

Her anxiety was palpable. "No. *Querida*, you can ask anyone who knows me. I don't get angry. I'm extremely placid." He sent her his most patient smile.

"Now you're teasing me."

"Yes." His smile widened. "I have many attributes that make me the ideal candidate to father your child."

Her eyes widened. "Then you'll do it?" She gripped his hand with evident excitement. "You'll be my sperm donor?"

"Ah." He took exception to her terminology. "I think we may be skipping over some critical steps first."

"Like what?" she asked, withdrawing the warmth of her hand.

The question took him aback. "Like getting to know each other?"

He was dismayed to see her expression freeze. "Oh." He pulled back to look at her more directly. "You're asking me to father your baby without any more involvement? Is that what you're asking?"

He failed to disguise his incredulity—not to mention disillusionment and, yes, anger.

She flinched. "You make it sound like a crime. Women do it all the time."

"We're not talking about women in general," he replied with controlled heat. "We're talking about you and me and creating a child who deserves every advantage in life, which means a two-parent household. Are you saying I wouldn't take part in his life—?"

"Or *her* life," she interrupted, growing as hot under the collar as he was.

"Either way," he continued, "I'm not fathering a child unless I have full privileges as a parent with unlimited visitation."

Forcing himself to stop speaking, he barely kept himself from adding how he wouldn't father a child with her anyway unless they got married first. Yet talk of marriage had sent her running for the hills the last time he'd brought it up, so he withheld that caveat to be brought up at a later time, after she'd grown to love and to trust him.

Nina popped the entire cube of cheese in her mouth and chewed, presumably while considering his ultimatum. Then she emptied half her wine glass with a long draught.

"That might be possible," she finally said.

Exultation hit his bloodstream, making Santiago want to punch a fist into the air and bellow "Hooyah!" Knowing that would scare Nina away, he held out his goblet and proposed a toast, "To our future child."

Her gaze jumped from the goblet to his face, causing him to hold his breath lest she reconsidered.

At last, she touched her glass to his, creating a lovely chime, which, to him, sounded rather like a church bell.

"To Esme," Nina said, lifting her chin in a gesture he recognized as defiance. "That's her name."

"Short for Esmerelda?" Santiago guessed.

"Could be," she said with a shrug. "Esmerai is a Turkish name. My grandmother's name."

Ah, so she was Turkish American, hence her shiny black hair and almond-shaped eyes.

"Esme," he repeated. "I like it."

A dusky pink blush highlighted her cheekbones, making her so breathtakingly beautiful he ached to kiss her.

All in good time, he thought, checking that impulse. If he played his cards right, Nina would be the one to kiss him first. Then love, then marriage.

If God wills it, he added to himself.

CHAPTER 18

"*H*ello?" Putting down the book he was reading, Jonah answered his cell phone with a soaring of his heart. Eden! He'd called her a dozen times; at last, she was calling him back. Swinging his gaze out the big windows of Master Chief's living room, he saw it was nearly dark.

"Jonah?"

The way she said his voice had him scooting to the edge of the armchair in which he'd been reading. "What's wrong?"

"Miriam's not with you by any chance, is she?"

Jonah looked around Master Chief's empty living room.

"No. Have you tried Ian's?"

"Yes, she's not there, either. She left her cell phone in the bathroom. The dog had an accident in the house, which means she didn't walk her like she was supposed to. And now it's dark outside. I'm really getting worried."

Concern drove Jonah to his feet. "I'll come help you look for her," he offered, hunting for his shoes.

"You don't have to do that," she replied.

"Yes, I do. I'm probably the reason she's doing this. I'll be over as soon as I can."

Hanging up on her, he found his shoes under the chair and started putting them on when his phone rang again. This time, he didn't recognize the number.

"Hello?" He hoped it was Miriam, borrowing someone else's phone.

"Mr. Mills? This is Officer Hammond with the Virginia Beach Police."

Jonah sank back into the chair, alarm prickling along his spine. "Yes?" Hammond was the officer who'd caught Miriam buying cigarettes the previous week and, somehow, he'd gotten Jonah's number.

"I'm sorry to tell you this, but your daughter, Miriam, was caught smoking cigarettes at Back Bay Wildlife Refuge, where smoking is prohibited."

Stunned, Jonah recalled how Miriam liked going to Back Bay to look for wild ponies.

"I see," he said, disappointed. It was his fault she was acting out, he was certain.

"I need you to come collect her. She'll be fined, of course. And because she's a minor, you'll have to go to court."

Jonah didn't care what they had to do. Miriam had been driven by her emotions to break the rules. She was clearly crying out for help, which was why she'd given Hammond his number and not her mother's. What's more, he fully intended to be there for her.

"I understand. Collect her where?" he asked.

"I've detained her at the visitor's center. The park just closed, but you can raise the bar by hand and drive in."

Jonah glanced at his watch. Back Bay was at least five miles distant. Eden would have to pick him up and take him there.

"I'll be there by nine o'clock," he said, using civilian time.

An impatient silence followed. "Fine," Hammond said on a curt note and hung up.

Disliking the man's peremptory tone and worried for Miriam, who was probably frightened out of her mind, Jonah called Eden immediately.

"Hello?" she answered on a hopeful note.

"I know where she is."

"Oh, thank goodness."

"She went to Back Bay to look for ponies."

"All the way out there?" Eden sounded skeptical. "But her bike is here at the house."

Jonah stopped prevaricating. "Okay, truth is I just got a call from Officer Hammond. Miriam was caught smoking cigarettes inside the reserve."

"Oh, no," Eden cried, obviously distraught.

"But she's safe," Jonah soothed. "That's all that matters. He wants me to pick her up at the visitor's center."

Eden groaned. "It's a wildlife refuge. I can't imagine what the fine for smoking is out there!"

"Don't worry about the fine," Jonah said. "I told Hammond I would be there by nine. Can you come pick me up? I would ask Rivera but he's on a date."

"I'm leaving right now," she told him. "On a date with whom?"

He overheard the door shut behind her as she let herself out of the house.

"Your friend Nina. She came over this morning—mostly to check me out on your behalf, but then she took Master Chief up on his offer of a date."

"That's great! I'm happy for them." But her tone sounded distracted, and her happiness was clearly tempered by worry for her daughter. Jonah heard her shut herself inside the Jaguar and start the engine.

"Focus on the road," he urged. "I'll be waiting for you out front."

By the time he reached the mailbox, he could see the headlights of their car coming up the road. Eden had a lead foot on the accelerator. Not for the first time did he curse his inability to drive.

"Hey," he said, drinking in the sight of her as he slipped into the car.

She paused to stare back at him, her moist eyes reflecting the street lamps.

"Hi." The air in the car thickened with emotional tension.

"Let's go get our girl," he prompted, putting on his seatbelt. "She has to be feeling pretty intimidated."

"Hopefully enough to learn her lesson," Eden murmured, even as she accelerated swiftly, turning right onto the road that took them away from Sandbridge and toward the refuge. The sky grew darker as the road carried them from civilization into nature.

Approaching the entrance to the park minutes later, Jonah saw the bar was indeed down.

"Hammond told me to raise the bar and come on in." He hopped out of the car to do just that.

Seconds later, they pulled up next to a Park Services Range Rover and a dark blue sedan. At the other end of the lot, parked nearly out of sight, was a familiar-looking car.

"Oh, look down there," Jonah exclaimed. "That's Master Chief's car."

Eden followed his gaze and frowned. "He brought Nina on date out here?"

"I guess so." As he straightened from his own car, Jonah's gaze went to the blue sedan. It was an undercover cop car, he realized, identical to the one that had run him and Sabby off the road over a week ago.

Jonah's instinct for trouble twitched. He patted the Sig at his hip, relieved to have it in his possession. Wouldn't this remote area be the perfect place to do him in? Then again, Lowery had nothing to do with Miriam smoking at a wildlife refuge. Jonah had to be paranoid to think Lowery could arrange such an elaborate plot to get him out here, nearly alone, too.

All the same, he caught Eden's hand as she hastened toward the office, a wooden bungalow painted in driftwood gray.

"Slow down, honey," he begged her. "Something feels wrong about this."

The pitying look she cast him made him want to howl in frustration.

"Just stay behind me," he requested tersely.

With a huff she didn't bother to hide, she stepped into his shadow, letting him precede her toward the door.

Other than the crash of the nearby ocean and the whistling of wind through the sea grasses, the place was unnaturally quiet. Their footsteps reverberated on the wooden ramp. Sand crunched loudly under their soles. Just as they reached the solid door, it swung open. Jonah found himself looking up into the hard face of a uniformed officer.

"Evening," said Hammond curtly.

Oddly, though the sun was sucking the last hint of daylight from the sky, the man hid his face behind sunglasses. Even so, the distinctive line of his jaw, paired with the car out front, identified him as the driver who would have struck and possibly killed him a week earlier if he hadn't jumped off the road in time.

Adrenaline spiked his bloodstream. Prompted by instinct and ignoring caution completely, Jonah seized the man's shirtfront, yanking him off balance. Hammond stumbled forward, and Jonah drove a knee into his midsection. As the man doubled over, Jonah snatched the pistol from the officer's holster.

"What are you doing!" Eden railed.

"Trust me," he growled at her. With Hammond straightening on a groan, Jonah transferred the 9mm to his own shooting hand and released the safety.

"Back up," he ordered.

Eden tried again, clearly appalled by what was happening.

"Jonah! You can't do this!"

"Stay right here," he ordered her. "Back up!" he repeated when the cop didn't move.

With a look of fury and pure reluctance, the cop took three steps into the visitor's center.

"Stop," Jonah added when it was clear the man was looking for a weapon on the counter behind him. Stepping inside, Jonah searched for Miriam, but the modest room, comprised of a counter, bookshelves, and a bench, appeared empty.

"She's not here," he called to Eden.

"What?" she said, edging into the room to have a look for herself.

"Don't come in!" Jonah warned.

Taking advantage of his distraction, the officer reached for the nearest object at hand—a wooden pamphlet organizer—and hurled it at Jonah, who dodged easily only to find himself tackled a second later.

The cop slammed him into the wall, causing the gun in his hand to discharge, embedding a bullet in the ceiling. Eden screamed. Two things occurred to Jonah at once. First, the man wasn't only bigger than he was, he was obviously a trained combatant, probably ex-Special Forces. Second, he was entirely fit. If Jonah let the man get the better of him, he wouldn't live to tell about it, and Eden was probably next to be killed for witnessing the event.

"Go!" he managed to yell at her between hooks and punches and deadly choke holds. "Get Master Chief!"

Eden had frozen in astonishment. Somewhere between Jonah's unexpected offensive and the horrifying and unbelievable consequences, it had dawned on her maybe her husband's paranoia wasn't strictly in his head. Something weird was happening; otherwise, Miriam would be here, and Hammond would be reasoning with Jonah, not trying to kill him.

With spittle flying and furniture breaking, it was horribly apparent Jonah was fighting for his life.

"Go!"

His plea penetrated the shell of shock keeping her motionless. Eden backed out of the building, fumbling to extract her phone from her purse. She had no idea where Jonah's master chief might have taken Nina.

Please let them be close, she prayed, accessing her contacts and finding the number he'd given her back when everyone thought Jonah was dead.

As the ringer sounded in her ear, Eden cast a torn glance back at the visitor's center and the sounds of a terrifying struggle before leaping off the stoop and running as fast as her legs could take her, up the path leading toward the ocean. Where else would Rivera and Nina have chosen to picnic, but within view of the water?

Rivera's phone rang and rang in Eden's ear. Over the sound, she detected footsteps behind her and realized she was being chased. Fear galvanized her. *Was Hammond not alone, then?* She increased her speed, flying along a raised footbridge conveying her past several dunes and thorny brush.

"Master Chief!" she yelled, as her call to him went to voicemail. The wind carried her cry inland.

Reaching the end of the footbridge, she dared to look back. Under the twilight sky, the bridge was sufficiently lit that she could tell no one was behind her. Yet she was certain she'd been chased, at least for a while.

Crack! A second bullet discharged inside the visitor's center.

"Master Chief!" Eden cried again. Whirling toward the ocean, she sprinted across the soft sand in the hopes that he and Nina had gone right and not left.

Santiago's swim in the ocean had kept him from proposing to Nina before she was ready to hear it.

"You're lucky you didn't get eaten by a shark," she commented as he emerged from the sea and took the towel she offered him.

"You sound relieved that I'm alive," he teased, toweling his damp head.

"Humph." She refused to give him the satisfaction of saying as much. "You do swim well."

"Thanks." He paused in the act of drying his chest. "Did you hear that?"

Standing at the water's edge, they both pivoted toward the sound that had come to them over the foaming of the ocean.

"A car backfiring?" Nina wondered.

"A gunshot." Santiago looped the towel over his shoulders and grabbed Nina's hand. "Come with me," he said, tugging her behind him in the event of a stray bullet.

"That's Eden!" Nina cried, peering past his shoulder.

A mane of golden hair shone in the gloom, giving Eden away. Her frantic gait jumpstarted Santiago's adrenaline.

"Something's wrong." He broke into a run with Nina right behind him.

Within seconds, Eden crashed into them blurting unintelligible words about the visitor's center and a cop and Miriam and Jonah about to be killed, if he wasn't already.

"Stay here. No." Santiago changed his mind. "Go back to the blanket and stay there until I come get you."

Not waiting to see if the women would obey him, Santiago charged into the direction Eden had come from, cursing his lack of shoes—and weapon—as he leaped barefooted onto the rough wooden walkway.

All at once the silhouette of a man materialized at the other end. A firearm discharged, and the figured ducked, whirled and fired back, all in one graceful and familiar gesture.

It's Jaguar, Santiago realized. The person chasing him had just shot at him. *Madre de Dios!*

With no weapon of his own with which to return fire, Santiago yelled toward the shooter in the thickening darkness, "Hey, he has backup!"

A startled silence followed his assertion. Jonah seized his reprieve, sprinting toward Santiago in a full-out retreat while running in zigzags lest he got shot at again. Gaining Santiago's side, Jaguar grabbed his arm and urged him to flee.

"Where's Eden?" Jaguar huffed as they reached the beach.

Indicating the direction they should take and keeping to the dunes for cover, Santiago hissed his discomfort as sharp blades of grass cut into his soles. He pressed on, ignoring his pain, until they came upon the sheltered bowl of land where both women waited in silence for them.

"Jonah!" Eden leaped from the blanket and hurled herself into her husband's arms. "Oh, my God, you're okay. You're okay." She sobbed in her relief. Then she gasped, "Where's Miriam?"

Still holding onto his wife, Jaguar shook his head. "She wasn't there. At least, I didn't see her."

"What's going on?" Santiago needed an explanation of how his date night had gone from delightful to dangerous in mere minutes.

"I was targeted," Jaguar relayed in a gravelly voice. "Some cop in an unmarked car tried running me off the road last week—I thought it was just a fluke. But he's been following Miriam around and watching the house."

Eden added, "His name's Hammond. He caught Miriam buying cigarettes last week and called my number."

"He called me again tonight," Jonah continued. "Supposedly, she was smoking cigarettes out here this evening. Hammond claims he caught her and he told me to come and pick her up." He paused and looked at Eden. "I don't think they meant for Eden to come, though."

"Where is Miriam?" Eden repeated with panic in her voice.

Nina put an arm around her. "I'm sure she's fine."

"They?" Santiago prompted, trying to follow the story.

"Hammond wasn't alone." Jaguar continued. "The call was a ploy to get me out here. When Eden and I arrived at the visitor's center, I recognized Hammond as the cop who nearly ran me over, so I went on the offensive. He did his best to kill me, and I can tell you this for sure—he's more than a cop. He's had prior training. If I hadn't realized he had a bad knee, he would have choked me to death. I freed myself by kicking there and managed to shoot him. I think I might have killed him," he added hoarsely.

It was suddenly clear why Jaguar sounded so tense.

"Then who was firing at you just now?" Santiago demanded.

"Lowery," Jonah answered.

Eden stilled and looked at him. "I knew there was someone else! He chased me for a while, but then he let me go."

Jaguar nodded. "He was out there the whole time, waiting for a chance to shoot me."

Santiago wasn't yet convinced of Lowery's involvement. "Why didn't he fire on you when you first arrived?"

The question stymied Jaguar but only for a second. He looked at his wife.

"Because Eden was standing right behind me, and Lowery didn't want to kill her."

Eden touched his arm. "How'd you get away from him just now?"

"I went out the window at the back of the building."

"Did you actually see him?" Eden asked.

"Yes. He had camo paint on his face, but I'd recognize Lowery anywhere."

Santiago ran a hand through his wet hair. "And there's no one else out here?"

"Not that I know of."

Eden moved back into Jaguar's arms, seeking comfort and offering reassurance.

"We have to call the police," she said. "They can't all be bad. We have to find Miriam."

Santiago studied his lieutenant, standing stiffly in his wife's embrace, understandably in shock. If the man Jaguar had killed was an actual police officer, Jaguar could kiss his career on the Teams goodbye.

"Jonah," Eden pleaded. "We don't know where Miriam is."

He visibly stirred from a trancelike state.

"Right," he said and looked over at Santiago, whose heart hurt for him. "I'll make the call."

Less than an hour later, Eden sat in the passenger seat of the Jaguar as Jonah chased an ambulance from the wildlife refuge to Sentara Princess Anne Hospital. She had not stopped shaking since Jonah first attacked Hammond. It was probably a good thing Jonah slipped behind the wheel of their car without asking.

"Do you think they'll keep her overnight?" she wondered as they sped down the dark back-roads toward lights shining in the distance.

The police had found Miriam within minutes of their arrival, lying in the back seat of the undercover cop car, along with an empty canister of some kind of odorless incapacitating agent. What they *hadn't* found was an injured police officer or a second shooter, only signs of a violent struggle in the visitors center and lots of tracks in the sand.

Jonah glanced at the car's digital clock. "Given the time, they probably should keep her."

"She'll be okay, won't she?" Uncertainty put a wobble in her voice. Miriam had roused to consciousness when they'd awakened her, but then promptly vomited, making Eden fear about the long-term effects of the gas she'd inhaled.

Jonah reached for her cold hand, holding onto it.

"I think she'll be okay. That gas was probably Agent 15. It was stockpiled in large quantities in Iraq during the Persian Gulf War. It isn't toxic. I'd like to know how Hammond got his hands on it, but I'm sure he didn't hurt her. It was me he was after."

The words reminded Eden of everything that had transpired. The police, who'd been as incredulous as she'd been when they first arrived, had changed their tune the minute Miriam was discovered. They'd gone from wanting to arrest Jonah to proclaiming Hammond, who'd been off-duty that night, had no business drugging a teenager and leaving her in the back of his squad car. He would be in serious trouble when they located him.

Jonah and Eden were freed to leave with the ambulance, providing they brought Miriam to the police station the next day to answer more questions and give a statement.

Drawing a deep breath, Eden assured herself the worst was behind them. In their investigation, the police would discover clues backing up Jonah's story. She herself could not deny what she'd seen with her own two eyes.

Speaking through a tight throat, she uttered the words weighing heavily on her heart.

"Jonah, I owe you a huge apology. I thought—"

"I know what you thought," he cut in, keeping her from having to say it.

Fixing her gaze on the mesmerizing red lights in front of them, she tried to explain herself. "It's because I read an article at your psychiatrist's office, and it painted such a grim picture of PTSD—"

"Honey, you don't have to explain." He cut her off again, gently but firmly. "I don't blame you for not believing me initially. The entire situation is bizarre in the extreme. I'm kind of glad it happened. At least, now you know I've been telling you the truth."

She shut her eyes and shook her head. "I should have known it all along," she lamented, looking at him again. "I should have trusted you. God gave me a clear sign to recommit to our marriage, and I didn't have enough faith in Him. I'm so sorry."

He reached for her hand, threading his fingers through hers.

"You trust me now?" he asked.

"Yes." While she still couldn't picture Jimmy Lowery killing his own teammate, it made sense that he'd been the second adversary at the refuge. Eden's presence had thrown a wrench into his plan to kill Jonah.

"What is Jimmy so afraid of?" Eden asked. "What was in the notebook, Jonah? You can tell me. I promise I won't tell anyone."

He glanced over at her, then back at the road. "It explains how Lowery's been leaking top-secret intel, possibly to members of The Entity. I must have called him on it over a year ago, right before the op to Carenero."

"How's he leaking it?" she pressed.

"He was blind-copying recipients who shouldn't have been receiving any emails at all, deceased SEALs."

"But dead men can't read emails," she pointed out.

"Exactly. I'm guessing the accounts were reactivated, and someone else was reading them. I'm sure he's wised up and changed his MO."

"Even so," she replied, "NCIS will want to look into that."

"I'm not so sure." Jonah turned on his blinker and followed the ambulance turning at the intersection. "Someone wants Elwood's investigation scrapped, to the point of killing the investigator."

Eden had never met Elwood. Instead, she envisioned the old man Jonah had thought was following them from her parents' house. Given everything Jonah had been through, he could just as easily have been a hit man.

"Do you still think it was Jimmy Lowery who killed Agent Elwood?"

Jonah didn't immediately answer. "I don't know. I think this is bigger than Lowery. Someone at the top ordered Elwood's office cleaned out and his hard drive wiped. Lowery doesn't have that kind of authority."

A chill raked Eden's spine. "I don't like the sound of this."

"Things are getting intense," Jonah reflected. "Lowery has tried to kill me three times now."

"You never told me about the cop car trying to run you over. Why not?"

Jonah sent her a wry look. "That's obvious, isn't it? You didn't believe me when I told you Lowery fired on me after I left the gym. Besides, with everyone concluding that I had PTSD, I figured it might have been a hallucination. What kind of cop mows people down in broad daylight, anyway?"

Eden's outrage grew. "The same kind who lures teens into the back of his car and gasses them. I can't believe he told Miriam I'd been in a car accident."

Jonah adjusted his grip on the steering wheel and said nothing.

Eden studied his taut profile. "I'm so sorry I didn't believe you about Jimmy shooting at you the other day." Love for Jonah and admiration for his bravery overwhelmed her suddenly, causing her eyes to fill with tears.

"Don't cry, beautiful." Lifting her hand to his mouth, he kissed her knuckles, then concentrated on following the ambulance into the entrance to the hospital. "I'm a big cat, remember? I've got at least five lives left."

Realizing he was still a marked man, Eden swept a fearful look around the parking lot. "Lowery won't follow you here," she said, more to herself than to Jonah.

"We'll be safe," he agreed.

As the ambulance veered toward the sliding glass doors, Jonah zipped into the nearest empty parking spot.

"Jonah." Eden halted him as he went to take off his seatbelt. He glanced at Miriam's ambulance before giving her his full attention.

"I've been wanting to tell you this since we were at my parents' house." Even though her timing wasn't great, she had to say it now, lest—God forbid —she didn't get another chance.

"I love you," she stated, carrying his hand to her fast-beating heart and holding it there. Her voice thickened with emotion. "I love you for your patience with me and for your kindness to Miriam. You're an incredible man, and I want to stay with you forever. Please don't let anything happen to change that."

A moist sheen slipped over Jonah's eyes, reflecting the lights from the hospital.

"I love you, too, Eden. Nothing in the world has the power to change that."

Leaning toward her, he planted a brief, fervent kiss on her lips even as he reached past her to unlatch her door and push it open, urging haste. They both ran toward the entrance, reaching the hospital as Miriam was being wheeled through the sliding doors.

"Mom!" she called, lighting up to see her. "Dad!"

Eden gave a sob of relief to see her daughter sitting up, looking far less disoriented than she had at the refuge. This night, she realized, could have ended so much worse. God was obviously watching over them. She prayed He would continue His vigilance.

Some faceless evil seemed hell-bent on keeping Jonah quiet.

CHAPTER 19

$\mathcal{A}$ strange beeping noise roused Miriam from a light slumber. Slitting her eyes, she remembered where she was and the bizarre circumstances that had brought her there—though, in all honesty, she recalled very little beyond the sensation of going lightheaded in the back of Officer Hammond's unmarked car.

Questions sluiced through Miriam, bringing her wider awake. Lifting her head off the pillow, she could tell it was nearly dawn by the light framing the drawn curtains of her hospital room. The light revealed two lumpy forms sleeping on the cushioned bench in front of the window.

A smile tugged at her lips as she recognized her mom and dad, sharing the visitor's lounge, cuddling in their sleep. Lying front to back on a padded bench barely big enough for one person, they seemed to be sleeping soundly.

Adjusting the pillow under her head, Miriam watched them sleep as the room slowly brightened. She tried to make sense of what had happened the night before.

She remembered Hammond putting her in the car, but little beyond that. When the police woke her up hours later, they'd found an aerosol canister under her feet, suggesting Hammond had released some kind of gas that made her pass out. A blood test at the hospital had confirmed she'd been exposed to an incapacitating agent with an unpronounceable name. Jonah had called it Agent 15.

Her mother had explained how Officer Hammond had lured Jonah out to Back Bay Wildlife Refuge by telling him he'd caught Miriam smoking cigarettes out there. Through snippets of conversation between Jonah and the police, Miriam had come to a thrilling but also chilling conclusion: Jonah wasn't paranoid.

Hammond had attacked her father, who'd shot and maybe killed him. Another man, a teammate named Lowery, had also shot at him. Yet, miraculously, Jonah had escaped death once again. And, even more miraculously, he and her mother seemed to be reunited. At least, they didn't look to her as if they planned to separate, not snuggled together on the bench like that.

With a sigh of contentment, Miriam let her head drop to the pillow and closed her eyes. All her life she had felt God considered her a mistake, the same way her grandparents did. Consequently, God didn't look out for her the way he did for other people. But that wasn't the case, was it? It was true what Pastor Tom said at church: God did answer prayers, even Miriam's.

With a tear of contentment sliding toward her temple, Miriam fell back asleep.

∼

The sudden buzzing of a cell phone brought Jonah's head up. Memories of the night before flooded him with a deluge of terror, relief, and hope. Eden slept in his embrace, her sweet curves eliciting a night of sensual dreams.

"That's my phone," he murmured, dropping an apologetic kiss on her cheek as she stirred. He vaulted over her to retrieve his phone from the charger. "It's Master Chief," he whispered as he glanced at Miriam, whose eyes fluttered open.

"Yes, sir," he answered, throwing in the respectful title, not because it was protocol, but because the man deserved his veneration. He had been the very soul of reasonableness when the police had answered their summons the night before.

"Good morning."

Rivera's cheerful tone helped to allay some of Jonah's fears. Today he, Eden, and Miriam would report to the police station to give their stories. Surely, the police would conclude Jonah hadn't been at all in the wrong, and they would focus their investigation on Hammond and Lowery.

"What's up?" Jonah braced himself.

"I wanted to tell you I dropped your stuff off at your house because I think you should return to your family."

Jonah hesitated. It was obvious Lowery wasn't above using his family to get to him. Living with Eden and Miriam again could put them in serious danger.

Rivera continued. "Saul, Theo, Lucas, and Bambino have volunteered to do security detail. You'll run into a pair of them when you go home this morning."

Gratitude swelled Jonah's heart. "That's awesome." He turned his gaze to Eden, who had sat up to listen to his exchange. The thought of living with her, holding her in his arms whenever he wanted, filled him with deep contentment. He couldn't wait for Miriam to get released so they could all go home.

"Also, I'm going to the CO's house after church to bring him up to speed on what's happening," Master Chief added. "I'm going to show him a copy of LeMere's entries."

Anticipation gave way to a peculiar mix of hope and dread.

"I guess there's no way around it," Jonah replied. "Hopefully, he'll agree LeMere's journal implicates Lowery." If only it didn't appear that NCIS, or someone with authority over them, wanted the investigation of the leak to go away.

"There no other way," Rivera assured him.

"He's not going to be happy the leak took place right under his nose," Jonah realized.

"No, he isn't."

"Where'd you put the original?"

"It's locked in my desk at the office."

"Okay." Jonah blew out a breath. "Keep me posted on your meeting."

"I'll call as soon as it's over," Master Chief promised. "How's Miriam?"

Jonah looked back at the bed where Miriam had sat up and was now regarding him with an almost worshipful expression. "My daughter is awake and looking lovely," he answered.

Miriam's gaze dropped. He watched with satisfaction as her little smile appeared.

"Thanks for everything, Master Chief," he added, hoping his words conveyed the depths of his gratitude. "I can't thank you enough."

"*No hay de que.* It's nothing. I wanted to be there at the station when you talk to the police, but that's the only time Dwyer can meet with me."

"That's okay," Jonah assured him. "We'll be all right. Keep me up to speed on Dwyer's response."

"Yes, sir."

Pushing his cell phone into his pocket, Jonah looked back at his family.

"You guys mind if I live with you again? My teammates are going to protect us." He had total faith in their ability to do so.

"I don't mind." Miriam said without a second's hesitation.

Eden's eyes glowed with warmth. "We would love that," she said, sharing a special look with her daughter.

Two hours later, Jonah swung into his driveway to find Saul and Lucas up on his deck with their shirts off, hard at work.

"Now that is some serious eye candy," Miriam commented from the back seat.

"Miriam!" Eden scolded, trying not to sound amused. "Are they staining the deck?" she asked, peering up at them more closely.

Jonah grinned. "Looks like it." It had bugged him like crazy that he hadn't yet finished the project he'd started.

As he and his family exited the Jaguar, memories of the prior night's terror faded. It felt so good to be home again. The sky was a robin's-egg blue, the breeze cool enough to keep a body from sweating, even if laboring under the bright sun. They mounted the stairs to greet their personal bodyguards.

"Howdy." Saul saluted them with a wet roller. His long, mahogany hair was caught up in a braid, making him look like the Creek grandfather who'd taught him his tracking abilities. "Hope this is the same stain you started with." He indicated the four-gallon drum sitting open next to the rolling tray.

"It is," Jonah assured him, greeting Lucas who'd taped his roller to a long handle so he wouldn't have to bend over. "You guys don't have to do this, you know."

"Oh, yes we do," Saul replied. His tattooed, muscular arm flexed as he rolled stain on the railing. "You promised us a Labor Day party, and tomorrow is Labor Day," he pointed out.

Jonah looked over at Eden to gauge her response. "You still okay with hosting a party?"

"Fine with me," she assured him, but her eyes conveyed their shared concern that last night's misadventure would have unforeseen consequences.

Miriam hooted with enthusiasm. "Awesome! I get to decorate. We need to get out the tiki torches and buy some balloons."

Eden nodded. "We can do that, *after* our trip to the police station."

Her anxiety wasn't lost on Jonah, who prayed their plan for a party would come to fruition.

"Let me go change so I can help these guys." He started for the door.

"I want to help, too," Miriam piped up.

"You should rest," Eden told her as she unlocked it for them.

"Where's Sabrina?" Jonah was struck by the unusual quiet.

"Nina picked her up last night. I didn't know how long we'd be at the hospital."

"Nina has a key and I *still* don't?" he asked with exaggerated frustration.

Eden indicated the key still in her hand. "We're making you a copy today," she promised.

Jonah rewarded her answer with a quick kiss. "You know once you give me a key to this place, I'm never going to leave."

Looking deep into his eyes, she stood on tiptoe and kissed him right back in front of her daughter and Jonah's men.

"I'm counting on that," she retorted.

Jonah's heart sang. In spite of the threat still hanging over his head, he had never been happier.

Following Commander Dwyer from his front door to his kitchen, Santiago couldn't help but contrast the CO's suburban home to his own little seaside cottage. For one thing, the CO's house of whitewashed brick was located in a gated community and backed up to a golf course. The man often joked that his love of golf had cost him his marriage, but he didn't seem to be hurting financially.

Given the tasteful decor he glimpsed in the living and dining rooms, the absence of a wife was not at all apparent the way it was in Santiago's house. If there was a woman in the CO's life, though, he'd certainly never made mention of her.

Dwyer led him into his kitchen, a gourmand's paradise with a six-burner gas stove, glossy granite counters, and tall, white cabinets.

"Can I get you a drink? I have a bottle of Don Q rum I'm dying to open."

The question surprised Santiago. At work, Dwyer was the consummate professional, detail-oriented and exacting. Maybe on weekends, he finally relaxed. Given his lime green shirt and white slacks, he'd probably played eighteen holes while Santiago had been in church. It was good to know the hard-nosed CO occasionally let his hair down.

"No, thank you sir. Water would be great."

"You got it. Have a seat."

Dwyer waved at the oak dinette table, and Santiago sat where he could see the ninth tee. Filling two glasses with iced water from the state-of-the-art refrigerator, Dwyer laid Santiago's drink in front of him, then sat across from him with a drawn-out sigh.

"Soon," he said, "I'll be living like this every day."

Santiago smiled. "I'm happy to see you looking so relaxed." It was a shame the news he brought would ruin the CO's weekend, if not his plans for retirement.

"Can't wait to leave the office behind forever," Dwyer agreed with gusto.

"What will you do with yourself, sir?" Santiago put off his difficult news a moment longer.

The CO's overly dark moustache twitched. "I'm thinking of volunteering more, like in a community service organization."

An admirable idea, Santiago thought. Too bad he had to bring his CO such stressful news. He looked down at the envelope under his hand.

"Whatcha got there?" Dwyer asked, his pale gray eyes bright with curiosity.

Santiago had asked himself how to broach the entire topic and had decided to start at the beginning.

"Sir, these are copies of certain entries in Blake LeMere's diary."

Dwyer put his glass down suddenly. "LeMere! I was thinking about him just the other day."

"His death was tragic," Santiago added. "I know it was deemed an accident, but the final entries in his diary suggest otherwise."

The CO blinked, then frowned. "May I read them?"

"Of course." Opening the envelope, Santiago slid out the copies and passed them to the CO.

As Dwyer waded through LeMere's often cryptic handwriting, Santiago watched the emotions cross his face—first confusion, then suspicion, then outrage. At last, he lifted an incredulous gaze to him.

"My lord," he said in a hoarse voice.

"That's not all, sir." With apology in his tone, Santiago went on to explain how Jaguar now remembered reading LeMere's journal before his captivity. "He thinks he must have confronted Lieutenant Commander Lowery right before the op that resulted in his captivity."

"Why didn't he come to me first?" Dwyer blustered.

"Perhaps he was hoping Lowery could offer him a reasonable explanation?"

"And did he?"

"Jaguar doesn't remember, sir. But he believes Lowery is the one leaking intel to The Entity. What's more, he believes Lowery turned on him that night in Carenero. That he left him for dead—just as he may also have contributed to LeMere's death."

Silence seemed to echo in the CO's vast kitchen. All Santiago could hear was the ticking of a clock in one of the front rooms. Visibly stunned, Dwyer lifted a hand to his cheek, then looked down at the copies as one might regard something disgusting.

"This is unbelievable," he murmured.

"I wish that was all there was to it," Santiago added apologetically.

The CO dropped his hand and visibly braced himself. "What else?"

In as precise a manner as he could, and emphasizing everything he himself had seen and heard, Santiago relayed what had happened at Back Bay Wildlife Refuge the previous evening.

"Jaguar is certain, sir, Lowery was the second shooter. He is testifying as much to the police."

Dwyer had blanched beneath his golfer's tan. Santiago could tell what he was thinking—that SOCOM would hold him responsible for his XO's actions, possibly to the point of denying him retirement.

"All I want to do is to retire in peace," he muttered, confirming Santiago's suspicions. It was clear then that the CO thought about himself first and foremost.

"I'm sorry, sir. I know this couldn't be happening at a worse time."

Dwyer shrugged off his self-centered thoughts. "Oh, don't worry about me. I can roll with whatever is dished out—you know that. But I can tell you this, Lowery's got some serious reckoning coming to him," he promised.

Santiago nodded his relief. "Thank you, sir. Jaguar shouldn't have to be worried for his life after everything he's been through already."

"No, he should not," the CO agreed. "I'll reassure him in person. You think he'd be up to a talk with me tomorrow?"

"Of course," Santiago replied. "He'd be delighted."

Dwyer sent him a piercing look. "How's he doing otherwise? Are his memories coming back? Do you think he can ever be an active-duty SEAL again?"

Santiago brightened. "In my estimation, sir, I think him fully capable of returning to the Team."

"But what about his memory?"

Santiago grimaced. "You'll have to talk to his doctors about that, sir. All I know is he's forgotten nothing in regard to his training. He is every bit as capable as he was before his disappearance. If anything, his year in captivity has made him mentally stronger. He can easily rebuild his physical strength."

Looking encouraged, Dywer stroked his chin. His pale eyes narrowed.

"Do you think he would consider taking Lowery's place and becoming my executive officer?"

Santiago's eyes widened at the prospect. "I'm sure he would, sir!"

Dwyer thumped a hand on the table. "That settles it. I'll call him and arrange a meeting at my earliest convenience."

"Thank you, sir!"

Following his CO's example by coming to his feet, Santiago realized their meeting was over. Leaving the copies of LeMere's entries on the table, he followed the commander out of the kitchen and through the house to the front door.

Dwyer pulled it open for him. "Have yourself a wonderful holiday weekend, Master Chief."

"Thank you, sir. You do the same." With a spring in his step and eager to share the outcome of his meeting with Jaguar, Santiago hurried across the pristine lawn to his car, parked at the curb.

∾

At two in the afternoon, Eden pointed the Jaguar in the direction of Station 17, located right there in Sandbridge. A satellite office for the Virginia Beach Police was appended to the fire station, sparing them a drive into the city.

Jonah sat in the back seat with Miriam, leaving shotgun for Lucas, who needed the legroom. Saul had stayed at their house, pledging to keep an eye out for Lowery.

An electronic chime sounded as Jonah held the door open for them. With Lucas posting watch outside, Eden, Miriam, and Jonah stepped into an empty waiting room. The window to the receptionist's office stood open, but there was no receptionist to greet them.

"Be right there!" yelled a gruff voice from the back room.

Eden drew a nervous breath and watched Jonah tuck in his shirt so that the weapon he carried on his hip was blatantly apparent. Searching his face, she read worry banked behind his carefully neutral expression. Even though he'd acted in self-defense the night before, he had to be concerned that he'd killed an officer of the law. She was just about to suggest they say a prayer when the door to the back swung open, and a lanky man with a receding hairline and kind eyes swept a keen gaze over them.

"You must be Jonah, Eden, and Miriam Mills. I'm Chief Dudley. Come on back."

Leading them into a miniscule office, he gestured to the chairs opposite his desk and lowered himself into the chair behind it. In spite of its size, the office had a homey feel. Photos of children and a pretty wife were displayed on his desk, reassuring Eden.

Dudley roused the laptop in front of him, perused whatever he was looking at, and shook his head.

"I've read the police report, and I have to say, I'm baffled. I don't suppose anyone's told you yet that Officer Hammond's body washed up on the beach at Dam Neck this morning."

Eden's cheeks turned cold. She divided a startled look between Miriam and Jonah, both of whom guarded their reaction better than she.

"I should have an autopsy report within the hour. How about you give me your version of the story so I can make heads or tails out of this?" Dudley requested, sitting back in his seat.

For the next half-hour, Miriam, Jonah, and Eden took turns explaining how they'd all ended up at Back Bay.

"I can't explain at this juncture what Lowery's motive might be for wanting me dead," Jonah finished apologetically. "It's strictly a military matter."

Dudley's deep-set eyes gleamed with curiosity.

"But I can say I never meant to kill anyone. Officer Hammond was determined to take me out. He had the advantage of strength and size, and he was obviously trained in hand-to-hand combat."

Dudley nodded. "He's a former SEAL—he was," he amended. "That explains why he and Lowery knew each other," he added to himself. "You can rest assured we'll be bringing James Lowery in for questioning. If he hasn't got an alibi and the shell casings found at the scene match any weapon he might own, I'll be placing him under arrest."

Jonah nodded, murmuring his thanks.

The police chief looked back at Miriam. "You're quite a brave young lady. No negative effects of the gas used to incapacitate you?"

Miriam shook her head. "I feel fine," she said with a shrug.

"About that." Jonah searched Dudley's face. "How did Hammond get his hands on Agent 15? It's classified as a chemical warfare agent."

Dudley frowned back at him. "That's an excellent question, Mr. Mills—Lieutenant," he corrected. "I'll look into it." Just then, his desk phone gave a shrill ring. "Excuse me. This would be the autopsy report. Go ahead," he said, taking the call.

As the person on the other end spoke, Dudley's gaze darted toward Jonah.

"I see," he said.

Eden scarcely breathed as he thanked the caller and put the receiver down. He looked them both in the eye.

"Good news," he said, freeing Eden to breathe again. "The coroner says Hammond died from drowning, not from blood loss, though he did have a bullet in his thigh. Considering he was off duty and that he drugged a minor and basically kidnapped her, I can't see any cause for pressing any charges. You are all free to go."

Tears of relief sprang to Eden's eyes. Jonah hung his head for a moment and closed his eyes—his first display of emotion since their arrival. Miriam blew out a huge sigh of relief, causing Eden and Dudley both to laugh.

An abiding sense of peace, the likes of which Jonah hadn't felt in months, maybe in years, relaxed every muscle of his body. He lay on the quilted mattress in his and Eden's bedroom, with his wife snuggled up against him. Pulling her naked body closer, he kissed her forehead.

259

"It's like our wedding night all over again," he commented.

She stilled the hand that was stroking his shoulder. "Do you remember it?"

"No," he admitted, "but I can imagine it was pretty amazing."

"No better than tonight," she assured him.

Theo and Bambino, their body guards for the night, were taking turns standing watch on the deck and sleeping in the study.

Jonah pondered the contentment in his heart.

"Something tells me everything's going to work out for us," he said, amazed by the certainty that now girded him. "The CO has promised to hold Lowery accountable, and I might even get his job as the executive officer."

Master Chief had shared the good news with Jonah earlier that afternoon. Soon afterward, the CO himself had called and asked Jonah to meet him the next morning at Oceana Naval Air Base at the skeet and trap range. He'd been planning to do some shooting and figured he could talk to Jonah at the same time.

Imaging the CO welcoming him back to Blue Squadron, it took Jonah a moment to realize Eden had fallen silent. Pulling his head back, he studied her pensive expression.

"That has to scare you," he guessed, "the thought of me going back to work."

She smiled crookedly. "It scares me a little," she admitted. "But you were born to be a SEAL, Jonah. I'm not going to get in the way of your destiny."

"Spoken like a martyr," he teased with a smile.

She did not return it.

He sought to reassure her. "I am never going to forget that I'm a husband first, Eden. Then a father," he added, "then an operative."

She held him closer. "I believe you. But I'm still going to worry about your safety."

"Fair enough."

His assurances were interrupted as his cell phone did a dance on the bedside table. Wondering who would be calling this late in the evening, Jonah extracted himself from Eden's embrace and reached for it.

"It's Master Chief. Probably wants to talk about tomorrow. Hello?" he said, taking the call.

"Jaguar, I'm sorry for calling this late. I just got word of some tragic news."

Rivera's announcement, coupled with his odd tone, made Jonah push himself up to a sitting position.

"What is it?" He braced himself for a blow.

"Lowery was found dead in his apartment this afternoon. He lives in the BOQ's on base. One of his neighbors overheard a gunshot and called the MPs. He apparently shot himself."

Shock, sorrow, and even guilt raked Jonah's heart.

"Dear Lord," he muttered, aware Eden was digging her nails into his biceps. She had apparently overheard. "Does he have any children?"

"No, thank goodness, no children," Rivera answered.

Jonah closed his eyes and sighed. "Wow, I did not see this coming."

"It's sobering," the master chief agreed.

"I wonder if the CO knows yet."

"He does," Rivera said. "He's the one who notified me."

"You think he still wants to meet with me tomorrow?"

"He didn't mention canceling."

Jonah considered the reason for Lowery's suicide. "Jimmy must have realized that I'd seen him, and his number was up."

"That's likely, but you shouldn't blame yourself."

"No. No, I don't," Jonah assured him.

"There is one other possibility," Rivera murmured, hesitantly.

"What?"

Rivera kept quiet for several seconds. "I'd rather not say until I have more evidence."

The ominous words stripped Jonah of the peace he'd been enjoying only moments earlier.

"Okay," he said, trying to guess what was going on in Rivera's head.

"Things will work out," Rivera reassured him.

"They have so far," Jonah agreed.

"Well, you may not need any more security detail," Rivera stated, "with both Hammond and Lowery dead."

Jonah had almost forgotten about his teammates, who were elsewhere in the house, as quiet as mice.

"Should I send Theo and Bambino home?"

Expecting Master Chief to say yes, Jonah was surprised to hear him say, "Not just yet. I want to look into something first. What time do Saul and Lucas take over in the morning?"

"Oh-eight hundred hours."

"Take Saul with you to your meeting with the CO," Rivera advised.

Why? Jonah wanted to ask, but he didn't want to force Rivera into explaining himself.

"All right," he said, trusting the man's counsel.

"Good. Sleep well, then." Rivera hung up on him abruptly.

Puzzled, Jonah slowly put his phone down.

"You okay?" Eden pushed herself up to sit beside him.

Putting his arm around her, he sent her a forced smile. "Sure."

"You're not blaming yourself for Lowery killing himself, are you?"

The question confirmed she'd overheard Rivera's news.

"No." Jonah pulled her closer, loving the way her skin felt against his. "He had to know when he started leaking intel that there'd be hell to pay if he was caught."

"It seems so sudden, though," Eden reflected.

"Not really. He's probably been worried sick ever since I showed up at the hospital. Last night was his last, desperate attempt to get rid of me. When things didn't work out the way he'd hoped, he decided to take his life rather than face the repercussions."

"You're probably right," Eden agreed.

Jonah tucked a tendril of her hair behind her ear. "I don't want this news to ruin our first night together."

To his delight, she kissed his jaw and then his neck. "It won't. In fact, I know just how to take your mind off any bad news," she murmured with a demure downward sweep of her lashes.

"Oh, you do?" His blood raced with anticipation. "Show me then."

CHAPTER 20

*O*ver the grinding of the garbage disposal, Eden heard her phone ring.
Miriam looked up from wiping down the kitchen counters. Flipping
off the disposal, Eden dried her hands hastily on a kitchen towel and reached
for her cell phone. The caller's name caused her a pinch of dismay.

As soon as Jonah had left with Saul half an hour earlier, she'd decided to
leave Dr. Branson a voicemail informing him how wrong he'd been about
Jonah's diagnosis. She knew if she didn't get it off her chest, it would eat
at her.

Unfortunately, the good doctor was calling her back. Since only a coward
would avoid a frank discussion, she drew a breath and answered.

"Hello?"

"Mrs. Mills, I got your voice message," Branson said on an earnest note.
"I'm actually very pleased to hear I was wrong about Jonah having PTSD.
However, the danger you described may be related to something that's been
bothering my conscience for a while, now, and I'd like to talk to Jonah about
it. He's not answering his phone, however. Is he there?"

Eden distanced herself from Miriam, who was openly eavesdropping.

"No, he's off skeet shooting with his commander," she explained as she
shut herself quietly in her bedroom.

"Oh. I see." Dr. Branson sounded perturbed to hear it.

"What did you want to tell him?" Eden prompted.

"Could you...could you just ask him to call me?" the doctor stammered.

"I'm sure he wouldn't mind if you told me," Eden insisted. "We've become close again. I'm not going to leave him."

"Oh!" The doctor's tone shifted toward hopefulness. "Well, I'm very happy to hear that."

Eden nudged him again. "It has to be important for you to call on Labor Day."

Branson heaved an audible sigh. "You're right. In our last session, Jonah asked me if I'd spoken to his commander about his progress, and I told him no. But the truth is his CO's been monitoring his recovery very closely."

"How do you mean?"

"He asked to read all of my clinical notes on Jonah."

Eden frowned. "Well, maybe he just wants to know if Jonah's well enough for active duty."

"That's what I thought. And Spitz was the one who found me this job, so I felt obligated to do as he asked."

"Spitz?"

"That's what we called him in high school. We've known each other for years. I'm sure you're right. That's got to be Spitz's motive. Still, I owe it to Jonah to tell him the truth. Please have him call me. I'd like to apologize in person."

"I will," Eden promised. "Thanks for calling."

Hanging up, she pondered the doctor's words as she returned to the kitchen.

Miriam looked up from stowing the spray bottle under the sink.

"What's wrong?"

Eden walked straight through the kitchen and out onto the deck where Lucas was securing tiki torches to the deck's railing using plastic zip-ties.

He straightened to his full height with an enquiring smile.

"How's it going?"

"I'm not sure," she responded. Tipping her head way back to talk to him, Eden relayed the gist of her phone call with the psychiatrist.

"What do you think?" she asked, wanting an impartial opinion.

The lieutenant's eyes had narrowed. "That's not exactly ethical on either man's part."

"My thoughts exactly. What's more, if Commander Dwyer is retiring, why is he so interested in Jonah's memories returning?"

A crease appeared between Lucas's eyebrows. "You're right. That doesn't make sense." Consternation hardened his handsome features. "Oh, no. What if Lowery wasn't instigating the leaks to The Entity? What if he was acting on Dwyer's orders all along?"

Eden blinked at Lucas in confusion. "Why would Dwyer leak intel from his own squadron?"

Lucas's face hardened. "Who knows? But we can't ignore the possibility that Lowery was simply Dwyer's lackey, and look what happened to him."

Eden felt the blood drain from her head. "We need to get through to Jonah, but he may have turned his phone off."

Lucas whipped out his cell phone.

"I'll call Saul," he said, his voice grim. "Don't worry," he added, seeing the dread Eden couldn't hide, "Saul won't let anything bad happen to Jonah."

~

Pulling into the nearly empty parking lot at Spec Ops Headquarters, Santiago Rivera frowned to see only two cars parked out front, and not the ones he expected, either.

Jaguar had said he was meeting the CO of Blue Squadron at oh-nine hundred hours this morning, yet neither man's vehicle was present. The silver Jeep belonged to the duty officer, Ryan Larsen, who had to sit by the phone while everyone else had the day off. And the seafoam-green SUV belonging to the Spec Ops secretary made no sense whatsoever. Lucas's fiancée, Monica Trembley, definitely had the day off.

As Santiago neared her vehicle, her back-up lights flared and her SUV reversed swiftly out of its parking spot. It pulled away, making a wide berth of Santiago's old beater. Nonetheless, he caught a glimpse of Monica's set features as she zipped toward the main road, refusing to make eye contact.

What was that about?

Parking swiftly, Santiago let himself into the building and hurried to Larsen's desk in the main room.

"Hey, Master Chief." The young man's eyes rounded with surprise.

Santiago planted himself in front of him, crossed his arms over his chest, and considered the new SEAL's pallor.

"Where are the CO and Jaguar?" he demanded.

Ryan appeared baffled. "Not here," he stated the obvious.

"What was Miss Trembley doing here?"

Ryan turned an interesting shade of pink.

"She needed to get into the CO's office, Master Chief," he replied a tad too quickly.

Santiago glanced down the hall to Dwyer's office. His own office and the CO's were connected via a door with a simple turn-lock on the CO's side.

"Did she say why?"

"No, sir."

He looked back at the anxious third class. "Does Miss Trembley outrank you, Larsen? Is that why you let her in without the CO's permission?"

"I got his permission." Larsen gestured toward the landline phone next to him. "He called at oh-seven hundred hours this morning and told me to unlock his door for her. You can check the call log if you want."

Santiago let his arms fall to his sides. The seed of suspicion that had dropped into his head last night sprouted insidious roots.

"No," he said tersely. If the CO had given verbal permission for his secretary to enter into his office, then Larsen hadn't violated any policies. He might well have succumbed to Monica's flirting, however. Poor Lucas! Maybe he should have a talk with him.

Walking straight to his office door, Santiago unlocked it and flipped on the lights. The door between his office and the CO's was properly shut. Still, Monica could have easily turned the lock from the CO's side and let herself in.

Crossing to his desk, Santiago prayed his suspicions were wrong as he unlocked the drawer where he'd stored Blake LeMere's journal. It was immediately apparent someone had rifled through the drawer, then taken what they were looking for.

Santiago's heart beat faster. He doubled-checked that the journal was, in fact, no longer there before shutting the drawer quietly. Copies of all the keys for office furniture were kept by none other than Monica, whom the CO had cleared to enter his office.

The doubts that had entered Santiago's mind after relaying the news of Lowery's suicide to Jaguar solidified.

Lowery taking his own life right after Santiago went to Dwyer with damning evidence could not be a coincidence. Santiago's acute intuition told him the truth—the CO had made certain Lowery would never testify one way or the other. And now the original diary, critical in detailing how Lowery had leaked intel, was gone.

Breathing harder, Santiago's thoughts flew to Jaguar, who was even then with the CO—somewhere. He'd assumed they would meet at headquarters, but on a holiday weekend, Dwyer had obviously chosen a different location.

Spinning toward his door, Santiago hurried from his office, casting a disapproving glare at Larsen, who was still looking red in the face. He ran straight for his car to get his hands on his cell phone, as none were allowed in the building. He had to warn Jaguar lest the CO take drastic measures to keep his lieutenant quiet. If he couldn't get to Jaguar, then he could at least reach out to Saul.

∼

"You look good, Jonah," the CO declared as they helped themselves to two shotguns and a box each of shells from the equipment room.

"Thank you, sir," Jonah said, donning his eye protection. "I feel good. Thanks for having me out today. I haven't gone shooting in...I don't know how long," he finished with a rueful laugh.

"Memory is still an issue, huh?"

Dwyer nodded his thanks at the one employee in the lodge, a retired SEAL by the name of Bob. The man had unlocked the lodge door for Jonah but refused to let Saul in with him. Clearly, the CO considered Lowery's betrayal a private matter, not something everyone on the squadron ought to be privy to.

Jonah could see Saul through a window, sitting on the hood of his car in the parking lot, scowling. Then again, Saul, whose shooting skill had given him the codename Reaper, would make even the CO look like a lousy shot. Little wonder Dwyer hadn't asked him to join them.

He hastened to assure his CO. "I'm remembering more and more, sir."

"Glad to hear it." Dwyer gestured toward the exit. "Let's go."

Bob darted forward, holding the door for him. Nodding his thanks, Dwyer stepped outside first. On this federal holiday, he very nearly resembled the civilian he would soon become, dressed as he was in jeans and a light-blue polo. But the military was ingrained in him, as evidenced by the fact he'd expected Bob to hold the door.

Pausing to survey the large field, which included two skeet ranges, a wobble stand, and even an archery range, Dwyer said, "What do you say we do the five-stand range?"

Positioned at the farthest end of the field, the five-stand range consisted of a long, covered platform from which to shoot and up to a dozen unique wooden traps scattered about the field. The traps launched clay pigeons from every conceivable angle, either one or two at a time.

No doubt the CO wanted to see if Jonah had lost his edge. He wished, with a pang of regret, that he'd found some time to do a little target practice prior to their meeting. Then again, when the CO had asked him to meet him at the Oceana Skeet and Trap Range, Jonah hadn't realized he'd be invited to join in a round of shooting.

"Sounds good to me, sir," he replied.

Propping his shotgun over a broad shoulder, Dwyer struck out in the direction of the distant range, past the wobble stand, where Jonah had shot skeet once a long time ago. Bob, like a proper NCO, flanked Dwyer on his left side, just a couple steps behind him. Jonah quickened his step to fall in on the CO's right side.

The long grass whispered against Jonah's soles, filling the rather tense silence as they covered a distance of about a hundred yards. Casting a glance at his contemplative commander, Jonah ignored the phone buzzing in his pocket—probably Dr. Branson again, reminding Jonah of his Tuesday appointment.

At that moment, Jonah was fixated on his immediate objective—convincing Dwyer he was fit for active duty. Dwyer would bring that up when he was good and ready. Better to focus their talk on Lowery.

"I imagine Lowery's death shocked you as much as it did me, sir," he began.

Dwyer cut him a sharp look. "Yes, it did. Hard to wrap my mind around it."

"Yes, sir," Jonah agreed. "Master Chief showed you Blake LeMere's journal?"

"He did."

The man's tone did not invite more conversation. Jonah guessed he might not want to bring up Lowery's treachery in front of Bob.

"Nice day for shooting," Dwyer added, confirming Jonah's guess.

Jonah looked around, clearing his thoughts with a deep breath. Only a few fat clouds floated overhead. The breeze kept the sun from overheating them.

"Yes, sir, it is," he agreed, wondering when the CO was going to bring up Jonah's return to active duty.

By the time they arrived at the five-stand range and mounted the wooden platform, Jonah had broken into a light sweat. From there, they surveyed the field. It was littered with wooden traps of various sizes positioned willy-nilly around the open range. At the far end of the facility, the range butted up to an eight-foot, chain-link fence with signs hanging every twenty feet warning of live artillery.

Conscious of how far he'd walked from Saul and the parking lot, Jonah suffered a sudden twinge of vulnerability. There was nothing to see on the other side of the fence, only a thick line of bushes, then an open field dotted with pine trees.

Lowery's dead, Jonah reminded himself. So was his cohort, Officer Hammond. Jonah didn't need to worry either one of them was lurking nearby, intending to shoot him. All the same, he hefted his shotgun, glad to have at least one weapon, since he'd stowed his SIG under the seat of Saul's car—no open carry on the military base.

"Have you played five-stand before, Jonah?"

"No, sir. I have not."

Dwyer cocked an eyebrow at him. "You sure about that?"

Jonah hesitated. Maybe he had, during that year he couldn't recall, the same year he'd married Eden.

"We played once before, you and I," Dwyer informed him with a rueful smile.

Jonah blinked, digesting both the news he'd done something he couldn't remember, as well as the fact Dwyer had obviously been testing him in bringing him out here.

"No worries." The CO sought to reassure him. "Like you said, your memories are coming back. So you know how five stand works, there's a menu at each one of the five places where you shoot."

He stepped up to the first stand and read the laminated menu mounted atop the railing.

"This one says we've got a single pigeon coming out of trap five." Peering out at the traps, he located five for both of them. "Then a report pair is launching from twelve and three."

Bob spoke up. "Three's way back there by the bushes."

The CO consulted the menu again. "Then a true pair comes from nine and four, simultaneously." He looked up to identify them.

"Got it," Jonah said, with growing enthusiasm. "Let's load up."

Having selected a semi-automatic 12-gauge, Jonah slipped five shells into his shotgun, the most it would hold, perfect for five-stand. Dwyer, on the other hand, had chosen a pump-action riot shotgun with a standard choke. Jonah hadn't realized it was capable of holding extra shells until he saw the CO load at least ten. Then he gave his shotgun a pump, advancing the first shell.

"You first," Dwyer offered to Jonah, with a little smile.

With his heart pumping faster, Jonah lifted his protective muffs over his ears. *Please, God, don't let me botch this completely.*

Stepping up to the railing, he cleared his thoughts as he did prior to any mission. His being recommended for active duty apparently hinged on his ability to shoot, but no pressure, right?

Shouldering his weapon, he glanced at the menu, looked toward the fifth trap, and said, "Pull!"

Bob thumbed the remote control, and trap five ejected a clay pigeon. It sailed up at an angle far higher than what Jonah had expected. He corrected his aim, tracked the pigeon, fired, and missed it completely.

Bob made a snorting sound.

Way to go, Jonah railed inwardly.

Setting his teeth, he rechecked the menu then located traps twelve and three, the latter by the fence, the former on the opposite side of the range. Not knowing which would spit out a pigeon first, he drew a measured breath and slowly released it.

"Pull," he said.

A clay disk spewed from trap three. Jonah shattered it, pivoting just in time to pulverize the pigeon coming from twelve.

"Not bad!" he heard Dwyer yell through the muffs.

With a hopeful glance at his CO, Jonah applied himself to hitting the next pair, launched at the same time from targets four and nine. Nailing them both, he repressed a smile of relief and reminded himself they'd barely begun. Still, it was good to know he hadn't lost his expert marksmanship along with his memory.

Bob scribbled Jonah's score on a game card, then picked up the remote as the CO took Jonah's place. By the time the two men approached the fourth stand, they had both hit thirteen pigeons out of fifteen. The phone in Jonah's pocket buzzed again. Annoyed by the interruption, he took advantage of their transition to steal a quick peek at it.

Keep alert. Don't trust.

The text message, sent by Master Chief, set off warning bells in Jonah's head. He jammed his phone quickly back in his pocket and scanned the bushes outside the fence with renewed nervousness.

Don't trust whom? Lowery and Hammond were out of the picture. *Did Rivera mean the CO?*

Reeling in confusion, Jonah feigned concentration as he loaded his shotgun. Dwyer, who still had five shells in his larger magazine, waited for him.

All at once, his CO broached the topic Jonah had assumed was taboo in front of Bob.

"Lowery's suicide and his leaking of intel to The Entity is a bit of an embarrassment to Blue Squadron."

Jonah glanced up at the man's narrowed eyes. "Yes, sir. Just so you know, I didn't mention his treachery to the police, sir. I wouldn't want a scandal getting in the way of your retirement."

"I appreciate that, Jonah. As it is, I should've retired six months ago."

"I heard about that, sir." Master Chief had informed Jonah how the investigation of his disappearance had delayed the CO's retirement. Apparently, they both had cause to wish it had never happened.

"Yes, but that's okay. I got to see firsthand what you're made of. You're a survivor, Lieutenant. I could use a man like you."

The words confused Jonah. How could Dwyer possibly use him when he was about to retire?

"Would you like to be back in the squadron, Lieutenant?"

Jonah's heart beat faster. Now that he'd brought up the matter, Dwyer wasn't wasting any time. Hope pulsed in him.

"Yes, sir. Of course, sir."

"Then, maybe we can work out a deal. I can convince your doctor, your psychiatrist, and Vice Admiral Holland you're fit for active duty, provided you agree to be my eyes and ears in Blue Squadron once I've retired."

Jonah looked from the CO to Bob, whose face was carefully neutral, then back to Dwyer.

"I'm not sure I follow you, sir."

The CO sent him a patronizing look. "Allow me to share my political views with you, then."

Turning his shotgun over, he started loading more shells into the magazine—five more, giving him ten to Jonah's five. Turning the gun back over, he advanced the first shell with a decisive pump.

Sensing a shift of energy, Jonah wondered what was going on. In the same instant, Bob sidled just close enough to lay hands on him, should there be need for that.

Tamping down his rising concern, Jonah scanned the area to assess his options. The CO had evidently brought him all the way out there so no one would see them, especially not Saul, unless he climbed onto the roof of the lodge.

For Jonah to get away, he would have to vault off the platform, run across the five-stand range, then go up and over the fence, disappearing into the bushes on the other side—impossible to do when the CO had ten shots at the ready.

Dwyer kept talking, in a voice ringing with conviction.

"The problem with our country these days is that our leaders are weak. They don't want to do what's necessary to protect the people." He glanced at Bob who shifted even closer. "Take the Joint Chiefs of Staff, generals and admirals, all of them. You'd think they'd advise the president to take a harder line with terrorists, but they're too concerned with keeping their positions and their salaries to risk pissing him off."

Jonah's thoughts raced. There had to be a reason why the CO was talking politics with him. So long as he kept talking, though, Jonah had time to figure out what the man's intentions were.

"But a warrior such as yourself," Dwyer continued, "one who's been tortured and detained, surely realizes the importance of staying on top of our enemies. What we need is more operators and less politicians running this country, then maybe we'll get it right. But unless we burn Washington to the ground and start over, that's not going to happen, is it?"

He paused, waiting for Jonah to agree with him.

"No, sir," Jonah said to appease him, though the words *burn Washington to the ground* smacked of subversion.

"The only option, then, is for men like us to take this nation's security into our own hands. Our enemies can't strike at us if we steal their weapons first. We amass them and we control them because, in the end, power means peace."

Who destroyed my warehouse?

All at once, Jonah's confusion vanished. The answer to the question *El Jefe* had asked over and over during his interrogations hit Jonah over the head.

Dwyer had given the order to blow it up, but only after his followers removed the four boxes of dirty bombs. Then they'd blown up the rest, so they'd never be used against the US at any future time. And what of the bombs? Had they destroyed them as the SEALs were going to do, or were they hoarding them to be used on terrorists at some later date?

If The Entity's methods weren't flagrantly illegal, not to mention nationalistic, they might be viewed as brilliant.

Holy smokes, Charlotte Patterson had been right. Lowery was merely the tip of the iceberg, serving at the CO's behest! It hadn't been Lowery's choice to leak intel; Dwyer had been directing him to do it. That made Dwyer the leader of The Entity, a rogue warrior who believed what he was doing was in the best interest of his country.

Reeling with his insight, Jonah gave a thought to Master Chief's text. Rivera seemed to have guessed the truth about Dwyer—how?

"You want me to take Lowery's place to leak intel like he did," he guessed.

Dwyer's eyes narrowed with contempt. "Lowery was weak. He made mistakes he couldn't afford to make."

"Like blind-copying secret recipients in his emails."

"Just so."

Jonah fought to keep his cool. "Was it your idea to kill Blake LeMere before he told anyone else?"

Dwyer gave a noncommittal shrug. "LeMere's death was ruled an accident," he retorted simply.

Jonah's righteous anger grew. "What about Lowery's death? That wasn't really a suicide, was it?"

Instead of answering, Dwyer's expression turned incredulous. "Are you going to defend him now? He should have finished you off in Carenero, not just bashed you in the face and walked away."

"You ordered my execution?" Jonah's heart pounded.

"Reluctantly, of course. I was still holding out hope."

"Hope?" The words disrupted Jonah's thoughts. "For what?"

"You don't remember a single word of our previous conversation, do you? We stood right here, over a year ago." Dwyer gestured to the platform they were on. "I asked you then if you would consider joining a few powerful men in saving the world, and you said you would think about it. Well, I think it's time that you made up your mind, Lieutenant."

Confusion fogged Jonah's thoughts, preventing him from thinking tactically. He couldn't recall any of what the CO was telling him. Nor did he believe he would have ever agreed to Dwyer's bizarre invitation—*or would he?*

He'd been so self-absorbed before his captivity, but surely he'd held the same convictions as he did now. Renegades going off and doing their own thing—even in the supposed best interest of their country—was form of treason. He could not have condoned Dwyer's actions. Of course not. If he had, Dwyer wouldn't have ordered Lowery to turn on him.

"I'd have thought," Dwyer added, adjusting his stance and raising his shotgun so it now pointed at Jonah's thighs, "your experience as a prisoner would have hardened your heart against the enemy and helped you to make up your mind."

Jonah said nothing as he weighed his options. All he had to do to walk away was to agree to Dwyer's demands. He could then go straight to NCIS and tell them everything Dwyer had just told him. Then again, NCIS seemed to have an insider looking out for Dwyer. Why else had Elwood's hard drive been removed? What's more, agreeing to join Dwyer, whose hands were covered in the blood of LeMere and Lowery, was like signing a pact with Satan himself. Jonah couldn't bring himself to do that.

Still, refusing to cooperate was going to get him killed. His recent resurrection from the dead would be for nothing. He would miss out on the live he and Eden had rediscovered. Lowery's death would remain labeled a suicide. LeMere's death and even Officer Hammond's would never be answered for. Dwyer would retire, never once having to pay the price for murder. So which was the better choice?

This can't be happening, Lord. I was supposed to make things right. That's why you brought me home, isn't it?

"Enough of this." The CO's tone signaled the end of their talk.

All at once, Bob wrested Jonah's shotgun out of his hands. As Jonah lunged to get it back, the point of a blade pricked the flesh between his fourth and fifth rib. Stymied, Jonah could do nothing but watch Bob toss his shotgun aside. It landed on the back edge of the platform, in the opposite direction from where Jonah wanted to go.

"Either you agree to work for me," Dwyer said on a reasonable note, "and I get you back in the squadron before I retire, or you die here today. Which is it? Think carefully."

"I have questions," Jonah countered, biding his time. If Master Chief knew he was in danger, he would seek him out as quickly as possible or, at the very least, alert Saul, who was closer, to intervene. *God will work through his people,,* Jonah assured himself.

"Who has ultimate control over this stockpile of weapons? Is it you?" he asked. "Or do you answer to someone else, and, if you do, how do you know that person isn't a power monger, another Hitler or Mussolini?"

Dwyer sneered at him. "I know what you're doing, and it won't work. I'm disappointed in you, Jonah. You were a promising SEAL before you were debilitated. But now you're weak, like so many others in our profession. I feel absolutely no guilt in sending you to your Maker."

The words chilled Jonah to the bone. "Too many people know I'm here at the range with you. You can't just kill me in cold blood and get away with it."

"Kill you?" Dwyer affected shock at Jonah's words. "I will have shot you in self-defense, Jonah. You went crazy, snapped at the sound of gunfire, as Bob will testify." He shook his head with false lament. "PTSD is such a crippling syndrome. That's why I told Bart Branson to diagnose you with it."

The CO's perfidy stunned Jonah. Infuriated by Dwyer's manipulations, he roused from his paralyzed state and rammed his elbow back into Bob's arm, dislodging the knife. Throwing himself into a rolling dive, he managed to grab his shotgun as he slid fluidly under the railing.

Falling off the platform, he scrambled underneath it into the crawlspace, relieved it wasn't covered by latticework. A blast from the CO's shotgun blew off the end of the planks right behind him.

Beneath a flimsy and temporary shelter, Jonah plotted his escape. He would have to run across the skeet field to reach the fence, using the traps along the way for cover. The odds of succeeding were next to nothing. Dwyer would blow him away on his first sprint to trap four.

"You gotta help me out here, Lord," he begged under his breath.

Two things happened simultaneously. First, the CO moved to stand directly over Jonah. Jonah rolled out of harm's way just as buckshot drilled through the planks over his head, peppering the earth right next to him. In the same instant, the report of a second shot rang through the air. Jonah gasped. Bob and the CO both swore in surprise. *Thwack!* The entire platform shuddered as a lead shot tore through a supporting post.

It's Saul! Jonah realized, recognizing the distinct report of Saul's hunting rifle from the few times they'd tracked game together. Fitting it with a scope, Saul could hit targets up to a mile away.

Thank you, Lord! He *knew* God would find a way to rescue him.

Only problem was, Saul had to reload his Weatherby after every shot he fired, and the CO had a semi-automatic.

Go! Taking advantage of his adversaries' surprise, Jonah bolted out from under the shelter, sprinting in a zig-zag line toward the nearest trap.

With audible curses, Dwyer fired twice at him and missed because Saul fired simultaneously, sending the CO into a tapdance. Jonah dropped safely behind the lumpy trap number four, about as wide as he was and half as tall. He had to crouch down to cover himself while Dwyer's fourth shot strafed the top of the trap, sending splinters flying in all directions.

Jonah waited for Saul's next shot to ring out. Like a sprinter at the starting line, he exploded into motion. Halfway to trap three, with Saul reloading, Jonah turned and fired to cover his retreat, then spun around and sprinted the remaining distance to the trap beside the fence.

Dwyer's answering shots sliced through the air, mere inches away.

Jonah ducked behind trap three with his heart galloping and his lungs straining. With his back pressed flat against it, he paused to catch his breath.

Saul wouldn't shoot to kill, just to debilitate, he realized. This wasn't a war, after all, and it would end his career to kill either man, even to protect his teammate. But would the CO suffer the same compunction? How could he justify shooting Jonah in the back?

Eyeing the eight-foot, chain-link fence, Jonah decided he should risk it, providing he had the strength to clamber over. Assuming Saul could see him, even though he hadn't even glimpsed Saul, Jonah propped his gun against the trap, drew one more deep breath, and nodded his readiness.

Seconds later, Saul's Weatherby rang out a third time. The CO let out a howl of frustration as Saul apparently hampered his firing capabilities.

With another quick prayer, Jonah leaped onto the fence, managing to seize the bar at the top, scrabbling for a toe hold. Finding the links too small for the tips of his shoes, he relied entirely on his arm strength, discovering he wasn't as weak as he'd feared.

In one move, he pulled himself up and over the bar, managing to land on his feet on the other side. As he forged headfirst into the line of thick bushes, the CO fired off one more shot. It ripped through the slender branches next to Jonah's head, narrowly missing him. So much for not shooting a man in the back.

Saul's rifle gave a final report as Jonah wrestled his way out the far side of the shrubbery. The roar of an engine drew his gaze to an unlikely sight: Master Chief's antique car jiggling across the field in his direction.

As the Ford Falcon lumbered up to him, Jonah yanked open the door and leaped into the passenger seat. Rivera ran a quick gaze over him, then turned them around and floored the accelerator, speeding them away as fast as his old car could go.

"The CO tried to kill me!" Jonah exclaimed, trying to wrap his mind around it.

Driving them toward the road, Rivera cast another worried glance at him.

"He sent Monica Trembley to the office this morning. She took LeMere's journal."

"Monica?" Jonah spared a thought for Lucas. "Maybe she was just following orders."

"Perhaps," Rivera said with skepticism. His old car lurched onto pavement, putting them on the road that led away from the skeet and trap range toward the front gate.

Jonah swiped a shaky hand over his face. "How did you find me?"

"I called Saul, who told me where you were. He'd just heard from Lucas not to trust the CO."

"How did Lucas know?" Jonah exclaimed. Everyone seemed aware of the CO's treachery but him.

"You'll have to ask your wife. Something about your psychiatrist calling."

"My psychiatrist?" Jonah held his breath as they approached the base's exit, but the guards paid no heed to the cars leaving the post.

"What do we do now?" he asked Rivera. "Who's going to believe us that Dwyer's been stealing weapons in advance of his own squadron?"

Rivera shook his head, clearly at a loss. "Not NCIS," he said grimly.

Just then, Jonah's cell phone buzzed. Dreading a call from Dwyer, with what could only be twisted threats and sick reasoning, Jonah pulled his phone from his pocket.

"It's the NCIS intern, Charlotte Patterson. Hello?" he answered.

"Lieutenant Mills?"

"Yes, it's me."

"Patterson here. I have excellent news."

Jonah sat up straighter. "Good. I'm in need of that right now. My CO just tried to kill me."

Silence betrayed her momentary shock, but then she said, "I'm not surprised. I should have called you immediately, but I was on the phone with the DIA until the early hours of the morning. I recovered Lloyd's iPad from a morgue in the Northern Neck yesterday. The coroner found it in his jacket when his body was brought in."

Jonah perked up at the possibility of more evidence. "That's great. I hope there's something conclusive on it. LeMere's journal was stolen from Master Chief's office by Dwyer's secretary."

"Ugh. You're kidding me. Well, not to worry," Patterson assured him. "I've got everything we need on this iPad to put Commander Dwyer in jail for good. Lloyd's got video and voice recordings of conversations between Dwyer and various other men, including Lowery. All of them are incriminating."

An enormous weight lifted off Jonah's shoulders. He closed his eyes in silent gratitude.

"For obvious reasons," Patterson continued, "I don't trust NCIS to pursue an investigation. DIA is going to handle this for us. I'm on my way to deliver the iPad to my contact now. Based on what I've shared with him, he's made arrangements to arrest your commander by nightfall."

Jonah opened his eyes again. "That's incredible! I can't thank you and Lloyd Elwood enough. You're going to make an incredible special agent, Miss Patterson."

"Thanks," she said. "Do me a favor, though. Keep close to your friends until you hear from me that Dwyer's behind bars."

"Yes, ma'am," Jonah assured her.

"I'll be in touch," she promised, ending the call.

Keeping his phone in his hand, Jonah grinned his relief and met Rivera's hopeful glance.

"Patterson says she has Special Agent Elwood's iPad and there's enough evidence on it to incriminate Dwyer. She's already spoken with the DIA, and they're planning to pick him up by nightfall."

Rivera's tense expression abruptly relaxed. "Thank God."

"Yes." It couldn't be more obvious to Jonah that God had looked out for him that morning. "You were right, Master Chief," he marveled as they drove through the gate without being waylaid.

"About what?"

"You told me God would take care of me. I could so easily have been killed just now and everyone would've believed Dwyer's version of the story. He told me he was going to say I flipped out and attacked him because of my

PTSD. His buddy who works at the range would have said he'd witnessed the whole thing, and that would have been that. He killed Lowery, too, Master Chief. He practically admitted to it."

Rivera nodded as if he'd guessed it already, then looked back at the road where something in his rearview mirror caught his eye. "Saul is coming up behind us."

Jonah peered over his shoulder, relieved to see Saul's sleek, midnight blue Camaro. "He saved my life today. You both did."

"What did Dwyer say to you? What's his excuse for stealing weapons from right under his own squadron's nose?"

Jonah gave a humorless laugh, then summarized Dwyer's motivations in a single sentence. "He thinks power means peace."

Rivera turned right at the intersection, headed in the direction of Jonah's home.

"You'd better call Eden," he suggested. "I'm sure she's frantic by now."

As he dialed Eden's phone number, Jonah drew a cleansing breath and let it out again.

"Jonah, thank God! Tell me you're okay," she said by way of a greeting.

Her alarm suggested she'd somehow guessed the danger he'd been in.

"I'm okay," he reassured her.

She heaved a huge sigh of relief. "I got the strangest call from Dr. Branson. Apparently, he and your commander went to school together, and Dwyer got him his job so he could keep tabs on what memories you were recalling. After hearing that, my imagination went nuts."

"Actually," Jonah told her, "you were right to be worried. The CO actually told my psychologist to diagnose me with PTSD. That way no one believes what I have to say. I'll tell you everything when I get home."

"Are you sure you're okay, honey? You don't sound like yourself."

"I'm okay." Her concern shot a warm ray of love through him.

"Do you still want to have everyone over?"

Jonah searched himself. Patterson had told him to keep his friends close. What better way to do that than to have them over for a party?

"Absolutely," he replied.

Whatever ultimately happened, he was sure of one thing: God would continue looking out for him. Jonah's eyes stung with the force of his gratitude.

I love you, Father. Thank you for protecting us.

EPILOGUE

The summer sun beat down on the small group standing on Eden and Jonah's deck—Theo, Bambino, Lucas, Saul, Master Chief, Miriam, and Jonah. Nina would arrive at any moment, and then everyone Jonah and Eden cared about, except her parents, would be here in this one place. Even Sabby was lounging in a small patch of shade, waiting for potential treats.

To no one's surprise, Monica, who'd been invited as Lucas's fiancée, had messaged him that she was visiting her sister up in Williamsburg and couldn't make it.

Eden broke a sweat as she'd hurried about, laying out the side dishes and the utensils while Jonah saw that everyone had drinks.

Once they'd all settled in, Jonah began to relay, as he manned the grill, what had happened to him that morning. On hearing how closely her husband had come to being shot by his own squadron commander, Eden glanced at Miriam and found her blowing up balloons with a scowl on her face.

Master Chief followed up Jonah's story with his own version. The suddenness of Lowery's death had sparked suspicions, causing him to drive to HQ that morning to sit in on Jonah's meeting with the CO. Instead of running into them, he'd brushed into Monica, who was just leaving. Likely acting on Dwyer's orders, she had entered Rivera's office via the CO's and had taken

LeMere's journal, their best piece of evidence regarding his treachery, with her.

In the reflective silence following Master Chief's story, Eden looked at Lucas, as did everyone else. With a crestfallen expression, he rose from his chair and crossed to the far side of the deck to stare out at the ocean.

Just then, Eden heard Nina pull up out front and went to help her carry up the kit for making homemade ice cream. On their ascent to the deck, she sketched Nina a quick explanation of what was going on.

The aroma of charcoal and barbecuing meats filled the air, but it couldn't penetrate the cloud of disillusionment hanging over Alpha Troop. As he turned the meat, Jonah added a commentary onto his story.

"What's crazy is that Dwyer believes he's acting in our country's best interest. He asked me to join him in saving the world. Those were the words he used."

Saul spoke up from the chair he was brooding in. "Where's he putting all the weapons he's been stealing?" Sunlight glinted off the hoop in his left ear as he lifted his head.

"And how many people are working for him?" Lucas turned back to face the group. "Are they all former SEALs?"

"I don't know. Some may be active-duty like Lowery," Jonah said.

Master Chief tore his gaze off Nina to add, "He may think he's saving the world when he actually wants to control it. In Dwyer's mind, as long as he's in charge, terrorism doesn't stand a chance. What he doesn't realize is that *he* has now become the terrorist."

The youngest SEAL, Bambino, offered up an insight. "That's why he's been wantin' to retire."

"Exactly." Jonah gestured at him with the spatula. "Once he's free of SOCOM, he can live like a pirate, amassing his weapons in some off-shore location—provided he can still get intel now that Lowery's gone."

"Thank God the DIA is stepping in," Theo exclaimed. As dark as mahogany, with biceps at least twenty inches in diameter, Eden could see how he'd earned the code name Mr. T.

"Yes, thank God," Jonah agreed. "Hey, since the meat is just about ready, how about we say a prayer? Master Chief, would you do the honors?"

"I'd love to. Let's form a circle," Rivera proposed, backing up and holding out his hands.

Looking confused, Nina set down the bag of salt for the homemade ice cream mixer.

Master Chief gestured for her to join him. With a glance at Eden, she nonetheless crossed to Rivera's side and slipped her hand into his.

Eden seized Jonah's hand and pulled him away from the grill. With her newfound happiness threatened that very morning, Eden wanted nothing more than to feel the hand of God upon them.

Jonah took Nina's free hand. Lucas stepped forward, adding to the circle. Theo linked hands with Lucas and Bambino. But Saul, looking ill-at-ease, stayed put in his chair.

"Come on, Saul," Eden urged.

"You don't want me in that circle," he said with a shake of his head. "I made a pact with the devil years ago."

Master Chief waited patiently without speaking. Miriam, tying off a balloon, grabbed up Saul's hand on her way by him and forced him out of his chair.

"My dad needs you," she informed him firmly.

With a self-conscious grimace but unwilling to let Miriam down, Saul closed the circle and hung his head. Eden hid a smile and closed her eyes, letting Master Chief's voice with its lilting accent wash over her.

"Heavenly Father, we all thank you for keeping watch over our brother, Jaguar. Your wisdom and your compassion are beyond compare. You alone know what will happen now. Protect us in your loving kindness, Lord. We see forces of darkness at work everywhere we turn, and we fear for ourselves and for our families. Therefore, we turn to you, our defender and our very great help in times of trouble. Fill us with your peace. Strengthen us to be vigilant of each other. Cast your protection over Charlotte Patterson and hasten the DIA to bring about justice. And most especially, Lord, safeguard and bless Jaguar and his family. We pray all this in the name of our dearest advocate, teacher and savior, Jesus Christ. Amen."

"Amen," repeated everyone, even Nina and Saul.

Reassured to the point of relaxing, Eden turned to her daughter and gave her a hearty hug. To her delight, Jonah put his arms around them both.

"I love you guys," he said in a gruff voice.

Over his shoulder, Eden mouthed her thanks to Master Chief, who winked back at her.

From a distance of a hundred yards, waves crashed over and over onto the shore, calling to mind something Eden had once read—the words of the medieval mystic Julian of Norwich.

All will be well and all will be well. All manner of things will be well.

Optimism lifted her spirits. She couldn't help but consider how much her life had changed since getting the call that Jonah was still alive. She had thought herself happier without him. How wrong she'd been. With God anchoring her marriage, her family, and her friendships, this was what true happiness felt like.

She and Jonah had a weapon unlike any weapon Commander Dwyer had ever tried to amass: the Love of God.

All manner of things will be well, she assured herself, enjoying the embrace of her dear ones.

The End

EVERY SECRET THING

ACTS OF VALOR, BOOK 2

The monotonous droning of a fly roused Charlotte Patterson from an unnaturally deep sleep. Fighting the unwanted drug that fouled her system, she forced herself to sit up. Her sluggish respiration quickened as she failed to recognize the antique bed in which she lay, on sheets damp with sweat.

Her gaze rose to high papered walls. More details came into focus as she blinked—a window with plantation shutters currently propped open at the bottom, an adjacent bathroom with old-timey fixtures, and a tray on a table by the door with food that had been delivered, she assumed, while she'd been sleeping.

Where am I?

The only sound besides the buzzing fly and the beating of her heart was that of a downpour outside the window. She recalled waking up once previously, long enough to sense the pitching motion of a boat. But that feeling was gone. She was back on dry land.

Compelled by her full bladder, Charlotte swung her feet to the floor. The drug that had caused her to sleep so deeply also made the walls shift closer, the floor jump up. As it hit her bare soles, she wondered when and where she'd lost her shoes.

Nausea roiled up suddenly as the memories rushed back.

She'd been driving up Rt. 301 in Virginia en route to the headquarters of the Defense Intelligence Agency outside of Washington DC. Although midday on Labor Day, she remembered being one of just a few people on the road. The black SUV surging toward her in her rearview mirror had come out of nowhere.

As Charlotte swore and increased her speed, the female in the passenger seat stuck her head out of her window. A pistol flashed in the sunlight—Charlotte's only warning before her Mustang's rear tire blew with a pop.

The steering wheel jerked in Charlotte's grasp. In that same instant, she realized her attempt to get time-critical information to the DIA was being thwarted.

"No!" she remembered raging. Her supervisor had been killed less than a week earlier while carrying the same information. She'd been so certain no one had seen or followed her.

In her fury, Charlotte jammed on the brakes by way of reprisal. The SUV plowed into the back end of her car with a terrific crash.

Her Mustang was still moving when she opened her door and leaped out of it, sparing a thought for the iPad she'd hidden under her seat. It was supposed to be in the DIA's possession within the hour, but saving her own life took precedence for the moment.

She ran toward trees as fast as her long legs permitted. A fearful backward glance revealed a man in hot pursuit. Even as fit as she was, he overcame her within seconds, threw his arms around her, and tackled her into tall grass, all without hurting her.

The same could not be said for him. As she flailed and scratched and bit him, he overcame her struggles with difficulty, then pulled a syringe from his back pocket. Using his teeth, he freed the needle and jabbed it into her thigh, injecting her with something that blurred her vision instantly.

Charlotte's head lolled. Looking back at the two cars, she watched the woman duck inside of the Mustang. It wouldn't take her long to find the iPad containing critical evidence, hidden under the driver's seat.

The last thing Charlotte could recall was being lifted like a ragdoll off the ground and carried to the man's SUV. She'd figured the man was going to kill her, just as he'd probably killed her supervisor, for knowing too much about Navy SEAL Commander Derek Dwyer.

Only she wasn't dead—not yet, anyway.

Instead of killing her, he'd gotten rid of her, apparently by putting her on a boat and sending her . . . *where?*

Charlotte forced herself to rise on legs that jittered. She had to hold her head with both hands to keep the room from shifting. Crossing in a wobbly line to the bathroom, she stared at her ghastly reflection as she splashed water on her face.

Revived by the water, she headed straight for the bedroom door and found it locked from the other side. As she suspected, she was a prisoner, albeit a well-fed one, given the sumptuous fare left out for her. Remembering the drugs that had kept her unconscious, she cautiously helped herself to the glass of fruit juice, slaking her thirst as she gulped it down. Picking up a strip of chicken cooked in pineapple, she chewed it carefully.

How long was I sleeping? She didn't know. *Days at least.*

Abandoning the food, Charlotte approached the screen-covered window. The partially-open shutter admitted a humid breeze. She realized she was standing on the second story of what appeared to be a plantation home. Rain spattered the lush lawn below her. Vegetation quilted the landscape in a tapestry of lilies, fronds and blooming bougainvillea.

Ducking to see under the raised shutter, Charlotte discerned, farther afield, a walkway leading from the home's main entrance to a massive moon gate. Two mulatto men smoked cigarettes in an adjacent gate house.

The gate was appended to a stucco wall that appeared to encompass the entire estate. Peering past the wall, through the fronds of palm trees sloping downhill, she gasped—first with appreciation, then with dismay—at the aquamarine body of water darkening to turquoise and stretching as far as the eye could see.

Given the architecture of the home, the striking hue of the water, and the dark-skinned guards, she determined there was only one place in the world where she could be—somewhere in the Caribbean.

Despite the warmth and humidity, Charlotte lowered her heels to the floor and shivered. The Caribbean Sea covered more than a million square miles and consisted of at least seven hundred islands. Considering the bizarre events that had brought her here, no one was about to find her.

She might as well have fallen off the edge of the earth.

~

Available in Paperback and eBook From Your Favorite Online Retailer or Bookstore

ALSO BY REBECCA HARTT

The Acts of Valor Series
Returning to Eden
Every Secret Thing
The Lost is Found

ABOUT THE AUTHOR

Rebecca Hartt is the *nom de plume* for an award-winning, best-selling author who, in a different era of her life, wrote strictly romantic suspense. Now Rebecca chooses to showcase the role that faith plays in the lives of Navy SEALs, penning military romantic suspense that is both realistic and heart-warming.

As a child, Rebecca lived all over the world. She has been a military dependent for most of her life, first as a daughter, then as a wife, and knows first-hand the dedication and sacrifice required by those who serve. Living near the military community of Virginia Beach, Rebecca is constantly reminded of the peril and uncertainty faced by US Navy SEALs, many of whom testify to a personal and profound connection with their Creator. Their loved ones, too, rely on God for strength and comfort. These men of courage and women of faith are the subjects of Rebecca Hartt's enthusiastically received *Acts of Valor* series.

RebeccaHartt.com

Sign up for the Rebecca Hartt Newsletter Here

https://rebeccahartt.com/contact